# The

# DARK
# WING

# The DARK WING

*Walter H. Hunt*

**TOR**

A Tom Doherty Associates Book
New York

THE DARK WING

Copyright © 2001 by Walter H. Hunt

This book is printed on acid-free paper.

Edited by Brian Thomsen.

Book design by Jane Adele Regina

A Tor Book
Published by Tom Doherty Associates, LLC
175 Fifth Avenue
New York, NY 10010

www.tor.com

Tor® is registered trademark of Tom Doherty Associates, LLC.

Library of Congress Cataloging-in-Publication Data

Hunt, Walter H.
    The dark wing / Walter H. Hunt.—1st ed.
        p.    cm.
    "A Tom Doherty Associates book."
    ISBN 0-765-30113-X (acid-free paper)
    1. Life on other planets—Fiction.    2. Space warfare—
Fiction.    I. Title.
PS3608.U59 D37 2001
813'.6—dc21                                    2001041533

First Edition: December 2001

Printed in the United States of America

0   9   8   7   6   5   4   3   2   1

These people have had the greatest influence upon me as this book has moved from thoughts to paper, and it is to them that it is dedicated: my parents, Earle and Clotilde Hunt, who did not live to see it reach publication; Mrs. Sandra Hawkes, a great and inspirational teacher at my high school, who truly taught me how to write; my own Bright Wing, my wife and best friend, Lisa, who has shared everything with me for half of my life; and my dear friend Susan Stone, who has championed this book from its earliest incarnation.

Thank you all for believing in me.

# The

# DARK
# WING

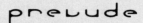

T-0 hours
2 February 2311
0342Hrs Std

IF YOU KNOW THE ENEMY AND KNOW YOURSELF, YOU
NEED NOT FEAR THE RESULT OF A HUNDRED BATTLES. IF
YOU KNOW YOURSELF BUT NOT THE ENEMY, FOR EVERY
VICTORY GAINED YOU WILL ALSO SUFFER A DEFEAT. IF
YOU KNOW NEITHER THE ENEMY NOR YOURSELF, YOU
WILL SUCCUMB IN EVERY BATTLE.

—Sun Tzu, *The Art of War,* IV:18

The sharp-edged silhouette of the starship *Lancaster* was just coming into view on the shuttle's forward screen when the system-wide alarm was broadcast on the gig's main comm. Sergei Torrijos, captain of the *Lancaster,* had been reclining comfortably in a passenger seat, taking a few moments away from the rather boring duty of reviewing inspection logs to look at the ship—*his* ship.

The midshipman piloting the craft acknowledged the alarm right away, as Sergei quickly set aside his tablet and came forward.

"Hail the *Lancaster*," he ordered the pilot, slipping into the other command seat. The young midshipman did so, and a small holo in the console dissolved to a view of the bridge.

"This is the captain. What's happening, Chan?"

"Enemy vessels incoming, sir," replied the voice of his exec, Chan Wells. "Jump points four and five are in the thick of it. Admiral Bryant's given the scramble order, and I have a pending call for you from Commodore McMasters."

The *Lancaster* had arrived insystem the day before yesterday, as a part of Admiral Coris Bryant's flag squadron. Even in peacetime, the need was great to show the flag here in the New Territories; while politicians and pundits back home talked of downsizing the military now that the zor threat was past, the Imperial Navy had strongly resisted, spending taxpayer credits on cruises that took them to places like this.

Less than an hour ago, Sergei had himelf been planetside, accompanying his squadron commander, Commodore McMasters, and the senior admiral on station on an inspection tour of the Down Base. Though it had been good to breathe real, unfiltered air and feel sunlight beating down on him, he knew that he would only be at ease when he stepped aboard the deck of his own ship.

"What's our ETA, Ensign?"

"Twelve minutes, sir, at present speed. With a little help from the *Lancaster*, I can cut that in half."

"Do it, Chan," he said to his exec. "Jump points four and five?"

"That's correct, sir."

Jump points four and five: eighteen and twenty hours Right Ascension. Antares-ward.

"Patch the commodore through to the gig. I'm on my way." The view of the bridge of the *Lancaster* dissolved away as the small craft began to accelerate.

Sergei again cursed his luck for being away, but probably half the captains in the fleet were in their gigs, or in their skivvies right now. The worst fear for any ship's captain, of course, is that his vessel will come under attack while he is not even aboard. Far worse than simply being off duty, it is the gnawing concern that a commander feels whenever he is far from his own deck. That he was in a ground-to-space shuttle, in visual range of the orbiting *Lancaster*, rather than several hours away on the other side of the system, was some consolation.

"Sergei, this is Ted." His commander's voice sounded hurried and tense against the backdrop of the General Quarters alarm.

Visual caught up with sound. On the small screen, he could see the busy hive of activity on the *Gustav Adolf*'s bridge behind Commodore Ted McMasters, his direct superior; the squadron flag was already under way. "Reporting, sir. I'll be aboard the *Lancaster* shortly."

"They've broken the damn treaty, Sergei. We're looking at—" He turned to examine the pilot's board before him. "We're outnumbered two-to-one, with half the Border Fleet on maneuvers."

"They don't have that many ships!" Sergei replied, glancing aside to see the *Lancaster* beginning to fill the forward screen.

"They've got forty or fifty ships on this side of the Rift, but we just didn't think they could get them all together without us noticing. We were wrong."

Just over five minutes later, after the *Lancaster*'s internal traction field brought the gig onto the hangar deck, Sergei was running through his ship's corridors, ignoring the dignity of rank in his haste.

McMasters' words echoed through his head: *We were wrong.* As he rode up in the lift, he thought about the implications. There had been less than twenty months of peace this time;

the Government back in Sol System had granted generous terms to the zor, believing they were too weak to consider launching another attack. As it had always been, it seemed ludicrous that the zor would ignite the war anew, bringing their small dominion into conflict with a larger, more powerful Solar Empire . . . but there had been intermittent war for more than half a century.

They had been too outnumbered, too outgunned, weakened by the victories scored by the fleet before the Treaty of Efal brought the campaign to a halt.

*We were wrong.*

The lift door opened and Sergei stepped out. "Captain on the bridge," Chan said, rising; those not engaged in duties associated with clearing dock came to attention. He waved them down and took the pilot's seat. Chan handed him a 'reader, showing the ship's status.

"All sections report," Sergei said, looking at the display.

"Engineering cleared for action."

"Helm onstation and ready, Captain."

"Gunnery sections ready for action, sir."

"Navigation ready for action." That last was a formality, since they weren't about to jump outsystem—the primary responsibility of navigation section—with the zor bearing down on them; maneuvering belonged to the helm while in normal space. The whole thing was a formality, really: Chan had ordered the ship to Beat to Quarters almost ten minutes ago and they were now ready to clear moorings, five minutes sooner than the regs said they needed.

As they locked on to the flight path being sent from the squadron flag, Sergei watched the mass-radar blips multiply on his pilot's board. There were already more than forty enemy vessels on the screen, and more were appearing as he watched.

*Ten minutes.* Mass-radar, unlike light-based radar, was instantaneous: it registered point-mass distortion of the local space, showing how large objects like planets and even smaller objects like spaceships wrapped the continuum around them as they moved. What he was watching was effectively real time, slowed only slightly by the processing of the *Lancaster*'s computer, even though the *Lancaster* itself was hours from the edge of the system, where the battle was already joined.

*They've got forty, almost fifty ships insystem in less than ten minutes,* he thought. *Only one way they could be that precise: if they all came from the same origination point.*

Based on their vector and momentum when they materialized, it would be trivial to calculate their starting position. "Chan—" he began to ask; but his executive officer had already considered that point, and gestured to a screen above the Ops station.

"It's about fifteen parsecs out, just within the Antares Rift. The star field is fairly sparse, but the computer has identified three or four likely choices. It looks as if they jumped from the neighborhood of a dark sun—but I'll bet next month's salary that there's a base out there."

When a ship appears out of jump, making the changeover from translight to sublight speeds, it carries with it the vector describing its orientation and velocity at the moment that it entered jump. The "jump echo," which consists of this vector plus a value indicating the amount of spatial disturbance generated by the jump itself, makes the calculation of the origin point a trivial exercise.

"A base big enough to handle more than fifty ships? It would take years to build something like that, especially in secret." Sergei grasped the arm of his chair with one hand as the idea hit home. "But it'd be easier in peacetime."

Chan looked back up at the plot, showing fifty-odd plotted entry paths, their hind ends crossing at a point deep in zor space, within the dark scar of the Antares Rift.

"We were set up."

*T−28 hours, 27 minutes*
*31 January 2311*
*2315Hrs Std*

"Where the hell did they dredge that up?" Commodore McMasters said, *sotto voce,* as the piped music on the orbital base's hangar deck shuddered to full volume.

Like the rest of Admiral Bryant's command, they stood at stiff attention as the admiral exchanged pleasantries with the commander of Pergamum Base. It was obviously a courtesy of some sort, since even the elderly admiral—who was known to be tone-deaf, and who rarely showed emotion of any kind in public—seemed to be experiencing a sort of painful recognition; but it was no tune Sergei recognized. He raised his eyebrows and gave an almost imperceptible shrug to his commander.

He'd been aboard ship too long, Sergei decided after taking a few moments to look around. The deck of the Pergamum orbital base was a huge container, big enough to swallow the *Lancaster* whole (*two or three times over,* he told himself, imagining three starships set nacelle-to-nacelle); it was bigger than any single compartment on any ship he'd ever been aboard, including the huge fleet-carrier *Ponchartrain,* on which he'd served his first tour. Its height defied description: lost in the diffuse overhead lights, he guessed it to be six or seven hundred meters away, while the breadth and width could be measured only in kilometers. Almost at the edge of his range of vision, etched sharply against the nightblack backdrop of space held back by pressure-field, he could make out a good-sized vessel—a close escort, maybe half *Lancaster*'s size—entering through the 'lock. From this distance, it looked like a toy.

" 'My Old Kentucky Home,' " McMasters whispered, interrupting Sergei's visual survey.

"Sorry?"

The last strains of the music worked their way out of the sound system. " 'My Old Kentucky Home.' For Bryant. He's from Kentucky, in North America on Terra. That's the damn song."

"Never heard of it." It certainly wasn't popular in the Buenos Aires arcologies where he'd grown up, the last place he'd spent more than a two-day layover on his home world.

"Old folk song. Nineteenth, twentieth century. Can't imagine how they found it. It's—"

Whatever it was, Sergei didn't have a chance to find out, since the admiral, accompanied by the officers of the base, had finished the opening pleasantries, and was approaching to begin the extended series of introductions.

It took long minutes for the group to reach the row where Sergei stood next to Ted McMasters, but by the time it arrived, he'd already committed the names of the chief officers onstation to memory. *Sir Stefan Ewing, Lord Governor of Pergamum.* Ewing was clearly a popinjay, a nobleman dressed in a Navy uniform, cut ever so slightly different from regulation; this was the privilege of an admiral, and Ewing was only a commodore, but Admiral Bryant didn't seem to find fault: nor could he, really, considering the importance of the Ewing family here in the New Territories. It irked Sergei to think that the most-forward naval base, even in peacetime, was in the hands of a noble fop who (if he remembered right) had purchased his commission.

*What the hell,* he thought to himself. *Wasn't the first one, won't be the last one.* Smiling with military precision, he exchanged a salute and extended his hand to shake that of the Lord Governor of Pergamum.

"Heard a lot about you, Captain," Ewing said in a growling voice, sounding as if he'd told each officer that in turn.

"All good, I hope, my lord." Ewing rated no more than "sir," but the noble honorific was more polite, if not more correct.

"Quite good, quite good. *Lancaster,* isn't it?"

"Best ship in the fleet, my lord, if I may say so. Perhaps the commodore would like a tour."

"We'll see what time allows, Captain."

Ewing took another long look at him—measuring him, sizing him up—and then moved on to Cory DeWitt of the *Pembroke*. Admiral Bryant gave him a sharp, curious glance before moving his attention to the next officer.

"I wonder what was that all about," Sergei said to McMasters quietly when the admiral and governor were well away.

"Venturing a guess . . . I'd say Ewing has a position open, and he's sizing up candidates."

"A staff officer's post?"

"No, I doubt it—he'd expect you to chafe at giving up command for a desk. I'd guess it's something to do with the naval base. Quite an honor, I'd say."

"Would you take it?"

"It wouldn't be offered to *me*. Been across the decks a few too many times to bring much prestige to the likes of Sir Stefan Ewing. He's looking for a 'bright young man.'"

Sergei colored slightly at the characterization, but didn't relax from attention to look at McMasters' face. He could, however, almost hear the smile. "I'm nearly forty-one, for God's sake."

"Exactly."


*T + 2   h o u r s ,   1 1   m i n u t e s*
*2   F e b r u a r y   2 3 1 1*
*0 5 5 3 H r s   S t d*


While things got hot on the Riftward side of Pergamum volume, the *Lancaster* and her sister ships scrambled from dock, headed at one-seventh of the speed of light for a rendezvous outside the orbital of the asteroid belt, three-quarters of a billion kilometers away. The battle, like all conflicts viewed from deep in a gravity-well, seemed to move in slow motion; shifts and watches would change twice more before Sergei's ship reached the primary battle zone.

Even with the tension of approaching combat, the five hours' gap between the first Beat to Quarters and the first visual contact lent an air of calm and almost normalcy on the bridge of the *Lancaster;* though there was still some risk that a zor captain with a severe death-wish might try to jump deep into the well to catch a human opponent unawares, the fact that it hadn't happened so far conveyed a certain sense of balance and proportion. The enemy was out *there,* at the edge of the system (where it was supposed to be).

Except, of course, that until two hours ago there hadn't been an enemy, at least in the minds of the Admiralty and the Government: this visit to Pergamum had been a peacetime mission.

The ships of the zor attacking force had materialized in normal space near two well-defined jump points outside the last planetary orbital of the Pergamum solar system. The system had been mapped originally by the zor, when it had belonged to them, and the jump points represented areas of low mass concentration and low probability of navigational hazards such as asteroids, comets or dust. In space, nothing is static, and the jump points drifted along with everything else; but these defined locations represented the safest places to materialize.

Sergei sat uncomfortably in the pilot's chair, studying the engagement that was hours from his present position, noting the ten blips that represented McMasters' squadron, heading as fast as they could for turnover—the point at which they would begin to decelerate toward the battle zone.

"Squadron conference is ready for you, Skip," Anne Da-Napoli said from the comm station. Sergei exchanged looks with his exec, who stood and came over to take the pilot's seat as Sergei walked off the bridge and into the ready-room.

Around the polished conference-table, four commanders were already present in holographic form: Bert—Sir Bertram—Halvorsen of the dreadnought *Mycenae;* Cory DeWitt of the starship *Pembroke* (a ship almost the *Lancaster*'s twin); Von Singh of the *Concordance*-class starship *Harrison* (an old and venerable vessel); and Adolfo Schaumburg of the squadron's carrier, the *Cambridge*. McMasters' place was still unoccupied at the head of the table.

Sergei nodded to his fellow captains as he took his seat.

At the head of the table, an image of Ted McMasters was coalescing. Within a few seconds the other four captains' images had appeared. McMasters looked around the room—where the commodore was actually sitting, aboard the *Gustav Adolf,* nine holos looked back.

"As I told each of you a few hours ago," he began without preamble, "we're outnumbered out on the edge of the system. Your mass-radar analysis will have told you that it's even worse than we originally imagined: there are ninety-two enemy vessels deployed near the Riftside jump points. The zor may well have abandoned every base on this side, and maybe even some in the Home Stars, to launch this attack.

"What was at the jump point . . . isn't there anymore." He looked down at a display in front of him, vaguely visible in holo image. "Fleet-carrier *Zambezi* reports losses of eighty percent of its fighter wings. It's moving under emergency power and is headed for dock, just outside the battle zone. Patrol command additionally reports the loss of several small craft, as well as the following vessels—" He touched the display and peered at it over the end of his nose. "*Alma-Ata, Aldebaran, Via Appia* and . . . *Sun Tzu*. All reported lost with all hands." This last name elicited surprised noises from everyone present; the *Sun Tzu* was a fifth-generation starship, one of the biggest and most heavily armed ships in the fleet, and had carried the flag of the senior admiral on station, Sir Graham DeSaia.

"Given the current situation, Admiral Bryant has assumed

command at Pergamum. If Admiral Lord Ralston returns with any part of the Border Fleet, or if Admiral Carson arrives, flag command will pass to them. For now, the flag is aboard the *Royal Oak*. Admiral Bryant's revised orders for the squadron are as follows." A display of the system came to life in the middle of the table, and McMasters began to detail the projected line of zor attack.

"This is their present position and concentration," McMasters indicated. "And this is where the admiral projects them to be in four to six hours." The display changed, showing the zor ships dispersed over a wider volume of the system, and much farther down into the gravity well. "Admiral Bryant believes that they will try to destroy the base, since they couldn't hold it even if they were able to capture it.

"One and a half squadrons are being deployed within the asteroid belt against this contingency. In the meanwhile, the rest of us have as our primary mission to keep the zor attacker from coming in range."

"Sir—" Cory DeWitt looked angry. "Are you suggesting that we're holding at least fifteen ships of the line back, while the rest of us try to protect a third of the solar system? We're outnumbered three-, four-to-one as it is, but without the squadrons deployed down in the well, it's—"

"That's right." McMasters didn't look too happy about it either. "The admiral has issued a Class One alert, and we're expecting imminent reinforcement from Sha'en."

"We could all be dead by then, if the commodore pleases."

"These are *my orders,* damn it!" He rounded on her. "This is where we stand. What's holding the zor at the periphery of the system is going to be gone—disabled, destroyed or in our laps—within six hours. Doesn't take an Imperial War College tactician to figure that out. Admiral Bryant has concluded that the zor are targeting the base, and he means to protect it. We are to do everything in our power to help achieve that goal, and we have everything in our favor . . . except numbers. We're faster, smarter and more heavily armed. Also, every ship in this squadron has seen enemy action. There are some ships—some already destroyed in battle—for which this engagement is their first.

"That may be why we were chosen to engage the zor out here."

"Sir," Sergei said. "Does anyone have any idea about why the zor attacked?"

McMasters looked across at him, leaning slightly back in his chair. " 'Why?' Who the hell knows," he added, more a comment than a rhetorical question. "Do you have some insights on the subject?"

"No concrete information, sir, merely conjecture."

"Out with it, Sergei."

"Well, sir . . . it's reasonable to assume that they didn't just strike at random. Pergamum's a valid target, an important naval base, and they must believe that destroying it, or the fleet that defends it, would be a blow to the Solar Empire.

"But why *now*, sir? Why would they strike at this particular time, unless there was something they wanted?"

"No one understands the zor," Von Singh of the *Harrison* interjected, "much less what they want."

Several others muttered assent. McMasters pyramided his hands in front of him. "Make your point, Sergei."

"Sir, there are a large number of ships stationed here at Pergamum, or making a peacetime visit to the base. Many of these vessels are on maneuvers right now, and unavailable. Furthermore, yesterday most of us were eating canapés and making small talk with each other planetside at the Governor's Mansion. Us . . . and two fleet admirals. Do you think that the zor might have known who was here, and chosen to attack right here, right now, because of that?"

"They'd need someone to spot that. A spy, or a coast-watcher."

"Or a traitor, sir."

No one had any response to this comment.

Still, it seemed that Commodore McMasters was aware of the unease around the table, and added, "The ships within the orbit of the asteroid belt are under the command of Lord Governor Ewing. The *Royal Oak* is out here, with us. Until we get in range, all we can do is prepare . . . and wait."

*T–16 hours, 12 minutes*
*1 February 2311*
*1130Hrs Std*

Waiting, of course, is part of the job in His Majesty's Navy, but Sergei sometimes found the long periods of inaction at peacetime social engagements almost too difficult to bear.

Sir Stefan Ewing's palatial mansion was located on an escarpment overlooking Pergamum's small capital city. Like nearly every other prominent building on the world, it had been shaped from a peculiar lavender-colored stone, quarried from the nearby Emperor Willem Mountains that towered over the capital's lush valley from scarcely a hundred kilometers' remove. Set out on the hillside and fashioned into a three-story edifice with rounded turrets at the corners, it looked like some sort of dream-palace at a distance. The luminous exterior of the turreted castle splendidly caught and reflected the rays of Pergamum's sun.

In accordance with strict protocol, the Lord Governor of Pergamum had issued an immediate invitation to the newly posted commanders and their staffs, and in equal conformity, they had responded in the affirmative; now, after a short aircar trip up to the castle on the hill, they stood about in the lush courtyard, sipping cool drinks and exchanging pleasantries.

Sergei had chosen to have his exec accompany him to this reception. The manual of naval etiquette indicated that he rated two additional officers in his entourage, since Ewing only exceeded him by one rank; but there was another difference that separated the two men: the patent of nobility held by the Lord

Governor, a distinction that some officers of captain rank held—but not Sergei Torrijos. His exec, Chandrasekhar Wells, a quiet, soft-spoken native of Stanton—New India—a half-dozen years his junior, was the perfect company at a gathering such as this; Chan was personally ambitious, but not at the expense of loyalty to his captain, and trustworthy, with no more friends at court than Sergei himself (which was to say, none). In the rarefied social atmosphere of Lord Governor Ewing's reception, Chan could serve as Sergei's second pair of eyes and ears.

Sergei and Chan had arrived on the aircar with Sir Bertram Halvorsen of the *Mycenae,* and Chan began to mingle with the other guests while Sergei and Bert stood together, admiring the quality of the governor's gardens and the strength of his drinks.

"This is quite a setup," Bert said, sipping thoughtfully and looking around the enclosed courtyard. "These border governors really know how to live."

"You're saying that the governor of New Chicago doesn't have a villa like this?" New Chicago was an oligarchy, and had been in the control of the same few families since it was first colonized.

"Well, of course he does, but . . . that took years to get to. New Chicago's pretty much settled now: big cities, arcologies, industroplexes . . . But out here the Governor does what he wants, the way he wants it. Goes where he chooses—" Bert gestured with his drink and added quietly, "Taxes as much as he chooses."

Sergei drew the conclusion Bert was aiming at, but shrugged. "The Ewing clan owns three or four seats in the Imperial Assembly. Certainly they're rich enough to afford a place like this."

"How d'you think they got to be this rich? This palace was built with public funds—don't doubt it for a moment.

"Well, it's a bit baroque," he added after a moment, nodding toward one of the corner towers, visible beyond the foliage in the garden, "but he does have a good eye for architecture."

*Too gaudy for me,* Sergei thought to himself, but reflected that he was no expert on the subject. Not wanting to venture an opinion, he merely sipped his drink sagely, and exchanged greeting glances with Cory DeWitt of the *Pembroke,* who stood in quiet conversation with Terry DeWitt, her husband and chief engineer.

Before Bert Halvorsen could continue, however, their host came into view, and noticing them, strode immediately up, exchanging a handshake with each of the officers.

"Gentlemen," Ewing said, holding the handshake just a bit too long. "I hope you're enjoying yourselves?"

"Very much so, my lord," Sergei answered, cutting off an opportunity for Bert to be glib. "Captain Halvorsen and I were just commenting on your residence."

"'My lord' is hardly necessary, Captain," Ewing replied. "At least in such friendly company. As for the house . . . yes, indeed, Felice and I have tried our best to make it comfortable.

"So, tell me, Captain Torrijos . . . How have you come to be posted here?"

"I think I'll get this refreshed," Bert said, looking from Ewing to Sergei, as if he'd caught some subtle signal that Sergei had missed. "If you gentlemen will excuse me," and he slipped away before Sergei could say a word to stop him.

"I . . . the *Lancaster* has just completed a three months' cruise near the edge of Imperial space, my l—sir. Commodore McMasters' squadron has been assigned to Admiral Bryant's fleet for peacetime duties in the New Territories."

"Policing, surveying, that sort of thing?"

"By and large, sir. Fairly routine activity, really, though it is important for us to be here, to show a strong presence to the zor."

"I've heard the admiral mention that rationale as well. What do you make of it, Captain? We hit them pretty hard at Scandia, and they sued for peace quickly after that. There are some who say"—Ewing looked from side to side, and lowered his voice, conspiratorially—"some who say that the zor threat has diminished enough that such a large presence out here in the New Territories is nothing more than a provocation."

Sergei knew this line of argument: it was the main plank of the Commonwealth Party, the opposition group in the Imperial Assembly. Any naval officer with a gram of sense knew what the Commonwealth Party wished to do to the armed forces, if a lasting peace was achieved with the aliens beyond the Empire; it would eviscerate it, deprive it of funding, put a large percentage of personnel on the beach with retirement bonuses or half-pay. In short, it would do what civilian governments always seemed to want to do to military establishments as soon as the peace broke out.

There was, of course, one basic flaw in this strategy.

"I appreciate the commodore's concern for the sensibilities of the zor, but I believe that it is a bit early to assume that the threat is over."

"We signed a treaty with them nearly two years ago." The governor's response wasn't especially combative, but it seemed clear that he wanted to see what Sergei's reaction would be; for his part, Sergei wasn't sure where Ewing was going.

"The Treaty of Efal is only the latest one in a series of 'permanent' arrangements with the zor, sir. It was concluded over the objections of the Admiralty Council, and against the recommendations of a large majority of line and staff officers. The Treaty of Las Duhr was abrogated less than three years after it was signed, and we had nearly nine years of war after that, before the zor fleet was mostly destroyed at Scandia. I am unconvinced of the good intentions of the zor as yet, sir."

"But each time the zor break a treaty with the Empire and fight with us, we push them farther and farther back, is that not correct? Pergamum was captured more than thirty years ago, and now it's twenty parsecs inside the Imperial volume. Surely even alien minds must realize that they are fighting a losing battle. They simply *cannot* win."

"I . . . am not sure that they think in those terms, sir."

"We have no idea what terms they think in, Captain. Certainly no one in the Navy seems to know."

*Or the Government,* Sergei thought to himself, but didn't choose to add it to the conversation.

"Torrijos, I have a great deal of admiration for officers such as yourself. Your experience as a commander is considerable, and your record commendable. But if the zor cease to be a threat . . . Well, there are more planets to govern than alien enemies to oppose."

"Sir?"

"Pergamum is still—essentially—a naval preserve. Even though the border is almost seventy light-years away, the presence of the Border Fleet here makes this more of a military world than a civilian one, but a . . . prolonged peace may well change all of that." Ewing looked around again, as if someone was listening in. "By the time Pergamum applies for representation, the people who helped bring that condition about will have benefited from their circumstances.

"I'm looking for the right sort of officers now. There won't be anything to offer for a time, but in six months, or a year perhaps . . ." He let the sentence trail off, as if he were trying to tantalize Sergei to tell him more. "Even if the fleet relocates, there will still be vessels on assignment here. His Majesty's Government will need someone to command them."

"Commodore, I—"

"Nothing to offer," Ewing repeated. "Nothing yet. Think about it, Torrijos." As if suddenly noticing someone else across the garden, Ewing turned and, without another word, strode away, aiming for another group of officers.

*T + 7 hours, 36 minutes*
*2 February 2311*
*1118Hrs Std*

Sergei kept one eye on the forward monitor while he and Chan went over departmental reports in the ready room. When the first flashes of weapons fire and the first glint of ship hulls became visible on extreme magnification, the captain of the *Lancaster* and his second-in-command went back on the bridge. The acting Admiral of the Fleet was already hailing them while Sergei took his seat and Chan relieved the gunnery officer of the watch.

"Yes, my lord," Sergei said, answering the hail.

"You have your deployment orders already, Captain, so I'll just wish you good shooting. The carriers up ahead have already taken heavy damage, so you may have fighters seeking cover while they try to reach the *Cambridge;* Captain Schaumburg is already trying to take them on. I want as many of them saved as possible, but for God's sake don't take any unnecessary risks!"

"Aye-aye, sir. *Lancaster* out." He swung toward the comm station, not taking his eyes off the forward screen. "Arte, hail the *Gustav Adolf* and tell the commodore we're coming into position. Chan, go to battle ready; report on weapons and defensive fields."

"All hands batten down, prepare for battle," Chan said to the shipwide. He looked at his displays. "Torpedoes armed and ready, Captain. All gunnery stations status green; absorption fields, distributors and travelers all report status green."

Pam Fordyce, his chief gunnery officer, came onto the bridge and took her station; Chan Wells moved to stand behind the helm officer.

"Helm, report on bogeys."

"Nearest bogeys are eighty thousand kilometers downrange. Two *Eclipse*-class vessels, bearing three-five-two degrees and zero-one-seven degrees, both negative one-zero degrees from

the plane of travel. The Imperial vessel . . ." The helmsman examined the transponder code carefully. "The Imperial starship
*Anson* is engaged with them. She appears to be heavily damaged."

"Comm, hail the *Anson*. *Lancaster* to the rescue," Sergei said,
noting the positions of the *Harrison* and *Odessa* on his flanks.
"Chan, pick us a target."

"Aye, sir," Chan answered, studying the pilot's board. The
comm officer nodded to Sergei.

"*Anson*, this is the *Lancaster*. We read you as heavily damaged; prepare to get under way."

There was a burst of static, coincident with a barrage from
one of the *Eclipses*. "—copy." A voice emerged from the noise.
"We're at about thirty percent, *Lancaster*, and I'm not sure . . ."
Another burst of static. ". . . have enough energy to maneuver
and still keep defensive—"

The comm channel dissolved completely into noise. The
comm officer worked the board, but shook his head.

Then there was no time for careful analysis. Combat between
space vessels was nothing like a vid, all noise and disruption; internal gravity prevented crew from being thrown from their seats
by a violent enemy broadside, and it took a considerable amount
of time for gunnery attacks to do anything more than build up
absorbed energy in defensive fields. Ships fired from gun-
mounts and torpedo tubes located all over the hull, targeting
from all directions.

On attack, the objective was to overload the enemy capacity
to absorb incoming fire, a slow process that would eventually
lead to shutdown—or even catastrophic failure—of defensive
fields. On the other hand, every ship defensive field had a complex structure like a crystal, that could be detected, analyzed,
and—if struck just right—penetrated by a single shot, piercing
the defensive field all the way to the enemy ship's hull. The enormous force and heat of an incoming shot could be devastating
against bare metal.

On defense, ships engaged in combat committed a large fraction of their power to radiating absorbed energy from their defensive fields. Due to the pseudo-crystalline nature of the fields, however, incoming energy was not always evenly distributed throughout the field, so a properly functioning defensive system was equipped with externally mounted devices—distributors, to carefully realign the field's lines of force as energy poured into it, and travelers, to equalize areas of energy absorption within the field itself. Thus a ship receiving incoming fire only from forward, starboard and above could redistribute that energy port, aft and below, greatly increasing the radiation capacity of the ship's field.

The activity of these devices, along with constant, semirandom maneuvering of ships engaged in combat, made analysis of a field's structure vastly more complicated; gunnery sections had to predict the structure that would be present when a precise hit struck, and the best gunnery officers combined a flair for the tortured mathematics of field dynamics with an intuitive feel for the pattern and flow as it swirled in their e-m and gravometric displays. In a way, top gunners were a throwback to more primitive times, when a master siege engineer used his intuition and experience to compute azimuth and distance, trusting more heavily to indefinable factors than the primitive instrumentation of the day. Good captains learned to trust their gunners, even if they mistrusted their rather unscientific methods.

"She's coming about, Captain," Chan said. Pam Fordyce was sweating over the fire-control boards at gunnery section, as two of her crew tried to calculate the field of the nearer *Eclipse.*

"Good. Maybe she'll let go of *Anson* for a minute." The Imperial ship's defensive fields were radiating well into the white, indicating that they were close to overload. "Looks like he's taken a breach aft on the port side, at about forty degrees."

"Copy on the breach, sir," Chan answered. "Mass-radar shows *Anson* as having been at the jump point when the attack started. Must have had his fields down."

"Damn fool." It was a common-enough tactic to fly "clean," without defensive fields, to conserve power; but it wasn't recommended when an attack was likely. *Well, there wasn't an attack likely, was there?* he asked himself. "Gunnery, lay down a pattern. Let's get his attention."

"Ready to fire, sir," Pam's voice came back. The other two gunners continued to work on the field problem, and Sergei could see that she hadn't completely loosed her attention, either.

"Fire at will."

Six superhot spheres of energy surged from launch tubes in the *Lancaster*'s belly and streaked across the intervening space to their target. Sergei imagined that he felt them go, though he knew intellectually that plasma torpedoes have no recoil . . . all six struck the field of the enemy *Eclipse,* between its aft section and roughly amidships.

"Brace for return fire."

But while the *Eclipse* had aligned itself better to receive the incoming fire, it had not changed its target, and continued to pour energy into the nearby *Anson*. Sergei ordered another barrage, and it, too, found its mark, while the *Anson*'s fields began to register brighter and brighter.

"*Anson*'s taken damage to distributors and travelers, Captain," Chan reported. "I estimate that she's got five minutes, on the outside, unless we knock out one of the opponents. Even then . . ."

"Helm ahead one-quarter. Comm, hail the *Anson*. Tell them to fold their tent *now* and get the hell out." He heard the hail go out, not sure if it would be received, as he watched the *Eclipse*-class zor vessel grow in the forward screen. They were coming into direct-fire range now.

"Forward batteries fire at will. Pam, we need to try that field."

"I'm trying, Skip," she said, again without turning. The *Lancaster*'s batteries were striking accurately; the enemy was starting to glow orange and then yellow. The *Anson* was clearly trying to withdraw, but its normalspace drive had been damaged by the hull hit, and didn't seem to be responding.

The *Lancaster*'s target, though clearly starting to feel the effects of the barrage, had not sent a single erg of energy against its attacker: it continued to fire on the *Anson*, which was blossoming patches of deep violet across its defensive fields.

"She's going to blow," Chan said, his voice level.

"Comm, hail the *Anson*, tell them to abandon. *Lancaster* will provide covering fire for escape craft. Helm, close with the *Anson*—"

"No time," Chan interrupted . . .

. . . And suddenly, the forward screen polarized to white, then bright blue and violet, then shut down altogether for a few seconds. "Beginning evasive maneuvers," helm said, "on your order, Captain."

"Do it," Sergei said immediately. The viewscreen came back on, showing the two *Eclipses* beginning to navigate around the expanding ball of blue-hot gas that, moments before, had been the starship *Anson*. Now it was just debris, a casualty of the battle.

The *Lancaster* applied reverse thrust to reduce her velocity as she closed with the battle scene, but it strained her inertial dampers somewhat; also, once lost, velocity can only be regained through the expenditure of energy, and much of her power was being devoted to other systems. Thus, while the remains of the *Anson* dispersed, the *Lancaster* simply veered around her, and after Sergei noted the close position of the *Odessa*, he nodded in approval as his ship bore down on the two enemies.

*Eclipse*-class zor starships were by no means the top of the line, and had been fighting with almost no propulsion velocity: they were drifting, maintaining position with attitude controls alone. As the *Lancaster* bore down on them, Sergei knew that his ship was going to be able to destroy them before they could escape, and that they must have known it, too. The *Anson*, a generation newer than the *Lancaster*, would have been more than a match for both ships if it had been uninjured.

The zor who had just destroyed it were waiting to die now as if their mission had been completed.

"Those bastards," he said quietly, to himself. As the *Lancaster* closed in, debris from the rapidly cooling explosion fell across the ship's path, gave up its kinetic energy, and drifted along, as if it had nowhere else to go.

*T–8 hours, 6 minutes*
*1 February 2311*
*2036Hrs Std*

There had been a day of briefings at the orbital base, followed by the governor's reception at his estate and then a dress-blues dinner at the Pergamum Down Officers' Club, a lavish, wood-paneled hall that had been built twenty years ago, when Pergamum was near the edge of the New Territories. It was almost as lavish as the governor's residence in the hills above.

Now Pergamum was almost a rear-area base, with more amenities and less strategic importance—still, the Border Fleet was based here, even though most of it was out on maneuvers. The hall was far from filled that evening, and the table talk had seemed to echo too loudly into its empty spaces. It had been a relief to get away from it, as groups of officers moved off to the gaming-rooms, or outside for a breath of night air, or—as Sergei had done—to the roof garden to look at the stars.

They left each other alone, the stargazers on the roof of the Officers' Club. Shielded from the ambient light of the capital city and the naval base, the starry panorama shone clear and bright, a strange and alien panoply, yet familiar in some undefinable way. Sergei knew, as he stood there looking up at the stars, that the world he stood on was somehow confining: that he belonged *up there,* aboard his ship, surrounded by the familiar fixtures that had constrained and defined his life for almost a quarter of a century. Down on the ground he felt bound, vulnerable, and didn't completely understand why.

Antares was visible in the night sky; it lay at the topmost point of a bright crescent of stars that had been nicknamed "the Boomerang." It had taken Sergei a few minutes of fiddling with Pergamum Down's database to identify the word—it was a Terran word, referring to an ancient weapon, later a sort of toy, that could be hurled away and would, if thrown properly, return to the thrower.

Antares, the bright red-orange star near the ecliptic, was the home star of mankind's enemy, the alien zor. He'd never met a zor in the flesh; none had ever been taken alive, and there wasn't much opportunity on the deck of a starship to step on, or over, a zor corpse. Few scholars had traveled in their space; to the average naval officer the zor were what briefings and 3-V said they were: alien, birdlike things, with beaks and wings and claws at the end of their arms and legs. They could fly, though apparently that was limited to worlds with half a g or less, and they were supposed to be lightning-quick, with—of all things—swords.

So here they were: aliens from the point of the boomerang, ever returning. They'd fought five wars with humanity, and they'd started every one, and lost every one—each time the boundary between zor and human space got a little farther out. Once, according to captured star-charts, the entire area of space that was now the New Territories had belonged to the zor—a rough cube more than forty parsecs on a side, with Pergamum near the center, stretching inward toward Sol System from a vast area of virtually empty space called the Antares Rift. On the other side of the Rift, 150 parsecs from Sol System, was Antares, at the center of a group of eleven stars that were the home worlds of the zor. Four or five of the others could be seen in Pergamum's night sky; none of the rest were visible unaided from mankind's home world.

Ever returning. It was a chilling thought, although it never quite left the mind of a naval officer.

*T+13 hours, 27 minutes*
*2 February 2311*
*1709Hrs Std*

"Incoming from the *Gustav Adolf,* Skipper."

The pilot's board showed nothing within two hundred thousand kilometers. Sergei nodded to Chan, who took the conn. "I'll take it in the ready-room."

"Aye-aye."

"Go ahead, sir," Sergei said, as the door slid shut. He dropped into his seat, trying to shed fatigue; he'd only taken two hours off since the last time they'd been in battle nine hours ago.

A holo representation of McMasters appeared in the adjacent chair.

"I can't raise the *Odessa,* the *Segontium* or the *Indefatigable.* The *Pembroke* reports heavy damage, but Cory says they can work high guard for the carriers. The *Cambridge* is on-station in the ionosphere of the gas giant. Everyone else seems to be all right. How are you doing?"

"We're at eighty-five percent efficiency, sir, but we'll have shed most of the excess field energy within half an hour."

"Good. From what I read, your sector is pretty much clear; our orders are to converge in the vicinity of the *Genève;* we're probably looking to fall back a bit, but the zor look to have taken huge losses."

"They don't seem to care about losses, sir." Sergei described the destruction of the *Anson,* and a similar scene involving the remains of the *Karakorum,* where the *Lancaster* had arrived a trifle too late. "My gut feeling, sir, is that they're looking to destroy ships, and don't intend to attack the base at all."

"Hmm." McMasters ran a hand over his unruly thatch of

hair, and rubbed his neck. Eleven and a half hours had elapsed since the first scramble from Pergamum base; he looked as if he'd spent the whole time in the pilot's seat aboard the *Gustav.* "There might be some validity to that position, but the admiral is still assuming an attack on the base."

"So the reserves stay inside the asteroid belt."

"For the present, yes. We're holding the line, Sergei, and giving better than we're getting. Make for the *Genève,* and if you're there before I am, report to the admiral."

"Aye-aye, sir."

Just under two hours later they came in visual range of the admiral's fleet flagship, the *Royal Oak.* A quick inspection of the ship, especially its energy gradients, showed that it had seen some action; the admiral had clearly had his ship in the line of battle. The *Gustav Adolf* had beaten them there; altogether there were more than two dozen ships assembled, including most of McMasters' command, and what remained of two other squadrons. The zor that the *Lancaster*'s mass-radar could detect had withdrawn as well, unwilling to approach the flagship and the firepower surrounding it.

Relative calm prevailed, as ships lumbered into new formations, radiating excess energy from their defense fields; still, Sergei could see, or detect, evidence of the battle that had raged for more than thirteen hours. Many ships—more than half— were radiating energy into the white, while more than half of them showed irregularities or deformations in their fields, indicating faulty or malfunctioning equipment. The *Lancaster* had lost two starboardside travelers due to overload, but hadn't taken any direct hull hits. All in all, they were in fairly good shape.

"Message from Captain Schaumburg for you, Skip," Anne DaNapoli said from the comm station. She'd come on watch four hours ago, and had waved off relief since then; she looked grim and tired, but probably a lot better than Sergei assumed he looked. After the communication with McMasters, he'd forced himself to grab a few more hours' bunktime, but hadn't really slept very well.

"Open the channel. —Dolph, what can I do for you?"

"*Lancaster*'s luck is still with you, Sergei," Dolph Schaumburg said. "You look like you haven't seen the battle at all. Hope that luck holds out. I'm ready to take your stranded flyers aboard, anytime you're ready."

"I haven't got orders to form up yet, so this is a fairly good time. You sure the *Cambridge* has enough berth space? I've got eight of them on the deck."

"We lost a quarter of our fighters during the battle. We've got plenty of room—in fact, those flyboys better be ready to go out. My crews are dead tired, the ones that aren't in sick bay . . . or the morgue."

*Or floating in space with the rest of the debris,* Sergei told himself. "I'll give the order."

"I'll be waiting for them. *Cambridge* out."

"Hangar deck," Sergei said, touching the intercom on his armrest. "This is the captain. Get those fighters launched and en route to the *Cambridge*. Bruce, tell them they've got fifteen minutes to get clear of the *Lancaster* or they'll be watching the rest of the battle from the cargo hold."

Within an hour the Imperial ships were formed up in a concave wedge, with the Royal Oak and the fleet-carrier *Genève* in the center; this configuration provided the largest concentration of firepower in the middle, and allowed the deployed ships to quickly englobe attackers if they made for the center of the formation. The *Lancaster*'s nearest neighbors were the fleet-carrier *Cambridge* and McMasters' flag, the *Gustav Adolf,* with the *Phaedra* and the *Harrison* nearby as well.

It was clear that the zor ships intended to engage the entire formation. Spread out loosely like a skirmish line in three dimensions, the zor vessels accelerated toward the Imperial positions, reached turnover and began to decelerate, firing almost at random as soon as they were in range. The admiral had deployed fighters out in front of the capital ships, intending to slow down the zor advance, but the enemy made no effort to get out of the way of the tiny craft, even losing a few of their own ships to lucky hits by the fighter pilots.

By the time the zor were at engagement range, most of the fighters were berthed again. Small craft might be useful once the zor were pinned down, so Sergei's orders were to make that possible—fend off zor attacks on the fleet-carrier by engaging whatever came close.

The zor seemed to know that, too. Avoiding a head-to-head confrontation with the *Lancaster,* two *Sunspot*-class battleships, somewhat slower and heavier-armed than an *Eclipse,* tried to turn the corner on Sergei's ship and reach the *Cambridge.*

"Fire at will," Sergei said as they closed in. The gunnery sections began to target and fire; on the pilot's board, ships were battling the zor vessels as they closed in on the larger ships, heedless of incoming fire.

The forward viewscreen was tinged dull orange as one zor vessel concentrated fire on a small segment of the defensive field.

"Cease fire! Helm, come about to new coordinates," Sergei ordered suddenly, and named a direction off to starboard, placing the ship so that it presented the port and underside travelers rather than the damaged starboard ones. "Ahead one-quarter." The ship began to execute the course change, and a bright yellow-white spot bloomed just ahead on the screen: the concentrated fire, aimed at "cracking" the *Lancaster*'s defensive field and scoring a hit directly on the hull, had been dissipated by the abrupt alteration in the structure of the field caused by the maneuver.

"Belay course change, all stop. Gunnery sections, resume fire. Pam, report on field strength."

"Down twenty-three percent," Pam Fordyce, his gunnery chief, answered, having anticipated the question.

"Anne, hail McMasters. Inform the commodore that the zor may be looking to make penetration attacks. Advise evasive maneuvers as necessary. I—"

"Excuse me, sir, incoming urgent from the *Genève*," DaNapoli interrupted.

"Let's hear it."

"—all ships. Fleet flagship is under attack by a large number of enemy vessels; repeat, large number of enemy vessels. Concentrated fire on the flagship. Calling all ships, flagship needs help." The message began to repeat; Sergei held up his hand and it cut off.

"Anne, try to raise the *Royal Oak*. Helm, report on the status of our two assailants."

"The closer one is at about forty percent, Cap'n, and has lost some maneuverability. The farther one is at about sixty, but he seems to have backed off to dump some field energy. He's almost out of fire range."

"Give him some torpedoes, and try for a penetration on the near guy."

"*Royal Oak* seems to have lost comm, Captain," Anne DaNapoli interrupted. "I was able to reach Commodore McMasters, sir, and he advises that we should be able to close up in this part of the battle volume and reinforce."

Sergei took a moment to look at the pilot's board. The zor force, perhaps half again as many ships as the Imperials, had begun to concentrate toward the middle of the Imperial formation, as if they were trying to englobe the flagship. Even the two enemies that had been trying to reach the *Cambridge* appeared to be standing off, changing their courses toward the *Royal Oak*.

"Helm, new course. Get us to the flagship, ahead one-third."

The *Lancaster* and the *Pembroke* accelerated toward the center of the Imperial deployment. As Sergei watched, the holo patterns on the pilot's board began to resolve: the attack was a clever exposition, considerably different from zor tactics in the past.

The zor ship-captains were just as heedless of danger and overly aggressive, but their tactics had been much more subtle, aimed at keeping the peripheral ships in the Imperial formation occupied long enough to concentrate fire on the ones in the center . . . as if it had been their plan all along.

"Pam," Sergei said into the relative quiet of the bridge, as the *Lancaster* began the long deceleration toward the *Royal Oak*'s position. "See if you can isolate the flagship's condition."

"It's hard to tell," she said at once. "There's a lot of noise . . . huh." Her fingers flew over the board, and then she seemed to replicate her movements, as if rechecking the information. She turned her chair to face Sergei. "They're radiating in the blue, sir. The *Royal Oak* is going to lose field power."

Sergei's hands clenched the arms of the pilot's chair. *They know. They must know.* "What's our ETA?"

"Six minutes, Cap'n. We'll be in firing range in less than two."

"Helm, ahead one-half."

"That'll take us well past the battle zone, sir—we won't be able to dump velocity in time."

"We'll have to execute a tight turn. I want to be in firing range—"

A large area of the screen became bright, expanding and licking out. Three other explosions bloomed—

"—before—"

The scene up ahead was confusion: the chain-reaction explosion took in another, much larger ship—a carrier, perhaps—and both human and zor ships were maneuvering to get out of the area. Only ships in extremely close proximity—hundreds of meters—could have been affected, unless the energy output was huge.

". . . Belay the order, helm. Pam, can you get a fix on the *Royal Oak*?" He thought he already knew the answer. The brightness began to fade ahead, as they got closer to the center of the confusion.

"No, sir. And I can't find the *Genève*, either."

The *Lancaster's* bridge was absolutely silent, except for the background noise of the ship. The pilot's board in front of Sergei began to sort itself out: transponder codes, perhaps a half-dozen on each side, disappeared as the mass-radar failed to locate the ships to which they belonged.

"Pergamum Base, this is the *Gustav Adolf*." The *Lancaster* was receiving a systemwide transmission; Anne DaNapoli moved to cut it off, but Sergei held up his hand. "Base, this is McMasters aboard the *Gustav*. Do you read?"

"Pergamum Base here."

"Base, send up the reserves. The *Royal Oak* and the carrier *Genève* have been destroyed by enemy fire. We need reinforcements."

"Repeat message, *Gustav Adolf;* did you say the *Royal Oak* is destroyed?"

"Affirmative. Reinforce our position immediately."

"Aye-aye, sir, I'll relay the request to the Lord Governor."

"That wasn't a request, Base. That was an order. Admiral Bryant was aboard the flagship and is presumed dead. I'm in command. Send up the reserves!"

"I—" The comm officer at Pergamum Base was clearly under orders to the contrary. Sergei sat forward in his chair; Ted had made this a system-wide broadcast, so every ship in the Imperial Fleet was listening. Maybe the zor were listening, too, but apparently that wasn't important at the moment. "I'm afraid I'll have to contact Lord Governor Ewing, sir, as he gave specific orders—"

"Listen, and listen good. This is Commodore McMasters, boy, acting commander of all forces in this system. I rank the Lord Governor by seniority, and I outrank you as well. Raise those vessels and get them under way for the asteroid belt *at once,* or there won't be a fleet here to defend. Do you read?"

"I read, sir, but I—" The transmission from the base halted

abruptly, as if it had been switched off. After a moment, it came back on, but the voice was different.

"McMasters, this is Governor Ewing. You have no authority to order the Pergamum defense force; they were given into my command by Admiral Bryant."

"Bryant's dead, man, and we will be, too, if you don't get those goddamn ships out here—"

"Their mission is to protect Pergamum Base, McMasters, and they'll stay right here to do so. You have no authority."

"Listen here, Ewing. I rank you, and this is a war situation. This isn't some kind of exercise, where you'll get a bad mark for violating regulations. The zor aren't here to take Pergamum Starbase."

"The admiral believes—believed—differently."

"It doesn't matter a damn what he believed! The zor are after *ships,* man. They're trying to disable the fleet."

"If that is the case, why should I commit additional ships to the battle? The zor will certainly try to target them as well."

"You should commit them, *Lord Governor,* because I'm ordering you to."

"As I have explained," Ewing answered, as if he were giving a lesson to a petulant and annoying schoolboy, "I do not recognize your right to give me orders."

"Admiral Bryant—"

"—is dead. You have already mentioned that. When an admiral appears here at Pergamum, I am sure orders will be given. Until then, my command remains where it is. Ewing out."

From a few thousand kilometers away Sergei could practically see the steam rising from his commander's head. Gunnery was still trying to make a target from the approaching zor, and helm was receiving instructions from the new flag. The *Lancaster* and the other ships nearby were trying to take up positions in a web pattern, so that they could provide covering fire.

Meanwhile the zor seemed to be milling about, firing randomly at anything that came close. It seemed to Sergei that they had completely abandoned line-of-battle.

"Wait a sec," he said, watching the pilot's board. The zor were beginning to cluster in a pattern that was still forming, moving toward the *Gustav Adolf*'s position.

"Anne, get me the *Gustav*." *The fleet flagship,* he told himself. "They're going to try and do it again."

*T+17 hours, 6 minutes*
*2 February 2311*
*2048Hrs Std*

A searing blade of fire swept across the underside of the *Gustav Adolf,* cutting away its hangar deck, and setting off a chain of explosions. Sergei could imagine bulkheads slamming shut, as the internal systems aboard the starship sought to localize the damage. Shuttles and lower-deck occupants tumbled into space, some still on fire, though the oxygen that fed that burning would soon be exhausted, reducing them to nothing more than debris at absolute zero . . .

*T+17 hours, 30 minutes*
*2 February 2311*
*2112Hrs Std*

The *Lancaster*'s pilot's board registered vessels jumping into the system: ten, twenty, thirty ships flying in a wedge formation, headed immediately for the inner system, where the two contending fleets were tearing each other apart.

The transponder codes winked to life: they were Imperial vessels of the Second Fleet . . .

*T+17 hours, 54 minutes*
*2 February 2311*
*2136Hrs Std*

Again the pilot's board registered vessels coming into realspace, even farther down in the gravity well. This time, though, they registered as zor vessels.

Enemy reinforcements.

Without looking, Sergei could guess their probable point of origin: the location out in the Antares Rift, where the other ships had come from. Again it occurred to him that the zor were employing new tactics: for the first time, they'd held back some of their force, waited for the Imperials to bring in reinforcements, and then sent in their own.

As he issued orders, bringing the *Lancaster* about in the absence of a comm link with his commander aboard the *Gustav Adolf,* he began to wonder if there would be any survivors of the battle here at Pergamum. The image of the boomerang suddenly returned to mind—the constellation in Pergamum's sky, with Antares, the zor Home Star, at its tip . . .

*aLi'e'er'e*

# CHOOSING THE FLIGHT

PART ONE

chapter 1

WE BELIEVE THAT THIS TREATY WILL FORM THE BASIS
FOR A PERMANENT AND LASTING PEACE WITH THE ZOR
PEOPLE.

—Baron Reichardt of Denneva, Secretary of State,
on the Treaty of Efal (2309)

WHILE WE USE PEACE TO RELAX, THEY USE IT TO RE-ARM.

—Timoniel Narada, Lord Laughton,
First Lord of the Admiralty (2309)

The public became aware of the battle at Pergamum as a rather significant military defeat, though it was by no means a complete loss; if anything, it was, in strategic terms, more of a loss for the zor than for the Solar Empire. The huge quantity of debris left floating in the Pergamum solar system after the last of the zor had withdrawn provided Naval Intelligence with a vast amount of additional information about mankind's enemy, and there was ample evidence that the zor had set aside, and committed, a considerable amount of resources to be able to make the attack in the first place.

Pergamum remained in Imperial control. Sixty-three and a half light-years—about twenty parsecs—from the Antares Rift, well within the limits of the Solar Empire, control of the 46 Cygni system had never really been in question. The naval base had not been the objective of the attack: it had been the intention of the zor to destroy the mobile fighting force stationed there. What was still operating when the last of the zor were destroyed, or withdrew, remained to guard that base; what could make the short jump to the dry dock at Mustapha, made the jump. Cleanup began; funerals were conducted, many in space. A week passed without further attack, and then a month more.

The Solar Empire returned to war.

Sergei Torrijos, commodore in His Imperial Majesty's Navy, waited for the retinal scan to verify his identity; then, as the last set of security doors slid aside to permit him passage, he made a few minute adjustments to his uniform and walked down the brightly lit corridor.

Both walls were adorned with portraits of naval heroes, staring down with imposing frowns, their dress uniforms emblazoned with decorations and honors. It was part of the atmosphere of the Admiralty: it was intended to overawe junior officers, to bring the weight of hundreds of years of hoary tradition down on their shoulders.

Though he'd rather be on the bridge of a starship, Sergei knew what he was here for. *Any one of those frowning portraits would change places with me*, he thought. *Better to be a living commodore than a dead admiral, any day.*

He came at last to a pair of double doors, decorated with the sword-and-sun of the Solar Empire. The doors had brass doorknobs set in the middle of the polished wood, relics of some past age.

He knocked, and from within he heard a familiar voice respond, "Come."

He entered the office. It was wide open to the view of Greater St. Louis: the skyline, the steady stream of 'copter and aircar traffic, the huge spaceport. The openness made him slightly uneasy; fifteen years aboard a space vessel had induced a mild agoraphobia.

At the far left side of the great panoramic view, a figure turned to face him. A broad smile spread across his face, and he limped over to where Sergei stood with his cap tucked under his arm.

They exchanged salutes and a firm handshake. "Good to see you again, my friend," the other said. "A commodore's uniform suits you nicely."

"Thank you very much, Admiral."

"So formal." Rear Admiral Theodore McMasters moved slowly over to a sideboard, gesturing to comfortable armchairs in a corner of the office. "Come, sit down. Can I pour you something? Vodka, wasn't it? Or gr'ey'l?"

"No, thank you, sir."

"I'll just have one myself, then." McMasters made himself a whiskey-and-soda, gave it a good stir, and raised it in the general direction of the control tower.

" 'To the everlasting glory of . . .' Well, you know the rest," he finished, and drank, then set the glass down beside his chair, and settled carefully into it. "So. Does your new command meet with your approval?"

"Surely the admiral does not need to ask. It's more than I ever could have hoped for."

"You're a damn good officer, Sergei."

"As you know, sir," Sergei replied, "being a 'damn good officer' means nearly nothing in His Majesty's Navy. Without friends in high places, 'good officers' never become more than helmsmen or junior engineers."

"My old friend and comrade, you now have a friend in a high place." He winked and smiled, spreading his arms wide as if he could encompass all of Greater St. Louis. "I, too, didn't expect to be sitting where I am, but after— Well, it was the least I could do to find you a new set of shoulder-boards to wear, especially if you have to fly that old rustbucket."

"'Rustbucket'?" Sergei sat forward. "'Rustbucket'? The *Lancaster* is the best damn ship-of-the-line in the fleet!" After a moment's hesitation, he added, "Sir."

McMasters smiled. "Every captain in the fleet will say that about his ship, but I'm glad to see that you take such pride in the old girl. She was mine before she was yours, and I hope you'll retain her as your flagship when her overhaul is complete."

"Aye-aye, sir!" Sergei had feared that he would be assigned a newly commissioned fourth- or fifth-generation vessel as his flagship. He'd freely admit that he preferred the old *Lancaster*, with crew and systems he could rely upon. Without that crew, and those systems, he would most likely be dead—along with the men and women of the *Royal Oak*, the *Pembroke*, the *Sun Tzu*, and others—twisted metal, flesh and bone, destroyed by explosion or decompression, debris adrift in the empty spaces of the 46 Cygni system.

Pergamum.

The dying echoes of the battle that had taken place several weeks ago still rang in his ears, and the scenes of destruction continued to play themselves out before his mind's eye, like a 3-V documentary.

The inevitable result of having trusted the zor once more, of having believed in the inimical aliens' "sincere desire for peace."

The gloom of remembrance must have shadowed his face. McMasters raised his glass again. "I remember it, too, Sergei old man. The *Gustav* was in even worse shape by the time we got her to Mustapha."

An explosion aboard the *Gustav Adolf*, McMasters' squadron flagship, had shattered his leg. At the time, he had been the senior officer in the battle zone—a commodore with no admirals alive to answer to.

"I assume, sir," Sergei said, after a moment, "that you didn't ask me here to reminisce about the good old days."

"No, something far more important."

McMasters sat forward and placed his hands on his knees. They were thick and knotted, an engineer's hands, pitted by burn- and scar-marks the admiral had accumulated in his long ascent from junior engineer to chief engineer to technician and beyond. "Sergei," he said, looking down at his hands, "I have important news for you, about something which could change the course of this war. Do you remember a captain by the name of Marais?"

Sergei thought for several seconds. "An aristocrat? Family owns—an agricultural combine?"

"Marais-Tuuen, that's right. He was kicked upstairs to flag rank a few years ago, during the last war, before Efal. He had made some statements about the conduct of the war which did not endear him to his superiors. He chose voluntary retirement with a promotion to vice admiral, and was removed from active duty.

"All the flap was about a book he wrote." McMasters reached into a drawer and pulled out a book disk. He slid it across the desk at Torrijos. "Have you read it?"

Sergei shook his head. "Never had the pleasure, sir, though I understand it's some sort of diatribe about the zor." He flipped the book in his hand and looked at the back cover, which showed a small 3-D picture of the author.

Graying at the temples, dressed in a captain's uniform, Marais did not appear to be a raving maniac, which was (Sergei recalled) what the critics made him out to be.

"Just some crazy?" he asked.

The admiral took a sip of his drink and replied, "Maybe. Let me review the theme of the book for you.

"Marais offers an analysis—perhaps a madman's analysis, perhaps not—of every step the zor have taken since they attacked Alya sixty years ago. He's gotten a look at zor sources, mostly myth and religion, but also some of their public records. I checked on him: his references are authentic, and he seems to be fluent in the language. This was written almost *two years* before the attack on Pergamum, but he knew that zor had no intention of keeping the peace—not in the Treaty of Efal or in any other treaty they have ever signed with us. This is not because they are a pack of lying bastards—on the contrary, he believes them to be extremely honorable."

"Then—why do they continually break those treaties?"

"They don't really break them, he says. Rather, they ignore them. To the zor, treaties with 'lower forms of life'—meaning you and me, Sergei—mean nothing at all. Mankind is outside the zor parables of creation, and is therefore an abomination that must be destroyed.

"We've always suspected that there was a rationale for their terrible ferocity—their entire pattern of destruction, especially high-density civilian areas and agricultural worlds instead of areas with more military or industrial value, suggests that their objective was the destruction of population rather than combat units or resources. In any case, they take advantage of peace, he says, to re-arm and ready themselves for further combat.

"The problem, of course, is that we always offer generous terms, and leave the zor their army and their fleet, when we defeat them. We are only setting ourselves up for the next attack, a year or two down the line.

"The zor have contempt for any enemy that would do that," McMasters finished.

"I'm not surprised the book wasn't well received," Sergei said. "It makes us look—well, spineless and weak. It also totally ignores the sort of media pressure brought to bear once the war was hot."

"Groups which never saw the sort of destruction the zor wrought . . ."

"Neither did Marais."

"That's quite true. He served in the rear areas mostly, and was only posted once or twice in combat zones, and then only as a staff officer. But the point of bringing all of this up, Sergei, is that the most biting and acid criticism his book, *The Absolute Victory,* hinged on his statement that the zor would attack again, and soon. No one in authority believed that the zor could or would attack the Solar Empire again.

"Even Admiralty analysis said that it would take them at least a dozen years to get back to fighting strength, after the beating they took at Scandia."

McMasters leaned back in his chair and took a sip of his drink, and then pyramided his hands in front of him. "It seems that the Admiralty—and everyone else—underestimated the zor. Everyone, that is, except Ivan Hector Charles, Lord Marais, Vice Admiral, Imperial Navy, retired."

"In other words—"

"In other words, my old friend, Marais was right, in at least one aspect. More importantly, someone—God only knows who—made sure a copy of *The Absolute Victory* was placed in the emperor's hands. As a result, Marais was summoned to the Imperial Court last week."

Torrijos snorted. "He asked for an active-duty assignment, I suppose."

McMasters smiled once more. "Aye, he did.

"Lord Marais asked to be appointed Admiral of the Fleet, with authority over all other officers and their commands."

A troop transport began to taxi along the main runway, which had been cleared for it; the reverberation made the floor and windows thrum from a kilometer and a half away.

"He did *what?*"

"While most of His Majesty's Court was gasping and sputtering, the emperor said that he would take the matter under consideration. Apparently, enormous pressure was brought to bear on the First Lord of the Admiralty—because the request was granted. As of April 1, 2311, three weeks from this date, Ivan Lord Marais is your commanding officer, and mine. And everyone else's—naval, marine, airborne, and ground support. In the combat zone, Marais will be unchallenged in his authority."

"Sir—this is an insult—an outrage! Will you stand for it?"

"What do you suppose I should do? Resign? Arrest Marais when he sets foot on the deck of a vessel? Call him out and challenge him to a duel? Hire an assassin?

"This isn't 3-V, my friend. I have no choice *but* to stand for it. Either Lord Marais will be competent, or better, and we will benefit by it; or he will be incompetent, or worse, and my presence may help to prevent total disaster.

"You see, I have been offered the position of chief of staff."

"By the emperor?"

"By Marais himself."

"Off the record, Admiral, he certainly has gall."

"You're right. But he also has the confidence of His Imperial Majesty.

"Which brings us to you. Sergei, I'm out to pasture now, unfit for duty. The line they feed you at the Academy about how a line officer has to be some kind of superman, strong, brilliant, and so forth—it's a load of crap. But a line officer does have to be able to walk, not hobble. They'll grow me a new leg, but I'll be out of action for a year, maybe more: certainly enough time to make me obsolete. Especially in wartime. I fly a desk for the duration, and it might as well be the desk of Marais' chief of staff. For one thing, it permits me to advise him. Especially on his choice of flag squadron commander."

Sergei had been listening quietly, but McMasters' last statement jolted him back to complete attention as the implication of it hit home. Before he could sputter out an answer, McMasters added, "I told him you were the best in the fleet. He told me he thought you were too young and inexperienced, but I assured him that fifteen years on the bridge of a starship was enough experience for anyone of your talents. You were my helmsman, my exec, and my wing commander, Sergei, and frankly, you've been the best damn officer I've ever been privileged to serve with.

"A month and a half from now Admiral Marais is going to lead a foray into zor space that will either be the greatest accomplishment in more than half a century of war, or will be a total disaster. Perhaps it'll be Marais' strategy that makes the difference. But maybe it'll be your skill. I want you to be there, to be his flag commodore."

"I . . . don't know what to say, sir. I didn't really know what to expect when you called me here, in the middle of a stint on the beach, but . . . Well, what I mean to say, is . . ." He let his voice trail off.

"I assume you'll take the post, then."

"If I may have the *Lancaster*, sir, then I accept."

"I'd be disappointed if you accepted without it." McMasters stood carefully and crossed to the sideboard. "Have that drink now?"

"I think so. If not for now, then for an hour from now, when I realize what's just happened."

## chapter 2

The St. Louis Admiralty complex covered hundreds of square kilometers of what had once been rolling farmland. Originally built around the even older Lambert Field, it had been extended and expanded over the centuries, absorbing more and more of the remains of the original city that bordered it. It was just as well: much of St. Louis had been reduced to rubble during the War of Accession that had created the Solar Empire, and the city itself had become something of a wasteland.

The skyline hallmark of the old city, the famous Arch, had faded into history, partially destroyed by the bombings and then razed to its foundations by Seabees brought in for that purpose. Even had it not been deemed a hazard due to the undermining of its foundations, it would have been a traffic obstacle or (worse yet) a reminder of an earlier age, before emperors and the exploration of interstellar space. In any case, the skylines of cities looked different now, more hunched and lonely. The massive arcologies that towered above the vast agroplexes of Arizona and Nevada, or perched off the Virginia and Carolina coasts, had proved to be more attractive than the four-hundred-year-old urban shells that dotted the continent.

Sergei had first visited St. Louis when he was beached near the end of the third Man-Zor war in 2295, when the carrier *Ponchartrain* was badly damaged and put in dry dock. The Treaty of Las Duhr, an even more foolhardy peace than Efal, had provided the Assembly with good pretext to slash the budget of the Imperial Navy not long afterward; he, like many others, had been left ashore with a commission and half-pay, with the dignity of a naval officer but no ship to call his own. Then, as now, he had been billeted in a suite in the BOQ (bachelor officer quarters) on the northeast side of the complex, ten minutes by aircar from the flight tower and the Admiralty offices.

At that time there had been very little hope for an aspiring, but less than influential, first lieutenant with no friends at Court, back from the wars and a long way from the poor megacity of Buenos Aires. He was twenty-six, as out of place in St. Louis as he had been back home. After flying a *Wasp* fighter against zor fleet-carriers and living to tell about it, a groundhog's life simply wasn't appealing. There had been a chance to resign the hard-won commission and retire into private life, as a cargo pilot or a security guard or something; separation benefits were raised a few notches to encourage this: *"His Imperial Majesty having no further need of your services, it is my pleasure to award you the Order of the White Cross and an Honorable Discharge from Imperial Service."* Or so he remembered it.

If His Majesty's Service was especially interested in discontinuing the commission of a particular officer, there was the technique known as "riffing"—from the officialspeak term "reduction in force." Officers with spouses or partners on the outside gladly took up civilian life, unwilling to take the chance on being participants in another war.

For Sergei, there had been no spouse or partner, and no other real choice. The path that had led him here had not been easy or without danger; he had escaped the sanitized poverty of his native city of Buenos Aires by entering the Coast Guard Academy there, graduating with honors after a training tour in the Sol System, and serving with distinction aboard His Majesty's fleet-carrier *Ponchartrain*. He was long past the decision to make the Navy his career, but the untimely cessation of hostilities had placed that in doubt.

It was here, in the St. Louis complex, that he had first gotten to know Ted McMasters. Commander McMasters then, they had first met when Ted had been appointed Judge-Advocate to prosecute him in a court-martial aboard the *Ponch;* it had been a charge of theft, trumped up by a venal officer of the watch after Sergei, a poor commoner from Buenos Aires, outscored all of the barons' sons in practice runs and outflew them out there where it was for keeps. Even though it would have been far easier to accept the perjuring testimony of the real culprits, Ted had decided that the honor of the Service demanded the truth. He accepted the collapse of the Imperial Navy's case with grace.

Ted was fortunate enough to have a posting when the peace broke out. Through some contacts at Court, he had gained the support of the *Lancaster*'s previous commander, the legendary tactician Sir Malcolm Rodyn, and had obtained the appointment as that vessel's new captain. Orders in his pocket, shiny new captain's bars on his shoulders, Ted McMasters had come back to Sol System looking for officers to fill his key staff positions; Sir Malcolm's key senior officers had either become his aides when he was appointed a staff officer at Court, or with his help had obtained promotions of their own. In any case, they were gone from the *Lancaster*'s roster.

At the time, Sergei had believed that his meeting with Ted in the officers' mess was purely accidental; later he learned that the transfer orders had been filled out well in advance, and only awaited Sergei's agreement and signature.

"I need some good officers," he had said. "Las Duhr will keep the zor happy for eighteen months, maximum." It was a commonly held belief in the armed forces; only the civilians seemed unwilling to believe it. "Be ready to ship out in a week."

Sergei mentioned the names of fellow officers, just as good (or better) than he believed himself to be. McMasters had dismissed all of them. "Sorry," he'd said; "not on my list." It had seemed terribly unfair to Sergei: without such a patron as Captain McMasters to rescue them from dry dock, they'd be stuck in place until they lucked out or gave it up.

"It *is* unfair," McMasters had said. "Nobody said otherwise. I didn't make the damn system, but I have to play by its rules. Whatever influence I have, I'll use, to my best advantage. When you have my seniority and my rank, I'm sure you'll do the same."

And he had, over the years. McMasters had picked most of the key people on the *Lancaster,* from Chan Wells down, that way. Fifteen years later Sergei was back in the same place, with completely different prospects. He had come full circle, in a way: now it was *his* responsibility to get a command ready for space. The circumstances were vastly different than they'd been in '96; the war was hot, and the Government was calling up every available officer. The prospects for his career were far brighter; the twenty-six-year-old First Lieutenant had become a forty-one-year-old commodore, even more well respected and even more battle-hardened than Ted McMasters had been then.

It was one of the privileges of a commodore to requisition a lavishly appointed dining-room to conduct mealtime conferences. Sergei had made the reservation by 'phone, late at night, and had been taken aback at first by the deference shown by groundside bureaucrats to flag officers—even newly appointed ones. The warrant officer who handled the transaction didn't even ask for a charge number, though he did ask a hundred other questions: about the seating arrangements, the menu, the wine, even the color scheme for the tablecloths and china. Sergei had dealt with this sort of thing before, as Ted's exec and as captain of his own ship, but never on this scale; things had moved so quickly since his return from the war front, he could hardly muddle through it. He realized that he would have to add a staff officer to deal with such things in the future.

At 1130 hours on the morning of his staff meeting, an aircar arrived and took him at breakneck speed from the BOQ to the Rickover Building, a thirty-five-story administrative structure, mostly glass and steel, that housed the line officers' mess. Fortunately the driver was a quiet rating, who had the good sense not to interrupt a commodore while he was deep in thought.

Sergei had a lot to think about. In the few days since his meeting with Admiral McMasters, he had been forced to move at double-quick time to obtain orders for the officers and vessels that were to make up his command; as the most junior flag in His Imperial Majesty's Fleet, he'd had to mention the new fleet admiral's name to overreach similar requisitions by other officers, looking to fill vacancies created by the recent battles at Pergamum and elsewhere along the periphery. Unlike obsequious staff officers, every active-duty line officer had influence to exert and an ax to grind. He knew that heavy-handed tactics had created resentments; perhaps he had even gained an enemy or two. There was too much at stake to worry about that now.

As the aircar flew along, he considered his efforts of the last few days. After some maneuvering, he had filled all ten command positions in his squadron; it required more string-pulling than any negotiations he'd experienced in the Navy. The small craft had been easiest to get; the sudden return of the war had severely disrupted cruiser formations, making them available in ones and twos. The larger ships, especially ones with commanders who had actually seen battle, were a bit harder, but he had finally done it.

The transition from cold to hot war had caught everyone by surprise (*even the people on the frontier,* he reminded himself). It had taken him several days to reach Sol System and be confirmed in his promotion and new orders; the tendrils of privilege had already taken hold, taking advantage of the chaos in the chain of command created by Pergamum and what came after. There were plenty of officers on the beach, so obtaining staff was no trouble—but getting orders for ships in His Majesty's Navy had been another matter indeed.

He had passed on his own prerogative to replace any of the commanders of the new vessels under his command, trusting that the ships and their crew would be best served by those men and women currently in command. Still, he knew so few of the officers he was about to dine with that he knew they would be nervous with anticipation.

Rickover was filled with smartly saluting officers. He made his way through them and to an elevator marked AUTHORIZED PERSONNEL ONLY. It went directly to the thirty-fifth floor.

Though fifteen minutes early, he was the last to arrive; his ten new subordinates snapped to attention as he entered, remaining so while he crossed the thickly carpeted floor to the head of the table. An orderly tried to help him into the huge, high-backed armchair, but Sergei waved him off and the man stepped back.

"Be seated, please," he said. The officers slipped stiffly into their seats. His eyes fell on a small monogrammed card in front of him: CDRE. S. TORRIJOS. The various officers, many of them previously no more to him than names on a roster, looked tense, faced with the unknown quantity of a new commanding officer. He took a deep breath, and let his gaze travel around the table.

On his immediate left: Uwe Bryant, the most junior of the ten, commander of the *Indomitable*. He looked uncomfortable in his immaculate dress blues, interrupted only by the solemn black armband. Admiral Sir Coris Bryant, his grandfather, had died at Pergamum, leaving Uwe to carry on the legacy. The *Indomitable* (and its twin, the *Inflexible*) had been chosen from what had remained of Admiral Bryant's command after Pergamum; its former commander and exec had been visiting Admiral DeSaia aboard the *Sun Tzu* when the zor attacked, leaving the younger

Bryant to command the small ship through the entire battle. He had a reputation as an intelligent officer, if somewhat overcareful.

Next to Bryant was Alyne Bell, captain of the carrier *Gagarin*. Her dress blouse was decorated with the ribbons of a dozen years of campaigning. Bell, he knew, had served for a short time aboard the carrier *Ponchartrain*, Sergei's own first posting. By comparison to her younger colleague, she appeared to be prepared for what was to come. The *Gagarin* was a newer *Eridanus*-class carrier, replacing the old squadron carrier, the *Cambridge*, which had been badly beaten up at Pergamum. Dolph Schaumburg's carrier was expected to remain in dry dock at least four or five months, but with Sergei's help he had managed to make sure that it obtained a repair requisition rather than being scrapped entire.

On Captain Bell's left was Roger Fredericks, commander of the cruiser *Inflexible*. Fredericks, a longtime line officer, had revolutionized cruiser tactics while serving in Admiral Bryant's command, but a sharp tongue had always stood in the way of his promotion to the rear echelon. He looked on sourly, perhaps resenting Sergei's presence at the head of the table.

The next position was occupied by Senior Captain Yuri Okome of the close escort *Ikegai*. Okome was a natural choice for this squadron; he'd been on active duty more than twenty-five years, and had turned down senior command positions to stay as captain of his own ship. During peacetime, he was a logistics instructor at the Naval Academy, where his scarred face and demanding nature tended to scare hell out of cadets studying under him.

At the other end of the table sat Senior Captain Marc Hudson, captain of the starship *Biscayne*. He had acquired quite a reputation in His Majesty's Navy for innovation and coolness under fire. His service dossier had been thick with commentary, balanced about equally between people he'd impressed and people he'd offended in the twenty-odd years since becoming the youngest officer ever to command a starship (the old *Boadicea*, crippled at the battle of Anderson's Star).

The captain of the starship *San Martín*, Sharon MacEwan, sat next to Hudson. She was a younger scion of the famous Fighting MacEwans. It would have been headline news on the 3-V if a foray into zor space took place without a MacEwan in command; more than two dozen officers of the clan served in the Imperial Navy, carrying on a family tradition that was already old when Bonnie Prince Charlie had returned to try and claim his British throne. Sergei noticed that Sharon had already acquired the patented MacEwan glower that had daunted many a senior officer.

To MacEwan's left sat Tina Li. She commanded the starship *Sevastopol*, a ship with a long history and tradition; the original ship of that name had accompanied the first emperor from Halpern Starbase to Sol System, distinguishing itself repeatedly during the War of Accession. Two facts had stood out from Captain Li's record. First, her officers and crew were fiercely loyal to her—at least three or four of her most senior subordinates had turned down independent commands after Pergamum to stay aboard the *Sevastopol*. Second, she had acquired a reputation for getting herself—and her command—into and out of tight situations. At Pergamum, outnumbered by enemy vessels and cut off from the mass of the fleet by an enemy maneuver, she had executed a daredevil turn in the high atmosphere of a gas giant and then flown through an enemy formation at high velocity to escape destruction. While some, more conservative superiors had labeled her as foolhardy early in her career, it was hard to argue with success; clearly the men and women of the *Sevastopol* knew a good thing when they saw it.

Next to Li sat Sir Bertram Halvorsen, the commander of the starship *Mycenae*. Sergei had served with Bert for nearly four years under Commodore McMasters, and was glad to have him along. Bert was heir to an earldom and a vast industrial fortune, and had acquired a reputation for being soft largely because of the lavish appointments of his vessel; other than the former fleet flagship the *Royal Oak*, the *Mycenae* set the best wardroom-table in the fleet. Sergei had dined often with Bert Halvorsen, finding him a gracious host (*even toward a commoner*, he reminded himself)—and had fought beside him, finding him extremely competent. There weren't too many people Sergei trusted more in a fight.

Sir Gordon Quinn of the starship *Helsinki* sat on Sergei's immediate right. Quinn also came from old nobility, British peerage as well as Imperial; he claimed a lineage of more than a thousand years. Given the choice of any ten ships and any ten commanders in the Fleet, the *Helsinki*—and Sir Gordon—would not have been among them. She was an older vessel, a refitted *Lyonesse*-class starship; the keel had been laid down a dozen years before that of the *Lancaster*. Quinn was an insultingly arrogant nobleman, who had never passed up an opportunity to remind his more humbly born colleagues of the difference in their stations. When Sergei's options on ships to fill his ten positions had run short, he had obtained orders on the *Helsinki*, intending to replace Quinn as commander; unfortunately, Quinn's staff aboard the *Helsinki* shared many of the captain's least desirable attributes, with less command experience. Placing someone he trusted in command might make the *Helsinki* undependable in a fight; instead, Sergei left Quinn in command, placing him at his right hand to closely observe the other's annoyance at being subordinate to a lowly born commodore. As for the *Helsinki* itself, adding it to his command—along with the *Biscayne*, the *Sevastopol* and the *San Martín*—was only necessary because so many ships, like McMasters' own flagship, the *Gustav Adolf*, had been destroyed or crippled at Pergamum. At least it had survived, unlike the *Pembroke*, the *Harrison* and the *Odessa*, and the many others that had been reduced to slag and vapor.

The memory of the loss of so many friends and colleagues made Sergei pause for a long moment before beginning to address his new officers.

"Let me begin by thanking you all for being here on such short notice," Sergei said, folding his hands before him. "I realize that you have been kept a bit in the dark. I assure you that so have I until recently. My commission is quite new, my orders even newer.

"This is not the time or place to dwell on the past, except as we may pay our respects to the departed dead and the everlasting glory of the Service. I have to direct my attention to the future; you must as well. I have obtained orders for you, and the vessels you command, in order to form a new squadron, one that will carry my flag and the flag of the new fleet admiral." He stopped, cleared his throat, and took a sip from an elegant fluted water goblet. He looked from face to face, all paying rapt attention, waiting for his next words.

"I have been chosen for this command by the new admiral, with the advice of Admiral McMasters. I admit that some of you have more time in service, or enjoy a greater reputation. Nonetheless, I am the admiral's, and therefore the emperor's, choice. I intend to do my best to fulfill that trust.

"By asking to have you and your vessels placed in this command I have expressed a similar confidence in you.

"Some of you have served with me before, under Admiral McMasters' command; others of you are known to me only by the admiral's good recommendation and your exemplary service records. You each have the option of refusing, of course, but I hope that you will all accept. It will be a pleasure and an honor serving with you. With my best wishes let me say, welcome aboard."

He stopped again and took another sip of water. The subordinate officers in turn exchanged glances, slowly returning their attention to him.

"I'd like to review the strategic situation, and then I'd like to discuss assignments within the squadron; but before we proceed, I'll be glad to field any appropriate questions."

"There's a rumor that the Admiralty has appointed a civilian as fleet admiral. Is that true, sir?"

Sergei looked up to find the source of the question, as the silent waiters delivered the onion soup au gratin. He located the speaker: Captain Marc Hudson of the *Biscayne*.

"Captain?"

"I . . . should like to know who the new fleet admiral is, if the commodore pleases."

*Maybe,* Sergei thought, *he just asked too damn many questions.*

"Our new admiral is not a civilian, Captain. He is Rear Admiral Ivan Hector Charles, Lord Marais," Sergei replied quietly. "He will be coming aboard at Tuuen."

"Lord Marais is a . . . staff officer," Hudson observed.

"Lord Marais is Admiral of the Fleet," Sergei replied. He knew exactly what the older man must be thinking: *A staff officer in command of the fleet?—a disaster in the making.* Sergei had had that thought himself.

Still, he felt obliged to defend his new commanding officer. He added frostily, "He is our emperor's choice. I don't suppose that you have some objection, Hudson?"

The table fell silent. The tension in the room went up dramatically.

Sergei took the round-bowled spoon with the Admiralty crest on it, and lightly touched his soup bowl. He cursed himself for mishandling the situation.

"I beg the commodore's pardon," Hudson said after a moment. "I did not mean to cast aspersions on the admiral or, God forbid, His Imperial Majesty. I meant . . . only to take note of Lord Marais' combat experience. If I recall, sir, his lordship has considerably more academic than combat credentials."

"I am aware of that, Captain Hudson."

"This is no training exercise, sir. This is war—war with a ruthless enemy that *we* all know."

"I am aware of that as well. Your point?"

Hudson looked at his fellow officers. Certainly the rumors about Marais had made the rounds; Sergei guessed that this had been under discussion before he'd arrived and Hudson had been chosen to pose the question.

"I meant no offense, sir. I— Nothing, sir."

Sergei thought of pursuing it, and then discarded the idea.

"If there are no further questions, I suggest that we proceed. We have quite a bit to review." The officers shifted in their seats. He picked up a stylus and touched a control-pad beside his place setting.

The lights dimmed, and a 3-V projection appeared above the center of the table, showing the war zone: the New Territories, a volume of space reclaimed from zor hegemony over the past sixty years. On the Solward side of the display, a glyph identified Mustapha, the territorial capital and site of the Territories' largest repair facility; other symbols indicated naval bases and strategic points. Sergei moved the stylus to highlight a point near the edge of the smooth curvature that represented the treaty border between zor and human.

"About eight weeks ago the zor committed a large force to an attack on the Pergamum naval base. Without complete intelligence on their deployment, we can only guess at the way in which they were able to assemble enough tonnage to mount such an attack; this report"—he displayed an icon—"indicates a common origin point of incoming jump vectors during the battle, located somewhere in the Antares Rift.

"It seems clear that a number of other sites on this side of the Rift were essentially left uncovered in order to undertake this attack. The tactic has been used before, but . . . for whatever reason . . . it came as a surprise that the zor might do so again.

"The attack began at 0342 Standard on 2 February. Seventeen and a half hours after the initial arrival of zor forces, elements of the Second Fleet arrived; less than half an hour later, a substantial reinforcement of the zor attack took place, indicating that the enemy had expected our own reinforcement.

"From the results, and the tactics used at the battle, it is apparent that the zor objective was to disable or destroy as much of the Imperial Fleet as possible. Data on casualties and equipment loss have been kept strictly on a need-to-know basis; I have reviewed them, and I understand why. Given the enemy's limited resources, they achieved remarkable success.

"Pergamum was more than a slap in the face. It was a punch in the gut; as we are all well aware, the violent attack cost us all of our admirals onstation, along with twenty-six other command officers, dozens of other officers of lower rank and more than three thousand enlisted men and women. First, Second and Fifth Fleet tonnages have been reduced by an average of forty-five percent. One-third of the vessels in that count will be returned to active service, but it will take at least four months to bring most of those online. We didn't lose Pergamum, but we might as well have; based on what's out there now, we couldn't hold it—or anything Riftward of it—if the zor were to attack again.

"We believe that their casualties were equally frightening. But if they could mount such an assault on Pergamum, they might well try another such assault elsewhere.

"They must know what their attack accomplished. However, very few people outside of this room know it. Our mission is thus made even more difficult by the limited margin for error, and the need for the potential danger to be kept secret."

"Do you really believe that the danger is that great, sir?" Sharon MacEwan asked. Sergei caught her gaze.

"Don't you, Captain?"

"I don't see how this is any different from any other change from peace to war footing, Commodore. A sudden attack by the zor after a negotiated peace is commonplace enough. *We* certainly expected it. What makes this any different? Sir."

"There are at least two differences, Captain. First, no zor attack—even the attack on Alya sixty years ago—ever had this much impact. Compare the battle at Pergamum with the attack on the Boren industrial worlds in 2291. Even though there were half again as many enemy vessels, we lost less than a third of what we lost at Pergamum. We also lost no admirals at Boren."

He caught Uwe Bryant looking up at that, and kicked himself for his choice of words.

"The second reason, however, outweighs the first. As you are all aware, the emperor's civilian Government convinced His Imperial Highness that the zor had neither the resources nor the will to make further war upon the Empire. After the Treaty of Efal, despite Admiralty advice, bases were closed, crews were beached, ships were dry-docked and defenses were neglected. More such actions were planned, even at the time of the attack." He paused, remembering a conversation with Sir Stefan Ewing, and he forcibly put aside his anger, thinking about Pergamum again.

"Even if the losses at Pergamum had been less severe, the Empire that opposes the zor this time is on less of a war footing than at any time in the past."

"I beg your pardon, Commodore." Roger Fredericks raised a hand, looking back at MacEwan; she inclined her head, yielding the floor. "If the commodore pleases, the picture you paint is of a rather strong zor force opposed by a dispersed and largely unprepared Imperial Navy. If that is true, sir, what difference could a squadron make? There are many targets to defend—and we can only guess where the zor will strike next."

"That would be a valid argument, Captain," Sergei answered. "But it only would apply if we were going to serve garrison duty. But look at who is sitting at the table. Does this look like a garrison staff to you?"

For his part, Roger Fredericks kept his dignity and aplomb intact while Sergei looked slowly from face to face. He gauged the facial expression of each of his subordinates: some—Li, Quinn, MacEwan—looked surprised and annoyed; some—like Halverson, Hudson and Bell—were suddenly much more attentive.

Sergei caught Yuri Okome's eye as he looked around the table. The old scarred dragon was leaning back in his high-backed chair, his arms folded across his chest. His face was impassive, but his eyes were alight, as if to say, *All right, I'm surprised. But I'll be damned if I'll show it.*

Sergei let the moment drag out, and finally said, "We'll be jumping for Tuuen in less than three weeks, and from there to Mustapha. I do not have orders for you from the admiral as yet, except that we should prepare for an attack on the zor at once."

"With ten ships, sir?" Alyne Bell asked. She had been making notes on her 'pad, looking from Sergei to the strategic disposition and back. "I mean no disrespect to yourself or to the admiral, sir, but this force is insufficient for—"

"I would be inclined to agree, Captain Bell, if I knew what our orders were. I assume that the admiral is predicating our success upon the element of surprise."

"Based on the information we have at our disposal, sir, it seems that any installation we choose to attack can be reinforced by a force at least equivalent to our own. Given the zor ferocity, we'd be cut to ribbons trying to escape afterward. I don't see how surprise can work in our favor for very long."

"It cannot," Sergei replied. "By that point, I assume, there will be some overall plan."

Nepotism and favoritism in the Service make officers less willing to speak their minds. It was hardly a surprise to Sergei that his new officers mostly refrained from critical comment; in a way it was reassuring, since he wasn't attracted by the idea of creating dissension between his command staff and his new CO. Still, their reticence seemed to cloak an uneasiness that he did not expect would be easily dispelled—until, and unless, he gained their trust.

Hudson waited for him when he dismissed the meeting. Sergei tensed as he nodded and exchanged salutes with the other officers, taking his time gathering his notes as the orderlies bused away the remains of lunch.

"What can I do for you, Captain?" he said at last, when Hudson approached.

"You can accept my apologies, sir," Hudson said. "I'm sorry to give you trouble in your first staff meeting."

"No apologies are required." He took the proffered hand and clasped it. "I'm happy to have someone aboard who's willing to speak up."

"I'm not the only one who'll speak up, Commodore. I'm just the orneriest." He smiled, and it was infectious; Sergei found himself smiling too. "I was surprised, actually," he continued, as Sergei picked up his briefcase and they made their way to the lift, "that the commodore was willing to consider my résumé. I hadn't expected to be back in the saddle so soon."

"My report indicated that the *Biscayne* is at nearly a hundred percent."

"She's a fine ship, sir. But as you know, you could have had the *Biscayne* without me. It's not really a hardware issue." They stepped into the lift.

"Oh?" Sergei regarded Hudson. The older man was a trifle taller, graying at the temples, with a distinguished visage crowned by a thatch of Navy-cut, but somehow still unruly, hair.

"I ask too many questions," Hudson said. "Usually at the wrong times. Bad habit for a naval officer. 'Course, it would only really matter if I still gave a damn about it." The lift door closed.

"Lobby," Sergei said. The lift began to descend. "It's probably impolitic to tell your superior officer that you don't give a damn."

"I'm five or six years older than you, sir. If I was going to be a flag, I'd probably be one now. Especially with all of the promotions going on. Now, maybe if I had a friend higher up—"

It was a none-too-subtle jab, and Sergei turned to look at the older man, his eyes filling with anger.

"Now—" Hudson said, holding up one hand. "Now, sir, don't take it the wrong way. I have a lot of respect for you, Commodore Torrijos. It takes more than the patronage of Ted McMasters to make a body worthy of respect."

Sergei looked away, watching the floors tick by. "You have a strange way of showing it," he said levelly.

Finally the lift stopped in the lobby, and the doors slid aside. "If you'll excuse me, Hudson," Sergei said, and began to move away.

Then, not sure just why, he stopped, letting the lobby crowd swirl around him, and turned, to see Hudson standing by the lift doors. Sergei realized that he was letting annoyance get the better of him; Hudson had chosen to seek him out, and clearly had some motive for bringing up a sensitive subject.

It made sense to find out. He walked back toward the older officer.

"All right, Captain," he said. "Let's take a walk."


Hudson told him a great deal about the mood of his command as they walked around the Admiralty grounds. The rumors about Marais had been flying around for nearly a week; that sort of information wasn't going to stay quiet for long. The Imperial Court might be isolated, out on Oahu, but the communications network that spanned Sol System had been crackling with speculation from the moment the word on Pergamum had first arrived.

Sergei's initial reaction to the Marais appointment had been surprise and shock; his own jump to commodore had been unexpected, but the new responsibilities and duties had given him little time to speculate on the consequences. Hudson described the feeling of most of the officers he'd met toward Marais' appointment: it was nothing less than outrage. The choice of consensus had been Ted McMasters; the officers of the line didn't give a damn if he had to be rolled onto the bridge on a hospital gurney. The officers of the line didn't get a vote, of course; it was up to the emperor and the general staff, and they had chosen Marais.

As they walked, and Hudson talked, Sergei remembered Ted's words: "*A month and a half from now Admiral Marais is going to lead a foray into zor space that will either be the greatest accomplishment in more than half a century of war, or will be a total disaster."*

Hudson's opinion leaned toward the latter outcome: he expected it to be a terrible mess, a fitting testimony to the venal, corrupt Imperial Navy. Unless, of course, Marais' staff did what any good staff should do: cover for him to prevent mistakes that might cost them all their lives.

"I don't know what I dislike most," Sergei told him. "Your defeatist attitude or your intended insubordination."

"It isn't like that at all," Hudson assured him. "It would simply be a matter of taking vague or contradictory orders and carrying them out in a way that makes sense. If Marais is clever enough to claim the credit, all the better. It's certainly fine with me."

"So we'll have a squadron with eleven admirals instead of one."

"No," Hudson answered. "There'll probably only be ten by the time this is over."

Sergei spent the afternoon in his quarters, reading. He'd started with a sheaf of documents dispatched him by Marais, by way of Admiral McMasters. There were notes on previous campaigns against the alien enemy, careful annotations of the sort a scholar might be expected to make; analyses of formations and small-unit ship tactics. The introduction told him very little that he didn't already know:

FYEO: Cmdr S Torrijos                    KEYWORD: zor
FROM: R Adm I Marais

PHYSICAL DESCRIPTION: Bipedal mammals, 1.3 to 1.7 m tall. Two arms, two legs, each ending in a set of gripping taloned claws with opposable thumbs. Coasting wings, wingspread 2.5 to 4.0 m; will function without mechanical aids in environments of less than 0.65 g (Standard). Facial features resemble

Terran eagle: bony crest on skull, beak, eyes with nictitating lids.

SOCIETY: Zor are a sentient species which developed interstellar travel independent of its discovery by humanity. They are a warrior culture, based on the central principles of "inner peace" and "outer peace"; the "inner peace" derives from a sense of oneness, of harmonious union with one's self, said to be a result of meditation, a sort of nirvana, while the "outer peace" is a result of harmonious union with one's society, the upholding of a rigid code of honor. It is known that some small percentage of zor violate this ethic, either by descending too far into contemplation (and violating the "inner peace" through achievement of false nirvana), or by interacting harmfully with society (and violating the "outer peace" by friction with one's fellow zor). The offender is most often outcast (*idju*) and nearly always commits suicide.

ATTITUDES: Zor view the world as the creation of their Maker, *esLi,* and the existence of another race suggests to them that *esLi* has turned his face from them. The continued existence of mankind will eventually break the mystic circle of inner and outer peace and thus destroy the zor as well. It is this drive that motivates the zor to such excesses of violence against mankind, and it is this that must be addressed.

*end of text*

Marais' extensive analysis had also included a compendium on culture and society. It was clear the admiral was well informed about the zor; he had apparently traveled through the zor worlds on the near side of the Antares Rift just after the Treaty of Las Duhr, gathering information and studying the language and culture. While the presentation was less cut-and-dried than the style to which Sergei was accustomed, he had to admit that there was a lot of information available about mankind's enemy.

Few humans had ever met a zor, and none had ever been captured in battle, but Marais was as knowledgeable as anyone could be: there were references to every known source of authority on the zor, from the first robot-probe records of the attack on Alya, to the last negotiating session of the Treaty of Efal. There was particular emphasis on the vast amount of data accumulated from the captured base at Mustapha.

In addition to the report there was, of course, Marais's book. Sergei had read the damned thing twice from beginning to end, noting the rhetoric and the phrasing that had seemed almost too careful. Some of it was a tirade against humanity's weak will, but other parts seemed to ring much more true. As the sun drowned in the western sky, flooding his sitting-room with pale light, he reread the passages he'd marked.

"We are always forgetting that our opponent is not human," Marais had written.

> Zor and man are two separate species, whose similarity of appearance may be coincidental, or a result of evolution in similar environments. But similarity of appearance does not in any way suggest a commonality in thought patterns or racial motivations.
>
> It is wrong—fatally wrong—to set out a strategy for fighting the zor without considering their view of the universe. We have tried to fight them on our terms, and for sixty years, despite winning battle after battle, we have failed. As unpalatable as it may be, we must begin to fight them on their terms.

Did he seriously expect to bomb civilians, or refuse to consider treaties?

Not only would none of that wash with the Admiralty or the public, Sergei thought; it probably was next to impossible, with anything short of extermination of the whole race. And that was worse than impossible —it was unthinkable.

## chapter 3

The current *Lancaster* had been commissioned in 2292, an altogether fine year for shipbuilding; its keel was one of nine laid down for ships of the line in the graving docks at Mustapha shipyards during the course of that year. It was wartime, midway through the third and (at that time) the most violent of the conflicts between mankind and the zor; the prime minister had asked for and received a large appropriation for shipbuilding, to strengthen and supplement the Imperial Navy, much reduced by the recent battles with the enemy and the corruption and graft of the previous administration.

In keeping with naval tradition, the brass nameplate of the previous vessel of the same name was installed, with much ceremony, on the curved rear wall of the flight bridge on 23 September 2292. The earlier *Lancaster*, a *Lyonesse*-class starship that had served the Solar Empire well and nobly for two and a half decades, had been mostly reduced to a pile of scrap metal and misshapen plastic in one of several fierce battles in the outskirts of Boren System; she had been decommissioned with equal ceremony just before Christmas of the previous year. Also in keeping with naval tradition, the unfortunate captain and officers of the vessel were put out on the beach at half-pay, with no alternative but to scramble for any posting that they, or their patrons at Court, could manage.

Since starships are not designed for planetfall, they need not be aerodynamic or even symmetrical, though the smaller the total surface area, the more readily a defensive field can cover a ship's hull. Starship design revolves around ship mass, normal-space engine power, and efficiency of jump drive. In the first case, a more massive space vessel requires a larger outlay of power to operate defensive fields and internal systems such as inertial dampers; in the second, the more powerful the engine, the more a ship is capable of accelerating and maneuvering; in the third, more efficient jump drives allow greater distances to be traversed in shorter times, giving jump-vessels greater range.

The new *Concordance*-class *Lancaster* was a stunning ship, of a completely new design, making improvements in all three areas. For more than thirty years, naval architecture had emphasized armament and shielding at the expense of maneuverability, attributes that made Imperial line vessels almost invincible against planetary targets or weakly armed system boats of rebellious colonies, but vulnerable to the onslaught of zor squadrons, which attacked heedless of the odds or their own losses. It had taken several years for the tradition-bound rear echelon to admit to its error, and years after that to bring about a change in design—of which process the *Concordance* and the other ships of its class were the leading edge.

Its first commander, Captain Sir Malcolm Rodyn, took the *Lancaster* on her shakedown cruise shortly after it was commissioned; it was a scouting mission, intended to evaluate the conditions along the periphery of the Empire, and perhaps to instill some confidence in the demoralized colonists by "showing the flag." The crew and officers, veterans of the protracted struggle against the zor, but new to the ship, got more than they bargained for.

A squadron of three enemy vessels jumped insystem while the *Lancaster* was in orbit at New Patras, and immediately tried to englobe the Imperial ship, using the swarm tactic that had served them so well in the past. The wily Rodyn engaged the zor at the lumbering pace of a *Lyonesse,* and then suddenly came about, outmaneuvering the lightly armed opponents and disposing of two of them immediately, and the third shortly thereafter, well before enemy fire could overwhelm his defensive fields.

Spacers, most notably officers and crew of the line, are a very superstitious lot, an attribute inherited from their wet-navy antecedents. Gunners aboard a vessel of war have their favorite side or orientation, and will sometimes even offer a bribe to a petty officer at a new posting in order to retain a port, starboard, aft, fore, or top- or bottom-side assignment. Helmsmen and navigators will perform redundant and unnecessary scans and equipment checks, a nervous habit that will exasperate a ship's captain no end. Engineers are, of course, the worst: they are attuned to the subaural hum of the ship's power system like a concert musician to his instrument, alert to the slightest skip or inconsistency.

Individual idiosyncrasies aside, spacers of all ranks and professions are very superstitious about the ship on which they serve. Like every other aspect of the Imperial Navy, tradition and previous history are inescapable; for ship and officer alike, reputation and "luck" play a vital role. The *Lancaster*—the previous one, at least—had been hung with the collar of a bad-luck assignment; equipment failures, indifferent leadership, and a series of less-than-desirable postings had culminated in the worst bad luck of all—destruction by surprise attack. The hangar deck had been depressurized, making the ship nearly impossible to steer. The next broadside had collapsed the superstructure of the main Engineering deck, breaking the ship nearly in two and blowing more than a third of the crew into space.

New Patras completely reversed the fortunes of the *Lancaster* name; it was the beginning of a series of "lucky breaks" that were just as fortuitous as the misfortune of the earlier ship.

While the earlier *Lancaster* had been regarded almost as a cursed ship, a testimony to spacer superstition that seemed to be self-fulfilling, the new *Lancaster* earned itself a reputation as a luck-bringer, a distinction that it would live up to repeatedly in the years to come. As for Rodyn, he earned himself the White Cross and a spot in the Academy textbook.

The *Lancaster*'s captain had obtained his commission, and the command of his ship, the old-fashioned way: he'd bought it. Perhaps the luckiest break for the new vessel was that he turned out to be one of the best ship's captains of his, or any other, era.

His luck seemed to travel with the *Lancaster* when he turned it over to Ted McMasters in 2296. Rodyn, the toast of the Imperial Court, died of a sudden and violent heart attack within six months of being promoted to His Majesty's staff, while his vessel, in newer but no less capable hands, went on to further enhance its reputation as the best ship in the fleet. That reputation was intact when the *Lancaster* was handed to Sergei Torrijos in 2304, when the promotion of Commodore Sir Coris Bryant to admiral made Ted McMasters a flag officer. With reluctance, McMasters turned the *Lancaster* over to his exec and took command of Bryant's old ship, the *Gustav Adolf*. Unlike Rodyn, McMasters survived his first year away from his old vessel, and went on to serve His Imperial Majesty well and wisely in his new command . . .

Until Pergamum.

Alone, with the *Lancaster*'s hum a persistent sound in his ears, Sergei Torrijos lay on his back and let his mind stray far away.

Without much initiative on his part, his memories ran back thirty years. He remembered Buenos Aires, his first home. (Even in the despair of the dark, with the unutterable *nothingness* of jumpspace just a metal hull away, he retained enough of himself to realize that B.A. wasn't his home now—that the Navy had be-

come his home, and his family as well.) Buenos Aires: a megacity of eighty-five million people sprawled on both sides of the
mouth of the Río de la Plata, a monument to the sanitized
poverty that the common people of the Solar Empire had inherited. Poverty, in fact, was a bad word for it, because that implied
all sorts of things that had all but vanished—uncleanliness, star-
vation, disease . . . and Buenos Aires had, really, none of those
things. If a simple problem like disposal of waste had been a
stumbling block, B.A. would have choked on it a century ago.

B.A. hadn't been choking on waste when he left it. It had
been choking on self-negation, something that was easy to feel in
a high-rise welfare prison. He'd felt it press on him, most especially because his parents worked for the Ministry of Construction, prisoners extending the prison with their own sweat. He
had left it at age seventeen, knowing that, whatever future he had
in His Majesty's Service, he would likely never again be a
groundhog. By the time he'd received his commission and grad-
uated flight school five years later, he was sure of it. His career
and his life were with the Navy, and he had never regretted having left the other life behind.

For the moment, he was leaving his responsibilities aside,
both as commander of the starship *Lancaster* and as the commander of the admiral's new squadron. While the *Lancaster*
cruised through jump, isolated from its companion vessels and
from the rest of the universe, there was nothing that urgently required his attention on the bridge; he could leave Chan in charge
of combat-readiness drills, though this was a task that he normally relished. Of course, in the seven years he had conned the
ship, his responsibilities had never extended past its hull—and
now that had all changed.

In light of the events of the past few weeks, Sergei thought
about the war. It was always "the war" to him, even though the
public perceived it as a series of independent conflicts, with their
own causes and effects. To those whose lives had been dedicated
to fighting it, though, it was all of a single piece, with only one

real cause. It was a long and bloody war humanity had fought with the aliens since encountering them somewhere beyond the fringes of his own dominion. Since there were no survivors, the exact location had never been determined; but the information obtained from that brief and violent contact had been sufficient to provide the aliens with the layout and approximate military strength of human space.

That was the beginning of it. The religion of the zor had driven them forward from that point; a few months later, in the fall of 2252, their wrath was directed at humanity.

Aʟya was a peaceful agricultural colony near the fringes of human space, with incredibly fertile soil and a much-improved photosynthetic cycle due to unique spectra in Alya's primary. It took the zor six hours to reduce the settlement and the sown fields to a heap of molten slag, as recorded by robot monitors within the system that had evaded the attacking ships' notice. There were no human survivors of the Dark Dawn of Alya.

The story of the Dark Dawn belonged to the nightmares of history. It had happened more than a generation before Sergei was born, but the event—and the legend that had grown up around it—had helped to galvanize the human race for the greatest fight it had ever known. And yet, despite superior technology and greater numbers, the killing stroke—if such a thing could truly be conceived—had been withheld by the Imperial Government, which continued to believe that, somehow, an accommodation could be reached. The memories, and recurring images, of Alya . . . and Anderson's Star . . . and Pergamum . . . were so easily pushed aside by treaties and so quickly recalled when the treaties were broken.

As he lay on his bunk, Sergei wondered to himself whether this latest venture would yield anything different or whether it, like all of the endeavors of the past, would result in no more than another temporary peace treaty.

He stepped onto the bridge, which was in the usual state of feverish activity that immediately preceded the end of a jump. The engineering station was crowded (there'd been some irregularities when they jumped from Sol—no sense in taking chances); Chan Wells, his first officer, sat in the pilot's chair, rechecking the course in the holo display. He looked up to notice Sergei's arrival. "Captain on the bridge," he said, and everyone who wasn't critically occupied stood to attention.

Ahead on the forward screen was the utter dark of the jump-space night, impenetrable, as no light could reach its domain. It was still powerfully frightening, despite two centuries of FTL travel, to look into that darkness and wonder whether there would ever again be light.

That wasn't the only reason for tension, of course. Because a ship in jump was isolated from the universe, there was never any way of telling whether there were enemy ships in the target volume. The dynamics of stellar travel almost encouraged surprise attacks—war (especially against the zor) was an enormous shell game, with time delays: offense was powerful, and defense consisted of trying to have enough strength at the right place at the right time. The Admiralty made educated guesses about the total strength of the enemy, used sophisticated computer simulation to evaluate the site of the next attack, and moved enough strength there to repulse it.

Those same simulations had convinced the Imperial Government two years ago that the zor did not have enough strength to attack any installation anywhere. The simulations worked fine: it was the assumptions that were wrong. In order to mass enough strength to attack, the zor stripped their defenses at a half-dozen important worlds, something the simulation had never considered as a possibility.

*Because a human admiral would never do it.*

The engineering and navigation crews made their reports to Sergei, and he gave the order to proceed with end-of-jump. Beat to Quarters rang over the system intercom, followed by the end-of-jump alarm.

The navigator began the sequence, ready to rejump if the *Lancaster* materialized close to another ship. The inky blackness of jumpspace gave way to quicksilver, and then the Tuuen system appeared: eight planets, including three Earthlike worlds with impossibly fertile soil. It was owned by the Marais-Tuuen agricultural combine, two families allied for mutual commercial benefit. The Tuuen, to whom the system had originally been granted, had sold sixty percent of the corporation to the larger Marais family when they ran into money problems a century ago; since then the system had prospered, with a seat on the Imperial Assembly, a lucrative sutler's contract with the Navy and the regular patronage of all of the connections of the powerful, rich Marais clan.

The *Lancaster* proceeded into the system, with the squadron ordered behind her.

⌐en-SHUN," said the bosun, as Torrijos entered the waiting area, his department chiefs in his wake. The hangar deck was brightly lit and empty, slowly being depressurized in preparation for the deck doors to be opened. The waiting-area was separated from the main deck by a glasteel bulkhead, which was capable of withstanding enormous pressures though completely transparent; an honor guard of officers and the requisite number of marines waited in spotless full dress for the admiral's barge to come aboard.

Torrijos stood for a few moments, looking at the familiar deck of the *Lancaster*. Ted McMasters had made him swab the blasted thing, years ago, when he was a midshipman. All the time he had kept one eye on Bruce Wei, the marine lieutenant who had been on hangar-deck duty that day, wondering if Wei would open the deck doors and vent him into space.

They'd not exactly been best of friends then. Now, of course, Bruce Wei was Major of Marines, second-in-command of the *Lancaster*'s ship's troops to the captain himself . . . and was in the chair up above the deck now, waiting for Torrijos' command to open the clamshell doors to admit the barge. Bruce was no less a bastard now than he had been a dozen years ago, but they had come to be friends as Sergei came to recognize the marine's virtues—bravery, loyalty and a cool head, such as he had shown at Pergamum . . .

He was halfway remembering that day, when the comm interrupted his reverie. Keith Danner, the comm officer, answered the call.

"Admiral Marais' barge requests permission to come aboard, sir."

Torrijos signaled to Bruce Wei. "Tell them they're cleared to come ahead."

"Aye-aye, sir." The great clamshell doors slowly began to open, folding out upon themselves. Beyond, a discerning eye might be able to pick out a thin, streamlined craft, splayfooted and needle-nosed.

The honor guard was still at attention; Torrijos and his officers stood at attention as well, as the barge coasted slowly through the hatch and onto the deck, coming to a stop almost exactly in the center. The doors were already closed as it came to rest.

"Admiral Marais is aboard, sir," reported Wei, as protocol required.

Shortly, the green lights came on across the hangar deck, indicating that the area had been pressurized and restored to normal atmosphere, and the glasteel bulkhead rose. Unlike a naval base, the *Lancaster* didn't pack enough internal power to carry out this activity with energy fields alone. The access door opened, and a stairway was lowered. Torrijos and his retinue crossed the open space and waited at its foot.

Marais, followed by an almost emaciated man in a captain's uniform, came down the stairs. He was the perfect match for the pictures Sergei had seen: tall, strikingly handsome, with a stern face. He silently exchanged salutes with Sergei and his officers, and then shook Sergei's hand.

"Permission to come aboard, Captain," Marais said, observing the traditional rule: no one short of the emperor could set foot on an Imperial vessel without reciting this age-old formula. Sergei nodded, smiling to himself, knowing there was no answer other than the affirmative.

Marais looked up and down the row of sideboys, and the ranks of officers and off-duty crew mustered to receive him, whites and blues. The other officer examined them also, and it seemed to Sergei that he was taking inventory.

"Commodore, it's a pleasure," he said, breaking the silence. "I've heard a great deal about you."

"All of it good, I hope, sir."

"Quite good, I assure you. Admiral McMasters was most insistent about you when I consulted him.

"Though I am sure you are skeptical about this venture," he continued without preamble, "I assure you that it is of critical moment. We are at the most important juncture in this entire war, and whether we wish to recognize it or not, the actions of this fleet will decide the future of our race, whether we will live . . . or die."

*There is absolutely nothing subtle about this man,* Sergei thought to himself, hoping that his face betrayed no emotion.

"You have the full cooperation of all of my command, Admiral. If there is anything we can do, now or in the future, to assist you, be assured that we will be ready and willing to do so."

With the formalities out of the way, Torrijos introduced his chief officers, and Marais, his adjutant: Captain Stone. Marais was escorted to his quarters, on the same deck as Sergei's.

"I'd like to see you here when you come off the bridge," Marais said, as he was about to leave.

"Admiral?"

"It is most important, Commodore. We have a great deal of logistical work to do. At . . . shall we say, 1900? We can take dinner together."

"It will be my pleasure, sir."

Marais smiled, and there was something about it that Sergei didn't like. Stone, the adjutant, hovered close to the admiral's shoulder.


Sergei and the evening meal arrived at Admiral Marais' cabin almost at once.

He had supervised the entrance into jump, a two-week interval which would bring the squadron out at the naval base at Mustapha; until then, the crew and officers would be marking time. Yet the admiral was in a hurry to begin planning.

*What the hell,* Sergei thought to himself. *Marais is a staff officer. Doesn't know anything about line duty. Probably wants to go over provisioning schedules or something.*

Dinner followed him into the cabin. As Stone showed him into the sitting-room, Sergei reassured himself that this would be nothing more . . . though somehow he didn't really believe that.

The dinner sat on its warming-tray. Sergei dismissed the steward, and he and the adjutant were left alone.

"The admiral—" he began.

"Admiral Marais is meditating," Stone interrupted him. It was the first time he'd heard the man speak; the voice was silky-smooth, as if it had been designed to put the listener at ease; instead, it made Sergei even more on edge. "He should be finished in just a few moments. I have strict orders"—Stone smiled, revealing a row of perfect teeth—"not to disturb the admiral when he meditates."

"You needn't concern yourself with it."

They both stood, and turned to see Marais emerging from the sleeping-room. He was informally dressed, and had a far-off look in his eyes, which gradually cleared as he scrutinized them, and then various points in the room, taking it all in.

He crossed the room to the warming-tray, uncovered a dish, and smelled the fragrant scent that rose from it. "Kung pao chicken. My compliments to your galley, Commodore Torrijos. I'm sure it will taste as good as it smells."

They ate, slipping into polite conversation about the squadron and the fleet: personnel mostly, and the reliability of the ships of the line—both had been severely battered at Pergamum, scarcely more than two months earlier. Sergei felt as if he were being drained for all useful information, wrung dry like a sponge.

The dinner was set aside, and the three officers adjourned to the viewing-area before the wallscreen. Marais took the small access tablet in his hand, and brought the screen to life. It initially depicted a volume of space roughly thirty parsecs in radius, with Pergamum at its center. Mustapha, their current destination, was at the fringes of that sphere.

Marais called forward a locator arrow and moved it idly about, first to Pergamum, and then to Mustapha. He left an indicator marker showing the fleet's current position.

"Commodore, we have a great deal of work to do, and a very short time in which to do it. Somewhere out here"—he flicked the arrow to the zor-space side of Pergamum—"is a zor fleet, badly battered from what I understand, but still a coherent force. They will assume that, as in the past, we will be heavily arming all worlds in the area, waiting for another strike. Furthermore, they will expect that it will take us some time to assemble a fleet suitable for our usual purpose—to overawe the zor, defeat them in one major battle, and sign a truce. However, this time, all of their expectations and assumptions will be wrong.

"I understand . . ." Marais glanced at Stone and then returned his attention to Sergei. "I understand that some of your staff is dubious of the effect that this command might have in prosecuting the war against the zor."

"I believe that they might be more comfortable, sir, if we awaited reinforcement from the Denneva or Charlestown naval bases. Some of my officers believe, and I am inclined to agree, that ten vessels would seem to be wholly inadequate to the task of defeating the zor."

"What do you expect it would take to . . . defeat the zor?"

"I could not say, sir, except that less than twenty ships is far too few."

"And what do you mean by 'defeat,' Commodore?" He looked at Stone, with an expression that seemed to indicate that he had expected the conversation to go this way.

"I . . . In the past, Admiral, defeat has—"

"In the *past,* Commodore. In the *past.* Any terms, any treaties or agreements with the zor, any basis for judgement of our performance thus far must be laid aside. So the question remains: What is necessary to defeat them? What constitutes victory?"

Sergei thought for a moment, and then decided on a textbook reply. "Defeat of an enemy is the effective elimination of his ability to carry out acts of belligerence."

"Then by your very definition we have never defeated the zor. Each time we have signed a treaty with them, we have only given them the capability to continue fighting. Though the first time they sued for peace, the Empire extended to here"—he pointed with the locator to an area near the destroyed colony of Alya—"and the second time, here"—he moved it farther out, about fifteen parsecs, to the Pergamum area—"and so forth, so that our treaty line is now here"—he pointed to the region of space near Eleuthra, the system that marked the boundary agreed upon two years ago—"which seems like a gain. But each time, though we have gained territory, we have not effectively defeated our enemy . . . by your own definition."

Human space, extending out from Sol System in all directions, was an irregular ovoid about 275 parsecs across its long axis. It extended farthest toward Antares, the zor home star; thus humanity's home was not quite in the astrographical center of the Empire.

Near the Antares Rift, an area almost devoid of stars, the Empire bordered on a cluster of zor worlds that were separated by the Rift from the zor home stars. Compared to the known extent of zor space, human space was huge; the aliens were outnumbered, outsized and—based on Sergei's own experience—outgunned.

Sergei sat silent, looking at the locator arrow on the screen, reviewing Marais' comments in his mind.

*Winning battles means nothing if you lose the war,* he thought. *And if all of humanity's efforts against the zor, all of the "wars" which it had "won," had not defeated the enemy, then it had not won them at all.*

"We must defeat the zor this time, Commodore Torrijos. We must eliminate the zor capacity to wage war against us, by destroying not only their ability, but also their will, to do so. In short, we will wage war on their terms."

"Sir . . ." Sergei looked at Marais, then at Stone, who sat impassive, and then back to the admiral. Some emotion had been kindled in Marais' eyes, and Sergei wasn't sure he wanted to know what it was. "Sir, the zor 'terms,' as I understand them, hardly stop short of annihilation of the enemy."

"That is correct." Marais toyed with the access tablet, turning it over in his hand. "We must consider all of our options . . . and we must do whatever is necessary to implement them. If that is our most logical path . . . then so be it."

## chapter 4

THERE SEEMS TO BE LITTLE DOUBT IN THE PUBLIC MIND THAT THE CONTINUING WAR WITH THE ALIENS HAS BEEN A BENEFIT AS WELL AS A BURDEN. SINCE THE FIRST VIOLENT CONTACT WITH THE ZOR AT ALYA, THE BOUNDARIES OF THE EMPIRE HAVE CREPT EVER OUTWARD, ENCLOSING MORE AND MORE SOLAR SYSTEMS ALONG THE AXIS BETWEEN SOL SYSTEM AND THE ZOR HOME STAR OF ANTARES.

DURING THE REIGN OF EMPEROR PHILIP II, A VOLUME ALMOST TEN PARSECS IN DIAMETER WAS TRANSFERRED FROM MILITARY TO CIVILIAN RULE. THE "NEW TERRITORIES" SPANNED TWENTY-TWO HABITABLE WORLDS AT THE OUTSET; BY THE TREATY OF EFAL IN 2309, THAT NUMBER HAD GROWN TO MORE THAN FIFTY, FROM THE COLD INDUSTRIAL WORLD OF ELEUTHRA ON THE RIFTWARD SIDE TO ALYA ON THE SOLWARD. IN ADDITION TO EXTENDING THE TAX BASE OF THE EMPIRE, IT ALSO PROVIDED A NUMBER OF NOBLE FAMILIES (SOME OF THEM NEWLY CREATED) WITH REAL ESTATE TO GOVERN, EXPLOIT AND FORTIFY AGAINST FURTHER ENEMY INCURSION.

THAT DIDN'T MAKE THE NEW TERRITORIES SAFE BY ANY STRETCH OF THE IMAGINATION. THEY WERE STILL THE BATTLEGROUND FOR THE INCREASINGLY VIOLENT CONFLICTS BETWEEN THE SOLAR EMPIRE AND THE ZOR

HEGEMONY. STILL, AS EACH PEACE TREATY WAS
CONCLUDED ANOTHER GROUP OF CAPTURED WORLDS
WAS ADDED TO THE NEW TERRITORIES, MAKING THE
INNER REACHES MORE AND MORE SETTLED.

DESPITE FRIGHTENING LOSSES, THE ZOR HELD
TENACIOUSLY TO A NUMBER OF COLONY WORLDS ON
THE SOLWARD SIDE OF THE ANTARES RIFT, A STARLESS
REACH OF SPACE A DOZEN PARSECS ACROSS; THIS SPREAD
OF PLANETARY SYSTEMS WAS LIKE A GIANT SPLAYED
CLAW, A LIMB CROSSING THE RIFT IN DEFIANCE OF THE
HUMAN PRESENCE THERE.

*—By Fire and Sword: A History of the Man-Zor Conflict,*
by Ichiro Kanev (Gleason Publishing, Adrianople, 2310)

Pergamum Base was well within the New Territories, but had been rendered almost useless following the zor attack—the orbital and ground-level bases remained, but it had no current strategic or tactical importance, and with much of the fleet reduced to debris in the outer reaches of the system, it was indefensible for all practical purposes. The home port of the Imperial Navy in this area remained Mustapha, the ducal seat for the Territories, located on the Solward side.

Mustapha had been captured from the zor twenty-eight years earlier. The story of its conquest was typical of a border world: it had been heavily fortified by the zor, serving as a naval supply depot. When its position became untenable, the Imperial Navy closed in, and the zor forces pulled out—except for a few hundred doomed warriors, who perished to the last soul defending it. Considering the losses to personnel and equipment during the eradication of those defenders, the zor High Nest doubtless felt the expenditure well worthwhile. After the last zor had been rooted out and the rubble had been cleared, the Navy had brought in the Seabees to refit the base to serve humans instead.

In addition to the obvious strategic advantage that an intact base provided, what the zor left behind provided significant insight into the way in which the aliens thought and the things in which they believed. Mustapha proved to be something of a

Rosetta stone for xenologists studying the alien race. It was the most intact zor facility ever captured, and from its layout and the equipment left behind, humanity learned a great deal about the aliens: their social structure (pyramidal, with most space communal except at the highest ranks); their command organization (highly dispersed—the limited comm facilities suggested that most ships were on their own in a battle zone); even their eating and drinking habits (and, thereby, some additional information on their physiology). It was all there, laid out like a complex puzzle, though many of the keys were still missing.

The most prominent feature in the Mustapha system was an enormous torus of metal, a fabricated ring that completely encircled the tiny moon of the system's only habitable world. The ring was anchored to the moon's surface by wide spokes a quarter-kilometer high, and was itself more than a hundred meters in diameter, large enough to be readily discerned by the naked eye from the surface of Mustapha. This huge structure, a marvel of engineering, had evidently been designed as a dry-dock and ship-repair facility, and contained numerous graving docks fitted with the heavy equipment needed to handle zor warships. It had required a tremendous effort and expense to retrofit the facility for human hands and human ships, but it had amounted to a fraction of what His Imperial Majesty would have had to pay to build one from scratch. Besides, the propaganda value alone had justified the drain on Admiralty resources.

Even after the reworking, Mustapha Base had retained evidence of its alien origin; the odd, disturbing angles of its external structure, as well as the fine-etched traceries the construction engineers had left swirled across its inner walls, pointed undeniably to the zor.


When the fleet reentered normalspace at Mustapha, the base was scarcely visible—a point of reflected light in the inner system, almost lost against the backdrop of the stars. A command to the helm officer presented Sergei with a long-range magnified view that picked out the details of the base. He could make out seven ships nose-in to the outside of the torus, further enhancing the dock's bizarre appearance—a sort of naval architect's fever-dream in black-and-silver. The image was too indistinct to pick out silhouettes or markings, of course, but Sergei could name off the ships in his mind—*Banff, Ulysses Grant, Phaedra, Victoria, Lacus Solis, Philip III, Wu Shih*—under repair, soon to rejoin the Imperial Fleet and the war against the zor.

They had been two weeks in jump getting here, during which time Sergei had become accustomed to the logistical aspects of his new command, and the scholarly, almost fanciful plans of his new commanding officer. Now, as the great former zor base hove into view, Sergei felt as if the war was about to begin in earnest.

As soon as the *Lancaster* had assumed orbit trailing the station, the admiral had expressed a desire to visit the repair docks. Sergei formed up an honor guard, including himself and three of his senior captains; in order to conduct the admiral and his escort from the *Lancaster* to Mustapha Base, the *Lancaster*'s gig was rigged as a barge, fitted with the official ID pennon of Admiral Marais. The gig—or barge—crossed the open space quickly, directed to an open dock on the ring by the base traffic control.

The entourage debarked from the barge into a large airlock, and after it cycled, they emerged into a wide, bending corridor. Fine traceries decorated the walls, catching the overhead fluorescents and glowing eerily. Three officers in full dress were waiting for them; the bosun's whistle sounded over the intercom.

"I'm honored, Admiral," the senior officer said, stepping forward with a salute. "Captain Henry Alvarez at your service, sir. Welcome aboard."

"Thank you, Captain," Marais replied. "My squadron commander, Commodore Torrijos," he said by way of introduction, gesturing to Sergei; "Captains Alyne Bell, Marc Hudson, and Sir Gordon Quinn of the squadron, and my aide, Captain Stone," he finished, indicating each in turn. Alvarez introduced his chief engineer and his chief naval architect.

"If the admiral would follow me," Alvarez said, and began to direct Marais toward the inner dock; but before he took a step, Marais held up his hand and walked to the inboard wall, which curved gently away from where they stood. Crouching slightly, he began to examine the traceries both visually and with the tips of his fingers.

"Admiral—" Alvarez began, sounding perplexed, but Marais did not seem to notice. The young captain caught Sergei's eye, looking for explanation, but Sergei shrugged his shoulders.

After a few moments, Marais straightened and returned to where the group waited respectfully. He had a faraway look in his eyes. He turned to Stone.

"Interesting," he said, and Stone nodded solemnly.

Then, he turned to his entourage and Alvarez. "*hRni'i.* The engravings." When they still looked a bit baffled, he continued. "The zor that staffed this station left behind evidence of themselves. I have made a study of the patterns used."

"You can read them, my lord?" Alvarez asked, surprised. The admiral nodded. "What do they say?"

"They say . . ." Marais looked away, at the *hRni'i* on the walls. "These were added very late, not long before the station was captured. They say that . . . the Nest is preparing to die."

Within the structure gravity prevailed, though it was somewhat less than half a g; through the glasteel portals, the battered hulks of starships stood in sharp profile against the star-strewn night, with firefly-images of spacesuited welders hovering around their hulls. Dark, irregular gaps in their smooth hulls told the tale of their demise: many of the ships had been caught unawares, defensive fields down, unprotected . . . It all came back to Sergei as he followed in the wake of the admiral, watching group after group of hastily assembled noncoms and specs as they answered Marais' questions and described the work they were doing on a battered vessel; the admiral slipped easily into their confidence, never asking the same set of questions twice, never talking down to them. The proud names of His Majesty's ships were listed on the status boards outside of the access airlocks, while outside in space the crews worked frantically to bring them back to spaceworthiness.

hose vessels are there because the zor did what no one believed they could," Marais said, watching the ring recede in the viewport. "From what I was able to learn, six more will be flightworthy by the end of the month. The zor won't be counting on that." He had offered them a sizable bonus, out of his own pocket, if they completed the tasks by then. Unusual, but not unprecedented. "We will jump for Pergamum in seventy-two hours. Commodore, please inform your command and the other squadrons. You will find orders keyed to your voice in the *Lancaster*'s computer."

"Seventy-two hours. Aye-aye, sir . . . Where do you plan to rendezvous with the rest of the fleet? The original campaign orders called for full deployment here at Mustapha."

"That situation has not changed. However, we will have badly damaged the zor at least once by that time."

"At Pergamum, sir?"

"At L'alChan, Commodore."

"L'alChan has no naval base, sir, unless I'm mistaken."

"That is correct. L'alChan is a *civilian* target. It should be sufficient for our needs: to draw out the zor fleet, and force them to make a mistake."

"The zor fleet surely outnumbers our force, sir. If I may point out the risk involved—"

"I am fully aware of the risk, Commodore." Marais turned away from the 'port to face Sergei. "However, there is no need to worry about the zor fleet. Aside from a few system defense vessels, we will face no serious opposition at L'alChan. Still, it will serve our purpose."

"Yes, sir. I am afraid I don't understand, sir."

Stone smiled, a dark and toothy smile.

"You will, Commodore," the admiral replied.

Marais had chosen to leave the Sha'en squadron with the responsibility for guarding the home front, including the Mustapha naval base, while his own command, such as he had thus far gathered, would bring the war into zor space. The ten ships of his squadron had made the jump from Mustapha to L'alChan in just under six days; as the admiral had surmised, the zor had not been expecting an attack so soon, and certainly not against a world with no military value.

The darkness of jump gave way to a swirl of mercury-gray, which resolved to streaks that became stars. The *Lancaster* was already at General Quarters by the time the forward screen showed normal; the admiral had taken up the chief engineer's bridge perch, with a good view of the pilot's board and the gunners' stations.

"Anne," Sergei said, without turning to face his communications officer, "give the signal to sound off." He turned his attention to the large 3-D display directly below and in front of his chair, displaying telemetry on nearby space from the *Lancaster*'s electronics. It showed the system in sharp detail, with small glyphs indicating the mass density near the seven orbiting worlds and the primary, as well as survey data indicating navigational hazards and unusual features. The course chosen for the squadron put them at thirty degrees azimuth, in a plane transverse to the main plane of the planetary orbitals; the jump point was inside the last orbital, with the sixth and seventh worlds at conjunction, on the other side of the sun.

As soon as the rest of his command materialized in the system, it would begin to take in readings from the other ships. At the edge of detection range, the board registered three small enemy vessels pushing hard toward the jump point.

"Aye, sir," Anne DaNapoli replied, keying a signal. A bo-sun's whistle cut through the silence on the bridge.

"*Gagarin* reporting, sir." The fleet-carrier had already appeared on the pilot's board as Bell's voice came through.

"*Biscayne* reporting, Commodore." After a moment Hudson's vessel appeared on the board.

"*Helsinki* reporting," said Gordon Quinn. "Sir," the nobleman added, after a brief pause. Sergei ignored the intended slight; there was no time for him to deal with it now.

"*Ikegai* onstation, sir," came Okome's voice. The close escort had already started to match velocities with the flagship, even though less than a minute had passed since the ships had begun emerging from jump.

"*Mycenae* reporting, Commodore."

"*San Martín* reporting, Commodore." Sharon MacEwan's voice came across the comm. "Cleared for action, sir."

"*Inflexible* reporting, sir."

"*Indomitable* reporting, sir." The small craft all appeared on the board and immediately began to maneuver toward their designated positions. General Quarters had already brought defensive fields up on all of the ships.

"*Gagarin,* begin to deploy," Sergei said. "Anne, hail the *Sevastopol*. I don't have it on the board yet."

"Aye-aye, Commodore. *Sevastopol,* this is the *Lancaster*. Do you read?" Sergei watched his board as the comm patter was patched on to his bridge. The first carrier wing was away and free of the *Gagarin* in a matter of fifteen or twenty seconds, while the ships of the line—the *Biscayne,* the *Helsinki* and the *Lancaster* itself—took up formation. The close escort *Ikegai* deployed aft and starboard of the flag, the two ships' defensive fields shimmering where they touched. The smaller craft formed a secondary group aft of the first-rank ships, guarding the flanks of the carrier, though there was a gap where the *Sevastopol* should be.

"*Mycenae,* close it up." The board showed the three zor vessels still accelerating from their base in the outer system. The projections indicated that they were near turnover: the point at which they'd have to start to decelerate, to avoid streaking past the human invaders. "All ahead one-half," he ordered. It would cost a bit of fuel, but by closing quickly it would force the zor ships to decelerate more suddenly, placing more stress on them.

"No response from *Sevastopol,* sir."

"*Mycenae,* countermand all ahead one-half, go to one-quarter. Bert, do you read?"

"Aye, Commodore."

"I'm not picking up the *Sevastopol.* If Tina comes out near the jump point, I don't want her flanks left uncovered. If you pick her up, let me know at once."

"Acknowledged." The *Mycenae* began to slip behind the other six vessels as they moved to intercept the defenders. Sergei could identify them now: *Stalker*-class armored patrol boats, heavily armed and maneuverable, but without jump capability. The fighter wing from the carrier had nearly reached firing range.

"Zor vessels, this is Commodore Sergei Torrijos of the Solar Empire, representing Admiral of the Fleet Lord Marais. I call upon you to surrender your vessels and this system in exchange for quarter."

The bridge was silent again, except for an occasional comment between the fighters. After several long seconds, the zor replied in their usual fashion: lances of energy burst from the oncoming vessels toward the lead fighter craft, which maneuvered out of the way.

Sergei exchanged glances with the admiral, who didn't seem

surprised by the response. "All right, Captain Bell," Sergei said into the air, leaning on one arm of his pilot's chair. "Let 'em have it."

The advantages of fighter craft are maneuverability and speed, which are achieved at the expense of almost everything else, beginning with the pilot's comfort and culminating with the lack of defensive fields around the fighter. The pilot wears a pressure suit and helmet, on the odd chance that, if his craft is blown out from around him, he may actually survive; he sits in a seat that is just comfortable enough for him to fly for a few hours at a time, but not enough for him to shift from side to side more than a few centimeters. Everything is close to hand: attitude controls, weapon actuators and readouts on the current position of the ship, the mothership and the present target. Flying a fighter is the most exhilarating duty in the Imperial Navy, and by far the most dangerous. It requires superb concentration, excellent reflexes and a personality quirk that undervalues human life.

Alyne Bell knew all of this from personal experience, of course, as did her commodore. The bridge of a carrier is a little different from that of a starship: the pilot's board is huge, and there is a "traffic director" in charge of it, usually the carrier's exec, to whom the wing leaders report. When all four (or, in some cases, six) fighter wings are deployed, things are changing so quickly that, without such an officer, the bridge would quickly become a madhouse just trying to keep track of the movement of the carrier's own fighters.

"All right, Captain Bell. Let 'em have it."

"You heard the man, Lew," she said to Lew Cornejo, her exec, who was monitoring the deployed wing on a headset. "Send the second wing whenever you're ready."

"Aye, Captain," he said. "Second Wing, prepare—" He stopped for a moment, watching as one of the transponder codes for a first-wing fighter winked out. On the forward screen, there was a sudden explosion, almost at the edge of visual range. "Prepare to launch," he said at last.

Gagarin reports the loss of two fighters, sir," DaNapoli said a few minutes later, as the main force dropped farther into the gravity well. "One of the enemy boats has lost maneuver capability."

"How long to firing range, Chan?"

"Just under six minutes, sir, at present velocity."

"Where's their base? How far are they from cover?"

"I'm plotting their trajectory, sir . . . I make out a base in the fourth orbital, approximately at opposition. If they retreated at full velocity, it would take them about three-quarters of an hour to reach firing range of the base." The trajectory appeared as a thin line of light across the pilot's board; Chan rose from his station and came to stand beside Sergei's chair. "They'll never get home."

While the body of the squadron closed in, the two fighter wings buzzed around the three larger zor defenders, looking for the correct shot. Almost simultaneously, two of the fighters found it. Narrow laser-fire struck the shifting, luminous defenses and arced in toward the hulls, spreading like summer lightning as it cascaded through the field, multiplying rather than dissipating. The warning went out from the lucky shooters to their wing-companions, and as the zor vessels twisted and maneuvered to try and ward off the shot . . . which sometimes worked . . . the fighters veered off, trying to put as many kilometers as possible between themselves and fiery detonation. The defensive fields on the two zor ships grew brighter and hotter, running from red to yellow into bright blue-white before a sudden and violent explosion . . .

A cheer rang out across the *Lancaster*'s bridge as the viewscreens polarized and the detection equipment became ineffective. Twin balls of energy expanded outward across the path of the oncoming ships, which changed course to avoid it. As the visual and tactical displays came online again, the *Lancaster* picked up the remaining ship. Rather than retreating for cover, it was headed for the jump point and the *Mycenae,* left behind to wait for the *Sevastopol,* still missing.

"*Helsinki,* come around and go get it," was scarcely out of Sergei's mouth when the *Lancaster*'s jump sensors registered an incoming vessel—

The *Sevastopol* was bearing down on the zor vessel from its port side and aft. With scarcely enough time to bring up its own defenses, the just-arrived Imperial vessel opened fire. Between the *Sevastopol* and the *Mycenae,* the zor ship had no chance.

The squadron bore down on the inner system. L'alChan's primary world, the fourth in the system, had an orbital base that had been home to the three boats: it was no match for the massed firepower of the human ships. With a substantial portion of its hull collapsed, the station quickly lost gyroscopic stability, and its orbit decayed, sending it hurtling into the planet's upper atmosphere; pursued by the attack ships, it careened planetward, and the remains that were not consumed by the searing heat of reentry crashed into the world's northern ocean several hundred kilometers from land.

Sergei had been prepared, then, to accept a surrender from the groundside forces, and had begun to issue orders to open a comm link to the planetary base; but before it could be carried out, Marais belayed the order.

"They have already refused the opportunity to surrender," he said quietly, his hands folded in his lap.

"The situation has changed somewhat since then, sir," Sergei had pointed out. The gunnery computer was already identifying and keying in targets down below; most of them were population centers and industrial complexes.

"You have your orders, Commodore. Carry them out."

Sergei had considered objecting. There was no real reason to destroy the planet's facilities, after the military strength of the system had been neutralized. No reason . . . except Pergamum perhaps, or Alya.

After a moment that seemed to stretch out to infinity, Sergei ordered the attack.

In the peace and quiet of his cabin afterward, with only the soft touch of his fingers on his keypad or the scratch of his stylus to interrupt the silence, the violence the fleet had rained down on the zor agricultural world seemed impossibly far away. There was no firsthand record of the attack, of course, since no landing had taken place; but Sergei could close his eyes and almost visualize what it must have looked like from below . . .

Imagine a warm spring afternoon. Clear skies above, plants in bloom, crisp, clean air, a soft breeze. Perhaps the indigenous wildlife is audible in the background. Imagine all of that. Hold it in your mind for a moment, and savor all of it—the weather, the breeze, the chirping of birds (or whatever), the growing plants.

Then imagine it suddenly transformed into the seventh circle of Hell:

Fire rains from the sky. Vegetation is set aflame by chemical incendiaries. The ground is rocked by explosions, the air is filled with smoke and debris and the smell of burning—wood, plastic, even flesh.

He had let his eyes close as he imagined the scene, and just as suddenly as the visualization had come to him, he thrust it away, and the sights and sounds of the destruction faded back into his imagination; instead, all he saw was his half-written report staring back at him from the wallscreen.

It only took a few moments of reflection to decide that he'd rather think of something else; but the strength of the images continued to attract his imagination as consistently as he was repelled by the thought. Somehow he placed it in the context of a bombing of Buenos Aires or St. Louis, or London or Paris, instead of some alien metropolis on L'alChan. It was like Alya, the world that had been ravaged by the zor long ago at the beginning of this struggle. There was a continent on Alya that would be uninhabitable for several centuries; it would take about that long for half the radioactive by-product of what was dropped there to transmute to inert substance.

It didn't make the idea of having destroyed L'alChan any more palatable; it just made it easier to think about.

C ome."

The door slid open, and Chan stood there with Tina Li, captain of the *Sevastopol,* fitted out in a dress uniform. Sergei rose from his desk chair as they saluted, and beckoned Captain Li to an armchair, nodding dismissal to his exec. He took the chair opposite, giving his subordinate officer a few moments to get nervous.

"I suppose you know why I asked you aboard the *Lancaster,* Captain."

"I can conjecture, sir."

"It didn't seem like it was worthwhile to try and take you to task on an unrestricted comm line. Among other things, I have an admiral to deal with, and since this is the first major operation under my command . . . Do you read me, Captain?"

"Loud and clear, sir."

"All right." He leaned forward, elbows on knees. "That being said, let me be frank, Tina. I know you only by reputation, and I'm sure you've heard something about me. I have great respect for your ship and crew, and for you as its skipper. I'm sure that skill has contributed to your lifespan, and kept the *Sevastopol* online. But this isn't patrol detail, and it isn't everyone for himself or herself.

"The battle plan didn't call for what you did, and the ship you took out wouldn't have even been where it was if I hadn't detailed Bert Halvorsen to cover your ass. It was flashy, and it rang up another kill for the *Sevastopol,* but it could've destroyed it, too."

"War's a risky business. Sir."

"I'm not a damn desk officer, Tina! Don't give me that. Your job isn't just to take risks, it's to know which risks to take. L'alChan had three system defense boats and an orbital base; it was outgunned and outnumbered, and didn't warrant the risk of delaying jump. There are a half-dozen ships near completion at Mustapha that could take your place and whose commanders will follow my orders, and there are a hundred line officers to whom I could give the *Sevastopol.*"

"The commodore has those choices." Tina looked angry, her hands clenched into fists. Sergei could almost read what she was thinking: *I've got friends at Court, too.*

"I'd rather not make them. I want your ship, I want your expertise as its commander. But I want you to follow orders."

She seemed a bit relieved at that. "What do you intend to do, sir?"

"With you? Nothing. The *Sevastopol* had a nav failure, which I'm sure you'll correct. I'm not going to give out any medals for this carnage; perhaps the admiral will. But I'll expect my orders to be carried out in future.

"That's not up for negotiation. It's part of my job. If you let me do my job, Tina, I'll give you wide latitude to do yours." He stood and walked to a cabinet set into the wall of his quarters and opened it, revealing a tall decanter and glasses. He poured a bit of liquid from the decanter into two of the glasses and brought them over to where Tina still sat, not completely at ease, and handed one to her.

"Here's to success," he said, touching his glass to hers.

•    •    •

**M**arais made a speech to the squadron while most of it was still orbiting the ruined world of L'alChan. The echoes of that speech would haunt Sergei all during the trip back to Mustapha.

The admiral had dressed for the occasion. It was common practice for admirals, especially wealthy ones, to design and wear uniforms suited to their own tastes; these varied from the totally unadorned to the completely ridiculous. Mostly, however, the designs were nostalgic, after a fashion decades or centuries in the past.

Marais' choice for addressing the advanced guard was a simple black outfit, highlighted at collar and cuffs with silver embroidery, and adorned with service ribbons and medals, some of which (Sergei suspected) were inherited from the long line of Marais antecedents who had served the Empire. It set his profile off nicely, though, producing the desired austere effect.

When he began to speak, his eyes were lit with an intensity that was frighteningly powerful.

"Many times in the long history of our race, a tribe, a nation or a civilization has reached a crossroads from which two paths led. On the one hand was continuation, victory, wealth or power; on the other was destruction, defeat, poverty or slavery. On some occasions, the correct choice was made. On others, the wrong path was taken, and the entity was overwhelmed, left in the dust to be trampled by its successors.

"Some say that there is no escape from this pattern, no way to break out of the wheel of fate, which would forever pit one part of humanity against another. Indeed, prior to the unification of humanity beneath the aegis of our emperor, we went to the very brink of self-destruction in our wars against ourselves. That era is past. We have changed our course as a race, and no longer war amongst ourselves, but rather are united, seeking our destiny in the vast reaches of space. In the course of that expansion, we have encountered other races—the otran and the rashk, finding friendship and mutual understanding despite the vast gulf between our cultures, vaster indeed than between any of the societies of mankind.

"Then mankind and its allies discovered the zor.

"Despite our best efforts, we have never been able to attain an understanding with that race, which continues to pursue a course that aims at our ultimate destruction. Every treaty we have signed with their High Nest has been no more than an opportunity for them to rest and recover, to give them a chance to fight us again.

"This sanguine struggle continues, even in time of peace, despite our unwillingness to pursue it.

"It is not because we have something they want.

"It is not because we have colonized worlds that belonged to them.

"It is not even because they believe us to be intrinsically harmful to them.

"It is simply because . . . we *exist*."

Marais nodded to Anne DaNapoli. The admiral's face disappeared from viewscreens across the squadron, and was replaced by a display of the Pergamum system, littered with the skeletons of starships and the debris that had once been equipment, cargo and crew . . . the floating remains of the ships that hadn't survived. Everyone in the fleet had a friend who'd died there; the scene had been played back hundreds of times since the event.

All across the squadron, keeping station off the destroyed remnants of the zor colony world of L'alChan, throats tightened and fists clenched.

"We will never be safe from this menace as long as we refuse to defeat our enemy, the zor. Make no mistake: they are very much our enemies, and have *always been so*—in peace as well as in war. For half a century, we have tried to reach an accommodation with them; we have attempted to deal with them as our culture and history suggest, as human nations have always dealt with each other. But their perspective of the universe precludes the existence of another race side by side with their own."

The panoramic view of destruction was replaced by Marais' face once more. A careful observer might have detected some tension—or perhaps intensity—in his expression.

"The zor seek to destroy us. If we fail to recognize this painful fact and act accordingly, there will be no future generations to recognize or rectify our mistake. If we do not stop them here and now, decisively, finally, in the same way that they seek to stop us, the human race *as we know it* will cease to exist.

"We must win this war decisively or we will not win it at all. There is no halfway; there will be no terms of surrender. There will be no quarter. This is the most important moment in the history of mankind."

He gave the Imperial salute: hand to temple, then fist to breast. All across the volume, thousands of naval and marine personnel responded.

"Victory!" he shouted, and there was fire in his eyes now. Caught up in the moment, his subordinates aboard the *Lancaster*, including Flag Commodore Sergei Torrijos, responded with a shout of "Victory!"

And for a moment, the nagging doubts disappeared. But they would not be gone for long.

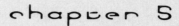

## chapter 5

*Transmitted on private channel, 12 May 2311, 2244 Standard*
*Encrypted SML/42A/113-1*                    *Key Nonrecoverable*
*Attachments: text, vid*

Orange:

The speech made by Alpha subject is enclosed for your review. It will reach the public within a few days, but you might wish to review it for semantic content. It was certainly effective: they stood and cheered and shouted "Victory." Subjects Beta/22 and Beta/19 have speculated on Alpha's intention to take a lead position in the Imperial Assembly; with the evidence from the overfly (attached), there might be accusations of atrocities: still, the polling psych analysis indicates that the public's tolerance for such acts is much higher than even subjects onstation believe.

I would remind you, however, that although subject Alpha's success enlarges our options, it also increases our concerns, since the possibility for escalation of the threat accompanies it. While suspicions of this problem can certainly be made known, particularly to those in the Assembly with whom we work, we should be careful to make no less, and no more, of it than it already has become.

>unsigned<


Private transmission, Priority 8:                    14 May 2311

FM:   Cdre Sergei Torrijos
       Pergamum Naval Base

TO:   R Adm Theodore McMasters
       Admiralty HQ Terra

Admiral:

The recording of Admiral Marais' address to the fleet at L'alChan is enclosed for your review. The text will probably reach you through more official channels in a few days anyway.

While I cannot find fault with Admiral Marais' conduct thus far—indeed, considering the success of the L'alChan operation, I cannot help but praise it—I feel a foreboding about the upcoming campaign. He's told us that this operation will be much different from anything we've experienced thus far, perhaps in our careers. I do know this: Marais was in complete control by the end of that speech, and the officers and crew of this fleet are ready (at this moment, anyway) to follow him to the ends of the universe.

Still, I cannot help but wonder what he will say when the zor approach us with peace terms, as they have in the past. No doubt the emperor will wish to consider them and will agree to an armistice. I am afraid that will leave us far short of Marais' "absolute victory."

The *Lancaster* is in fine shape. I know that you'd rather be out here than back there, but I also know that your thoughts and hopes go with us.

>*Sergei*<

The Chamber of Meditation was as silent as death, interrupted only by the sound of the High Lord breathing, and the occasional breezes that stirred through his wings. He could feel his heart beat, and almost sense the pumping of blood through his veins. He had performed the breathing techniques and cast his mind to the Eight Winds . . . but still the dreams would not come.

Dreaming was the duty of the High Lord, the bond between the High Nest and the Lord *esLi*. Ever since the time of A'alu and Qu'u, when the Nests were first united, the race had been guided by the prescient dreams of the High Lord.

The father of the current High Lord, like all of his predecessors, had approached his great responsibility tentatively, with awe and fear; but he had gradually become accustomed to reading the signs given him in those dreams. The unity of the Inner and Outer Peace had been complete . . .

Until the dream that changed the course of the High Nest forever.

The High Lord remembered as he perched in the Chamber. It was a dream that had been given him by his father with his *hsi*, just before he went to *esLi*; he held it in its totality, as if he had dreamed it himself. *esLi* had spoken to his father (or to him? The bounds of time were always stretched and hard to perceive when dreaming). The Lord had not shown His visage in the dream, but had spoken with the echoes of the Plain of Despite.

"Behold, High Lord," *esLi* had said. "I have given you the universe to rule; I have taught you the ways of Inner and Outer Peace. I have united you with My talon, and guided you with My words.

"But you have allowed this abomination to stain the world I have given you."

In response to the High Lord's unspoken question, the image of an alien appeared before him: a pale, wingless creature, hung heavy with flesh, unattractive and unpleasant.

"This abomination, High Lord, this race has appeared beyond the borders of the zor dominion, and honors neither the Inner nor the Outer Peace.

"It must not be permitted to exist, High Lord. It is an affront to you. It is an affront to me.

"I charge you with a great and serious burden. You must exterminate this race, scour it from the face of the heavens.

"For if you do not . . ." the Lord *esLi* then turned to him at last, gripping him with a fearsome, iron visage. "If you do not, High Lord, this is the last you—or your successors—will ever see of me."

. . . There the dream ended. It had not been the last dream his honored father had experienced, but it had been the signal tocsin of His Lordship. Out there—beyond the Chamber of Meditation, beyond the zor home worlds—his brothers and cousins sought to carry out the mandate that *esLi* Himself had directed. Tentatively, carefully, the High Lord's father—and then the current Lord himself—had reached back into the muddy ocean of prescient dreams, and the race had been guided by them.

The memory of that terrible dream had never left him, and from time to time it echoed with particular strength, as if something in the dark half-world of dreams sought to emerge, or as if something had happened in the world of light that had repercussions in the High Lord's dreams.

While he perched in the Chamber, waiting for the dreams to come, the High Lord wondered which—if either—it was.

Against a more reasonable opponent than the zor, the strategy of the last sixty years—playing for a draw—would ultimately be the least costly and the most likely to convert the enemy from belligerents to allies. While the zor campaigns became ever more daring and aggressive, humanity had become predictable, disdaining risky but potentially victorious strategies in favor of those that might retain or extend the status quo.

The Empire had lasted nearly two centuries by employing this technique to great effect against rebellious colonies; if the insurgents could not be suppressed by the application of limited, *affordable* force, the demands of the colony—generally improved political status within the Empire, more favorable trade relations, even representation in the Senate—would be granted, taking the renewing energy of the rebels and harnessing it to the defense of the establishment. The present emperor's grandfather had declared the highest maxim of this policy when counseling restraint against the zor in the immediate wake of the destruction of Alya. "Never completely alienate a potential ally," the old emperor had said, "even if he happens to be your enemy at the moment." For more than half a century, while man and zor fought to a bloody standstill several times, the Solar Empire continued to play for time, hoping to convert the zor into that ally.

The destruction of L'alChan contributed little to the defeat of the zor in either the short or long term, but it was a clarion call that the admiral had dispensed with that strategy completely. It was the first clear evidence of the difference in this war. Of course, the sensitivity of the destruction of a completely civilian installation did not escape the notice of the censors, who dutifully purged any mention of the event in mail and in dispatches. This further enhanced it in the eyes of fleet personnel, whose political conservatism was reinforced by the fleet command's decision to withhold information from civilians. The Senate and the emperor's ministers would wait, whether they liked it or not. As for the public, 3V and the Red Cross, they were even more remote from the "real world" of the war, and were thus not even a concern.

The officers of the *Lancaster* convey their respects to Commodore Torrijos, and have the pleasure of requesting his presence for reception of Captain Bell of the *Gagarin,* in the wardroom of the *Lancaster* at low watch on the sixteenth of May.

RSVP to R. Chandrasekhar Wells, Commander.

●    ●    ●

Sergei emerged from the shower, toweling himself, and passed the desk where the invitation lay open. Despite electronics, it had been handwritten on cream-colored stationery with the sword-and-sun of the Empire surrounded by a pair of white roses, emblem of the *Lancaster;* it had been delivered in person some hours ago by a nervous first-cruise midshipman, who had looked as if he were ready to dash out of the cabin if his commodore said "boo." While maintaining the solemnity appropriate for a flag officer, Sergei was secretly amused as the young man had stammered out Commander Wells' compliments, delivered the letter and waited to be dismissed.

He sat in his desk chair, leaning back and letting it conform to him, and took the invitation in his hand. "*The officers of the* Lancaster *convey their respects to Commodore Torrijos . . .*" The proper form, for a ship's captain, would have been: "*The junior officers of the* Lancaster *convey their respects to the Captain . . .*" Except, of course, that his responsibility extended beyond the skin of the ship. It had taken them weeks to get around to inviting him to the wardroom, a courtesy usually extended during the first jump; perhaps they had assumed that he was too busy, or that they needed a special occasion. Well, they had it: the squadron's most eligible captain had caught the eye of every unattached officer onstation, and despite carrying the admiral's and commodore's flag, the *Lancaster* hadn't yet had the pleasure.

He set the invitation back on the desk, and tossed the towel in the direction of the clothes-hamper. *Rank has its privileges,* he thought wryly, knowing that an orderly would be in at the watch-change to pick up after him. He walked to his closet and selected a clean uniform and began to don it in front of a mirror, and thought about the evening to come.

Of all traditions in the Navy—and there were certainly enough of them!—the wardroom was the most enjoyable. In the days of the wet navy on the homeworld, the captain of a ship had his own cabin and his own domain; often the other officers had no private cabins, and no place of refuge to study, relax or be entertained. In the first generation of FTL ships, the engines were huge and inefficient, making ships' interiors cramped and crowded. Other than the captain, officers bunked cheek by jowl with crew; the privilege of an officers' wardroom was jealously guarded.

The passage of time had changed all that. Fitting out a wardroom these days, even aboard a ship of war like the *Lancaster,* reflected on the ship, its officers and especially its captain; wealthier commanders might even pay for it out of their own pockets. Sergei and his immediate predecessor, Ted McMasters, had benefited from the largesse of the original captain of the new *Lancaster,* Sir Malcolm Rodyn, who could afford it. Sir Malcolm, it was said, set one of the best tables in the Navy, and Ted and, later, Sergei had done nothing to sully that reputation. During Sergei's first cruise, the wardroom had hosted a full-dress dinner for Admiral Boulanger, and it had dazzled him; even Ted McMasters had seemed subdued and nervous. Later, of course, Sergei had learned that by favorably impressing the influential admiral, the *Lancaster* had obtained an active posting. It was his first opportunity to experience the political aspects of wardroom fetes.

Fleetingly he wondered whether there was some overtone to this dinner that he hadn't caught. It was an opportunity to meet the principal officers of the *Gagarin,* of course—Alyne Bell, Lew Cornejo and Anne Marcos—in a neutral setting, where they would all be guests of the *Lancaster* officer corps; certainly his junior officers would want to make a favorable impression ... but perhaps there was something else that he was missing, something to which he had to pay closer attention.

Without concentrating on it, he had gotten dressed, and now was properly attired as a Commodore of the Fleet. He took a moment to examine it all, as if he were preparing for an inspection; he brushed a fleck of dust from his right forearm, and made a minute adjustment to his uniform blouse. The slight graying of his hair was becoming noticeable but didn't trouble him; yet the weathering lines around his eyes showed the signs of worry even more than the signs of age. Maybe it was part of the wages and benefits of a flag-rank officer. He shrugged into his uniform jacket, picked up his cap and made his way out of his cabin.

Come *a long way,* he reminded himself. *Years since I was impressed by this sort of thing.* But it did still impress him, and while he watched the junior officers direct the setting of the table, he let his mind wander, thinking about the many hours he had spent here, on the best damn ship in His Majesty's Fleet.

Not long after his arrival, Alyne Bell arrived, escorted by the middle-watch officer of the deck. She was flanked by her two subordinate officers: Commanders Anne Marcos and Lewis Cornejo. Sergei knew Cornejo from flight school, and later from time together on the *Ponchartrain;* Lew had demonstrated a strong survival instinct that many of his more headstrong colleagues had lacked. That was a good attribute for an executive officer (his current posting on the *Gagarin*) but it was something of a stigma for one aspiring to command, enough to give him a reputation as unwilling to take risks of any kind. As for Marcos, Sergei knew her only through her service record, one of hundreds he'd reviewed while assembling the squadron. She had achieved some renown as a technical wizard, and it showed in her eyes as she surveyed the room with the glance of an architect or structural engineer.

Chan Wells greeted each of his fellow officers warmly, offering each of the ladies a beautifully formed white crystal rose— symbolic of the old Terran royal house after which the *Lancaster* was named. He presented Cornejo with a white parade baton, into which the hammer-and-sickle/star-and-sword insignia of the *Gagarin* had been worked in silver. Sergei silently complimented his exec; it was a nice touch.

Presently the officers were standing in small groups, exchanging before-dinner pleasantries, sipping wine from tall, fluted crystal goblets bearing the white rose of the *Lancaster*. After some maneuvering, during which he had to exercise commodorial rank at least three or four times, Sergei found himself in conversation with his carrier commander.

"Your wardroom sets quite a table, sir," she said, indicating the spread of china and glassware on the dining-table.

"Legacy of Sir Malcolm, mostly. Plus, of course, the additions of later captains, myself included."

"What did you add?" she asked, surveying the room.

Sergei gestured to the long table. "The first year I commanded the *Lancaster*, I had the opportunity to buy it from the captain of the old *Armitage*. She'd been pretty badly beaten-up over near Boren, in some kind of zor ambush, and was headed for the scrap heap. It seemed a shame to let a fine piece of Amazon tallwood go to waste, so I scraped together the money for it. I've never regretted it."

Captain Bell regarded him with what seemed to be genuine appreciation. "You have good taste, sir. Something as beautiful as that on a warship sounds ostentatious, but . . . having seen it, in its surroundings"—she gestured to the decorations of the room with her goblet—"it seems natural."

He smiled and raised his own goblet to sip, but before he could taste a single drop, there was a sudden crash, followed by the sound of breaking glass. Immediately the area was cleared but for the culprit—a young ensign in dress uniform, frozen in place like a deer caught in a hunter's sights, his face trapped in apology and surprise.

The room broke into song, led by Chan Wells, president of the *Lancaster*'s wardroom.

"Here's to Ensign Elway,
   Here's to Ensign Elway,
   Here's to Ensign Elway,
   Who's with us to-night,"

began the officers of the *Lancaster*, ringing out a song boasting of the young ensign's clumsiness, foolishness and lack of sexual prowess. At each chorus, the officers clicked their goblets together to toast the young man, who became more and more embarrassed. During the last verse, the youngest officer of the vessel took down a broad-brimmed floppy hat from a corner shelf and moved from person to person in the room. Each of the *Lancaster*'s junior officers dropped a sheet of scrip into the hat; at the end of the song, the hat was nearly full, and the junior man presented it to Chan Wells with a flourish.

Wells walked over to Ensign Elway, who had remained still during this entire procedure. "By order of the first captain to command this vessel—" he began.

"—may his immortal soul smile upon us—" the other officers intoned.

"—on behalf of the officers and captain of the *Lancaster*—" with a respectful bow to Sergei . . .

"—may our throats never be dry—"

"—I present to you, Ensign Pedro Marion Elway, the Ransom." Chan held the hat out to Ensign Elway, who took it, thanked Chan quietly and handed it back, his face still red from the attention directed at him.

The officers broke into applause, with cries of "Nobly done!" and "Taken like a gentleman," and the room returned to conversation. An orderly had been summoned at some point, and now began to clean up the mess left by the broken goblet.

"What was that all about?" Alyne Bell asked, as she watched the glass being swept up.

Sergei smiled. "Old tradition. These goblets are Corcyran crystal, incredibly beautiful and prohibitively expensive. They're also extremely fragile, which means that they'll tend to break— usually in the hands of young ensigns on their first cruise." He turned the goblet in his hands, so that the light caught the pale rose etched into the surface. "Since we don't want to bankrupt our junior men, and since we *do* want to use the crystal and china, there's a simple rule: the first time an officer breaks a piece of the dinner service, the wardroom collects to pay for it. After that, he's on his own. Our young Elway just got his free one."

"I . . . see. Tell me, Commodore, did you—"

"Oh, yes. My first cruise on the *Lancaster,* I was selected by the Number One to help supervise laying out a special wardroom dinner for Commodore Bryant. I knocked a Delft soup tureen off the table and received the song from just the exec and the Officer of the Day. They told me I'd used up their good graces for five cruises to come."

Captain Bell could not help but laugh. Sergei found himself noticing that he enjoyed the sound; not knowing really what to do with the information, he filed it away.

"I'd be interested in knowing what you make of our new admiral," Sergei ventured.

"I've always felt, sir, that it is bad policy to express opinions of one's superiors, especially *to* one's superiors."

"Very adroit, Captain. My compliments." He tipped his goblet and took a long sip. "My curiosity isn't motivated by policy, though. I simply wonder how all this appears."

"Wardroom privilege?" She glanced about, as if to see who might be listening. Sergei thought he noticed some sort of hand-signal pass between Bell and Lew Cornejo.

"By all means."

"Thank you, sir." She drank slowly. "With respect to the admiral, I would say that Lord Marais has accomplished a great deal in a short time, enough to convince most of the senior officers that he won't lead us into a disaster."

"'Most?'"

"Well, nearly all. Command-rank officers are skeptics by nature, sir, with all due respect."

"You sound like Marc Hudson."

She looked up suddenly when Hudson's name was mentioned, giving the Sergei the impression that he'd somehow echoed her thoughts. "I'm sorry to interrupt. Please continue."

"As . . . soldiers, sir, we have a job to do, and we tend to believe that the—that we should generally be left alone to do it. Fighting the zor has been the burden of two generations, and the war might have been won before if . . . it had been prosecuted more vigorously." She was watching his reactions, gauging him, as if she were treading on dangerous ground with her comments. The courtesy of the wardroom—that nothing spoken between fellow officers should ever go beyond its walls, excepting only treason, and that left to the discretion of the officer—protected her, but she had no way of measuring the sincerity of her commodore.

"The past is impossible to change," he replied, and an image of Pergamum crossed his mind: the sight of the hangar deck of Ted McMasters' ship, the *Gustav Adolf,* shearing away, toppling shuttles and repair-craft into space in a silent, agonizing dance. "If you were admiral, Captain, what would you do?"

"Hit 'em hard, sir, and not let a peace be signed until we were damn sure that they couldn't get up again."

"We've been talking about that for sixty years, Captain."

" '*Talk*' and 'do' are different things, Commodore. We have never been given a chance to *do*."

"There's still an emperor and an Imperial Assembly, Captain Bell. We'll still have to answer to them, sooner or later." He gestured around the room. "You can have the best damn officers in God's own universe, but there's a point at which the emperor and the Senate will decide whether the war is over or not."

"They're not out here."

"I fail to see—"

"*We're* out here, sir. If the admiral is as good as his word, we will decide the outcome of this war." Without further comment, she inclined her head slightly and withdrew, walking across to have a word with her exec.

•    •    •

The officers rose as Admiral Marais entered the room, flanked by his adjutant and his squadron commander. He took his seat at the head of the large oval table and activated the wallscreen behind him. Images came to life above the table-surface as the subordinate officers took their seats.

"This will be our last opportunity to review the strategic situation before we jump for R'h'chna'a," he began without preamble. "The address to the fleet at L'alChan was primarily for the troops, as I am sure you understand; still, I cannot help but emphasize the importance of this endeavor." Marais folded his hands on the table in front of him. "In short, I meant every word I said."

"Begging your pardon, Admiral." Captain Marc Hudson sat forward. "May I invoke wardroom privilege?"

Marais leveled a gaze at him, as if in challenge. "Granted, Captain," he said, after a moment.

"Thank you, sir." Hudson cleared his throat. "I'm not intimately familiar with the inner workings of court politics, seeing as how I've been walking a ship's deck for the high side of thirty years." Sergei, sitting to the admiral's left, winced: it was a subtle jab at Marais' nobility and his lack of line experience. Marais let it pass. "In any case, sir, I'm aware, as we all are, that your mandate . . . if we choose to call it that . . . your mandate comes from this book you wrote that it seems our emperor—long may he live—had on his night-table the night he was choosing fleet admirals."

The rest of the officers shifted uncomfortably in their chairs; still, Hudson was protected, theoretically, by wardroom privilege. "Now, this book, sir, fully outlines your plan of attack."

"Indeed it does, Hudson. I'm afraid, however, that I—"

"By your leave, sir, I expect you want to know what all this is leading to. Really very simple, Admiral. Your book—which I read, sir, and found quite interesting, may I say so—your book implies that we intend to pursue this campaign till we have destroyed not only the zor capability, but also the zor will, to fight. All rhetoric aside, Admiral . . . and I'm not criticizing your speaking voice, you understand, sir . . . but, all rhetoric aside, you understand the ramifications of what you imply?"

There was a long moment of silence. Hudson was one of the most experienced officers in the fleet, and his folksy style tended to distract the listener from his impressive list of academic credentials, including a Ph.D. in theoretical physics and jump dynamics.

Marais nodded. "Captain Hudson, I understand completely. There is a strong possibility that this campaign could take months or even years to complete."

"See, sir, all it takes is enough angry zor to pilot a jump-ship, and millions of human beings go up in an H-bomb cloud. Or worse. Intelligence reports say how the zor seem to be a few notches ahead of us in biological warfare.

"Now, this book of yours has a fine idea in it, sir, but I can't help but ask you, how long do you think you'll be able to keep at this before the emperor—long may he live—will decide to call it off? I mean, sir, the longer this goes on, the more likely a suicide mission will be aimed at Paris or B.A. or St. Louis. And the zor have always given up before. You're ready to fight months or even years. What about the emperor, Admiral? What happens when he calls time?"

"It doesn't matter, Captain. The prosecution of this campaign is in my hands."

"You mean—"

"I mean," Marais said, looking from face to face, "that this campaign will end when I deem that it has finished. General Orders 6 will support me in this regard: it places me in the position of overall commander of this fleet, until my assignment is complete, or until my death. The emperor is a hundred parsecs away."

"Regardless of the situation."

"Correct." He looked again from face to face, sizing up each of the officers in turn. Later, Marc Hudson would remember it as having seemed rather like an undertaker measuring for coffins. "Ten days from now, this fleet will engage the zor forward fleet at R'h'chna'a. As you know, the reinforcement of our strength here at Pergamum, combined with an estimate of the damage done to the enemy during the last engagement here, gives us a substantial advantage both in firepower and in total numbers. We should have no trouble eliminating their threat. Now, as there will be no line of retreat, we—"

"I beg your pardon, Admiral," interrupted Captain MacEwan. "What do you mean, 'no line of retreat'?"

"Please review the orders for this mission, Captain," Marais replied coolly. "We do not wish to cause the zor to retreat from R'h'chna'a, as they most certainly will do, despite that system's strategic importance as a naval base. Instead, we wish to destroy their force. In short, the fleet will deploy in the vicinity of the jump points and prevent the enemy from escaping. Tactical simulations estimate something on the high side of eighty percent probability of success, with minimal losses. If component parts of the fleet perform their assigned tasks, there will be virtually no enemy vessels to withdraw."

Sergei thought about the plan later that ship's-night, when the staff meeting finally ended. To him, the plan *seemed* articulate, based largely on simulation and probability distributions. This was not an original idea; the general staff had been directed by computer simulation for decades.

For instance: a very pessimistic simulation had predicted the zor would be too weak to fight a war for several more years. Some estimates placed the figure as high as ten or twelve years . . . yet they had attacked Pergamum. That simulation had not thought like a zor thought, unlike this one.

In any case, the fleet was to penetrate zor space, seeking the zor fleets as objectives rather than specific world-targets. The only target was the enemy's naval strength. Without it, there would be no war.

That was something he could believe in. He had been born when the conflict with the zor had been a new and frightening thing; growing up in Buenos Aires had meant daily air-raid warnings, news articles describing the fate of colony worlds attacked by the enemy, learned political-science dilettantes on the 3-V proving, for billions of viewers, how duplicitous and dishonorable the zor were. But the thing that scared Sergei the most, yet attracted him as well, was not the brutal violence of the war with the zor, but, instead, the magnitude of the conflict. It was mankind's first truly interstellar war, excluding the Colonial Suppressions of the early 2100s that had led to the War of Accession and the founding of the Solar Empire; but even these conflicts had been almost completely local to one system or another. Battles in this war could occur anywhere.

But if there were no zor navy, and the Solar Empire made sure no new one was built . . . then that threat would disappear forever.


Twelve Standard hours before the jump, the officers' club at Mothallah Starbase was crowded. Sergei had given his crew liberty in four-hour shifts, leaving only a skeleton crew aboard. Both officers and enlisted personnel of the fleet often needed to get tight in order to listen up. Like most of the commanders, he knew he could recall his people in a matter of minutes; he realized that relaxation was important, considering the gravity of the situation and the eight days of jump ahead. He also knew that getting off the ship, if only for a brief time, would have a tonic effect for him as well.

As he approached the serving-area, he made out the figure of

Marc Hudson. The older man saw him coming, and used rank and elbows to clear a place for Sergei at the bar.

"Here you go," Hudson said, offering him a just-poured mug of dark brown liquid. "I got a second one coming anyway."

"Thanks," Sergei replied. "I'm not really a beer drinker." He took a long swig of the stuff.

"Well, it's not really—" Sergei began to redden, and broke out in a fit of coughing. "—beer," Hudson finished.

"What is it?" Sergei whispered.

"Acheya. Hundred-sixty proof, local stuff. I sort of like it."

Sergei didn't reply. Hudson tipped his mug back, draining most of it on the first try. The younger man tried a more cautious sip, and was greeted by a pleasant maltlike flavor, with a nutty tang to it. This time the kick was just as strong, yet considerably more gradual.

"Arm my torpedoes again, son," Hudson said to the young bartender, who began to refill the glass. "Good to see you in friendly surroundings again, Commodore. How's the *Lancaster*?"

"Running smooth, Captain Hudson—"

"Marc. If you'll allow that level of familiarity, sir."

"Sergei."

"Glad to hear the ship's in good condition. Ted McMasters raised a stink about the idea of beachin' the old girl and breaking up the crew, and I told our admiral that it'd be a damn shame if he did that; that a refitted *Lancaster* was worth three fourth-generation ships crewed by youngsters who don't know each other well and probably couldn't find their—"

"I get the picture. You told Marais—"

"Well, not exactly." Hudson placed his thumbprint on the credit tablet, took his drink, and began to lead Sergei through the crowd to a less-crowded area of the club. "Actually, I told Captain Stone. But it seemed to do the trick."

"Stone? The admiral's adjutant?"

"Yeah. Strange character. Real quiet, but never misses a beat. Knows everything and everyone. Eidetic memory, you know."

"I didn't."

"Oh?" They found a quiet area, in one corner of the room. Hudson exercised rank on a marine lieutenant and her date for the evening, and the two officers slid into seats. Hudson took a long drink of acheya and leaned back. The seat conformed to his contour. "Stone's a career staff officer, about my age. Some colonial family; gotten everywhere by someone's coattails. He's been Marais' adjutant for five or six years, since before the last peace."

Sergei smiled. "We used to say 'before the war.' Now we say, 'before the last peace.'"

"Well, Marais wants to change all that. —But back to Stone: I tried to run down his service record, but it was classified at the flag level. Now, there are only two flag admirals who have that access—Ted McMasters and our own Marais. I wonder what Stone's got to hide."

Sergei sat in silence, swirling his acheya in front of him.

"Somethin' bothering you, Sergei?"

"A lot of things, but especially . . . Well, it's the whole tone of the war so far. The attack on L'alChan after we'd destroyed its defenses—it runs counter to everything I've become accustomed to. It's done wonders for morale, God knows; everyone in this fleet seems to have a friend or relation who's died in the war . . . but it seems like we're being primed for something, something terribly destructive and violent."

"War *is* destructive and violent. You know that as well as I do." Marc Hudson sat forward in his seat, which came forward as well, returning to its original shape. "Look, you've been in the Navy for a number of years, so I shouldn't have to give you this speech, but it may be that you need to hear it.

"We like to think of ourselves as an essentially peaceful race: 'Turn the other cheek,' 'Do unto others . . .' and all that. But in fact the emperor's will sometimes has to be carried out in violent ways. His Majesty says, 'Go to such-and-such a system and clobber the piss out of these colonists or those rebels,' and we do it. We say no once—*once only*—and one of two things happens: either we get hanged for traitors, or the Empire disappears as an entity.

"It's not on the application forms or the draft registration, but part of every soldier's obligation to his emperor is the willingness to kill—when necessary, where necessary, and whom she or he is told is necessary. That's the way it is. Doesn't matter whether you use a crossbow or a ship's laser cannon; you pull the trigger, or push the button, and somebody dies. But you don't have to justify it: you can leave that to the one who gave the orders.

"Now, not everybody can accept the idea of killing, even in the emperor's name; but then not everybody's a soldier, either. But you and I *are*. Right now, the situation mandates that we go after the zor, we pummel them good—so good, in fact, that they can't fight back anymore. So good that they never come after us again. No peace terms until we're done with 'em. No armistices, no treaties. We'll carry it on until there isn't a spaceworthy vessel available on the other side. Then we tell 'em what we want, and they'll give it to us. Because they'll know what'll happen if they refuse."

"And if they refuse?"

"They won't. No sane race would, not without any way of defending against a space navy."

"And what about . . . L'alChan?"

"A demonstration. Just to show 'em we mean business." Marc Hudson leaned forward, clenching a fist in front of him on the table. "And we do, Sergei. We mean business. We're not gonna let the tail wag the dog anymore."

"And you think . . . Admiral Marais will be satisfied with that."

"Sure he will." Hudson drank off his acheya, and slid the mug onto the table. "He's going to win this war and go back and be prime minister for life. And good luck to him, too. As for the rest of it, let the politicians sort it out." He came to his feet and left the table, weaving through the crowd in the general direction of the bar, leaving Sergei alone to gaze at his own reflection in the half-finished mug of acheya.

chapter 6

ONLY THE WISE SHALL BE ABLE TO
RECOGNIZE THE DARK WING FROM        *(Respect to esLi)*
THE MINION OF *ESGA'U* THE DECEIVER.

HOW SHALL YOU IDENTIFY THE SHADOW
OF *ESHU'UR*'S WING?        *(Stance of Revealed Fear)*
BY THE SIGNS THAT HE DISPLAYS.

—*hiShthe'e YaTur, The Flight Over Mountains*
(from the Shthe'e Codex,
by Loremaster Shthe'e HeChri)

From his vantage point, behind a one-way screen on a platform overlooking the Council Chamber, the High Lord could view the angry discussions of the dignitaries that had already arrived.

He could understand their anger, and even trace it to a likely source: it was the progress of the war, indignation, frustration and fear . . . unaccustomed emotions, especially given the character of the ongoing campaign against the *esGa'u Yal*, the alien servants of the Lord of Despite. Even with the outstanding victory that had begun the most recent phase, the progress of the campaign had been unacceptable, and for a change it seemed that they had not been eager to come to the bargaining table.

There had even been whispers of . . . something else.

The High Lord of the zor had sought to find solace in dreams, to ask advice of the Lord *esLi,* as many of his ancestors and predecessors had done, but to no avail: there were no dreams to behold, no matter how strongly he concentrated on his own Inner Peace. He had taken counsel with his nearest advisors, from his close cousins to his *Gyaryu'har,* the bearer of the *gyaryu,* the HeYen sword of state, but none could give him the answer that he desired.

*Perhaps,* he thought to himself as he watched the Councillors argue, *I could not properly form the correct question.*

Down below him, the last members of the Council of Eleven to arrive, old Lord Makra'a HeU'ur and Lord Riyas HeChra, flew into the chamber and took up their perches. There were twelve zor below: one representing each of the eleven original Nests, collections of clans that had originally occupied the home world of Zor'a, and a twelfth Lord, representing all of the other clans and independent *L'le* scattered across zor space. In truth, while the eleven Lords of Nest commanded the greatest dignity in Council, tracing their lineage back sixty-fours of sixty-fours of years, the Speaker for the Young Ones was the emissary for sixty-fours of times more individuals . . . though the other eleven might oppose him, it was his voice that, perhaps, carried the most weight.

Both were silent as they took their positions, but from the positions of their wings the High Lord could tell that they, too, were angry. Clearly some of the discussions were taking place outside the Chamber. The High Lord composed himself, making a mental note to consult with the hall-guards afterward to see if they had overheard anything. Then, without further pause, he stepped through the one-way screen to stand out on the platform. Within a few moments, all discussion ceased, and the twelve Councillors took their posts. All arranged their wings in the Posture of Polite Deference, as befit the honor due the High Lord by a Lord of Nest, and as one they uttered the ceremonial, "*Karai'i esShaLie'e, esLiHeYar.*" Be welcome, great Lord. To the everlasting glory of *esLi.*

"My Lords," Sse'e HeYen began. "I beg eight thousand pardons for separating you from your concerns and responsibilities to meet here, in time of war. It is not custom for the High Lord to summon the Council once we have embarked upon a course of battle, but the High Nest has begun to receive reports of a most disturbing nature, and it behooves a Nestling such as myself"—the High Lord's wings adjusted themselves slightly to indicate a faint bit of humor—"to consult with the eleven Lords of Nest, and our distinguished Speaker for the Young Ones"—this with an inclination of the head toward the zor Lord perched at the far end of the Chamber—"to obtain their views."

"The Eleven thank the High Lord for the courtesies extended them," Makra'a HeU'ur replied formally. He looked briefly around the Chamber, exchanging glances with several of the other Lords. He bowed slightly to the Speaker for the Young Ones, and added, "as well as to the Speaker. As much as your nestbrothers of HeYen, we are ready to serve the High Nest."

"Have you been chosen to speak for the Council, Lord HeU'ur?"

"*esHu'ur*'s wing struck my Nest first, High Lord."

The name *esHu'ur* echoed around the chamber ominously, and several of the Councillors tensely adjusted their wing positions. The clans of L'alChan were, indeed, members of Nest HeU'ur; but the doctrine of the High Nest had portrayed this attack as coming from the *esGa'uYal,* the Lord of Despite's alien servants, rather than from *esHu'ur,* the Destroyer, the Dark Wing.

"Your Nest was first attacked, Lord HeU'ur. Why do you propose to suggest that it was the work of the Dark Wing?"

"High Lord," Makra'a HeU'ur began, adjusting his wings carefully into a posture that denoted some combination of polite patience and vague deference, "I have loyally served you, your revered father and your august grandfather for many eights of years. When I first belted on my *chya*"—he placed one clawed hand on his ornamental weapon hanging at his waist—"the alien *esGa'uYal* were a new, and threatening, phenomenon. Always we have viewed their existence as an affront to ourselves, an insult to *esLi*—a creation of the Lord of Despite, sent to test our Outer Peace, as your august grandfather taught us. There had never been a reason to adopt any other stance toward them, other than to view them as *hsth*-flies, to be swatted away, or *artha,* to be hunted down and killed. Always, they would demonstrate that they were intelligent, but ultimately *idju,* for staying their hand.

"Always . . . until they attacked L'alChan.

"They have never before attacked a world that was not, in some sense, a military target. This I can readily accept, High Lord: L'alChan had value, both from its resources and as a result of its location. Since they have a new commander, new tactics might well be expected—"

"To the point, my Lord of Nest," the High Lord interjected. The older zor turned and looked up at him for a long moment, made a minute adjustment to his wing-position—a slight bit more patience, a trifle less deference, and inclined his head.

From ten paces away, the High Lord thought he might have heard the vague empathic snarl of Lord HeU'ur's *chya*. His own sword, the *hi'chya* of the High Nest, seemed to respond, its annoyance at effrontery tangible within his mind. He ignored it.

"L'alChan was not simply attacked, High Lord. It was not merely destroyed. It was leveled, scarcely one stone left standing on another. Not one of the People was left alive; not a single crop was left unwithered. As I am sure you have seen, robot broadcasts from the system recorded scenes which are completely at variance with the pattern heretofore established by the *es-Ga'uYal.* It was an *e'ChaReU'un,* a ritual bloodletting."

"You attribute properties to the commander of the aliens that he cannot possess, Lord HeU'ur. No servant of the Lord of the Cast Out can perform such a ritual."

"Their commander understands the Highspeech."

"Blasphemy!" interjected one of the older members of the Council, and several others readily agreed.

"You fly over dangerous ground here, Lord HeU'ur," the High Lord said, his wings rising to the Posture of Formal Indignation. "He learned the Highspeech during his travels in our worlds when we were at truce with the aliens, and though he cannot speak with all of the proper inflections, I understand that he is quite well read in the literature, and can even understand the *hRni'i* in a rudimentary fashion."

"Why does it *matter* that he can understand our language? Even Sr'can'u, who guards my garden, understands the Highspeech. That does not make him one of the People."

"The human commander made a speech to his followers after the destruction of L'alChan. He told them that there will be no terms of surrender in this war, no quarter. In short, High Lord, he has chosen the flight of a warrior."

Pandemonium erupted in the room, with shouts of outrage and clawed hands hovering near *chya'i*. The High Lord did not speak, but waited for the noise to subside; no formal duels were declared, nor oaths given or taken, and after several moments, the room was quiet again.

"A single attack on an outpost, followed by empty rhetoric from a servant of the Deceiver, is also insufficient to confer the status of zor warrior on this human. You are old and wise, my Lord; I cannot believe that you would not have other reasons for making this assertion."

"I thank the High Lord," Lord HeU'ur answered, his wings arranged more to deference now. "An attack against L'alChan was followed by another against R'h'chna'a, and another against S'rchne'e. Six naval depots, with minimal garrisons, were also attacked and destroyed. Not captured, my Lords: destroyed utterly. Not a single *hRni'i* was left behind to speak the laments of the warriors who died there.

"This is more than the heightening of violence in our war. This has gone further than the efficient prosecution of a campaign. Our enemy begins to assume the proportions, and the role, of the Destroyer.

"The commander of the *esGa'uYal*, my Lords, is the avatar of the Dark Wing."

The room threatened to erupt again, but the voice of the Speaker for the Young Ones cut across the noise. "We have seen the humans succeed before. Even the aliens know something of tactics and strategy. I have two replies for my august colleague Lord HeU'ur.

"First, it is hardly surprising that a member of the aliens might destroy *hRni'i*, dismissing them as decorations only. That has certainly happened before.

"Second, regardless of the ardor, or even the worthiness, of one individual human, the Lords of Nest of the enemy will certainly call for peace sooner or later. They always have before. Even with the destruction of the worlds and bases described, we still have A'anenu, *Ka'ale'e* Hu'ueru, the Core stars, and the colonies beyond the Core away from the Rift. The attack on their naval base at Ilya'aHyu—the system they call 'Pergamum'—was a great success. Nothing, in my estimation, has changed."

"High Lord," HeU'ur began, then looked at the Speaker, then at his fellow Councillors. "High Lord. I can well believe that some in this chamber perceive me to be an old fool, seeing shadows of the Dark Wing, the Destroyer, in the actions of our enemies. I grant them their opinions."

There were murmurs in the chamber; Lord HeU'ur ignored them. "I have seen many battles, I have fought the humans myself. Now, as evening shades decline upon these old wings, it might be well taken that I could be seeing patterns that are not there, flights that do not come my way.

"It might be . . . but it is not.

"I am a warrior of the People." He stood straight, his wings taking on the precise Posture of Deference to *esLi.* "I have faced the enemy, and I have also studied the legends. This flight follows the path of the *Lament of the Peak,* and it is not the flight we had originally chosen. The longer this campaign continues, the more likely I am to be correct. This time, the commander of the humans has taken on proportions greater than a servant of the Cast Out."

"If we offer peace," the Speaker answered, quietly, "they will accept again."

"And if they do not?"

"We have not flown that path!" the Speaker answered angrily. "My Lord of HeU'ur, you choose to see the touch of the Dark Wing in the pattern the Lord *esLi* weaves for us. Well and good. But if we offer peace, and the aliens accept, then your—circumstantial evidence—will vanish like mist, and there will be no *esHu'ur* after all."

"Is that what you counsel, Lord Speaker?" the High Lord asked.

"It is indeed, High Lord. It would be necessary, of course, for you to consult with your commanders to determine the correct time to make the peace gesture; but it should be done quickly, before further . . . rumors"— he looked briefly at Lord HeU'ur, then returned his attention to the High Lord—"begin to circulate."

"How say you to this, Lord HeU'ur?"

"I . . . bow to the distinguished Speaker for the Young Ones," HeU'ur replied. "But I warn the High Lord that this pattern is yet forming, and if the humans *do* refuse to discuss peace, there may be more to my assertion than mere . . . mist."

The High Lord could see the expression in the old Lord's eyes as he looked away, to fix his gaze on the Speaker.

*I will not forget,* HeU'ur's glance and posture seemed to say.

•   •   •

Rear Admiral Theodore McMasters, Imperial Navy, sat uncomfortably in a plush armchair and thought about time.

Across the room, a grandfather clock kept the beat, mirroring the movement of the earth in its lazy back-and-forth swings. It was a true antique, four hundred years old: from the pre-electronic age, it seemed, with no internal or external power supply. An Imperial functionary came by at precisely eight-thirty in the morning and wound it with a special key. The clock had outlived several functionaries, and a skilled jeweler in Waimea had recently crafted a new key to replace the old one that had finally worn down.

The waiting-room was decorated in the twentieth-century style: deep pile rugs, abstract art, Bauhaus and rococo furniture, an ancient 2-V set in the corner. From his limited recollection of art history, McMasters knew that the decor represented an appalling clash of the many contradictory styles of that century, but also knew how gauche it would be to point it out. It caught the emperor's fancy to be a connoisseur of classic art, and there was no one in the Solar Empire who would gainsay him.

It was time that made it all interesting: centuries ago, all that surrounded him, from the 2-V to the big grandfather clock, was commonplace, a part of everyone's life. Now no one could do without their autokitchens or readers.

Sitting here, trussed up in his dress blues in the waiting-room of the prime minister in the Imperial Palace on Oahu, time passed very slowly, a tick at a time from the great old clock; and yet it seemed that the last thirty years had passed by so quickly, that only a few days ago he had been a midshipman aboard the *Charlestown,* destroyed twenty-three years ago in a skirmish at Anderson's Star. He had become fire-control officer aboard the *Lancaster* not long after, and was in the process of becoming the best poker player in the Second Fleet . . . He had to smile, remembering how he'd lost that title and half a year's pay to Bruce Wei in the match held in the upper launch tube of the *Lancaster.*

The *Gustav Adolf* had come later, of course, and the fleet action at Pergamum... The leg was nearly healed now, but it twinged in sympathetic pain, remembering the violence done it during the battle.

Time: it had taken all of what had gone before and flushed it out the tubes, and continued to do so, as the present continued to happen. The past was gone, and all that remained was the evidence, to be counted out in neat stacks, catalogued, and placed in archives and museums and waiting-rooms.

The door opened, and McMasters looked up to see a liveried footman enter. "Admiral? His Excellency's compliments, sir, and his apologies for having kept you waiting. If you will accompany me?"

McMasters stood and followed. A few months as a staff officer had not made him much more comfortable in dress uniforms or in dealing with politicians; better, he thought, to be on the deck of a starship somewhere, than at another damned policy meeting.

Still, it wasn't every day that even admirals were invited to the drawing-room of the emperor's prime minister.

The footman showed him in to a large sunlit room. Near the bay window, the tall figure of the prime minister stood drinking tea, looking out over the water far below the lip of the Imperial enclosure of Diamond Head. From the doorway, McMasters could see the waves roll in from the Pacific, and the beautiful blue sky of Hawaii overhead.

"My dear Admiral," the prime minister said, placing his teacup on his desk, and crossing the sun-dappled carpet to shake McMasters' hand. "His Majesty kept me in conference somewhat longer than I had expected. I trust you were not inconvenienced."

"No, sir," McMasters replied. He followed the minister to the opposite side of the room, where they settled into armchairs while the footman served them drinks.

"Let me begin by saying, Admiral, that His Majesty is quite

pleased with your efforts, and that he realizes that you have made the best of a difficult situation."

"You refer to my rank?"

"You needn't be coy, Admiral. Your willingness to continue on active duty after Lord Marais' appointment demonstrates true devotion to the Crown."

"You needn't flatter, Your Excellency."

The prime minister smiled. It was the sort of expression that suggested appreciation of a worthy opponent. "Touché, Admiral McMasters.

"Now that the preliminaries are out of the way, let me enlighten you about my reasons for bringing you out here, when a simple 'phone call might have sufficed. I can trust my own safeguards in this office, but if the subject of our discussion became public knowledge . . .

"In any case, a few members of the Assembly seem to have excellent sources, both in the fleet and in the Red Cross, and the reports they have received about conditions in the battle zone are most disturbing—enough so that they are threatening to bring their information to the House floor. I know it is not necessary to elaborate in detail what they have described: suffice it to say that Admiral Marais' actions have repeatedly violated Chapter 17 of the Articles of War. His Highness is very concerned about all of this, of course."

"Of course, sir. But have the admiral's actions indeed violated Chapter 17?"

The Prime Minister let his smile harden. "Admiral Marais' assignment is to *carry out* policy, not to *determine* policy, McMasters. Destruction of nonmilitary targets, killing noncombatants, attacking civilian installments without prior warning all constitute violations of that Article—the emperor's law."

"I would be inclined to agree, sir, except that these are zor installments and zor civilians."

"Surely you do not make a distinction between—"

"The zor have attacked civilians and nonmilitary targets, Excellency. Why should it be so unpalatable for us to do the same?"

"But—" The prime minister sputtered a bit, and reddened, as if he had not been expecting the conversation to turn this way. "Where is your humanity, man?"

"I'm not sure I understand you, Excellency."

"Human beings do not fly about bombing civilians. Regardless of their race. It is not the emperor's will to conduct wars in this fashion, Admiral."

"Perhaps not, sir. But wars are, ultimately, mechanisms for mass destruction of the enemy. I believe Admiral Marais has whatever authority he requires—to do whatever he deems necessary to secure the victory he was asked to obtain."

"As I said before, Marais has the power to implement policy, not to determine it. He has already overstepped his bounds."

McMasters settled himself in the chair a bit, and considered his words. Then he said, "I would remind Your Excellency of General Orders 6. Admiral Marais has been granted complete latitude in his authority, for the duration of the emergency—"

"The zor fleet has been defeated and dispersed: first at R'h'chna'a, and then at S'rchne'e—"

"*For the duration of the emergency,*" McMasters repeated across the prime minister's words. "The admiral believes that the current emergency will not be resolved until the zor are no longer a threat to humanity."

"When will that be? When every zor is dead?"

McMasters did not reply, but simply looked at his hands, folded in his lap.

"Admiral," said the prime minister slowly, "we are discussing xenocide here." He took a sip of his drink and set it on the side table. "We are talking about an act of brutality totally out of proportion to any such act in the history of mankind."

"Admiral Marais will do what he feels is necessary in order to prevent the zor from destroying the human race."

"Regardless of the consequences. Or the will of his emperor."

"Your Excellency, I am not a politician. I am a soldier, a loyal servant of my emperor, and the chief of staff of the admiral of the fleet. His Imperial Highness chose Admiral Marais, and vested him with the power to invoke General Orders 6. He has done so, and in no way has he compromised his loyalty to the emperor."

"I would dispute that, Admiral McMasters. In fact, a case can be easily made that he has acted in a manner unbecoming an officer. He can be replaced. Easily."

"Oh?" McMasters raised an eyebrow. "Who does His Highness plan to replace the admiral with?"

"With you."

"Me?" McMasters sat forward. "You cannot be serious."

"Why not?" The prime minister allowed his face to relax into a smile. He was accustomed to pulling the strings of power, and believed McMasters was ready for manipulation. "My dear Admiral, you have struggled long and hard to attain your present position. You have more friends at court than you realize."

"Or Admiral Marais has more enemies."

"Those are two sides of the same coin, are they not? The emperor is well pleased with the victories at L'alChan, at R'h'chna'a and at S'rchne'e, and is now desirous of an end to this campaign. Admiral Marais, it appears, does not wish to act in harmony with His Highness' wishes. It would be a simple matter indeed to relieve Marais of command and place you in his stead."

The prime minister fell silent. McMasters let the quiet drape the room for a long moment, until at last he spoke.

"Your Excellency, professional courtesy forbids me to tell you in my own words exactly what I think of that proposal. Despite my own feelings about Admiral Marais, I will not be used in a political ploy to remove him, if for no other reason than I would be your creature if I accepted.

"No, sir. Tell my 'friends' I will not do it." He picked up his cap and fitted it on his head. "If you brought me here simply to make that offer, then I believe that our business is done." He stood and walked toward the door of the suite.

Unperturbed, the Prime Minister remained seated and said to McMasters' retreating back, "There are other officers, Admiral."

McMasters turned at the door to face the prime minister. "Perhaps there are, sir. But Admiral Marais and his fleet are a hundred and thirty parsecs away."

"Meaning?"

"It is very simple, Your Excellency. The emperor, in his wisdom, chose Marais to be the admiral of the fleet. He placed that fleet far enough away and gave Marais enough power so that he can now conduct the war any way he wishes. Whether it is what he intended or not, His Highness is essentially no longer in control of the situation."

"What do you suggest, then?"

"'Suggest'?" McMasters smiled, briefly, wearily. "Tell the emperor to reread Marais' book. And this time, he'd better believe what's written there. It's going to happen, all of it." He opened the door. "Good day, Your Excellency."

Even before the echoes of McMasters' footsteps had completely receded, the footman stepped from around the corner of an alcove and walked to the bay window. He pulled the curtain carefully aside, as if watching something out across the beach; then he turned to face the prime minister, his face betraying the hint of a smile.

"Melodramatic," he said.

"You heard it all, then?"

"Better than that." He walked to one of the comfortable armchairs and dropped himself into it. He touched his right earlobe, decorated by a small, star-shaped earring. "I have it all, right here."

"Indeed." The prime minister let one eyebrow lift, and crossed his arms in front of him. "Well, what do you think?"

" 'Think'?" The footman put his feet up on a hassock, crossed them, leaned back in the chair. "I think you're in very deep trouble."

"You know exactly what I mean, damn you."

"What do I think about McMasters? Not that my opinion's worth a damn, not until I bring this back"—he touched his ear again—"and have it analyzed, of course, but . . ."

" 'But'?"

"I'm not sure he's bluffing. Now, before you start on me, understand that he surprised me as much as he did you. I didn't expect him to defend Marais, either. The psych profile indicated that he'd jump at the chance to unseat a noble-born upstart with no command experience, especially since His Imperial Highness didn't put McMasters in command to begin with. The service record and dossier all pointed to—"

"Listen here, Smith, or whatever your name is," the prime minister interrupted him. "You assured me that he'd be receptive. As I recall, the Agency didn't use terms like 'indicate,' or 'likely,' or 'pointed to.' You—"

"I didn't assure you of a damn thing." He rose quickly from the chair and strode to stand opposite the prime minister, casting off the lazy indolence as quickly as he cast off the role of footman. "The Agency didn't assure you of a damn thing. We projected that he would respond favorably to such an offer. That he didn't is probably as much a result of your own mishandling of the interview as our projection of its outcome."

"I—" The minister turned away to conceal his anger, then faced the agent again, his voice trembling with fury. "You are accusing me of *mishandling* the situation? I'll have your head!"

"Oh, I don't think so. More likely, I think, that His Imperial Highness will have *yours*." He smiled and walked back to the alcove from which he had come. "Good day, Prime Minister," he tossed over his shoulder.

The waves continued to crash in below the palace; and

though a warm breeze drifted in through the bay window, the prime minister felt chilled.

(From the *Record of the Imperial Assembly,*
June 24, 2311; Question Hour.)

MEMBER HSIEN: . . . Your Excellency, the Red Cross has reported numerous instances of civilian atrocities committed by the naval forces under the command of Admiral Ivan Marais. The documents relating to this matter have been filed with the Record and are available to members . . . [*identifying database information*] . . . Would the Government care to comment on these events?

PRIME MINISTER: The First Lord of the Admiralty will answer for the Government.

FIRST LORD: Certain matters concerning naval operations are classified, Mr. Hsien, and cannot be revealed in open session.

HSIEN: Your Excellency, the Government is avoiding the question. The matter under discussion is already in the public domain, and therefore may be addressed in open session of the Assembly . . .

PRIME MINISTER: The Government is aware of that, sir. However, the reasons for these actions touch upon classified naval operations.

HSIEN: There is an established precedent concerning the Assembly's right to know—

PRIME MINISTER: There are also established rights of the Government to withhold information pertaining to Imperial security in time of declared emergency.

HSIEN: The emergency is hundreds of light-years distant—

PRIME MINISTER: The gentleman clearly does not recognize that, at any time, the enemy could launch a massive strike against Sol System itself. We did not believe the zor capable of launching such an attack before, but they proved us wrong at Pergamum. Our assumption at that time was that the zor would not strip their own defenses in order to launch such an attack. Yet they did exactly that. As long as a single zor jump vessel exists, the emergency exists, and Admiral Marais has the power and authority to take whatever actions he deems necessary to deal with it.

HSIEN: Is this to say that the Government condones these atrocities, Your Excellency?

PRIME MINISTER: The Government refuses to describe any action taken thus far by Admiral Marais' fleet as an "atrocity," sir.

HSIEN: Will the Government then dismiss the evidence provided by the Red Cross?

PRIME MINISTER: Insofar as it bears upon the propriety of the Navy's actions, Mr. Hsien, yes.

Ted McMasters toyed idly with the tablet, scanning the disposition reports of the Navy's dozens of warships. His mind was only partly on his work: hardcopies of the last few days' Record sat on his desk, marked in several places.

The prime minister and his Government were in a most uncomfortable situation, all things considered, McMasters thought to himself; whether he liked it or not, the Government was being forced to defend Marais' actions, since it could do nothing about them. To the prime minister, it was more than a matter of principle: it amounted to political survival, since any admission that Marais was out of the Government's control would be to commit political suicide.

Yet it was true. Marais could do virtually anything he wanted, a hundred and thirty parsecs from Sol System.

McMasters was not at all concerned about the number of zor, civilian or not, that were killed in the process of winning the war:

it was just retribution, after Alya and Pergamum and a dozen other battles. Marais was serious about his intentions—more serious than anyone had guessed. Yet his arguments did ring true, regarding the defeat of the zor: there could be no halfway measures, no armistices, until the zor were finally beaten. The reports of excessive violence did not have to be exaggerated, but war was like that, no way to soft-pedal it. Whether it was atrocity was hard to tell . . . Still, here he was, sitting in a comfortable armchair, watching the shuttles take off from Lambert Field and trying to second-guess combat decisions more than a hundred parsecs away.

But while the shadows grew longer over the Admiralty spaceport, and darkness crept into his office, Ted McMasters felt a chill, a fear that he could not brush away. Marais scared him: not because of acts against the zor, and not even because of the threat he potentially posed to the current ruling government. From the start, everyone had underestimated Marais, and had dismissed the book as a bit of pompous nonsense, a lot of blather about racial will and absolute victory through unrestrained violence. It had even impressed McMasters, temporarily suspending his natural cynicism about such things. Everyone had assumed . . . even he had assumed . . . that Marais would take charge of the campaign, and either succeed or fail, but get no farther than anyone had in the last fifty years.

Suppose he won, so totally that the zor did give up?

Suppose his campaign did result in the absolute victory over the zor, even if it meant xenocide, the death of billions of sentient beings? The idea was ludicrous, unthinkable. Even as he had sat, calmly discussing it with the prime minister, he had dismissed the other's concerns as merely a political ploy. There had never been anyone in the history of the human race who had committed such an act . . .

There had never been anyone with the power to commit such an act. Until now.

Read the book, he'd told the prime minister. That's what

Marais is going to do, if he can. *Admiral Marais will do what he feels is necessary to prevent the zor from destroying the human race.*

*Whatever is necessary.*

But what would he do after that?

He touched the access tablet and dialed a high-priority number. The tablet glowed faintly for a moment, reading his thumbprint. Shortly, an operator appeared on the wallscreen.

"Good afternoon, sir. Your business?"

"This is Admiral McMasters. I must speak with the prime minister."

"I'm . . . sorry, Admiral, His Excellency is in conference at the moment. If I could—"

"Get him out of conference. This is of the utmost importance: it deals with the defense of the Solar Empire. Do it."

## chapter 7

THE HERO DESCENDS TO THE PLAIN;     (*Glory to* esLi)
   HE HAS MADE HIS CHOICE
IN THE SERVICE OF HIS LORD.
WITHOUT FEAR HE DRAWS HIS *CHYA* (*Stance of the Warrior*)
AND CALLS DEFIANCE IN THE HEART
   OF THE STORM
WHILE THE DARK WING DESCENDS     (*Respect to* esHu'ur)
UNBIDDEN, UNCONTROLLABLE
A PART OF THE WORLD THAT IS
THE BRIGHT DARKNESS WHILE
   THE LIGHT FADES

—Final transmission from Qu'useyAn Main Base,
6 July 2311 (translated)
(from the personal files of Admiral Ivan Marais)

The blue-white diadem of the sun was just verging on the horizon as the fighter craft turned away from the city, reflecting light on their silvery fuselages for a few moments before they turned to the upper atmosphere where their mothership cruised at nearly orbital speed. An observer from below, if there had been one alive, might have seen something artistic in the scene—

the fast-moving aircraft streaking across the bright blue sky, catching the first bright rays of morning in anticipation of the ground.

But even if an observer had been alive, which was highly unlikely, he would have been a zor—and their perception of art was, no doubt, very different from that of humanity.

It was a moot point. Even as their swift craft left the planet behind, the pilots could look in their rearward screens and view the destruction they had wrought on what had once been a bustling zor city. The tall, graceful buildings that still stood, staggered drunkenly against each other; the suspended roadways had fallen, and the ground was pitted and scorched. A fine residue of soot and dust still rained down over the scene, swirling among the rubble and following the morning breezes along the wide avenues, invisible now to the pilots as they raced toward rendezvous, yet coating their planes.

Since the single squadron had jumped from Mustapha, the number of capital ships under Admiral Marais' command had increased from ten to thirty; the work at Mustapha, aided by generous bonuses, and further transfers from the reserve and training fleets stationed away from the battle zone, all contributed to this increase. Sergei was the most senior by time in service, and also had the admiral aboard, making his command the lead one. After the arrival of the other two commodores at Pergamum just a few hours after the attack on R'h'chna'a, he had directed the preparation of a thorough staff study for the admiral, detailing the intelligence reports on zor movements and providing recommendations for action. In addition to the senior officers, Sergei drew upon the talents of the commanders with the greatest staff experience—Bert Halvorsen, Gordon Quinn and Uwe Bryant—to complete the report.

It was delivered to the admiral late in low watch on the day after the arrival of the new additions, following a hectic session of preparation that lasted through ship's-night. It took only four hours for Marais to summon the six officers to make a presentation. Admiral Marais had the right of access to any space aboard any vessel in the fleet, but chose to conduct his conferences aboard the *Lancaster*. A room near the admiral's quarters had been refitted for his use—3-V chairs and tables were added to make it into a conference-room. It was here the admiral met his bleary-eyed staff.

The officers filed in and took their places. Marais made no comment, except to exchange a glance with his senior commodore. Sergei knew what was in the report, and had his suspicions of what the admiral thought of it, but kept his opinion out of his eyes and took his seat with the others.

"Gentlemen," Marais said when he had taken his seat as well. He placed his hands, palms down, on the black, reflective surface of the table. "I have reviewed the report you prepared. It is my belief, after consideration of its contents, that my inexperience at command has allowed the subtleties of your arguments to escape me." It was clear from the way he said it that he meant no such thing. "I should like you to present them here for my further examination."

Sergei was surprised. He had half expected a pro forma rejection; he wasn't sure what to make of this, except to treat the admiral's request as an order.

"Captain Bryant," he said, "can you make the presentation?"

"By your leave, sir," Bryant replied, looking at Sergei for support and then at the admiral, "I'm not really prepared for—"

"I'm aware of that," Marais cut him off. "It doesn't have to be polished. Please proceed."

Bryant stood up and took his copy of the report to the other end of the room and placed it before him on a small podium. He fixed Sergei with a stare, trying to elicit information; it was clear that he was unsure of the purpose of the demonstration—was it intended to embarrass him personally? Was he somehow caught between two contending forces?

"Activate screen," he said to the air, and tapped several keys on a tablet set into the table. The 3-V shimmered and resolved into a projected map of the New Territories and the adjacent, zor-controlled area of space.

Bryant cleared his throat and looked from officer to officer. "The most recent conflict began when the zor attacked the naval facility at Pergamum." He touched a key, and a point in the map acquired a label and glowed light blue. "Based on battle summaries and intelligence reports obtained at, and subsequent to, the battle there, we have estimated the total naval strength of the zor enemy fleet at that time to be fifty-one capital ships—twenty-six *Eclipse*-class battleships, eleven *Hawk*-class cruisers, eight *Nest*-class carriers, four *Talon*-class cruisers and two other craft of older vintage—and eighty-eight small craft, more than three-quarters of which were *Wing*-class destroyers. All of these are classified as having a jump range of at least ten parsecs. A complete summary of the capabilities and identifying characteristics of this force is provided in the printed report, and appears on the displays in front of you. The point of origin for the attack was a point in deep space, most likely a dark sun, located approximately one-third of the way from the Solward edge of the Antares Rift.

"In order to have sufficient force to mount an attack on Pergamum, the zor admiral stripped the defenses of at least six colonies on the Solward side of the Antares Rift. Naval facilities at R'h'chna'a, S'rchne'e, Ch'than, T'lirHan, B'tha'a and Qu'useyAn appear to have been completely evacuated for this purpose; additionally, the A'anenu naval base was reduced by at least fifty percent to supplement the force that attacked Pergamum. The defenders were caught completely by surprise, and followed expected tactics after the zor fleet was repulsed: the Second and Fifth Fleets, stationed in the war zone, spread to cover other military sites in the New Territories, particularly Mothallah, the most populous world in the Territories, and

Mustapha, the main naval repair facility. This all occurred before your lordship's appointment, of course.

"The zor expected a counterattack, though not as quickly as we did, and almost certainly not where we did." Bryant cleared his throat and highlighted the L'alChan system, just within the zor sphere of influence. "Coastwatchers' reports indicate that, following Pergamum, the zor fleet dispersed to cover exclusively *military* targets—about one-half to S'rchne'e and Ch'than, with the remainder returning to A'anenu. Several targets, including L'alChan, were left exposed by this maneuver. Our attack took advantage of this, even though we had no way of being sure whether reinforcement might occur while we were committed there. The zor who defended L'alChan certainly knew, though: when we attacked there, they knew that unless they surrendered immediately, resistance would equate to suicide. From our ... limited understanding of zor culture, we may presume that the alternative was far worse."

The room was cloaked in a heavy silence for a few moments before Bryant continued.

"The zor admiral must make some assumptions about our next logical move. If his intelligence on our strength and numbers is equal to our own on the zor navy, he must realize that we now have sufficient strength to meet and defeat any single defending force on this side of the Antares Rift. He also knows that the past history of conflicts between man and zor most often indicates increasing war-weariness on our part; thus, an extended campaign works to the advantage of the zor. That being the case, his objective must be to keep our force dispersed as long as possible, by making attacks at various places along the periphery of the New Territories, preventing us from concentrating on any of the obvious targets—any of the naval facilities, but especially A'anenu."

"A'anenu," Marais repeated, interrupting the presentation. Bryant had been poised to continue, but Marais held up his hand. The other officers shifted uneasily in their seats.

"Sir?" Bryant asked, his glance going to Sergei, who had no answer for him.

"A'anenu, Captain Bryant. What is the strategic value of A'anenu to the zor?"

"It's . . . Well, it's crucial to them, sir. It would be nearly impossible for them to conduct operations without such a base. None of the other bases would replace it."

"You would expect the zor admiral to be aware of that essential fact."

"Of course, sir, but I—"

"Of course." Marais stood in a single, fluid motion and strode to the other end of the table where the young captain stood, face tense, hands clenched. "Of *course* he knows the importance of that particular base, and he must realize that we know it as well. We capture or destroy S'rchne'e, R'h'chna'a, Ch'than, T'lirHan, and all of the rest and we *still* cannot neutralize the zor without taking A'anenu. Therefore, in order to *defeat* them—to eliminate their ability to carry out acts of belligerence—" He glanced at Sergei, held his gaze for a moment, and then returned his attention to Bryant. "—we must capture or destroy A'anenu. Since the zor have so little apparent regard for individuals of their own kind, military or civilian, they will not bother to reinforce any of those other worlds.

"Furthermore, attacking human worlds at this stage would do no more than waste valuable resources. Without A'anenu, the zor cannot carry on the war. With it, they cannot be eliminated as a threat. Both sides are aware of this, Captain—the only battle of consequence will be for the naval base."

"They will wait for us at A'anenu," Bryant said. It was more of a statement than a question, though it was clear that he was not convinced of it.

"More than that. The battle must assume a significance far greater than its military importance. It will have religious significance, and therefore political consequence."

"Religious significance." Bryant looked at Sergei, then back at the admiral. "Sir."

"*Everything* has religious significance to the zor, as I understand it, sir," Bert Halvorsen said, leaning forward. He hurried on, as Marais seemed ready to turn on Bryant. "Why should defense of a naval base—albeit an important one—hold any greater religious meaning? Especially since, as it has been explained, we are not even part of their cosmology. If the admiral pleases."

Marais slowly turned to face the table. He placed his hands on the table in front of him, and leaned down toward Sergei, who sat impassively at the other end of the table.

"Permit me to clarify the situation." Without looking away, he said to the air, "Computer, display the contents of my personal file, access code 14-A."

The diagram of the border stars vanished, and was replaced with the image of a page of text in zor computer script.

"This is a transmission from the zor base at Qu'useyAn, sent just before its destruction. It never reached its destination, for obvious reasons. I believe it is referenced in the appendix to your report, but based on what I have heard, I cannot but believe that you did not even read it."

Sergei stood up at his end of the table, straightening his tunic carefully. Marais stood up straight also.

"The report you requested *forty-eight hours ago* was to be based on projections of zor strategy and estimates of our ability to prosecute the campaign against them. In accordance with your orders, sir, that report was prepared and presented to you. The amount of effort was extraordinary under the circumstances, Admiral, and covered all of the *military* contingencies our analysis could encompass. Sir."

Marais appeared ready to reply, but Sergei pressed on, choosing his words carefully. "It is my pleasure to serve under your lordship. After many years in His Majesty's Service, the success we have enjoyed against the zor represents considerable satisfaction, and brings honor to the emperor and the personnel of this fleet. Defeating the alien enemy is highest in their priorities, sir, and I assure you that it is foremost in mine.

"When we were commanded to prepare the report for you, we did so in our capacities as military commanders, tacticians and soldiers. Our conclusions—namely, that the zor continue to be a threat to any world within their jump range, and that their most logical *military* strategy would be to seek to keep our fleet dispersed, covering a large number of targets—are in keeping with the most closely held precepts of military thinking, even in light of recent events.

"We considered these—" He gestured toward the screen. "Computer, translate this text to Standard." The screen rippled and then presented the text in readable form. "We considered these messages, sir, to evaluate what the zor strategic position might be. All we found was—mythology. Poetry. Nonsense, sir: the poetic sending of a commander about to die."

"It is not nonsense, Commodore. It is excerpted from the *Lament of the Peak,* and is—"

"I concede the point, my lord, and stand corrected. Nonetheless, sir, regardless of its cultural significance, we were not equipped to determine how it might bear on the strategic position between ourselves and the zor. It was simply not within the scope of our analysis. We were posed a military problem, and we responded with a military solution. If that is not what the Admiral wanted, perhaps he should have been more clear."

Sergei was visibly angry, trying to control his temper before another flag officer. Marais had been on the verge of taking the staff meeting to an entirely different level by humiliating a junior captain, and by extension, perhaps, the rest of the planning staff. For his part, Sergei wasn't sure exactly what had been intended, but he felt backed into a corner; in any case, he had put himself forward, and there was no retreating now. Bryant, who had been on the spot since the start of the meeting, looked visibly relieved at having been made to surrender the conn; the other staff officers seemed interested primarily in being inconspicuous. Only the admiral's adjutant, Captain Stone, looked engaged and somehow darkly amused as admiral and commodore held each other's eyes for a moment that seemed to stretch out forever.

The admiral had demonstrated a strong will before; perhaps he saw no need in showing it now, or perhaps he realized that—in command or not—he needed the cooperation, not just the obedience, of his chief officers.

"Captain Bryant, you may stand down," he said at last, looking aside. "You—and your fellow officers—have my compliments for your promptness and efficiency. It seems . . ." As his mood changed, double-time, his face seemed to fall, as if the confrontation had somehow burdened him with a great weariness. "It seems that I have not sufficiently clarified our own overall strategy, nor explained my view of the progress of this campaign."

Bryant and Sergei took their seats while Marais waited, and then he continued. "The document you see pictured there"—he gestured to the screen—"is extremely important because it represents a change in viewpoint among the zor. It may not be immediately clear why this is so: as Commodore Torrijos points out, there is nothing in this document but poetry from zor mythology, but it is absolutely in keeping with the zor worldview to use this method to communicate, even through official channels.

"The chosen passage is from the poem *Lament of the Peak*. It describes one of the journeys of the famous zor hero Qu'u, who is sent by the first High Lord A'alu to the Plain of Despite, a sort of . . . frozen netherworld, to recover some item from the keep of esGa'u the Deceiver, the fallen angel of zor mythology, who is trapped there. Qu'u has gone there as part of a grander design, but it is of his own free will: he speaks of aLi'e'er'e, or Choosing the Flight—that he has done what he must do, but it is still by his own choice. At the point described in the passage, he despairs of ever again seeing the world above, and feels the descent of the Dark Wing upon him."

" 'The Dark Wing,' sir?" Sergei asked.

"The destructive force. The Dark Wing is neither good nor evil: it simply exists, and eradicates whatever is in its path. *es-Hu'ur*, in the zor Highspeech, is a word full of overtones and connotations, many of which an alien human cannot hope to completely understand. In his own way, the sender of that message"—Marais gestured toward the screen—"was likening himself to Qu'u and, more importantly, comparing *us* to the destructive Dark Wing. For the first time, we have become a part of their cosmology, in the role of Destroyer."

"Begging the admiral's pardon," Sergei said, "but what does that mean in terms of strategy?"

"The zor are a fatalistic race." Marais crossed his arms in front of him, a gesture that looked like he was hugging himself. "They see signs and portents everywhere, and are supposedly directed by the prescient dreams of their High Lord. If they become convinced that we *are* the Dark Wing, their actions will respond to our movements. They will seek to test us, to prove or disprove that belief. We, for our part, must do everything we can to reinforce it, and widen it."

"Admiral," Bryant volunteered. "Are you suggesting, sir, that we choose to conduct this campaign by manipulating the misperceptions of zor beliefs? That we take advantage of some kind of loophole in their religion?"

"Not quite misperceptions, Captain Bryant." Marais leaned forward, placing his hands on the table in front of him. The translated zor message hung eerily above him on the screen. "If the zor continue to fight, and if we continue to defeat them, we will fulfill the role they have set out for us. We will be the Dark Wing, the destroyer of their race."

The last sentence hung in the quiet of the conference room for many seconds. Bryant, a young man by the standard of the other officers in the room, but still the son and grandson of an admiral, carefully straightened the papers in front of him and folded his hands atop them.

"You are proposing xenocide, sir."

"That is the logical conclusion," Marais said evenly. "I do not see any reasonable alternative."

"There could be a settlement—"

"No." Marais stood up straight again and pointed to the screen. "This is their view of us at the moment. *This* is the language they speak, the message they understand. There is no margin for a settlement—there is no settlement we could make that would earn their respect and command their adherence. We are not fighting that kind of war anymore: this has become a war of conquest. Do you understand, Captain? We will receive absolute and total surrender from the zor enemy, or they will be destroyed."

"They will never surrender," Sergei said quietly.

"Then we will do to A'anenu what we did to L'alChan and S'rchne'e and R'h'chna'a, and the rest of the smaller facilities, and then we will go to the zor home worlds and do it there. And that will be the end of the zor threat to mankind . . . forever."


The staff meeting did not go on much further. As the officers were dismissed and began filing out of the conference room, Marais said, "Commodore Torrijos, if you would remain behind for a moment."

The other officers seemed to quicken their pace. When the last of them had departed the room and the door had slid shut, only the admiral, his adjutant and Sergei were left. Marais settled into a chair and folded his hands in front of him. Sergei remained standing, scarcely relaxing from full attention.

"There seems to be a problem with my interpretation of zor strategy. I don't mind saying, Torrijos, that I don't like being called out in front of staff." He waited for an answer, but Sergei remained silent. "Perhaps the officers in the fleet believe that they can direct the conduct of operations better than I can."

Sergei didn't reply. He could sense a palpable anger from

Marais' side of the table, and knew that his reticence would likely fuel it even further, but with the admiral's adjutant standing by, anything he said would be on the record, and would probably dig him deeper. Worse yet, he could not really tell where this was heading.

"History has shown the opposite, Torrijos. Professional officers," the admiral sneered, "men and women like yourself, have been fighting the zor for sixty years, and have not yet succeeded in eradicating the zor threat." The way he said "eradicating" chilled Sergei as he stood trying to keep his face impassive. "Now, you Academy men are trying to undermine my command, both here and back home. I won't stand for it. Do you read me, Commodore?"

"If the admiral pleases—"

"Do you *read,* Torrijos?"

"Loud and clear, sir, except that I must point out that I am not an 'Academy Man,' sir."

"You're McMasters' man, Torrijos, which is the same damn thing."

"—Sir?"

"His protégé. You're McMasters' protégé. When he couldn't get himself onto this expedition, he made sure to place you here. Now at last I see why."

"My lord, I—I take exception to your imputations. I have no agenda, either on my own behalf or on behalf of Admiral Mc-Masters. I am willing to stipulate, for the record, that it is my impression that Admiral McMasters has no desire to undermine you, either. If you wish my resignation, sir, you may have it at any time. I had assumed, however, that we had work to do."

Marais held Sergei's glance again, his eyebrows slightly raised. "That is not the impression I received."

"If the admiral pleases, I cannot determine with accuracy what impression he might receive. For the record, sir, I believe that no comments I have made suggest defiance, insubordination or mutiny, and stand ready to respond to any formal accusation you choose to present against me."

"As opposed, for instance, to pushing you out an airlock with the other conspirators," a voice said quietly.

Both Marais and Sergei turned quickly to look at Captain Stone, who still had a faint smile on his face. Moments passed. Sergei, for the first time, began to feel nervous; it was as if he had been on solid ground up till now, and it was turning to mud beneath his feet.

"Though there is certainly precedent for summary judgement in a war zone, Stone, I hardly think it's appropriate in this case." The admiral looked back at Sergei; Stone's expression changed only very slightly, but it seemed to Sergei that there was the faintest glimmer of disappointment.

A very brief glance passed between Sergei and the admiral's adjutant at that moment, and briefly Sergei felt an unease that even the outrageous threat had not aroused. It was if Stone were somehow different, an interloper on his ship, in his fleet, serving his admiral.

Stone was the first to look away, and Sergei turned his attention back to Marais.

"My sources at Court tell me that a few weeks ago, the prime minister offered your mentor the post of Admiral of the Fleet. There have already been some stirrings of opposition to this campaign and to my methods, notably in the Imperial Assembly. Since McMasters has no great affection for me, I expect that a request for my resignation will soon be sent on its way, if it has not already been dispatched. Politics extends its tentacles even into a war zone, and before this campaign is over I expect to face insubordination and perhaps even mutiny.

"As for you, Torrijos, it appears as if I have misjudged you."

"Sir." Another mercurial change in disposition was more than Sergei could handle. It was bewildering, and it took him a moment to react. "By your leave, sir, I must return to my duties."

When the admiral inclined his head a centimeter or two, Sergei saluted, turned on his heel, and left the room and the deck as quickly as he could, seeking the familiar solace of the *Lancaster*'s bridge.

Go ahead, Chan."

The wardroom darkened, and the halo sprang to life, showing a survey holo of the world they had conquered a few days before, marking the major installations and settlements. They were all coded blue now, indicating that they had been "neutralized"— a polite and altogether rather gentle synonym for "destroyed."

"The report I received at 0600, sir," Chan began, "indicated that all known inhabited sites have been neutralized. In accordance with standard procedure, Captain Bell provided me also with the flyover log. I have prepared an excerpt, which I can play for you now."

"Will it tell us anything we don't already know?"

"I'm sorry, sir, I—"

"No, go ahead." Sergei looked down at the carpet. He was very tired—when he had the opportunity to sleep he hadn't been able, and now the responsibility of mopping up would keep him on his feet for several more hours. Modern medicine had kept his attention span up to acceptable standards, but could do little to alleviate the bone-weariness he felt throughout his body.

Chan moved his index finger on the tablet, and the holo disappeared. In its place was the view of one of the coasts of Qu'useyAn, near a large city. As the plane approached, the remains of the city became more visible.

The alien architecture that now lay in ruins had been graceful and striking; thin, tall buildings with entrances at many levels, with walkways, perches and balconies at various heights. In the low gravity—just over half a Standard g—it would have been possible for the zor to use their wings on this world. Now, the harsh, bright sunlight beat down on the debris of what had once been a great city. The ruin was almost timeless in its immobility, like some great monument to a long-departed civilization, except for the zor corpses draped and hung at odd angles and in caryatid poses, stilled by death.

Inland of the coastal city, the overfly showed a great swath of plain, evidently agricultural land. As he watched, Sergei remembered that he had read that Qu'useyAn's soil was exceptionally fertile: it had supported extensive agriculture—which further enhanced the world's value to the zor.

That was a thing of the past now; the phages had done their work efficiently, aided by chemical agents dropped during the battle over the nearby city. The tilled land was devastated and lifeless, strewn with crumpled and seared remnants of crops that would never see harvest.

The scene shifted as the plane moved inland. The ground grew more broken; rivers carved the land, separating rows of hills from each other by deep once-green valleys, marred by the drift of phage spores. Near the confluence of a river with its tributary, the skeleton of a zor town huddled; its graceful houses were leveled, bridges across the river were sundered, and the shell of what might have been a factory still smoldered. There had been no one to bury the bodies, of course.

The plane entered the mountains. The valleys were coated in shadow, out of the blue-white glare of the sun; at first it was impossible to resolve anything past wisps of smoke in the shaded darkness.

Gradually, however, the scene came into focus: a large complex of buildings climbing along the shelf of the cliffside, with the mountain-peaks crouching overhead; a heavily forested mountain valley spread below, cloaked in primeval shadow. Most of what was visible seemed intact, untouched by bombing or burning like other scenes they had viewed. Sergei was about to ask just what was being shown, when he noticed that much of the level ground was torn up, with large holes gouged out of the hard earth.

"This is a *L'le,* a Nest," said Chan. "Bacterial agents were used on the surface, along with heat-seeking burrowing missiles. Most of the casualties occurred belowground, in the galleries and . . . nurseries. The aboveground facilities were left intact because there was . . . no need to destroy them.

"Admiral Marais commented that this Nest would make an excellent infantry training facility."

*How pleasant,* Sergei thought. "Is there more?" he asked, as the screen faded to gray.

"The overfly log is substantially longer, of course. I thought this excerpt would be sufficient—it covers the primary areas of operations undertaken by the strike force: bombing industrial and military facilities, destruction of agricultural land, destruction of Nests. Due to the efficient conclusion of these operations, as you know, it was unnecessary to depopulate the oceans."

Sergei sat in silence, wondering what he should say next. Chan was nervously toying with a stylus, tapping it against the sole of one boot.

"Commodore?" Chan said, after a long pause. "Sergei? Is something wrong?"

"Chan, what were the total casualties from this operation?"

"Thirty-two killed, seven hundred twenty-eight—no, seven hundred twenty-*nine* wounded—"

"*Their* side."

Chan sat up in his chair. "I could only offer an estimate— about four hundred thousand, I would say, sir."

"I assume that's conservative."

"Based on our limited information and preliminary demographic studies, four hundred thousand is probably a lower bound. It *might* be as high as three-quarters of a million."

Sergei thought about the number for a few moments; then, gradually, his mind turned to Admiral Marais. He knew that the next step in the campaign was to attack the last remaining zor naval base in this sector, at A'anenu; it would leave the zor with nothing but their Core worlds, centered on the Antares system, and what lay beyond—uncharted by the Solar Empire.

It was almost certain that Zor'a, the name the zor gave to their homeworld, would ultimately be the target of an attack not dissimilar to the one just completed here on S'rchne'e. They would fight even more tenaciously for Zor'a, if such a thing was possible: and they would ultimately lose, since the human fleet outnumbered and outgunned them.

For the first time in the campaign, it was really coming home to Sergei in a very graphic way that the fleet was involved in the wholesale destruction of a sentient race—not defeat, not conquest, not subjection—but destruction. Xenocide . . . the end of the race itself.

Final death of the zor, so that humanity might live.

He could not even place an ethical framework around the concept: it was too far-reaching and monumental for him to assess it. As a soldier, he had always been able to accept killing as part of the task—as a twentieth-century general had put it, "The job of the soldier is not to die for his country, it's to make the other dumb bastard die for *his* country." Or something like that.

But it was quite another matter for a mortal to take a responsibility upon himself that should only be accorded greater beings. The destruction of the zor should not be the province of a single human; even the desire of the zor to destroy humanity did not make it right or just. It was too much, to be the death-angel for the zor.

Then a flash of insight struck him, bringing back the staff meeting, and Marais' comments on the direction of the war:

They were *already* the Dark Wing. The Dark Wing, the mystical Death of the zor, who leveled all differences, destroying indiscriminately, with no chance of negotiation, with no way of retaliation. They could be the Dark Wing . . . they would be the Dark Wing. With an awful certainty, he knew this, as he sat in the familiar wardroom; and suddenly everything felt unfamiliar and alien, as if he was seeing for the first time through a different set of eyes.

There was no turning back from this, for there was no way of undoing what had been done, and no way of preventing what was to occur.

"Pass a 'well done' to Captain Bell, Chan." He stood and walked to the door of the wardroom, then turned to his exec, familiar yet suddenly different. "And—if I'm needed I'll be in my cabin."

"Is something wrong, sir?" Chan repeated, turning his chair to face Sergei.

"No . . . nothing. Nothing at all." He stepped through the open door and walked away, down the corridor toward the lift, thinking about the Dark Wing.

## chapter 8

Two letters bearing the official seal and warrant of His Imperial Highness, Alexander Philip Juliano, were dispatched at the same time from the Imperial Compound on Oahu. The first letter, prepared on the personal vellum stationery of the emperor, was placed into the hands of a courier, who locked it into her dispatch-bag and immediately boarded a 'copter, taking her from the compound to the transcontinental shuttle landing field on the neighboring island of Molokai. As was customary, a shuttle was waiting, on standby for the personal use of the emperor. Within minutes the shuttle, with courier aboard, was moving westward toward a destination halfway around the world—the Imperial Assembly in Genève.

The second letter had a destination considerably farther away, and instead of vellum, the document was committed to electronic form, transmitted at high speed, encoded to an orbital communications satellite, which aimed its FTL tight beam squirt at a fifth-magnitude star in the constellation of Scorpio and emitted an energy packet that took less than a microsecond to form, expand and disappear into the nothingness of jumpspace.

As it happened, both letters arrived at their intended destination at approximately the same time.

It was a blustery afternoon in the city by the lake. An unseasonably cold day for August had descended on the Genevois, forcing them inside to watch the driving rain and swirling wind bring a taste of autumn to their city. To add insult to injury, the vine-covered shoulders of the Salève, a dozen kilometers away beyond the fashionable Carouge suburb, were dappled in early-August sunlight, as if to taunt the city-dwellers to whom the sun was invisible behind slate-gray clouds reflected in the mottled surface of Lac Léman.

The prime minister stood at his sixth-floor window and looked out at the storm. For a few moments, at least, he left the Assembly behind and was lost in the scene, enjoying the beautiful view that even inclement weather could not ruin. The surcease was only temporary; his agile mind quickly grasped the apparent onset of autumn as a metaphor for what had been happening in the parliamentary body he directed, what had been happening steadily all summer while he maneuvered about, trying to gain advantage.

It was coming to an end. He could not really hear or see it, but the ax was falling. He had not lost a key division on any matter of import, and was not likely to do so: his own Dominion Party had controlled the Assembly for more than three-quarters of a century, and was in no danger of losing its majority . . . even his erstwhile opponent, Assemblyman Tomás Hsien, could do little to alter that. Instead, his enemies were within the party, within the majority bloc in the Assembly.

He knew it was coming, but protocol—and dignity, for that matter—required that he not show it. After six years as prime minister, serving both the old emperor and the present one, he knew quite a bit about both.

*It wasn't supposed to turn out this way,* he told himself, rub-

bing his forehead and turning his back on the scene. The familiar
fixtures of his office seemed almost alien in the muted artificial
light, so at odds with the darkening day outside; he remembered
fonder days, with bright summer or winter sunlight pouring in
through the windows. It had been bright and sunny on that June
day when he took command of the Dominion Party and the
Government, replacing a discredited, disheartened predecessor
who had lost the confidence of the Party and (worse yet) of the
emperor. Constitutional monarchy or not, without personal support from the occupant of the throne in Oahu there was no way
to effectively govern in the Assembly.

It seemed like a long time ago.

It had been a long summer, and now it was ending. This afternoon, at the plenary session of the Assembly (held in the great
bowl-shaped chamber that had been built originally for the
centuries-dead League of Nations), he'd felt his control starting
to slip. In a few minutes, the leader of the opposition would be
here, circling like some carrion bird, smelling the kill. For more
than three months, reports had been finding their way to the
press and to the official journal of the Assembly, regarding what
was going on out on the fringes of the Empire. Without regard to
the politics of the matter, Admiral Lord Marais had taken the war
to the aliens in a way that was totally unpalatable to the general
public, placing the Government in an extremely uncomfortable
position: either condone the acts of violence and destruction, or
admit that the Navy was out of its control.

It was like a choice between suicide by hanging and suicide
by jumping off a cliff. In the end, it amounted to the same thing.

He'd even thought of a way out, a way to get control of the
war effort—by playing one officer off against another. Imperial
Intelligence was wily, though, and wouldn't take responsibility.
In the end he'd been made to look like a fool, and was the recip-
ient of a full-scale diatribe from His Majesty the emperor.

*"Do something,"* the emperor had said. *"Or else it's your ass."*

There wasn't much he could do now. The latest reports from

his sources, and from Intelligence, indicated that Marais had gone off the deep end, preaching—that was the word for it, all right!—preaching about the destruction of the zor. The evidence left behind indicated strongly that he would have no difficulty carrying out his plans, even if it led to xenocide. *It might well lead to that.* How far would it go?

How could he stop it?

The wind shook the trees outside, as if to mock him with the futility of his question. For the first time in his lengthy Parliamentary career, the prime minister felt totally helpless.

A soft chime sounded. A voice said, "Excellency, Assemblyman Hsien is here to see you."

"Two minutes. Then let him come."

The prime minister turned to look out the window, and caught a reflection of himself in it. *Christ,* he thought. *I look like I've been through the wars. Well, that won't do.* With a characteristic effort of will, he took a deep breath and stood up straight, running a hand across his thinning hair and a quick finger across his carefully trimmed beard. When he turned from the window to face his visitor, he seemed to have completely regained his vigor.

The door opened with a low hum. A younger man with coffee-colored skin and Oriental features walked into the office. He was fashionably dressed, and exuded an air of complete confidence. A smile was fixed on his face, the one he used so often with the public—and with his colleagues; and as he advanced toward the prime minister, his hand extended, his eyes darted from place to place in the room as if he were sizing it up, measuring it inch by inch, to see if it suited him.

"Tomás, so good to see you." The prime minister reached his visitor in the middle of the room and took the younger man's hand. Tomás Hsien, leader of the Commonwealth Party, allowed no change in expression.

"Thank you for taking the time, Georges. I realize that you have a busy schedule."

The prime minister beckoned his adversary to a pair of plush chairs that faced a massive portrait of the emperor hanging above an empty, untended fireplace. "Now," he said when they were settled, "how may I help you?"

"You know why I'm here. Don't be coy." The fixed smile seemed almost feral in the late-afternoon light. "I believe that you don't have long to live in the Assembly."

"I still have the votes. Nothing has changed." The prime minister leaned back, laying his arms on the arms of the chair.

"*Everything* has changed. You've lost control of the war."

"You have no evidence to support that claim, preposterous as it is. The war is proceeding according to the Admiralty plan."

"Which is?"

"I'm not at liberty to discuss it."

"We're not out on the floor now, Georges. This won't make it into the official journal, and I have an assemblyman's security clearance. You can't withhold this."

"I can, and I will. I don't think you have any say in it."

"The people—"

The prime minister leaned over one arm of the chair and took hold of Hsien's gaze. "The people have nothing to do with this. The people—" He gestured toward the window, where the wind was tossing leaves through the rain-soaked sky. "The people, my friend, do not sit in the Imperial Assembly. They do not make decisions, nor is their opinion desired, or asked for. Governments and corporations decide, and as long as there are consumer goods and the shuttles run on time, they will leave it in our capable hands.

"More than half of all adults in the Solar Empire have lost a relative during the last sixty years, either as a civilian casualty or while serving in the military. Do you know what that means? It means that more than half of *the people,* Tomás, have a grudge against the zor. Sympathy for the aliens exists among scientists and other intellectuals, not among *the people.*"

"Not when they hear how their grudge is being carried out."

"And how would that be?"

Now it was Hsien's turn for dramatic pauses. He rubbed his hands together and looked away. "Of course, I only know what my sources tell me, but I understand that your admiral has wiped out the civilian populations of several zor-controlled worlds, and is now planning the capture, rather than destruction, of the large facility at A'anenu, in order to stage an assault on the zor home worlds." He glanced at the prime minister to see if there was any reaction.

The minister showed no indication, but he was seething inside. *How the hell did he get all of this?* "Go on."

"I have also learned that your admiral's megalomania has reached . . . shall we say *mythic* proportions. He apparently thinks that the zor believe him to be the zor Angel of Death, or some such, and he believes it, too."

"Marais is something of a scholar in this area."

"Don't you find this sort of nonsense inappropriate?"

"Marais has enjoyed unparalleled success. It's hard for me to disagree with success, Tomás. What would you have me do? Restrict his options?"

"Then you condone what's going on. You're condoning *xenocide.*"

" 'Condone' is a very strong word."

"But that's what it amounts to. Unless . . . you really don't have any control over the situation."

The prime minister felt like telling Hsien: *Yes, that's it—we have a madman on our hands; we really* are *standing by while he does as he pleases*—but he knew that it would do no good with this sort of person, even if it were proper to do so. And it certainly wasn't proper, no matter how tight the noose might be around his neck.

*The bastard's right about that,* he thought. *I probably don't have very long to live. Not that it will really change the balance of power in the Assembly.*

"Portray the situation any way you like."

Hsien sighed, as if he had lost patience with a petulant child. "Really, Georges, I had hoped you would be reasonable. Perhaps the emperor will be more attentive."

"The emperor won't even give you leave to visit, Tomás, as you and I both know. Don't waste your time."

"I so hate to disagree with you." The leader of the opposition reached into an inner pocket and withdrew an envelope with the Imperial seal on it. The back flap had been delicately parted, as if it were something precious. "I already have my invitation."

While the prime minister sat, stunned by the admission, Tomás Hsien rose gracefully from his chair and tucked the envelope back into his pocket. "I expect that I will find dealings with your successor considerably more . . . fruitful. Don't get up—I'll let myself out."

Before he could rise to object, the other was out of the office, the door sliding shut behind him.

The storm continued unabated, battering against the windowpane, and shaking the branches of trees from side to side.

The Logistical aspects of the assault on A'anenu required considerable planning. It was to involve more than two thousand marines, all of whom had to be briefed, drilled and equipped; while the fleet kept station above what had been the zor colony of S'rchne'e, the troops practiced in the mountain warrens on the planet below. Aboard ship, the bridge, engineering and gunnery crews went through drills and simulations to hone their skills for the upcoming battle. The *Lancaster* was included, providing an additional burden for Sergei, but one with which he was at least familiar. Sitting in the pilot's chair on the bridge of his own ship, he felt more at ease than he had in weeks.

The crew had just finished an exercise involving a one-on-one battle against an *Eclipse*-class ship of the line, in which Sergei had employed a modified Rodyn maneuver to destroy it. Chan Wells was preparing a statistical summary when the lift doors opened; when he turned, he said, "Admiral on the bridge," and came to attention. The rest of the bridge crew, since they were not on battle station, rose as well; Sergei was not obliged to do so, captain on his own bridge, but he stood out of courtesy to Admiral Marais.

His first glance at his superior officer made him aware of an intense anger barely concealed behind the admiral's eyes. Marais beckoned to Sergei. "In your ready-room, when this exercise is finished," he said, and walked down the ramp leading to it. Sergei only glanced at the report that Chan placed in front of him, then gave his exec the conn and followed the admiral.

He entered and saluted when Marais turned to face him, looking away from the holo of the globe of S'rchne'e. "You wanted to see me, sir."

"How secure is this room?"

"I can voice-seal it, sir."

"Please do so."

"Computer, seal this room on my voice signal. Torrijos, Sergei."

"Commodore Torrijos: voiceprint confirmed," a voice replied, and a small light went on over the doorway, and though it was not visible to the occupants of the room, a light went on over the outside of the door as well.

"Before I proceed, Torrijos, I feel that I must apologize for the comments of my adjutant. He takes a somewhat . . . protective view toward me and my objectives. I still maintain that there may be certain officers in this fleet who do not agree with my methods, and feel that their political connections back home give them some leverage out here; they are wrong. I was incorrect in assuming that you were among them."

"Thank you, sir . . ." *I think,* Sergei added silently, wondering what psychological game, if any, Marais was playing this time.

"Your patron McMasters has turned out to be more of a friend—or less of an enemy—than I originally thought. He was offered the command of the fleet in my place, as I have told you, and apparently turned it down. This came as a rather rude surprise to the emperor, who had hoped to save himself embarrassment by removing me. Now he has tried another tack." Marais reached into a pocket of his uniform jacket and removed a dispatch, which he handed to Sergei. "This arrived just a few hours ago."

Sergei opened the dispatch. It was from Sol System: from Oahu, in fact. He glanced down at the sender's code, and saw the sigil and warrant of the Solar Emperor. After several moments of staring at it, he tore his eyes away and quickly read through the text.

Official transmission, Priority 21:                8 August 2311
TO:   R Adm Ld Ivan H Marais, Commanding
        aboard IS *Lancaster*   onstation

Admiral:

We send you our fondest regards and warmest congratulations for your success against the zor enemy. Your unparalleled victories have been applauded across the Empire, confirming our confidence in our choice of you as Admiral of the Fleet. A suitable welcome awaits you when you return to Sol System following the conclusion of hostilities. Congratulations are also due the many brave men and women who serve their Emperor under your command.

It is with great pleasure that we inform you that the zor plenipotentiary has placed a new proposal on the table, agreeing to offer greater concessions than ever before obtained, to wit: total withdrawal of the alien fleet from the TransRift area in exchange for a cessation of hostilities. This proposal, if accepted, would obviate the need for an assault on the naval site of A'anenu, thus avoiding further unnecessary bloodshed.

In order to expedite the negotiation, we have this day dispatched a negotiator to the fleet anchorage of S'rchne'e, who will immediately upon arrival seek to contact representatives of the High Nest to arrange this armistice in a way and manner acceptable to both sides. We expect that you will aid and assist this person to the limits of your ability and resources.

Once again, we extend our congratulations for your success.

>*Alexander Philip Juliano Imperator*<

*Imperial Oahu*
>*Imperial seal*<

"The emperor doesn't want you to win the war," Sergei said finally.

"So it would seem." Marais took the dispatch back and tucked it away. "This is a turn of events I had expected, but I still cannot help feeling angry about it. The zor emissary has offered to end the war, and withdraw their fleet from A'anenu—if we stay away as well. But since that would leave A'anenu in their hands, it would effectively nullify all of our gains on this campaign.

"And, of course, it would prove to the zor that we were not—that *I* was not—the Dark Wing. This is our best chance of defeating the zor—"

"Or exterminating them."

"That possibility always existed. They wish to exterminate *us,* after all. This is our best chance, and the emperor is succumbing to pressure by sending a plenipotentiary ambassador out here to talk peace with the zor."

"What can you do, sir? The emperor's orders—"

"In my opinion, the emperor's orders do not supplant my original directive. In my judgement, giving up A'anenu is not compatible with establishing the secure frontier of the Solar Empire."

"What will you tell the ambassador?"

"I do not intend to be here. When the ambassador arrives at S'rchne'e, we will already be at A'anenu. It will almost certainly result in a court-martial, but it could win us the war. Only one thing will prevent it."

"What would that be, sir?"

"*You,* Torrijos. You have the opportunity, at this moment, to relieve me of command and take control of the fleet. This action will also lead to a court-martial, but I suspect that you will be able to clear yourself with the help of my by-now numerous enemies.

"I trust that you will make the correct decision."

Now Sergei understood why the admiral wanted a secure room to reveal the dispatch to him. The choice was truly in his hands: to support Marais in carrying out an act that was strategically necessary, but counter to the present wishes of the emperor, and thus face court-martial for insubordination; or to remove him from his post and face a court-martial for misconduct.

It was like a choice between suicide by hanging and suicide by jumping off a cliff. In the end, it amounted to the same thing.

"What are your orders, sir?"

Marais had been examining the holo globe, but he turned and looked up. "You are aware of the jeopardy to your career."

"Winning this war is the *purpose* of my career, sir."

His face changed to a hard smile. "Very well, then. Call a staff meeting for 1400 hours. I'll be expecting to get under way before the end of low watch."

The assault on the A'anenu naval base had two main objectives. The first and most obvious was the capture, rather than destruction, of the base itself and its surrounding facilities. Capturing it put the fleet fifteen parsecs closer to zor space, and provided a convenient refueling point. Pergamum was far behind them, Mothallah even farther, and the intermediate staging areas—for instance, what remained of S'rchne'e—had proved inadequate to handle the volume of traffic created by the fleet. Since none of the larger ships could make planetfall, the seizure of the orbital base was the most critical part of the entire operation.

In a sense, the actions of the rest of the fleet were trivial compared to Marc Hudson's success or failure. It would have been far more prudent to destroy the zor base, have the Seabees set up a temporary installation, and then transship a space-station inside one of the big cargo tenders. That would take weeks, however, and it was clear that Marais did not wish to wait that long, either due to his own impatience, or because the Imperial negotiator was on the way. That left seizure of the base as the only alternative.

The second consideration was the destruction of the zor mobile fleet. Marais' conjecture was that the zor would not waste time and resources defending other worlds, but would instead withdraw to A'anenu to defend it against the coming of the Dark Wing. It made a twisted sort of sense strategically, all mythological considerations aside; with the additional forces the Empire could now bring to bear, a defense of the base was the only chance for the zor to approach numerical parity. Marais hoped that it could be pinned there and eliminated, leaving the way clear for the fleet to cross the Antares Rift and attack the zor home stars.

Movement of the fleet toward A'anenu had finally quashed the rumor that the war was nearly over. The issue was more than motivational: the fleet was full of officers with connections, or ambitions, or both; a successful naval career was an excellent leg up on a political career, while association with wartime atrocities would destroy such aspirations forever. In the past, the power of coercion had always been strong when exerted by officers of lower rank but higher civilian station, on the grounds that most officers would not be in the Navy forever. Sergei knew that as well as anyone.

Good sense said that the capture of the last zor naval base in the sector would capture the public eye and end the war with a victory; certainly Marais' successes thus far would more than erase any lingering memory of "massacres" or "atrocities." In many wardrooms across the fleet, Sergei knew well, there were nagging worries that carrying the war too deep into zor-space might render the entire campaign a Pyrrhic victory: if the zor caused the fleet too many casualties, and if there were other enemy vessels that had escaped attention and were now on their way toward the core of the Solar Empire . . . no victory would be worth a damn if St. Louis or Genève was bombed and the fleet that ostensibly defended it was four hundred light-years away.

Twenty minutes to intercept, Captain."

Marc Hudson nodded to the helmsman. Ahead on the screen, the form of the system's primary grew, partially eclipsed by the main inhabited planet. The orbital base was just coming into view.

"Jim"—he turned his chair to face the gunnery officer, Jim Allison—"scan the base." He slapped the intercom on his chair arm. "Marines to battle stations."

An alarm began to ring through the ship. On his transponder, Hudson watched his squadron deploy: the single heavily-armed wing formed up for battle, aimed at the planetary surface, while the remaining two prepared to take the orbital station.

"Station is at sixty percent power, sir. Defensive fields are operational."

"Any ships berthed?"

"No, sir. As far as I read, all docks are vacant."

"All right, Lieutenant. Fire at will." He turned slightly to face his comm officer. "Ensign Zhu, signal the go-ahead to all ships."

The assault began: interplanetary space was filled with lances of light. While the heavily armed base engaged two squadrons, the third dived into the atmosphere, strafing the nightside installations presently bearing on them. As soon as the ground-based artillery and rocket-launchers were neutralized, a wave of airborne marines would jump to secure the groundside bases.

It was chancy—the whole operation depended on a crucial evaluation by the admiral, who believed that the main zor objective would be to destroy the human fleet, leaving the rearward bases to fend for themselves. This cavalier attitude toward defending A'anenu worked to the advantage of Hudson's command. A grizzled veteran of the last two wars against the zor, Marc Hudson had a fair idea of the tactical capabilities of his opponents. While fierce and unrelenting in battle, they often fought with a single-mindedness that approached a blind spot.

In a strategy meeting early in the campaign, Marais had provided a sociocultural argument for why this was the case; Hudson had retorted that the only important facts were that the zor were goddamn stubborn and could be goddamn stupid. Rationalizing the cultural motivation for a given enemy action was no replacement for having met that enemy bow-to-bow.

Engaging the main body of the fleet was ultimately someone else's problem.

But if the main fleet failed to defeat the zor near the outskirts of the A'anenu system, the enemy would return to capture its bases, and Hudson's men, deep in the gravity well, would have no means of escape, with the zor standing between them and the Solward jump point. Hudson was a loner, and hated to have to depend on the tactical capability of a military theorist like the admiral, even with a good man like Sergei Torrijos under him; Marais could make some half-assed move at any moment that could jeopardize Hudson's entire command . . . and Hudson might not live to tell about it.

So while the battle raged on, Hudson kept a close eye on the mass-radar transponder, to make sure none of the zor slipped away from the main fleet near the jump point.

•     •     •

The defensive field polarized all the way into the infrared and then back, light-devils dancing over the ship's hull. It was already doomed, as the ordnance continued to concentrate its fire. It still took a few long seconds before the engine bulkhead blew, and the jump drive annihilated itself and everything in the immediate vicinity with terrible violence.

Into the cheer that erupted on the *Lancaster's* bridge, Comm Lieutenant DeClerc said, "Commodore, we just received a tight-beam message."

"From where?"

"Outsystem, sir."

Their battle plan had been prepared in secret; Marais had had no intention of giving away his timetable since the fleet had jumped for A'anenu. No information was to escape until after A'anenu was taken. No one, in other words, should have known they were there yet.

"File it," Marais said, without turning from his scrutiny of the forward viewscreen.

"It bears the Admiralty high-priority code, Admiral—"

"*File it,* Lieutenant," said Marais, turning. His face showed barely concealed anger. "I don't give a damn if it bears the personal code of God Almighty."

"Y-yes, milord." DeClerc looked a bit shaken: he wasn't accustomed to receiving angry replies for doing his job.

The *Lancaster's* bridge had become very quiet. Marais cast a glance from officer to officer, from station to station. "I am in full command here, and will remain so until such time as the threat is ended. Lieutenant, you will continue to accept all such external messages with no acknowledgement until further notice to the contrary. There will be no contact with the outside until further notice. Is that understood?"

DeClerc nodded, a bit unsteadily. "Yes, milord."

As he spoke, the forward screen showed another enemy vessel detonating. A bright halo, like a new sun, illuminated the screen above and around Marais' head before it polarized nearly to opacity.

Even with computer aid, matching velocities with another projectile in space is a skill-oriented task. Helmsmen must have an innate feel for the ship they are piloting, as well as the relative motion of their target, and of all of the other forces bearing on the interaction of the two bodies. The fleet Academy regularly washed out promising cadets who lacked or could not acquire this skill. It was a harsh judgement in many ways . . . except that a helmsman who could not dock with a moving body in a training exercise would jeopardize too many lives when trying to do it under fire.

Now, with the remaining weapons of the base pouring hellish energies into their defensive fields at close range, the *Biscayne* and its sister ships closed on the orbital base. It was roughly spherical in shape, with a wide torus-shaped bulge at its equator. The hull of the station was interrupted all along this torus by circular iris hatchways. These were designed to mate with the access panels of zor ships, but the *Biscayne* and its sisters were specially equipped with access tubes to clamp on at the hatchways and defeat the lock mechanisms. There was no doubt in his mind but that zor infantry would be waiting behind those hatchways.

Marc Hudson knew from hard experience that it was difficult to give an order that might send a third or a half of the personnel involved directly to their deaths; but he also knew that the base had to be taken, and that fact superseded all other facts.

The *Biscayne* maneuvered to within a hundred meters of the orbital base, near the slag of a destroyed weapon mount. On order from the bridge, a flexible metal tube, three meters in diameter, extended itself from the upper fore airlock on the port side of the ship. By firing attitude jets on the side of the tube, it was maneuvered into position over the station hatch, while the *Biscayne*'s defensive fields absorbed fire aimed at it.

"Marines in position, sir," reported his exec. Around the hub of the station, a dozen other ships signaled their readiness.

"All right, Dana," he replied. "It's up to them."

The Marines in the access tube crouched behind a laser-reflective barrier. Ahead, a tech gave the thumbs-up, indicating that he had defeated the hatch electronics.

"Open 'er up, Russ," said Christopher Boyd, the Marine sergeant in command.

The marines tensed, their weapons trained on the hatch, as the iris valve unfolded. A rush of pressurized atmosphere blew into the access tube.

They expected a rain of laser-fire, but their external audio picked up no noise other than the far-off hum of machinery. The sergeant waved two of his troops to either side of the hatch, to provide covering fire, while the rest of his command advanced quickly onto the station deck . . .

—From the ceiling and the walls, random laser-fire erupted—

Chris Boyd and his squad hit the deck. Boyd could hear comm inside his helmet: it was clear that all of the breached entrances had been trapped this way. Two marines had been killed instantly, and two more were on the floor of the compartment, their lives leaking out of their suits, while Boyd and the others fired at the weapon mounts, eventually knocking them out.

The room, a sort of antechamber, was bathed in a dim red light; Chris Boyd knew that the zor saw farther into the red than humans, and thus would find it well lighted. A small adjustment in his helmet's lens-filter confirmed it.

There were two exits from the room, other than the iris valve—a hatchway directly above, and another positioned opposite the valve, but three-quarters of the way up the wall. The wall sloped outward at forty-five degrees at this point. There were no ladders to either, although small handholds were spaced at seemingly random intervals on the walls and ceiling.

Then it suddenly made sense to him. The internal gravity was just over half a Standard g, and the hatches would be easily accessible to someone with wings.

Concentrated fire had destroyed the flagship of the A'anenu defense fleet. Like the others, it had failed abruptly, silently and violently, a bright fireball that blinded the attackers for a few moments. Command passed to a new zor commander, and aboard the *Lancaster* and the fleet carrier *Gagarin*, tactical commands sought to quickly identify which enemy vessel was issuing commands. For a few minutes, the zor tactics remained the same; the zor battle-fleet, drawn up in a formation which resembled a dispersed cone, had been exchanging fire with the Imperial fleet; far outnumbered and critically outgunned, it had been reduced by more than a third in a matter of a few hours.

Marais had assumed that, just as in previous battles, the zor navy would remain engaged until it was completely destroyed. This would give Marc Hudson time to fight his way onto the naval base. By the time he had secured his position, any zor which remained would be trapped—with Captain Sal Roberts' uncommitted force guarding the jump point and their base of operations in the gravity well in enemy hands, they would have no choices other than surrender, or, more likely, suicide.

The new zor commander seemed to have perceived that strategem, and realized the importance of the base to his enemies; therefore, instead of remaining in the outer system, he suddenly issued an order to break off the combat. His reduced force exchanged parting shots with the Imperial ships, and maneuvered at what must have been several g's, overloading internal gravitational controls—painful for humans, no doubt sheer agony for the lighter and more fragile zor—correcting their course for the inner system and the naval base.

The move caught the Imperials by surprise. At first it seemed as if the zor ships were simply weakening, as they diverted energy away from their defenses to commit to maneuver; almost at once, two vessels reached critical absorption levels, and the enemy fire boring through their hulls caused their engine compartments to erupt in a blinding instant of primordial violence. Perhaps this was in accordance with the zor commander's tactics: while the explosion and accompanying radiation numbed enemy sensing equipment, the rest of his fleet performed the necessary high-g maneuvers, changing course and heading into the gravity-well, several seconds ahead of its human counterpart.

Chamber by chamber the marines penetrated deeper into the station. It was surreal, almost frighteningly so: the walls were decorated with a fine tracing of swirling patterns that seemed random at first, but upon closer examination revealed a cohesion, the full nature of which seemed slightly too complex to grasp. It was art, of a sort, but it also seemed to give a clue to the form and function of the room it decorated, and the position of that room relative to the rest of the station. Bathed in the eerie reddish light favored by the zor, it seemed all the more alien.

They moved warily now. Twice since they had first entered the station, they had triggered an automatic trap; but the marines were on their guard now, alert to the slightest change in temperature or pressure, listening through their suits' external audio pickups to every click and whirr of machinery. There had to be live zor somewhere in the station, but it might take days to find them all. Until every one of them was found and either captured or killed, the station would not be safe. How many marines it would take to achieve that objective was something Chris Boyd didn't want to think about.

"All clear, Sarge," he heard over his suit-radio. Hans Loudon, his hardbitten old lance corporal, was beckoning from one of the doorways from the large chamber they were now in. Boyd signaled to the other soldiers in the squad to cover the exits, and he crossed the room to join Loudon.

"What the—"

He looked into the room. He was taken aback at once: it was so different from the room in which he now stood that he half expected it to disappear when he stepped into it.

The first thing that he noticed was the lighting. Instead of the indirect reddish glow of the other rooms in the station, this chamber was brightly illuminated by the semblance of a bright vermillion sun, hung low over the horizon, like a sunrise or a sunset. The walls had been made to appear indistinct, seamlessly blending with the ceiling to form a cobalt-blue sky. It was a casual illusion, the sort of thing one could find on the recreation deck aboard any Imperial starship; yet it was more startling, for it conveyed an alienness, a sense that this scene was not created by humans, and not created for them.

A torus hung in midair, somewhere near the middle of the room, supported by a null-grav plate. It seemed to be made of stone, and was intricately carved with the same spidery swirls they had seen elsewhere. It was big enough within for three man- or zor-sized figures to stand (or perch) abreast.

"Cover me," he said, waving to the two assault-riflemen, who instantly drew a bead. Boyd advanced slowly, one hand gripping his pistol, the other held out in front of him. Step by step he crossed the floor toward the torus, attentive to the slightest motion that might signal a trap.

After what seemed to be hours, he found himself standing beside the torus. When he looked away from the direction he had come, where the door's dark eye stared back at him, he could almost lose himself in the illusion of the pale blue sky and the distant, unmoving sun.

He always wondered afterward what had made him decide to do it, whether it had really been his idea, or if something in the room or the torus itself had put the idea in his head.

"I'm going to go up into the thing," he said, and heard an answering grunt from Loudon. "Anything happens, you evacuate the room and regroup outside it. Understood?"

"Aye, Sergeant," replied the corporal. The riflemen tipped their weapons to indicate they had heard.

With little effort in the low gravity, Chris Boyd hauled himself up to stand within the torus, noticing for the first time the roughness of the inner surface, totally different from the smooth exterior. Standing within the ring, he cast a long shadow from the false sun, which hung almost directly behind him. Within, there were no controls or other devices to indicate the torus' purpose. Baffled, he crossed his arms over his chest and thought to himself.

It was then that he began to hear a distant *something*. It was too far away, or too soft, to be made out distinctly; but it seemed to resonate through the torus and throughout the room.

He looked from trooper to trooper as he listened; none seemed to give any indication he or she had heard. He hesitated to mention it aloud, for fear of drowning out the sound; instead, he listened all the more intently.

It seemed like a far-off chorus, but it was not music—nor was it totally spoken: it seemed to be a sort of multitonal chanting, following a syncopation of pitch and chord, with the words sometimes accompanying the music, and sometimes the other way around. It swirled into Chris Boyd's ears and eyes, and chased through the corridors of his mind, music and words and the illusion of sky and sun assaulting him as he stood within the stone torus.

*esLi,* it said, and then, more clearly: *esLi, Creator, wielder of the Great Sword.*

Again he shifted from face to face, as he stood in the disk, his shoulders hunched, trying to see if anyone else could hear it, but unwilling to break the silence for fear of drowning out the sound that seemed to grow in intensity and in tonality as he strained to hear.

*From the Valley of Lost Souls and the Never-Ending Battle, from the very Plain of Despite we call you, esLi, esLi, deliverer of justice, bringer of the Bright Wing.*

Before his mind could react to ask what it meant or how he was hearing it, images came unbidden into his mind and before his vision, dimming the awareness of the room in which he stood until it became remote and unreal.

A bright, orange-red sun shone upon him, and the desert surrounded him. He was coming into awareness now: the flight was being chosen . . . he could hear the chanting as it swirled around the talons of his mind.

*The Inner Peace is Yours, esLi, the Outer Peace also; there is no truth without the balance of each.*

*For Your own purpose You created us, to go forth in Your image and to shape the universe according to Your plan.*

*esLi.*

*esLi.*

Somewhere outside, or above, or beyond, he sensed another, more powerful mind. It was alien, but somehow familiar, a strong and guiding force just beyond the limits of his conscious perception, like something not quite seen, out of view.

*We will hold fast to Your code,* esLi, the voices continued, rising in intensity, a chorus now, freezing him in place, gripping tightly to the sides of the contemplation-disk, as if he were the target and focus of the sound.

*We shall not dishonor ourselves in Your sight. None will live that mock Your way or disobey Your plan.*

*esTli'ir and esHu'ur, equal in Your sight, servants of Your Will.*

*esLi,* the chanting said.

*esLi.*

He felt himself suddenly thrust into motion, like a spring wound tightly and then released. He heard himself shouting in a tongue he did not understand, his pistol aimed high in the air, the powerful image of *esLi* hammering at his brain. He ran across the room in low gravity, toward his surprised companions.

Suddenly the room turned sideways as a loud noise and flash of light erupted behind him. He felt the stone floor coming up to meet him from a long distance away, colored like the sand on his native Zor'a. He extended his talons to gain purchase, but they were already too far under to do any good. He flapped his wings at full extension, but they seemed unwilling to function, except to block out the sun for a moment, a dark, shadowy wing growing closer and closer, until he could see nothing else. As the ground shuddered beneath him he fell, toppling end over end, losing consciousness somewhere along the way down.

chapter 9

THE SENSITIVE COMES TO HIS FULL
                                    (*The Strength of Madness*)
POWERS SUDDENLY. THE INNER PEACE
FLIES AWAY FROM HIM WITH WINGS
FULLY EXTENDED: BALANCE IS LOST,
EARTH IS SKY AND SKY IS EARTH.

DESPAIR PERCHES ON ONE SIDE OF HIM;
MADNESS ON THE OTHER. YET WITHAL
                                    (*Valley of Lost Souls*)
HE MUST FIND HIS INNER PEACE AGAIN
WITH NEITHER COMPASS NOR GUIDE.

—*hiShthe'eYaTur, The Flight Over Mountains*
(from the Shthe'e Codex, by Loremaster Shthe'e HeChri)

The High Lord's rest was interrupted by another troubling dream. He was in the Desert of Nresh't'lu this time, a Nestling still, engaging in his warrior's rite of passage. The mystical sleep had come over him, marking him as both warrior and Sensitive; that was how many Sensitives perished, having the full flood of prescient dreaming come when they were least prepared, in danger from the World that Is while their consciousness was filled with the world of dreams.

*esLi* watched, and the Bright Wing hovered, as he fought to regain Inner Peace while the dreams battered at him.

It seemed that he was surrounded by aliens, who had taken hold of him and were carrying him down to their underground lair. He felt the heat of the day on his wings and upturned face suddenly cut off as they descended, step by echoing step, into the earth. Stunned by the mystical dreams, he could not fight or transcend the Outer Peace; he could do no more than watch through half-lidded eyes and listen with the inner ear of a Sensitive.

We read you, Commodore. Go ahead.

Sergei Torrijos' face appeared in the air near the pilot's board. Behind him Marc Hudson could see the anger-clouded visage of the admiral, arms crossed before him, trying to appear aristocratic or something.

"Marc, what's the situation?"

"As far as I can tell, sir, the marine squads are making headway against token resistance. At least two squads are in the vicinity of what we believe to be the command bridge."

"How long till they get in there?"

"Insufficient data, sir, I—"

"That doesn't answer the question."

He felt like answering, *Well I'm just sorrier than hell, Sergei,* but restrained himself. "It's a tough job, sir. They'll take it when they take it. Pérez reports that the assault force has met almost no live opposition, just automatic traps and electronics."

"Sounds a lot like a trap."

"Doesn't it, sir. It's a bit late to do anything other than forge ahead, sir, which is just what the Marines are good at."

"You have the remaining zor vessels bearing on you, Marc,

approaching the inner system at high velocity. We are in pursuit, but they'll get there well ahead of us. Will you have control of the base by the time they arrive?"

"I see why you ask." Marc scratched his chin thoughtfully. "What's their ETA?"

"Two hours at the most, to come into main weapon range. But you should be on the lookout for missiles a lot sooner than that."

"Your advice, Commodore?" He asked it, already considering his alternatives. The pilot's board, in front of him, showed the scene: several discrete points of light hurtling into the gravity well, traveling at a quarter-light at least.

*And armed to the teeth,* he reminded himself.

"Deploy your half-squadron, Marc. Detach the *Biscayne* and the other ships from the base. We'll be there as soon as we can. And for God's sake, don't let them near that base while the defensive fields are down. If the zor get too close, it'll condemn a few thousand Marines to certain deaths." The words hung in midair, like the afterecho of a struck gong.

"I beg to remind the commodore . . ." began Hudson, breaking the silence. "To a Marine, there is no such thing as certain death." He paused and added, "Which is one reason I am not a marine. In all seriousness, sir, all interservice rivalry aside, the marines have their assignment, and they will execute it with consummate skill. At this point, there is nothing I can do to get them out of there."

It was difficult at first to resolve where the dream ended and reality began. A part of his mind observed, abstractly, as he traced the fine swirls of the *hRni'i* with his half-lidded eyes, making sense of them, reading names of commanders and clans in ordered, curved rows near the top of the wall, with other, more crudely drawn symbols indicating where perches extruded and the direction of the nearest emergency hatch.

In another part of his mind, Chris Boyd was slowly coming to consciousness, the realization reaching him that he suddenly *understood* what he saw, rather than simply observing it. It was an effort among all of that remembering who and where he was; it was like swimming in a deep ocean that heaved and rocked, kilometers from land known but far out of sight.

He must have started suddenly, since three of his men turned suddenly toward him, guns at the ready. He blinked and looked around him at the dimly lit room he was in.

"You all right, Sarge?" asked the gruff voice of Hans Loudon in his ear.

"What?" He looked up to see Loudon coming toward him, across the small chamber the squad now occupied. "Uh, yes, I'm fine. What happened?"

"Don't know. Maybe you can tell me." Loudon put his hands on his hips. Only a narrow quadrant of his face was visible, the rest lost in the shadow cast by his helmet; it held something halfway between a grin and a scowl. "You stepped up into that torus thing, stood there for a minute, and then came runnin' across toward us wavin' your arms and shoutin' in some language I'd never heard before."

"Language? I only speak—"

Then he remembered, and the memory struck him with an almost physical blow. He heard the voices, a dim echo now, pronouncing the invocation to *esLi,* echoing around the stone ring, coruscating through his consciousness. And suddenly he knew the purpose of that room, and the torus that hung within it.

*esLi,* the dim echoes called through his mind. Voices had called that name—in invocation, in prayer. *esLi,* he knew somehow, was the divinity of the zor, and somehow, through something he'd done, a manifestation of that divinity had . . . touched him? Spoken to him?

He had been a zor for a moment, on some sort of journey, and a second sight had descended on him like the shadow of a wing flying overhead. It remained with him still, dormant and waiting. He looked from Loudon to the other marines, and saw them as two overlapping images: first, a group of fellow soldiers, nervous and tense in the land of the enemy, and second, as *naZora'i,* as *esGa'vYal,* soldiers of the Lord of the Cast Out.

*This is the moment of aLi'e'er'e,* he thought to himself. *You stand at the decision point, and it is up to you to choose the flight.*

He shook his head to clear his sight, and they were just Marines again.

"What happened after that?"

"We destroyed it, Sarge."

"You—"

"We *blasted* it, Sarge, and then you collapsed. I took command. After I made sure you were okay, I found us a place to hole up while you came to."

Boyd looked at him, stunned. His stomach churned. "That place—that was a . . . shrine. A zor place of worship."

Loudon turned to face him. Boyd could see a single eyebrow arch itself.

"Was it indeed, Sarge."


Marc Hudson's sense of foreboding was growing. He had been at this for too long not to know that something was going to happen.

The Marines had penetrated the space-station nearly to its center, scouring the outer corridors and compartments as they went. Nearly all of the enemy encounters had been with automatic weapon mounts, or hair-trigger traps; they'd met no more than half a dozen live zor.

Marc was almost sure now that it was a trap, one big enough to catch two thousand Marines. The most likely possibility seemed to be destruction of the base by the zor, once it was completely invested by Imperial troops. It would only require a few zor warriors to stay behind, set the traps, and wait.

Now the *Biscayne,* and the other ships under his command,

stood off the base, deployed and ready for the advance of the remaining enemy ships. There was no way for the marines aboard the base to get off: they were stranded, caged with an uncounted and—in human terms—completely psychopathic enemy.

As he sat gripping the arms of the pilot's seat, watching the dim outlines of the advancing vessels grow larger in the forward viewscreen, Marc profoundly thanked God once more that he was not a marine.

Once men sailed on water-oceans on the surface of the homeworld and other worlds, in ships scarcely bigger than a modern-day gig—built out of wood, not metal, and powered by wind or muscle. Until the age of steam, the armaments these ships carried stayed far ahead of the vessels' ability to withstand them, so that often battles were reduced to getting the first effective shot.

In those days, a captain stood out on deck and felt the sea roll under him; he shouted out his orders and heard the report of the guns. He could tell, intuitively, whether he was winning or losing . . . and the danger of death in the sea was never far away.

Space was another matter. Internal gravitational systems compensated for external destabilization, so that even a broadside from an opponent's lasers would not topple a coffee cup to the deck—even if the ship was sent end over end. If the defensive fields ever failed, however, and the full force of enemy fire rained upon the hull rather than the energy net that surrounded it . . . that was a quite different matter.

Starship captains sat in the pilot's chairs and dispassionately dealt out mega-ergs of death, while scarcely noticing a flicker of movement on their viewscreens. Sometimes the defensive fields failed, or the energy-generation equipment failed, and it was over in a moment: a new sun in the darkness of space, and an abrupt and violent end to life. *You can never really understand death until it happens to you personally. And then it's too late.*

In the two hundred years of star travel humanity had experienced, rarely had a battle between humans come down to destruction of one side or the other. Like a chess game, the objective was not necessarily to destroy the opponent, but simply to make him incapable of further opposition. So much potential for destruction was available, and human life was ultimately so fragile, that capture had far surpassed annihilation as the prime directive for space fleets. In a twenty-year career, a competent commander potentially could successfully refrain from *ever* destroying an enemy ship, base or installation. It was a hard habit to break, this notion of capture rather than destruction, even when zor and human first clashed: the tendency was too deeply ingrained.

The zor were alien in tactics as well as appearance. Their disregard for individual lives was almost callous: in order to destroy a given human installation, they would often allow three smaller vessels to be destroyed in a delaying action in order to deliver a killing blow. Human strategists were content to believe that the zor admirals were unsophisticated and desperate . . . except Admiral Marais, who knew better from an extensive study of the zor culture. Severe population pressure had contributed to their selflessness and disregard for individuals as opposed to the entire race . . . but that really was not the half of it. It was an outlook, a way of life, something so basic and all-pervading that it was almost impossible for humans to understand.

Sergei had thought he had understood it, a hard lesson learned in this campaign, which had been unlike any other he had yet experienced . . . but he knew now how wrong he had been to believe that. His mind raced in accustomed detachment, analyzing the situation with the passivity and logic of an outside observer. He knew that his palms were sweating, itching to get out and try to push the *Lancaster* and her sister ships faster, to catch up with the rapidly retreating zor ahead of them.

He broke the current predicament into its component parts, considering all of the alternatives and options as he went. It was simple, really: if this were to be a stepping stone, rather than the ultimate objective, he needed to capture the zor facilities, especially the one in orbit. This required a concerted assault by marines, while most of the fleet kept the remaining zor navy occupied. All of this hinged on Marais' perception that the zor would attempt to destroy the obvious target—the fleet—rather than to deny the secondary objective—the base—to the Imperials.

But Marais had been *wrong*. And now, because of it, a major part of the fleet's assault troops were in grave danger. Too many scenarios existed for Sergei to determine the likelihood that they could be rescued: too many of them ended in the destruction of the base, either by suicidal zor within, or by parricidal zor without. All it took was one well-aimed missile to get past Marc Hudson and to target just the right spot on the base—and the battle would have been lost, regardless of the ultimate fate of the remaining zor vessels. There would be no way to pursue the campaign without troops or a base of operations: and even Marais, arrogant as he was, would likely not fly in the face of his emperor and try to carry out his original objective.

Here it was, win or lose. Marais seemed to realize the implications, and seemed also to know what Sergei was thinking. His eyes were intent on the viewscreen, as he sat, unmoving, near the engineer's station.

The haggard faces of Marines looked back at him through the faceplates of helmets: the faces of men and women who had crammed too much experience into too little time, shoulders permanently hunched, gloved hands clenching their rifles.

Chris Boyd, one of them after all, looked away and down into the small comp he held in his hand. It showed a three- dimensional diagram of the space station, indicating depth by variance in color. Parts of the diagram were brightly outlined, indicating the progress of his and others' squads through the station.

By his best estimate from the diagram they were one deck away from the large spherical control-bridge at the center of the station. A quick examination of the *hRni'i* confirmed this, but he could not possibly explain how he knew, or why; it was easier not to mention his understanding of the zor glyphs on the walls.

Other groups of Marines had penetrated almost as far, scattered at various points around the diameter of the ship; but his squad of seven survivors were the closest.

Loudon was squatting near the floor on the opposite side of the room.

"Far as I can tell, Sarge," he said, "the ceiling of the bridge should be about—here." He jabbed a point a third of the way up the wall with a thumb.

"What's above it?" He already knew the answer, but it wouldn't be politic to mention that—since it would require an explanation.

"Uh—ventilation duct, I think. Damn diagrams, I can hardly figure 'em out one from another." He stood up straight, and peered through the transparent aperture of a narrow hatch on the same wall.

Boyd looked at the hatch, and then at Loudon. "Open it up."

Loudon drew his pistol and burned a hole in the locking mechanism, and then knocked the hatch open with the butt. "Not sure we can all get in there, Sarge."

"We'll have to lose some weight, then. Move out."

One of the troopers gave Loudon a leg up, and he squeezed his way into the narrow shaft. He was followed by two more marines, with Boyd bringing up the rear. The three others stayed behind, guarding the exit.

Looking back from within the velvet darkness of the shaft, the dim red light of the station's corridors seemed very bright; Boyd tried to concentrate on the floor ahead of him instead, so as not to ruin his night-vision.

Their progress was painstakingly slow. Somewhere below—

it was hard to tell just where, the sound was so indistinct—they could hear the high-pitched voices of zor.

What were they saying? Boyd wondered. Offering prayers to . . . *esLi*? He shuddered then, remembering the shrine, and all that he now knew told him that they would not be praying; their preparations for death had already long been made. He understood that now, with more clarity than he would have expected.

"Sarge," he heard Loudon's voice distantly; the shaft opened out ahead, and red light showed, streaming from the floor. The other three were gathered there; when he reached them, Loudon gestured downward into the light.

Boyd looked down at the control bridge, and beheld an alien tableau which, at first glance, seemed totally incomprehensible. Eleven zor were arranged there in a roughly symmetric pattern, each wearing or holding a long, ornate sword which glowed faintly from a lattice of energy. Each zor wore a sash of a different color, and had positioned him- or herself in a particular stance: wings elevated in one way or another, clawed hands extended or at the sides of the body, head elevated or turned.

These were the first actual zor his squad had seen aboard the station, and he'd wager a year's pay that these were the only ones there were. From the look of them, their duty there was as much mystical as practical, but he wasn't quite sure what it was.

Eleven zor.

*Eleven is a mystical number,* he thought to himself. *Eleven Nests; eleven partitions in each wing; eleven Home Stars.* It came unbidden into his mind, as he looked from zor to zor, standing like statues below, until his gaze landed on the one in the center, wearing the crimson sash, who stood before a pedestal. The pedestal was topped by a small stone ring, hovering half a meter above its surface, a replica of the one Boyd had experienced in the place of worship.

It was as if they were well prepared for death, ready to meet it with personal honor, though there would be no zor who could ever take note of, or honor, their behavior. This in no way altered it: what they did, he knew, was for *esLi*, Who watched in any case.

The zor stood in silence, unmoving and at attention, waiting for the inevitable.

As Chris Boyd watched, the storm broke.

The main hatch blew open. Through it burst three Marines, diving for cover as they loosed bursts from their rifles. One zor went down at once, with a howl, while the remaining defenders leapt into action.

A hole appeared ninety degrees clockwise of the main hatch, and two more Marines came through. Almost instantly one of the zor defenders changed aim and fired coolly and precisely at one of the newcomers. The Marine's faceplate shattered, and his face exploded messily as he fell to the deck, dead.

Loudon fired a shot at the lock mechanism, and set about removing the hatch. Boyd continued to watch below, transfixed by the speed with which the remaining zor shifted from target to target, picking off the Marines as they tried to enter the bridge. Crouched behind machinery, they were well placed to hold off attacks from nearly any direction; the Marine attackers were having a difficult time approaching the emplacement. The zor were blindingly fast: though not as physically strong as their human counterparts, their reflexes were superior by an order of magnitude, enough to nearly offset their disadvantage in numbers.

"Son of a bitch," said Loudon, breaking Boyd from his reverie. The corporal and another trooper were wrestling with the hatch, which had somehow become jammed into place. He fired his pistol at the transparent portion—

—And was rewarded with a dozen ricochets as the blast gradually lost its energy in the walls of the ventilator duct—

Boyd glared at Loudon, who probably should have known better. He and the other trooper continued to fight with the hatch, trying to pull it up.

Below, the encounter had settled into a snipers' battle, the zor crouched behind their makeshift emplacements, the Marines using wallmetal sheets burned from an adjacent compartment as mantelets, trying to advance on the zor positions. The zor, for their part, were doing their best to keep to cover, away from the deadly human attacks.

But Boyd's eyes were drawn to the pedestal in the center of the room. Apparently unnoticed by the Marines pinned down at the edge of the chamber, the stone torus had begun first to vibrate, and then to spin end over end.

Suddenly, again unbeckoned, understanding came into his mind, and Boyd realized what the pedestal was for, and why the zor were fighting—and dying—to defend it. It was also clear to him why there were only a few zor aboard A'anenu Starbase, why there had never been more than a few. It was a monstrous trap, a game being played to the last piece while the zor lured the marines to the center of the station.

With a rush of adrenaline produced by the sudden, sick feeling in the pit of his stomach, he added his hands to those of the two others trying to pry up the hatch—and abruptly it came free, snapping with a howl of metal-fatigue, and falling into the control bridge from above: a slow-motion drop in the half-g, altered slightly by the aberrant turning of the station.

The torus spun faster and faster. A stray shot, aimed perhaps at the pedestal, glanced away less than a meter from the disk, and the air around it glowed faintly orange for a moment.

Almost too fast for anyone—including himself—to notice, Chris Boyd aimed and fired at the disk from above, as defenders and attackers started at the sound of the hatch clanging against the bridge deck. The air around the disk glowed orange and red, then white and blue-hot, too bright for the naked eye: and still he poured the energy of the pistol out, firing with his eyes shut, his outside "ears" filled with the baritone howl of a zor voice screaming in pain, calling the name of the Dark Wing.

The other zor, caught unawares by the sudden attack from above, died abruptly as the Marines leapt over their barriers, firing as they went. In the center of the room, the pedestal and its contents exploded, scattering shards of metal and stone throughout the room. Only then did Boyd cease firing, deaf and blind, slumped on the floor of the ventilator shaft. His pistol slipped from his limp hand, and drifted slowly down until it clattered on the bridge deck and lay still.

The High Chamberlain, Ptal HeU'ur, had done his best to isolate the High Nest from the tumult outside it. The comnet was full of apocalyptic pronouncements; the air fairly crackled with portents of disaster. Even Sanctuary had closed its doors for a time, leaving emerging Sensitives with nowhere to go.

As for the High Lord, if the Chamberlain could have thought of a place more calm and at least half as secure as the High Nest complex in esYen, Zor'a's capital city, he would have directed his Lord to go there at once; but there was no such place.

Makra'a HeU'ur had returned to the Nest's home world of E'rene'e, and had summoned Ptal home; but the High Chamberlain had not answered Lord Makra'a's demand, choosing instead to remain by the side of High Lord Sse'e. Ptal was no mindless functionary, but it still provided him some Inner Peace to go about the business of his office as if nothing were happening.

Less than an eighth of a moon after the word of A'anenu's capture reached Zor'a, Ptal went early in the morning to the Chamber of Solitude, hoping to consult with the High Lord on a matter of minor policy. S'tlin, his *alHyu*, informed him that the

High Lord had neither meditated nor used his sleep-chamber for nearly two turns. After some cajoling and threatening, the servant revealed that the High Lord was in his private gardens. This inner sanctum was rarely to be violated, since it was a place that Sse'e cultivated his own Inner Peace; despite this, Ptal felt moved to go there, if only to allay his own concerns about his Lord and old friend.

He found him in the *esTle'e*, the circular central garden that lay directly beneath a nearly transparent skylight. The vermillion light of the primary suffused the walls to the southeast, delicately painting the carefully tended flora and highlighting the gold-enameled circle that bounded the *esTle'e*. Sse'e stood on the central perch, eyes closed, *hi'chya* in outstretched hands, his wings arranged in the Posture of Surrender to the Will of *esLi*.

Unsure of how to approach, Ptal HeU'ur stood quietly on one of the manicured paths, prepared to wait all turn until the High Lord was ready to speak to him.

After only a moment, Sse'e opened his eyes, lowered his *hi'chya* and, after making the appropriate obeisance, sheathed it. His wings returned to a neutral arrangement, and he beckoned Ptal closer. When he approached, the High Chamberlain could see fatigue and strain in the other's eyes.

"Eight thousand pardons for disturbing you, High Lord. My business is not urgent—"

"It is of no moment, *se* Ptal. Come here and stand with me."

The High Chamberlain approached, and took up a position on one of the lower perches. He made a polite expression with his wings, and then shared a hand-over-hand grasp with his old friend.

"You need sleep, *hi* Sse'e."

"That may well be. I have not been so inclined of late, but my—efforts—have gained me little."

"You do not dream, then?"

"No—on the contrary. The Lord *esLi* troubles me with dreams I do not understand. I see through different eyes, eyes

which behold our people as aliens, and yet can still read the
*hRni'i.*"

"You—dream that you are the admiral of the *esGa'uYal?*"

"No, I think not." Sse'e rearranged himself on the perch, and
blinked several times, as if trying to clear something from his
eyes. "In the dreams I am one of the aliens, but a lesser figure, a
soldier of some kind. I am with him and he with me. He is no
more than a Nestling now but understands that we have already
reached a point of *aLi'e'er'e*. Reached it, and passed it."

The discussion of choosing the flight chilled the High Chamberlain, and Sse'e sensed his mood.

"Are you troubled, my old friend?"

"I fear for all of us, High Lord. Every indication—" He
paused, and looked around the garden, taking a moment to
phrase his words in a way that seemed appropriate. "As you well
know, the Speaker for the Young Ones made an appeal to the
aliens for a new peace initiative, as was agreed at the meeting of
the Council of Eleven.

"It seems as if the aliens have neither accepted nor rejected
the offer but simply ignored it. The campaign continued, and
they were able to take *Ka'ale'e* A'anenu before the rite of
*saHu'ue* could be accomplished."

"This is certainly not what the Speaker expected."

"No, High Lord, it is not. In fact, his treatment of my Lord
of Nest, Makra'a HeU'ur, was only a few eighths short of ridi-
cule when Lord Makra'a told him what the outcome would be."

"'It is only the brave who can admit cowardice,'" the High
Lord quoted.

"I thank you for your characterization. I think that it is only
my concern for calm within the Council of Eleven that keeps me
from wanting to call the Speaker out for so affronting Lord
Makra'a's honor, especially in view of the outcome."

"Do you believe that the aliens' refusal to discuss peace is
sufficient proof to acclaim their admiral as an avatar of *esHu'ur?*"

"I . . ." The High Chamberlain's wings assumed the Stance of

Earnest Meditation. "I would have to consider the matter carefully, High Lord."

"Choose carefully, *se* Ptal, and make no mistake. This flight leads toward an eventual conclusion past which there is no way to determine our fate. It will be in the hands of the Dark Wing, and the Lord *esLi*."

"You mean . . ."

"We are facing the same trial as the hero Qu'u, when he searched for the Bright Wing in the Mountains of Night. It is evident that at least some of our commanders in the field have sensed this choosing as well; I have seen dispatches quoting *aHu'sheMe'sen*—*Lament of the Peak*—already.

"In the legend, the Lord Qu'u is sent by the first High Lord, A'alu, to determine the cause of a great plague that has beset the land. She sends him on his way, warning that she has dreamed that his journeys may take him again to the Plain of Despite, as they did before to recover the *gyaryu,* the sword of state that united the clans and created the High Nest.

"After much journeying and adventure, Qu'u determines that the Bright Wing has been seized and captured by *esGa'u*, the Lord of the Cast Out, and that the Dark Wing is descending unrestrained in the world above. Unrequitable, unstoppable, and unforgiving, *esHu'ur* brings plague and death across the world much to the delight of *esGa'u* and his minions. Eventually, Qu'u does reach the Plain of Despite and while crossing the Mountains of Night finds the place where the Bright Wing is bound. At the height of the storm, he realizes an important lesson about the nature of the Dark Wing and the Bright Wing, he performs his Lament, and the world is changed."

"You believe that the situation is now analogous."

"I daresay we have no Lord Qu'u, and I am not the measure of A'alu . . . but yes, I see our predicament as similar. We must consider the notion that this is *esLi*'s will that *esHu'ur* rise to confront us, and that we, like Qu'u, must make the right choosing at the height of the storm.

"If we do not, then we may face destruction so total that nothing might afterward be known of us forever."

"How will we know?"

"If I am right, *se* Ptal, then *esHu'ur* will know us by signs and portents. If I am wrong, then we might well be doomed anyway, because the Lord *esLi* has turned His face from us. The *Lament of the Peak* confronts us, my old friend.

"We must find the Bright Wing, and the world will be changed."

*aHu'sheMe'sen*

# LAMENT OF THE PEAK

PART TWO

## chapter 10

(Begin vidrec 2311-UNS080861-0923.)

WIDEANGLE: view of L'alChan System. Sim of Imperial squadron engaging system defense fleet at periphery.

VOICEOVER: "At its first major engagement at L'alChan, the squadron under the command of Admiral Lord Marais skillfully engages the enemy. The timely arrival of the IS *Sevastopol* catches a zor vessel in a deadly crossfire."

OVERFLY: L'alChan 4, showing destruction of zor Nests. Scenes of extensive destruction.

VOICEOVER: "After the attack of the fleet, no structure was left standing, no alien was left alive on the surface. The agricultural capabilities of the planet have been completely neutralized."

(Excerpted from Imperial Admiralty Press Conference, 22 June 2311.)

CAPT. SEAN MORTON (*Admiralty Spokesman*): . . . . suffered minimal casualties as a result of the attack. The

Admiralty considers this to be a significant plus, Mr. Tsang.

TSANG (*Reuters/Masaak*): Captain Morton, is it true that no surrender was requested from the defenders of L'alChan?

MORTON: No, Mr. Tsang, that is false. The defending fleet was requested to surrender and did not respond. Next question—

TSANG: I beg your pardon, Captain, but a follow-up: there is information to suggest that the zor were only requested to surrender when Admiral Marais' fleet arrived insystem, but that no such request was made when it reached orbit around the habitable planet.

MORTON: The Admiralty has not released any information to that effect, sir. Nonetheless, it begs the question: how many times would you expect a command to request a surrender from an obviously recalcitrant enemy?

TSANG: Captain Morton, the zor at the edge of the system were military personnel; those on planet 4 were civilians. Surely there is a difference—

MORTON: The zor did not trouble themselves with such niceties when they attacked Alya sixty years ago. Next question, please.

A video of the scenes of destruction from L'alChan, Sr'chne'e, R'h'chna'a and other worlds somehow found their way to the administrative headquarters of the fleet at Mothallah. A microcapsule was concealed in a courier's uniform hatband and accompanied him on a routine transport of most secret dispatches to the Admiralty. Once outside the security zone of Marais' authority, the danger inherent in violating the code of silence imposed by the admiral's orders passed, and the courier was able to pass the capsule directly to a prominent member of the Imperial Assembly during a tour of the New Chicago repair facility.

• • •

As the summer waned toward autumn, the first sights of the destruction began to appear on the private viewscreen of the prime minister in Genève. The office itself was stark and nearly bare, with most of her predecessor's furniture and accoutrements moved out and her own effects still not yet arrived. The images that filled the office, practically empty but for the new prime minister, seemed to fit it well.

The comm system, at least, was installed and working. While the images poured themselves out, the prime minister pressed the special red-toned button on her comm. It was answered at once, half a world away.

Sergei turned to see Marc Hudson in the doorway to the *Gagarin's* overfull sickbay, looking warmed-over and old, his uniform rumpled and wrinkled as if he'd slept in it. The fleet-carrier was serving as hospital for the injured and morgue for the dead from the battle for the zor naval base; Sergei had left Chan in command of the *Lancaster* and had set up a command post on the carrier in order to get a clear idea of the strength of the fleet.

"I beg to report . . . mission accomplished, Commodore."

"Marc, for Christ's sake, sit down. I have the report already." He went forward to help the other, but Marc waved him off and walked tiredly to an examination couch, pulled himself onto it, and relaxed back to a full recline.

"God, I'm tired," he said, from the horizontal, his eyes shut and hands folded across his chest. "Flouts the hell out of protocol, Sergei, but I don't want to fall down in front of you. So court-martial me."

"I'll do no such thing." Sergei walked to the couch and pulled up a stool and sat on it. "But stay awake long enough to tell me what happened aboard the station."

"Hard to explain." Hudson did not move or open his eyes.

"We almost lost it. The zor were preparing to destroy it, using a sophisticated destruct mechanism, but one of the *Biscayne's* Marines—a sergeant named Boyd—took it out using his pistol. I don't know how he knew to fire on it, but it was the right thing to do. The marine techs were able to change the course of the station, putting it at conjunction with the planet and out of the line of fire of the zor ships.

"Between my command and the rest of yours, it didn't leave the zor much room to maneuver. In any case, they had no way to destroy their own base."

"And the prisoner?"

"He was one of the dozen or so zor left to defend the station. When the self-destruct exploded he was knocked unconscious; one of the Marine squads picked him up and brought him aboard the *Biscayne*. He should've already been transferred aboard the *Gagarin*—"

"Yes, he has. We have him in an isolation tank in the next room."

Hudson's right eyelid opened a few millimeters, and a blood-shot eye rotated to look at Sergei.

"Next room, huh?"

"Want to have a look?"

Hudson grunted and shut his eye. After a few moments he sat up and opened both eyes. "Yeah, what the hell. Been awake this long, I should be able to hold out another few minutes."

He followed Sergei through a sliding door into the main sick bay. It was half-full; some of the overflow from the fighter-carrier had been sent to the main fleet for emergency treatment. As Sergei passed through the room, a little cheer went up and he gave a somewhat hollow smile.

They went through a door at the far end of the room and into a larger compartment, one wall of which was glasteel from floor to almost eye level. An unconscious zor was within, resting in a null-grav cushion. Sergei supposed it was a *he*, and a quick check of the medical record on the wall confirmed it; the zor rested with both inner and outer eyelids closed, wings folded about him, the proud head inclined slightly backward. Draped across his midsection was a uniform, secured by a narrow crimson sash of fine cloth. At his right hip hung an intricately worked blade.

Looking through the etched glass of the pod, it was hard for Sergei to reconcile all that he had experienced, or had heard about, the terrible brutality of mankind's enemy.

"He's a mean-looking bastard," Marc said, holding his hand over his eyes to shield some of the glare. "Looks like they left him armed."

"They took his pistol away, but the sword . . . well, admiral's orders were to leave it with him. It's called a *chya*—indicates that he's a full warrior."

"Been doing your homework," Marc said, without looking away.

"Know your enemy." Sergei ran a hand through his hair. "An interesting idea, don't you think?"

"What?" Marc pulled his glance from the partition. "What idea is that?"

"Knowing the enemy. We've fought them for sixty years—" He gestured toward the zor. "They've killed us, we've killed them, and now that we're on the verge of exterminating them we're finally beginning to understand them. It doesn't make any sense."

"It made sense when we started. You weren't sure, but I sure as hell was. I probably shouldn't have dismissed your concerns so lightly." Marc walked over to a couch and dropped into it, stretching his arms out to either side. "Permission to go unconscious, sir." He closed his eyes and leaned his head back.

"Granted." Sergei turned his back on Marc and approached the wall. The zor had not awoken or moved: it was as still as a holo, or a wax effigy. Marc Hudson, splayed out on the couch, was reflected in the glasteel surface.

*What will it mean to this zor to wake up here?* Sergei wondered.

The chamber was dimly lit, orange-red to match the luminescence of the zor home world; the walls were covered with holo images of the fine, swirled carvings they had found in every zor nest and aboard their space-stations and (one must assume) starships as well—*hRni'i*. Of course, the technicians that had installed the environment probably just chose the patterns at random from video footage, with no regard to meaning or context. Intended to make the chamber more comfortable for the prisoner, it might amount to writing meaningless gibberish all over the walls.

The only zor warrior in captivity would be alienated enough without the crude mocking of his human jailers.

A flicker of movement reflected in the glass caught his attention, and he focused on the admiral who had just entered the room. He looked over his shoulder and inclined his head, making a gesture toward the gently snoring Marc Hudson on the couch.

"Just checking on the prisoner, sir," Sergei said quietly.

"I understand your curiosity." Marais crossed to the med chart and quickly examined it, then peered through the wall into the chamber. "Very good," he said after a moment of scrutiny. "We have some chance of learning something before he commits suicide."

"I beg your pardon, sir?"

"It may be the only way to obtain information from him, Commodore. Once he has told us what we need to know, I will keep faith with this zor by permitting him to end his own life."

"Such a prisoner is rare, Admiral," Sergei replied. "Certainly we can ill afford to allow such a one to—"

"It is the only way."

"I'm afraid I don't quite understand the admiral."

"It will be my pleasure to explain it to you, then." Marais turned to the wall containing the isolation tank, his back turned to the others. He placed his hands on the wall, in a gesture that in another context might almost have been a caress.

Without turning, he continued. "We do not have techniques sufficient to obtain information from him against his will. He would rather die." He turned now to face Sergei. "In fact, to his fellow zor, he is already dead—worse: he is *idju*, dishonored and outcast, since he did not die when it was meant that he should.

"But, like those who commanded him, he will believe humanity to be agents of a supernatural, mystical force—the Dark Wing." He paused a long moment, as if to gauge Sergei's reaction to his statement.

For his part, Sergei had no intention of betraying any emotion on the subject, and provided what he hoped was an impassive expression.

"And if we are to live up to his estimation of us, we must play our part down to the final detail. For this zor we shall be true. He will provide us with information . . . and then he will die. By his own hand, according to his own custom.

"Do you have any objection?"

Sergei noticed Marc watching carefully as this exchange took place. He had not moved a centimeter since the admiral entered the room, but it was clear that he hadn't been asleep all along.

"No, sir, I have no objection."


The outer door sighed slowly open, and Ted McMasters went through and down the steps to deck level. A row of immaculate dress uniforms were ready to salute him and shake his hand; he thought, half to himself, that they probably had officers in them—but to the Imperial Navy appearances were everything, and the uniforms were far more important than that around which they were wrapped.

"So glad to have you visit, Admiral McMasters," said the most-decorated uniform, which contained Captain Michael Mbele, the base commander. "Welcome to Pluto Base."

"I'd like to tell you I'm glad to be here, Mike." They shook hands and walked across the deck, the crowd of other officers trailing in their wake. "But this isn't the garden spot of Sol System. Still—" They passed through an observation deck which showed the mottled blue orb of Pluto, half-lit, against the bright swirl of the Sagittarius Arm of the Milky Way. "Still, it has a nice view."

"Admiral McMasters," began the younger officer, "I really appreciate your personal visit. We've heard all sorts of rumors, and frankly, we'd like to have them either confirmed or denied." He stopped walking and leaned on the railing, looking out at Pluto.

"Maybe this is something better discussed behind closed doors."

"As the admiral wishes." Mbele led him through a small maze of corridors, and past a vacant receptionist's desk into a spacious office also with a view of Pluto. He drew the curtains slightly, and directed McMasters to an armchair that faced a pair of seemingly comfortable couches. McMasters sat, and the rest of the officers dispersed themselves to positions on the couches.

Mbele turned to McMasters and smiled broadly. "There are no secrets here, not from my officers at least, sir. And Pluto Base is about as 'closed doors' as you can get and still be inside Sol System."

McMasters nodded and said, "Captain Mbele, my official reason for coming is to tour the System's facilities. But unofficially"—he reached into an inner pocket of his uniform jacket—"I'm here to give you this." He handed Mbele a thin packet, closed with the Admiralty electronic seal. Mbele touched his right thumb briefly to the seal and shook the packet open.

The packet contained a folded set of orders and another sealed packet. Mbele opened the folded document and scanned it. A moment later he looked up from reading.

"This is a full-scale alert, sir."

"That's right. It takes effect immediately—as soon as you can make arrangements to implement it."

"May I venture to ask the admiral why—"

"I expect Sol System to be visited by a space fleet."

"Which fleet?"

"I wish I knew, Mike. There is a possibility that some zor fleet escaped Marais' net and is heading here; in that case, we must be fully prepared to prevent even a single ship from reaching the inner system.

"However, there is also the possibility that Marais may return himself." McMasters looked away for a moment at the barren visage of Pluto and added, "He might return here as an enemy, Mike. He's out of communication with the Admiralty, and his fleet has left smoking ruins in its wake. An advanced scout I dispatched several weeks ago was due to reach A'anenu last week and never reported in . . . and now Marais' campaign has taken on a character which is beyond political or military expediency. I'm sure you've already read what Prime Minister Tolliver and Assemblyman Hsien have had to say about it."

"We'd assumed it was pretty much civilian hysteria, Admiral."

"It's not *just* that. It's true that there was a peace overture by the zor a few weeks ago, offering to withdraw from A'anenu if we did the same; but it seems that Admiral Marais ignored an order to stand off A'anenu while the matter was decided."

"Ignored His Imperial Highness, Admiral? That's—"

"Treason."

"Sir," Mbele said, and looked away, as if he were trying to encompass the idea.

"Armed treason is probably a better description. It's certainly not without precedent, as I'm sure you're aware." The Solar Empire itself had come into being when Admiral Willem McDowell, a frontier naval officer around whom dissent had gathered, brought his fleet back to Sol System and held it hostage while loyal troops took power. The War of Accession changed that act from treason to legitimacy, since he had won.

"The long and the short of it is, there's a reasonable probability that the fleet has taken out A'anenu and, without any orders to do so, is proceeding to the zor Home Stars hell-bent on the destruction of a large percentage of the zor race. I confess that such an event wouldn't make me so unhappy, but I'm concerned about what he might do next.

"With the political climate so unsettled, the range of opinion on Marais stretches from potential courtiers to potential assassins. For so much power to be in the hands of one man who is not already sitting on the Imperial throne . . . well, it's dangerous.

"Mike, your responsibility is to the Emperor himself. Any enemy that enters this Solar System is to be repelled, regardless of who commands it. Your standing orders, along with the alert orders I have just given you, are your prime directive. If it's Marais' fleet that enters the Solar volume, open those sealed orders and act on them."

". . . Aye aye, sir," the younger officer replied after a few moments.

In his dream, the long, agonizing disintegration of *Ka'ale'e A'anenu*, the great sky-fortress, was like a pleading scream to *esLi*, offering the deaths of hundreds of *naZora'i* as payment for the terrible destruction of the base. The People were, after all, a fastidious race, and decried the waste of anything that had consumed so much time and effort to build. Waste was shameful . . . except when it came to life. In the holy cause of *esLi*, life was indeed a cheap commodity.

*Ka'ale'e* A'anenu felt the shock of the triggered *saHu'ue* as Rrith's *gyu'u* reached out and caressed it. It tore itself apart along its long spokes, shivering into fragments along the edges, shaking apart the *naZora'i* vessels that were anchored to it like parasites, realizing too late that it was their own death that they were touching. In his mind's eye, Rrith saw the triumph of destruction that would hold the Dark Wing at bay and succor the zor. As he, too, was destroyed by the explosion, he found himself being hurled outward to gentle *fte'e* music, his body enveloped in vermillion light as he transcended the Outer Peace ... falling ... falling ...

Somehow, solidity returned to him. Half in the brightly tinted Sensitive's dream but aware as only a Sensitive can be aware, he felt the sleeping pallet beneath his folded wings and caught stray thoughts from his companions in neighboring berths, intermingled with his own. Concentrating on the Talons of the Inner Peace, he brought himself into a light sleep, just below wakefulness, and thought about his dream.

*Damn*, he thought. *That was a weird one. Wonder if the doc can give me something for it./*

*Got to go on duty in three hours, better get some shuteye./*

*Sarge is always saying a marine can sleep anywhere, anytime, 'cause he doesn't know when he'll get his next chance .../*

Rrith was awake, all at once, shaking his head as if to rattle the unfamiliar alien thoughts from his head. His claw felt down to his hip, where his *chya* still hung. His pistol was missing, which seemed not to surprise him.

Without moving further, he looked around him, surveying the room with his eyes and other senses. From appearances, it seemed as if he was in a Nest: the chamber in which he lay was dimly lit, and the walls were finely traced with *hRni'i*, indicating the rank and standing of the House. From the look of the tracings, he was in a nest on S'rchne'e. There was something subtle in the air, a smell perhaps, or an almost indiscernible sound, that made him suspicious, but the *chya* still at his waist convinced him that his hosts were at least observing the formalities.

He sat up and swung his legs onto the floor, clanging hollowly beneath him. Almost instantly he thought better of it, for a wave of vertigo and nausea swept through him: slowly and painfully he mastered himself, concentrating again on the Talons of the Inner Peace, and his vision gradually cleared. The manic grip with which he held his bed steadily lessened.

He stood and walked across the room. The gravity felt right but the atmosphere was subtly wrong and alien, and a terrible uneasiness crept into his gut. When he reached the wall and tried to touchread the *hRni'i*, the feeling was confirmed with an impact like a physical blow. The *hRni'i* were projections, three-dimensional holos, rather than engravings or embossings. They were untouchable.

*S'rchne'e, of course*—he thought. *S'rchne'e was destroyed by* esHu'ur, *two and three-eighths moons ago. And now he hangs the emblems of his trampled enemies on the wall, just as one of the People would.*

This was not a Nest. Nor was it an antechamber where he would await the judgement of *esLi*, as he also had been prepared to believe. He was not in the next world, but alive, and probably in the captivity of *naZora'i*. When he awoke, he should have realized it: there was no way to have survived the destruction of *Ka'ale'e* A'anenu. Somehow, in some unforeseen way, he had not accomplished its destruction and he had not perished, but had instead survived to become the captive of the enemy.

He had been willing to accept the possibility, as remote as it might be, that somehow he had survived the destruction of the base and had been returned to the People—but if the humans had him, he had almost certainly failed. Now his mind was being invaded by alien thoughts—the worst fear of a Sensitive—and he was *idju*, worse than dead: dishonored with the face of *esLi* turned away from him. It numbed Rrith: it was beyond any possibility of which he had conceived.

It angered him as well: suddenly he drew his *chya*, scabbard and all, and flung it across the room, so that it rattled off the wall and settled on the floor. He could hear it snarling—perhaps at him, perhaps at the treatment he'd just afforded it. It didn't matter—it was not his anymore. Emotion welled up within him as he tried again to touchread the *hRni'i*.

•   •   •

A few hours' sleep did everyone some good. During the time that A'anenu station was being secured, two squadrons from Fifth Fleet had arrived insystem and offered their loyalty to Admiral Marais; they had brought news from outside concerning the fleet and the Empire that Sergei had dutifully sent on to the admiral, who returned to the *Lancaster* and had left word not to be disturbed.

The news was exhilarating and disturbing. The proclamation of Marais' suspension had been circulated throughout the fleet, and the temperature within the Empire had begun to rise in reaction: people were taking up positions on both sides of the issue, either opposed to the destruction that had been wrought in the campaign so far, and calling for the Admiral's head, or firmly behind him and what he was doing.

Somehow—Sergei didn't know how, but was determined to find out—transcripts and vids of some of the campaign had found their way into the hands of the opposition in the Imperial Assembly, and the prime minister had apparently been forced to resign. A terrific row was brewing, with the Imperial Navy at the center.

As for the fleet, the Admiralty's official position branded Marais an outlaw and a traitor. Despite this, many commanders in the fleet supported his actions and were more inclined to be loyal to a successful admiral who did not believe in half-measures, than in a venal civilian Government hundreds of parsecs away. Sergei's position, in his own mind, was already clear; he had made his choice before A'anenu, by refusing to relieve his admiral of command. This Rubicon in his career had long since been crossed, and Sergei knew the penalties that would be enforced on Marais, should he return to the Empire, would be minor compared to those that would await Sergei, unprotected by the perks of flag rank.

It still behooved the admiral to make some decision on the

newcomers; and after bringing himself up-to-date with activities aboard the *Gagarin,* Sergei went back aboard the flagship to inform Marais of the current situation.

It was dark in the admiral's quarters but the emergency lights framed Marais' outline, sitting in the armchair by the viewscreen, his chin resting on his folded hands. Captain Stone sat by the entrance to the sleeping-chamber with a portable 'reader in his lap. The pale light from the 'reader made Stone's face appear more ethereal and skeletal than ever.

Stone looked up as Sergei entered, but said nothing. Marais did not change his position, but Sergei noticed his eyes slowly open and track him as he crossed the room.

"I'd like to bring you up-to-date, sir," Sergei said, standing at ease before the admiral.

Marais continued to look at him, moving nothing but his eyes, flicking from Sergei's face to some detail of his uniform, and then back to his face.

"Please sit down, Commodore."

He sat, facing the admiral. Stone had turned off the 'reader and was now watching the tableau, hands folded in his lap.

"The situation has become more serious, Commodore. I have received this dispatch, routed to S'rchne'e and sent on to me by the garrison commander there." He passed a 'reader to Sergei. It displayed a communiqué, bearing the official Admiralty seal.

Official transmission, Priority 18:        16 August 2311

TO:    R Adm Ld Ivan H Marais, Commanding
       aboard IS *Lancaster*   onstation

FROM:  R Adm T McMasters
       Admiralty HQ Terra

My lord:

It is my solemn duty to inform you that as of the date above listed, by the expressed order of His Imperial Majesty, I am commanded to relieve you of command of all ships and bases, men and equipment currently in your charge. By the terms of General Orders 23, as modified by Naval Regulations 23:XVIV, responsibility for the discharge of your original assignment devolves upon the senior ranking officer, Commodore Sergei Torrijos, until such time as your flag can be transferred to your lawfully designated successor.

You are further commanded, by express order of His Imperial Highness, to repair to the nearest naval base to surrender yourself to a general court-martial, which will elaborate the charges and specifications of which you stand accused. They include: willful violation of Imperial statutes concerning noncombatants and civilians, refusal to accept offered surrender, insubordination, and conducting operations out of direct communications with superiors.

Refusal of this direct order from your emperor constitutes high treason against the Solar Empire, the penalty for which is death.

>*McMasters*<

Sergei looked across at Marais. He remembered the first time he had seen that face, on the back of a book in Ted McMasters' office, months ago. It was still the same noble profile—the proud expression, the outthrust chin, the dark eyes lit with some inner fire—but it had aged and tightened, as if all of the excess flesh had been pared from it.

"Here is your second opportunity to relieve me of command. Although," he added, looking sidewise at Stone, "I don't really expect you to do anything of the sort."

"This is more than insubordination, if the admiral pleases."

Sergei placed the dispatch carefully down on the arm of his chair. "This constitutes an accusation of treason against the emperor."

"It changes nothing."

"That may be, sir, though I believe that the Admiralty is still able to prevent any unpleasant outcome to a court-martial. For us to have taken A'anenu was contrary to the desires of the Government—but for us to proceed from here is contrary to the wish of the emperor."

"Stopping now does not win the war, Commodore. We must carry this out to its conclusion, whether the Government, or Admiral McMasters, or the Admiralty, or the emperor himself, wants it or not."

"We are preparing to commit xenocide."

"If they do not surrender, yes, we are."

With absolute calm and total surety, Marais sat and spoke of the death of an entire race. It had been in the book; it had been in his addresses to the fleet and to his officers—and now it was days away. There would be no miracle to give the zor the victory, and there would be no surrender. The zor would fight to the bitter end and Marais would direct their slaughter: and millennia upon millennia of evolution, and thousands upon thousands of years of civilization, would crumble and collapse and there would be nothing to rise in its place. It was a deed of incredible magnitude.

"Eighteen ships jumped insystem last watch. They already know that you've been relieved of command and have offered to follow you anyway. In short, sir, they've decided that your orders are more important than those of His Imperial Highness."

"How widespread is the knowledge of my recall?"

"Rumors are afloat, my lord, but the new arrivals have been kept at anchor near the jump point, pending your orders."

"The fleet will have to know. I cannot keep this matter from them, especially with what lies ahead of us."

Sergei stole a glance at Stone, who was perversely smiling as if he were enjoying the situation.

"What's on your mind, Commodore?"

"Sir?"

"You clearly didn't expect things to reach this stage. On the other hand, I have seen this coming at least since S'rchne'e. Something is troubling you, Torrijos. Out with it."

"Admiral, our . . . capacity for destruction has been well demonstrated on the zor. Within a few weeks or months we can clear away any other settlements on this side of the Rift. The enemy will be just as tenacious regardless of cosmology.

"Even if you are able to do that, sir—and with all due respect, I don't see anyone capable or even interested in stopping you—I think you might find that others in the fleet and elsewhere might have another agenda in mind other than extermination.

"The newly arrived captains have gone out on a limb with their actions. They've mutinied against their commanding officers to join you. There is only one logical outcome that doesn't put them, and their crews, in prison or out an airlock: they want to make you emperor."

Marais smiled at this comment; it seemed to catch Stone slightly off guard, as he sat forward, listening intently.

"Emperor." Marais stood and walked slowly toward the autokitchen. He asked for a fruit drink, which emerged in silence; he took it, sipped from it, and set it on a counter nearby.

"Yes, sir."

"Well." Marais leaned against the counter. "That's how we got an emperor in the first place. It isn't what I had in mind, and it isn't what I'm planning to do. I still consider myself bound by my oath and my orders, but I can see why they might think the way they do."

"They have no choice but to believe it, my lord. Most of the officers and crew of those vessels are commoners, and will face death if they return to the Empire without a . . . friendly party sitting on the throne."

"Are you suggesting that I now bear moral responsibility for their actions?" Marais stalked angrily back to the armchair and sat down, leaning forward to bore his glance deeply into Sergei.

"Are you saying that because of the precipitous actions of some ship's captains, I must now seek the Imperial Crown?"

"I do not suggest anything of the sort, Admiral. You will do as you must. I have pledged to follow your orders, because I believe that the defeat of the zor—as we have defined it—is the most important task facing this command. But I can't return to the Empire, as I'm complicit in your defiance of direct orders from the Admiralty and from the emperor. We may have the philosophical high ground but our legal footing is unsure."

"General Orders 6—"

"Please, my lord." Sergei held up his hand. "You don't have to preach to the converted. I am behind you, sir, but I am not convinced that my support will be of any consequence. As you pointed out to me some weeks ago, I had an opportunity to follow orders from home and relieve you of command and I did not. If you are guilty, so am I. The rest of the fleet is off the hook, sir, but you and I would dangle from the yardarm if a court-martial chose to reject your arguments. They're unlikely to view you in a favorable light.

"As for the officers and crew who have chosen to support you, in defiance of orders to the contrary they will either be traitors or heroes depending on who sits on the Imperial throne."

"That was never my intention," Marais repeated, almost to himself. He turned his chair to face Stone, who had watched the whole scene impassively, never saying a word. Sergei had almost forgotten the adjutant's presence—almost, but not quite.

"This is all moot, until the war is over," Stone said quietly.

"I beg to disagree," Sergei replied. "This is pertinent *right now*, since the admiral must decide where his responsibilities—and loyalties—truly lie. I would guess that the majority of the fleet is ready to follow him wherever he leads, but they must know the truth."

Stone set his 'reader carefully aside.

"Commodore Torrijos is most eloquent in his comments, my

lord. But his naive appeals to populism have no place in the Imperial Navy. I cannot easily comprehend why he has not shed
them before assuming flag rank. The opinions of a few malcon-
tents . . ." He paused, turning his gaze to Sergei. ". . . do not alter
the basic fact that the fleet is totally behind you. It is not necessary to *consult*"—he sneered the word out—"with anyone other
than senior staff."

Sergei matched Stone look for look, trying to harness his
anger in some productive way. *This son of a bitch threatened to
put me out an airlock,* he reminded himself.

"Let me consider this in private. Commodore, I will speak
with you later; Stone, you're dismissed for the time being." He
took up his 'reader, and returned the two junior officers' salutes
with a nod.

In the corridor, Sergei turned his back immediately on the
adjutant, but stopped when his name was called.

"I'll thank you to address me properly," he answered angrily,
turning to face the adjutant, who was still standing outside the
admiral's door.

"I beg your pardon, *Commodore* Torrijos," Stone replied
with exaggerated irony. "And while we're being so courteous
and polite, allow me to warn you to watch your step. Sir."

"That's the second time you've threatened me, Stone. Maybe
you'd like to spend some time in irons?"

Stone emitted a laugh that was somewhere between a cackle
and a cough. "My, my, a populist with a sense of humor. You
seem to forget with whom you're speaking. Just keep this in
mind." His face dropped all pretense of smile. "You're in over
your head, *Commodore.* Admiral Marais knows exactly what
he's doing, and his methods, means and agenda are nothing for
you to question.

"You're just here to follow orders, and to give advice on military matters. That's the only thing you should be considering. I
don't have to threaten you—what would be the point? Just keep

this warning in mind: anyone who tries to stand in the way of the Admiral's mission will wish he'd never been born."

Without another word, Stone turned on his heel and walked in the other direction, leaving Sergei standing in the corridor, hands clenched, groping in vain for a reply.

## chapter 11

"The first guy I look for," Marc Hudson said, tasting his soup carefully, "is a top-notch fire-control officer. The second guy I try to find is a good cook."

He smiled. "Damn, that's good."

Murmurs of approval and agreement circulated around the dining-table. The *Biscayne*'s private dining-room was near the captain's quarters, not far from the wardroom; it was big enough to accommodate eight diners comfortably. This evening it held only five: Marc Hudson, host for the evening; Alyne Bell of the *Gagarin;* Bert Halvorsen of the *Mycenae;* Tina Li of the *Sevastopol;* and Sergei himself.

The food had been served, and Hudson had dismissed the orderlies and voice-locked and secured the room at Sergei's order. Within certain limits, they enjoyed about as much privacy as could be found aboard an Imperial ship.

Sergei sat back in his comfortable armchair. "I'd like to thank you for having us aboard, Marc. As most of you can guess, you're here at my request; rather than let you remain on edge throughout an excellent meal, I'm going to cut directly to the chase.

"First, a few formalities. I'd prefer that we dispense with titles and the word 'sir' during the balance of our conversation, in favor of first names. I would like to think that I'm consulting with a few close friends rather than conducting a staff meeting.

"In a similar vein, you can assume that you all have wardroom privilege to say whatever the hell is on your minds."

He picked up his soup spoon and poked it absently into the gently steaming soup in front of him. "There's something very serious that I have to discuss with you, and I'm taking you into my confidence because I badly need advice.

"First. The attack on A'anenu was carried out despite a cease-and-desist order from the Admiralty.

"Apparently the zor made a peace gesture, and the government ordered the fleet to stand off S'rchne'e and await a civilian plenipotentiary. The admiral ignored this dispatch, basing his action on General Orders 6—he claimed that there was no authority save himself in the war area."

"I beg your pardon, Comm—Sergei," Alyne Bell interrupted, smiling at the use of his first name. "We're here because the zor *broke* a treaty. They've made peace offers before and we've accepted them before. Or, I should say, the civilian Government accepted them. This had to be a ploy."

"I agree. But there's more to it than that: the admiral said that it was critically important for us to ignore it because it sent an important signal to the zor High Nest."

"'The Dark Wing,'" Bert Halvorsen said. When the other officers looked puzzled, Bert arranged himself in a more comfortable position, and gave an inquiring glance to Sergei, who nodded. "Before A'anenu, Marais ordered a staff report to be prepared, outlining what we thought the zor would do next. We looked at past performance, and concluded that they'd want to make it as difficult as possible for us by digging in all over the place. Then we'd have to send the Marines in over and over to root them out.

"I have to take credit for this lamebrained idea, as Sergei well knows, but Admiral Marais tried to string up that poor kid Uwe Bryant because of it. He asked for us to give him a live presentation, and Uwe got partway through—and then Marais essentially told us we had the whole thing ass-backwards. He told us that the zor would pretty much abandon every place other than A'anenu and concentrate their force there."

"He was right," Tina Li said, buttering a slice of bread.

"He was *almost* right. He said that A'anenu was crucial to their strategy and that they'd fight like hell to keep it. Instead it was intended to be an expensive trap. Ask Marc."

"They tried to destroy it, and take most of our Marines and four or five ships along with it," Marc said, nodding. "Came too goddamn close for comfort, too."

"That's crazy," Tina said, scowling. "Without A'anenu, they didn't—don't—have a prayer of carrying on the war on this side of the Rift."

"But they'd made a *peace offer*," Sergei answered after a moment. "The sense of the offer was essentially that they'd suspend hostilities and withdraw from some worlds if we left A'anenu alone. Of course, they'd pull most of their firepower out of there—"

"What government in its right mind would accept a stupid offer like that?" she asked, leaning back in her chair.

"Easy answer?" Marc asked Tina. He looked at Sergei also, as if trying to get approval. "How about a government that thought that it had lost control of the war? Remember that the destruction of worlds like L'alChan and R'h'chna'a and the others was brutal to us, but no more so than some of the attacks the zor have made. But back home, they're calling them 'atrocities.'"

"Civilian hysteria," Alyne Bell interjected. "The Government can disavow knowledge of the specifics; we win, Admiral

Marais gets a parade, everyone waves a flag. In six months the hysteria's all gone."

"You really think it's that simple."

Marc smiled, raising one eyebrow.

"Another glass of wine?" He poured into Alyne's goblet. "Well, it isn't.

"You see, there's the problem of pacifist opposition—academics, xenologists, even politicians on the make. The Commonwealth Party has been waiting *decades* for something to hang around the neck of the Dominion Party, and don't think they wouldn't—even if every flag-waving patriotic Imperial subject has a relative who was killed by the zor. Most of them do, by the way. We're not that accountable, but what we do and the way we do it impacts what's going on back home.

"The longer the war continues, the more violent the footage from the war zone, the worse it becomes for the Government. After Pergamum, everyone was on our side. After a few months, they'd like it all to be over. Of course it isn't, and it can't be yet." He poured himself another glass of wine, and settled back in his chair, done with his discourse.

"We're a bit off the subject," Bert said. "The most important fact about the admiral's decision to make A'anenu the next target of the fleet was the *reason* he'd reached that conclusion.

"Essentially, he'd thrown all of our logistical analysis out the airlock because of a dispatch sent from Qu'useyAn. A zor commander had used a mythological allegory to describe the Imperial fleet. By this argument, somehow we'd gone from being totally outside their culture and religion to being the agents of destruction—something called 'the Dark Wing.' We—especially the admiral—had suddenly jumped in stature." Halvorsen toyed with his wineglass. "*That's* why we attacked A'anenu."

Marc rubbed his chin. "That is the stupidest goddamn thing I have ever heard."

He looked up in the air, and then around at his fellow officers and smiled. "I sure hope wardroom privilege is in effect."

"It is," Sergei said, smiling as well. "What's more, I'm happy to confirm the following: Bert is right, and, to some extent, so is Marc.

"And so was Marais. This campaign has actually done what Bert said it has: Marais has become a mythical figure in the minds of the zor. They believe him to be the Dark Wing."

"That's the second-stupidest goddamn thing I've ever heard," Marc replied after a moment.

"But it's true, and Marais believes it. This is crucial, because of what happened while we were attacking A'anenu.

"The Admiralty has relieved Marais of command."

Spoons dropped into bowls. Chairs creaked. No one replied to this comment, but Sergei knew that the other four officers were listening carefully.

"I've seen the dispatch. It's circulated through the fleet, though obviously not here at A'anenu yet. But the ships that just arrived insystem have word of Marais' removal; that's why they're here."

"To arrest him?" Bert asked.

"To *follow* him," Sergei replied. "They're here in direct violation of orders. As am I: Marais had showed me the dispatch ordering him to heave to, and told me that I was the only person who could stop the attack on A'anenu—by relieving him of command then and there. He hasn't made a decision on when or how he's going to tell the rest of the fleet what we already know.

"As of now, Marais has crossed the line from insubordination to treason. Incidentally, by telling you this, so have I.

"For the first time in sixty years, we've achieved real success against the zor. We have them on the ropes and our presence has *cultural* significance . . . and we have the choice of either letting it all go or being branded as traitors to the Solar Empire."

"Why are you telling us all this?" Tina Li asked after several seconds of quiet. "Are we supposed to make this decision for you?"

"No, not for me. I've already decided." He wiped his mouth

with a napkin and folded it, setting it carefully and slowly on the table. "Marais has maintained all along that to go back on his policy, even if ordered to do so, would violate his primary responsibility—the safety of the Solar Empire, particularly the security of the New Territories and the other areas near the zor. We intend to do what he was originally ordered to do, by the emperor himself. The admiral cannot allow orders to the contrary to influence him if he wants to accomplish his goals.

"I believe in him, and have committed myself to follow this through to the end."

"The emperor's orders—including General Orders 6—were never meant to condone xenocide," Marc pointed out. "They were for a time when a commander in the field couldn't be asking what to do every week."

"I agree. Philosophically, the admiral's interpretation of General Orders 6 is wide of its intent. He would argue that the letter of the law applies, and it is not the place of the Admiralty or anyone else to interpret the intent. This is still a war zone, and certain regulations govern his powers out here."

"Such as summary executions," Marc Hudson said quietly. Sergei looked up sharply, wondering what the comment meant; Hudson didn't elaborate.

"In any case, Tina, I have decided that I can accept Marais' treatment of regulations, and cannot in good conscience follow orders that relieve him of command. If he truly has become 'the Dark Wing' to the zor, his removal would also endanger the fleet out here. It may well be judged as mutinous back home, but there you are.

"No, I don't want to have you make a decision for me; I want you to decide for yourselves."

"What happens if we decide that Marais is crazy, or that you're crazy?" Bert Halvorsen asked.

"I assume that you'll be sent somewhere to sit it out. But you won't be a traitor by the Admiralty's lights; refusal to follow mutineers' orders makes you a loyal officer."

"Not to the mutineers," Marc observed. "And when some of them want to put you out into vacuum, you wonder whether you have any options at all."

As the officers left to return to their own commands, Marc touched Sergei's elbow, indicating that he should wait a moment. When the other three had gone and Marc had checked the voice-lock on the room and changed the access code, he said, "I owe you an apology."

"For what?"

"For not having taken your concerns seriously, months ago. This isn't what we thought it was."

"It doesn't matter. Nobody could have known this is what he had in mind." Sergei picked up a wineglass, held it up to the light in the room, set it down again on the table.

"But is it what *he* had in mind? I mean, we talked about Marais: who he is and where he came from. He's a scholarly type, and obviously intelligent. I can see him writing the damn book. But this campaign has been carried out with a depth and scope that are totally out of proportion to what he wrote.

"*And* he happened to become admiral. *And* it happens that the zor, bless their alien little hearts, have started to believe that he's the Dark Wing, the angel of death."

"What's your point?"

"Something very strange is going on. With your news, it's starting to fall into place: Marais, a staff-officer nobody, has the whole fleet in a moral quandary—give up on the war we've all come to believe in, or do what's necessary and then make him emperor."

"He doesn't want it," Sergei said.

"He may not, but he's starting to run out of choices. And anybody who might be showing cold feet is threatened with . . . how shall I put this? . . . a chance to breathe without air."

"You've been threatened?"

"Not yet. But Uwe Bryant was, after the story got around that he sent the flyover logs from R'h'chna'a to some friends of his late grandfather in the Imperial Assembly. I don't think that boy is ever going to see home again."

"Who issued this threat?"

"Come on, Sergei, don't screw around. You know damn well who issued the threat. The same person who wouldn't mind seeing you meet an accident. The same guy who's been trying to infiltrate the *Biscayne*'s personal logs, and probably the onboards in the rest of the fleet.

"Watch your back. That's my best advice to you, Commodore—I'd rather trust a zor than expect *him* to play by any sort of rules."

Sergei still had a report to complete, and before leaving the *Biscayne*, he had one more avenue to pursue. He didn't know whether it was caution, or paranoia borrowed from Marc Hudson, but he decided that he needed a secure place to conduct an interview.

Hudson had apparently considered this possibility, and had prepared his study for Sergei's use. He gave the commodore the key to the voice-lock and left him.

Once alone, Sergei called up his half-written report in his 'reader and began to review it. It was a thorough treatment of the course of the battle, gleaned from his personal logs and the reports of his subordinates—but there was something essential missing. He couldn't pin it down, but he knew one person who could provide some insight.

You asked to see me, sir."

He was in duty uniform rather than dress whites, but Sergei concluded that the tall Marine had decided that it was more important to respond quickly than formally. That seemed to reassure Sergei; he nodded, and beckoned to an armchair opposite his own.

"Thank you for coming so promptly, Boyd. I realize that you've been shoved around a lot during the last few watches, but I need to ask you a few questions."

"I'm glad to help, sir," Boyd answered. He walked stiffly to the armchair and sat down, placing his uniform cap in his lap. He sat up straight, though Sergei noticed that his shoulders seemed a trifle hunched.

"Perhaps," Sergei began, when he had settled himself, "you can clarify for me just what happened aboard the base."

"Sir . . ." Boyd looked at him, a bit nervously. "I'm sure, sir, that my superiors have detailed reports—Major Pérez, perhaps—"

"I've reviewed his comments. I understand that your actions were critical to the taking of the command bridge; I'd like you to describe your experiences to me in your own words."

"My squad was one of several that penetrated the base, sir. We managed to find our way to an access chamber above the command bridge, and I destroyed the, uh, self-destruct mechanism by firing at it. I must have lost consciousness at some point, because the next thing I knew I was in the *Gagarin*'s sick bay. Sir."

"Is that all?"

"'All,' sir?"

"Is that all that happened aboard the base, Sergeant? You *managed* to find a chamber above the bridge, and you were *lucky* enough to fire at the self-destruct mechanism?

"How did you come to fire at it? Surely the chamber was full of such things."

"I knew, sir." The tall marine flexed his shoulders a bit, and looked at the floor. "I just knew."

"What do you mean?"

"I saw it."

"Where?"

"In the mind of a zor, sir."

Sergei gave Boyd a long glance, but his face betrayed nothing. "You'll have to clarify that point for me, Sergeant. Perhaps you should describe what happened aboard the orbital base. Every detail."

It was clear that Boyd had some information to convey but no one had asked him about it. It was also clear that he had a reason to hide it, and Sergei suspected why.

Boyd took a deep breath. "Let me describe what the taking of the station—*Ka'ale'e* A'anenu—was like." Boyd's casual use of the zor word caused Sergei to lift an eyebrow, but the Marine hurried on.

"It was largely deserted, sir. The zor had set up automatic defenses—mostly booby traps. All of the airlocks were set up that way, and we lost a few people from every squad finding that out.

"Our course was set up from an overall plan developed by General Harbison of the *Gagarin,* as you know, sir. We had a map-comp to help guide us from the outside in but it was slow going, with all kinds of perches and passageways. There wasn't much to distinguish a chamber from a corridor . . . which is how we found the shrine."

"What kind of shrine?"

"It was like a 3-V stage, sir. There was a holo projection of a desert scene, accurate down to the orange sun. It was a scene from a place on Zor'a, near—" He stopped, as if he wasn't sure whether he knew what he was about to say, or whether he believed it. "Near the capital city. The most important part of the shrine, though, was the *esLiHeShuSa'a.*"

"I'll leave aside how you know that word. What is an *es-LiHe*—" Sergei smiled inadvertently. "I don't think I'll try to pronounce it."

"An *esLiHeShuSa'a* is a disk, sir, used for worship or meditation. The one we encountered was big enough for a couple of zor to perch in upright. It was about a half-meter thick and hung

in a nullgrav field about a meter off the deck. It was covered with
*hRni'i*—"

"I'm familiar with them. Go on."

"I'm still not sure why, but I climbed up inside this thing and
something began to happen. I felt myself in contact with—" He
looked away, as if he were trying to duplicate the sensation by
bringing back a memory.

His shoulders straightened out and pulled back slightly, then
returned to their normal position. "A being. Maybe a group of
beings, intoning the name of *esLi.* Then something came rushing
into my mind and I believed that I was a zor. I think. I was
knocked unconscious somehow, and my squad destroyed the *es-
LiHeShuSa'a.* After some really strange dreams I woke up and
was back to normal. No, not quite." He straightened up, more
marinelike all of a sudden. "I could read the *hRni'i* on the walls.
I knew what the *esLiHeShuSa'a* was, and what it was used for.

"By the time we reached the command bridge, I was able to—
sense—what was happening. The Sensitives on the bridge were
attempting to complete the ritual of *saHu'ue,* self-destruction.
The *esL'en'YaAr* was like the *esLiHeShuSa'a,* though it was
much smaller; I recognized it, perceived one of them reaching
out for it with his *gyu'u*—"

"'*Gyu'u*'?"

"Er . . . '*talon of the mind*' is the best translation I can manage, sir. I saw him reach out and mentally activate the self-
destruct mechanism, and I fired on it. He . . . felt it, he was still
closely linked to it, and so was I. I was able to destroy it, even
though I could hear his mental screams as I did so." Boyd closed
his eyes and hunched his shoulders slightly, one slightly higher
than the other.

"You heard his *mental* screams?"

Boyd opened his eyes again. "I can still hear them, sir. I wish
that I could describe it better, sir."

Sergei picked up a stylus and jotted a note on his 'reader.
"Sergeant, I consulted your service record. It appears that you

scored very poorly on standard Sensitive tests, and that you show only average affinity for languages. How do you reconcile this with what you've described to me? Based on your experiences, you'd be the most skilled human Sensitive alive. I'm skeptical. Call me a narrow-minded old salt, but I'm *damn* skeptical."

"You have a right to be skeptical, sir. My lance corporal was, and I had to convince him I was okay after stepping inside an alien artifact and then running across a deck flapping my arms and screaming in the Highspeech. He thought I'd left my brain in the airlock.

"But now I can *understand* the Highspeech, Commodore. I can speak it a little bit. I can read the *hRni'i*. I am not the same person I was."

Sergei touched the 'reader with his stylus, and displayed a file in the complex zor script. He took the 'reader and turned it around, placing it in front of Boyd.

"What do you make of that?"

Boyd took the 'reader in his hand and looked at it. His posture changed as he studied it: his face clouded and his shoulders drooped. After a moment, he looked up at Sergei.

"This is a zor communication, sir, but it reads more like poetry. I'm not able to tell you its source, but it has to do with a confrontation between a mighty hero—Qu'u is the name given here—and some sort of evil. No, not evil: darkness. Destruction. A force of some kind. The word is *esHu'ur,* which means—" He seemed to be reaching for an equivalent, but could not find it.

"'The Dark Wing,'" Sergei interrupted. He took the 'reader back, and cleared the file away. "All right, I believe I'm ready to accept your story at face value. Who else knows of this . . . experience of yours?"

"My squad, sir. But as far as I know, they didn't pass it on, and I decided that it was best to leave the details out of my report to Lieutenant Hong."

"Why?" Sergei already knew the answer.

"They'd reserve a room for me at the happy camp, sir. Posttraumatic stress disorder. Battle fatigue. Not good for a career, Commodore."

"Sergeant, you realize that I could have your ass in a sling for not reporting this incident before."

"From your questions, sir," Boyd answered, sitting forward with his arms loosely at his side, "I thought you had already decided that something was missing. From what I'd heard about you, there wouldn't be any point in keeping the whole story from you. I just figured you wouldn't believe it."

"Oh, I believe it, all right." Sergei picked up a piece of pink crystal Marc evidently used as a paperweight, and began to play with it idly. "There's no way you could have seen that communiqué, especially in untranslated form. There are less than a dozen people in the fleet who could read it cold like you just did, the admiral included, you excluded—except now I know better.

"For sixty years the zor have been completely alien to us. A few zor—diplomats and scholars—have moved in the human world, and even fewer humans—our own Admiral Marais among them—have delved into the zor world.

"Now you're talking about a fundamentally different sort of understanding. You claim to have somehow crossed the line, by some means, to the point that you shared . . . what? Thoughts? Feelings? Now you can read the zor script, and you understand the zor language. You haven't changed physically, but you might have some kind of . . . metaphysical difference.

"That leads me to an important question, Boyd: are you truly human anymore?"

"Sir?" He stood up straight again in the chair. "I'm afraid I don't understand the question."

"It's very simple. Are you *human*? Do you consider yourself to be human?"

Boyd didn't answer, but looked away, focusing his attention on a wall graphic of the New Territories. The current location of the *Biscayne* at A'anenu, beyond the Imperial border, showed as a tiny blue light winking regularly in the deep darkness.

"How long have you been a Marine, Boyd?"

"Seven years, sir." He turned his face again to Sergei, his jaw set.

"How long on active duty?"

"I was posted to the *Cambridge* five years ago, sir, and obtained a position in the *Biscayne* ship's-troops almost three years ago."

"What do you think of the zor?"

"The zor, sir? I—" The rapid-fire questioning had apparently caught Boyd by surprise. He paused and looked at his hands, as if the answer might lie there. "I consider them the enemy, sir."

"You're absolutely sure of that."

"Yes, sir. I'm sure."

"Good." Sergei folded his hands in front of him. "I want to make sure that, completely human or not, you are clear on the position you *must* hold with respect to the enemy. Your expertise is about to become very important and I need to know that your loyalty is not incorrectly placed."

"I understand, sir."

Sergei stood, and Boyd did so a fraction of a second later. "Come with me, Sergeant. There is someone that you should meet."

Rrith alternately slept and exercised, not sure what awaited him. He was not even sure that he cared. Sleep helped him to heal from his wounds and removed much of his dizziness; exercise made him hungry enough to eat the poor substitute for proper food that appeared in his cell from time to time.

"Cell" was the right term for his current location; even if he had any right to be elsewhere after his humiliating failure, it was clear upon examination that there was no way out of the chamber in which he had been placed. So there he was, incarcerated like a caged *artha*, except that his dishonored *chya* lay in the corner softly snarling to itself.

*At least the light is not too bright,* he thought to himself, re-membering the blue-white illumination that the *esGa'uYal* pre-ferred.

As time passed, the light in his cell did not vary, and there was no way for him to measure it except by guessing and count-ing sleep-periods. When his first visitor arrived, he knew no more than that it took place during his third waking.

He had just begun to smooth out his wings from sleep when the door to his cell opened and a human of some sort entered—alone—and the door was quickly shut again.

A fury welled up from deep within him, an anger derived from years of practice and reinforcement: part of his mind was computing how quickly he could reach his *chya,* and how likely it was he could kill the servant of *esGa'u* before someone cut him down; but some lassitude held him back. Instead he simply stood straight, arranging his wings in the Posture of Cautious Ap-proach and folding his arms across his chest.

"I am Rrith of Nest Tl'l'u," he said in the Highspeech, though he knew it was no longer his right to use it.

"*esLiHeYar,*" the human replied clearly, though haltingly. "I am aware of who you are, *se* Rrith," he added, in a language that Rrith did not recognize—but, to his surprise, was able to under-stand.

"You speak the Highspeech?" Rrith asked, half appalled and half intrigued.

"Yes. Just as you can speak and understand my own tongue," the human replied. It was true: whatever barbarous form the hu-man's language took, Rrith found that he was able to understand it. It was clearly a Sensitive phenomenon, but not one of which he was aware.

"What is your Nest and lineage, then?"

"Christopher Boyd," the human answered. "Master ser-geant, Imperial Marines. I'm from Emmaus, Epsilon Eridani 3. I interrupted your ceremony of *saHu'ue* aboard *Ka'ale'e* A'anenu by destroying—"

"I recall," Rrith interrupted, turning half away to look at the wall, absently tracing the *hRni'i* with his eyes. "You are some sort of expert on my people, I suppose."

"No. Not hardly. I mean, not until recently. Something happened aboard *Ka'ale'e A'anenu, se* Rrith, something I don't completely understand. I hoped that you might be able to help me with it."

Rrith arranged his wings in the Arrangement of Contained Anger and turned again to face the human. "Why should I wish to help you with anything, unclean Servant of the Cast Out?"

The epithet took Chris Boyd aback for a moment. He knew that Commodore Torrijos was watching, and listening, to the exchange taking place here: had he really expected acceptance from the zor prisoner, especially one who come so close to the destruction of a half-dozen Imperial starships and thousands of marines?

"I am no follower of *esGa'u*," he answered after a moment. "Surely you would already know that." He glanced at the sword which lay incongruously on the floor in the corner of the chamber.

"My *chya*, and what information it might provide, is certainly no concern of yours," Rrith answered, his wings rising into another position. To Boyd's surprise, he perceived that the posture conveyed a hint of curiosity that almost contradicted the obvious hostility of his answer.

*I wonder if the commodore saw that,* Boyd asked himself.

"I must disagree with you, *se* Rrith. We fly together." The metaphor came unbidden into his mind, and he had spoken it.

"Fly together? Pah. How could this be? You have no wings, nor do you bear a *chya*. You are not a zor warrior, and you will never be what I once was. You are, if not *esGa'uYe, esHara'e,* reason enough for me to despise you."

Rrith turned completely away from the human, his wings arranged in the Cloak of Defense, his muscles tensed, listening carefully for an approaching attack. But none came. If the roles had been reversed, Rrith supposed that he would have sprung on anyone who dared to insult him thus.

He did not know what conclusion to draw.

"I have told you that I do not serve the Lord of Despite," the human said at last. "I am a follower of—*esHu'ur.*"

Rrith whirled so quickly that the human stepped back. "You presume much," he said angrily, but he held his wings in the Stance of Reverence for *esHu'ur.* The human held his ground, as if he recognized what the gesture meant.

"I speak only what is true. I will speak it in the presence of *esLi,* if you wish, since it is He who gave me the ability to communicate with you. I can only assume that it was done for some purpose."

"This oath cannot be taken lightly."

"I am aware of that, *se* Rrith. Though you have never accepted it, oaths are a solemn matter among many of my race as well. In my branch of service, our motto is: 'Forever Faithful.' I have never violated that oath, and I would not violate this one."

Part of Boyd's mind wrestled with the uncertainty of what an oath before *esLi* might mean; another part held reverence for the abstract idea of *esLi,* which had touched his mind as he perched in the *esLiHeShuSa'a.* As the zor pondered, Chris decided that if he believed it to be true, it probably couldn't harm him.

"*esHu'ur* is a mighty force," Rrith replied at last. "If it has truly manifested itself, why would it not come in the form of one of the People?

"Answer me that, wingless one."

"I am not studied in your culture, *se* Rrith, but from what I've learned, no one knows what *esHu'ur* actually *is.*

"How would *you* know? If someone claiming to be the Dark Wing were to step through that door at this moment"— he gestured behind him—"could you really say?"

"You insult me with blasphemy," Rrith answered angrily, his voice rising. "I will speak no more of this. I cannot order you to depart, nor coerce you, but I desire no further conversation with you." His wings rose to encircle him, in a posture that seemed to convey another meaning altogether: one of fear, and expectation.

Boyd couldn't be sure whether to believe the zor's words or his stance. After a moment, and without a further word, he walked to the door and knocked; it was opened by the guard, and Boyd left without looking back.


I'm returning to the flagship now," Sergei said as they walked along. "Successful or not, you're our best chance of communicating with the prisoner. I'll cut orders to transfer you to the *Lancaster;* I realize that upheaval in your routine is the last thing you need right now, but I want you aboard and accessible. The admiral will likely have questions for you as well."

"Aye-aye, sir." They reached the lift and entered, a pair of midshipmen giving way and saluting as they passed.

"Hangar Deck C," Sergei said, and the lift began to drop. "The zor seemed to be quite hostile to you, Sergeant, though he did seem to wish to carry on a conversation. At least until the end."

"Yes, sir, that's true, but . . . somehow, I'm not completely sure he meant exactly what he said."

"Explain."

"There were times during the conversation that he said one thing and implied another. For instance, when I told him that I served the Dark Wing he seemed insulted, but he obviously conceded that I might be telling the truth. And when he dismissed me at the end, there was some sense that he expected me to do or say something to show that I truly did serve *esHu'ur.*"

"Stop ascent," Sergei said, and the lift shuddered to a halt. "You *sensed* this?"

"Sir?"

"You're suggesting that the zor said one thing but implied another. How? How was this hidden meaning conveyed? How did you know?"

Boyd looked at Sergei for a long moment. "I read it in the way he held his wings, sir."

"Wings?" Sergei studied the young Marine's face. "His wing positions conveyed information?"

"Yes, sir."

Sergei ruminated for a moment. "Wings. They communicate with their wings. Gestural language. Every time they've met with humans, every treaty negotiation, they've been talking with their voices and their wings, I'd bet. They can't read our facial expressions, and we can't read their wings. If this is true . . ." He looked at the ceiling of the lift. "Deck twenty-three," he said, and the lift began to ascend again. "We're going to speak with this zor again, Sergeant. And this time, I have a few questions I'd like you to ask."

## chapter 12

(From the Record of the Imperial Assembly, August 16, 2311.)

SPEAKER: The Chair recognizes Mr. Hsien.

MEMBER HSIEN: Mr. Speaker, I ask unanimous consent for the presentation of a motion to make a presentation. *(note documentary attachment 2311-A231918-17.)*

SPEAKER: Without objection, it is—

PRIME MINISTER: Will the Member yield for a question?

SPEAKER: Will the gentleman yield?

MEMBER HSIEN: Certainly.

PRIME MINISTER: I thank Mr. Hsien for his courtesy. Mr. Speaker, if the Assembly would examine the documentary attachment that the Member has graciously provided for our perusal, they will find that there is little substance that would deviate from the Member's publicly stated position regarding the war and its conduct. I would ask the Member, Mr. Speaker, what he hopes to accomplish by making a further presentation before the Imperial Assembly?

MEMBER HSIEN: Mr. Speaker, I would ask if the prime minister has completed her question so that I may answer.

PRIME MINISTER: Mr. Speaker, I thought that my question was clearly stated.

MEMBER HSIEN: Very well, Mr. Speaker. I have asked to make a presentation before the Assembly because of information that has recently come to my attention. This information has become widely known: that our commander in the field has committed a series of atrocities in the name of the Solar Empire that besmirch—

(SEVERAL MEMBERS): Mr. Speaker! Will the gentleman yield? Hear hear! Let him speak! (*etc.*)

*(Gavel from the Chair.)*

SPEAKER: Order in the Assembly. Will the gentleman yield?

MEMBER HSIEN: I will not yield, Mr. Speaker, I'm sorry.

*(gavel from the Chair; continued requests for recognition.)*

SPEAKER: Members will be in order. Member Hsien has the floor, but he is admonished to restrict his remarks at this time to the procedural matter, which is to say, to answer Prime Minister Tolliver's question.

MEMBER HSIEN: I apologize for any disturbance I might have caused, Mr. Speaker. The prime minister asks why I wish to address the Assembly further on this matter. My response is that I have more to say at this time. I believe that the Assembly's time would be well spent in hearing my comments; and most importantly, my party has paid the necessary fee to accompany the application. It is not the custom—

*(Further interruptions and gavel from the Chair.)*

MEMBER HSIEN: It is not the custom of the Assembly to refuse an application to speak when the time has been properly purchased. Regardless of the Government's fear of the truth, it will come out. Mr. Speaker, I move the question.

Members of the Government of His Imperial Majesty Alexander Philip Juliano were well aware of what was to happen in the Assembly this afternoon, but were powerless to prevent it. The news of the fleet's course that had reached opposition leader Tomás Hsien had been spread to the public. Suspicion and speculation had given way to rhetoric and invective, and now there was nothing to do but to stand up and be buffeted by it.

It was a bright early autumn day in Genève. The flower-clock down by the harbor bloomed; the gentle waves on Lac Léman lapped upon the shore. The blue dome of the sky, framed by the encircling Alps, looked down upon a laconic, beautiful picture-postcard of a city.

Up on the hill where the Assembly stood, the groundskeepers were tending to the flowerbeds and the immaculate lawns. Within the building, though, the temperature-controlled climate had a feel to it more like an oncoming hurricane. If there was one person who personified that storm—at least in the eyes of Julianne Tolliver, His Majesty's new prime minister—it was Tomás Hsien, the self-styled populist leader of the opposition.

She would not have let him speak, if she had had any control over it; the emperor had called her on the carpet and demanded that the assemblyman not be allowed . . . and she'd been forced to point out to His Imperial Highness that the Assembly would not stand for such an exclusion—he'd paid for the time, and he'd have to get it—and that anyone he chose to replace her with would be forced to tell him the same thing.

So Hsien would be allowed to speak. She knew what he knew, and more: he was privy to more information than had been leaked to the press, and she had access to channels that kept her up-to-date on the fleet's actions. Just before coming to the Assembly this afternoon, she'd held a private meeting with Ted McMasters, nominally Admiral of the Fleet, that was even now jumping toward the zor Home Stars, its mission to eradicate mankind's most deadly enemy. It was a biting irony that the end result of this entire war would likely be what humanity had dreamed of for more than two generations, but humanity viewed the means as too distasteful. It was impossible to be blasé about it, but hard not to be sanguine.

Hsien entered the chamber during the noon recess and immediately began to glad-hand, circulating among friends and potential friends in the Assembly. The prime minister, who hadn't bothered to leave for lunch, sat on the platform and watched him move smoothly from one fellow Member to another, his sharply chiseled face animated by excitement. They knew: everyone knew what was about to happen.

Several minutes late, the Speaker of the Assembly at last gaveled for order and recognized Hsien. He stood and walked slowly to the speaker's podium at the front and center of the hall. He arranged notes in front of him and began to speak.

"Mr. Speaker," Hsien began. "As you know, I have long championed the rights of the people in this Assembly. From the beginning of my career, I have stood outside of the traditional fraternity of power and leadership here—" He paused and glanced significantly toward the platform, where the prime minister and members of her Government sat. "Not because of any lack of faith in my own ability to lead, nor indeed because of any false humility, but because I believed that the interests of my constituency and the constraints of my conscience could best be met by pursuing this course.

"I participate in colloquia and serve on committees here in the Assembly, yet I am not a chairman, nor a party leader of any

kind. I am merely a Member here, a representative and a subject
of His Imperial Majesty the Solar Emperor. It is in this capacity
I address you today, with a heavy heart, disappointed and angry
at the actions of this Government.

"For my entire political career—indeed for my entire life—
our Empire has been in conflict with our mortal enemy the zor.
War has taken its toll on both sides, both physically and psycho-
logically. I think it would be fair to say that the people are weary
of war, and of its consequences.

"It has touched all of us to extent or another, from one end of
the Empire to the other: from the center here in Sol System to the
farthest frontier planet in the New Territories.

"Therefore it seems reasonable to me that as the duly elected
representatives of this war-weary people, we should be willing to
treat with that hostile enemy, this alien race, to bring about a cessation of those hostilities as quickly and as efficiently as possible.
I know—" He held up his hands palms outward, as murmuring
began to echo back and forth across the chamber. "I know that
the duplicity of the zor enemy and their ferocity against remote
bases might make some Members less than willing to conclude
peace.

"To them I say, it is our duty *as human beings* to ever seek to
achieve peace by whatever means even if it means overcoming
our own unseemly pride. We should be willing to *discuss* peace,
Mr. Speaker, especially if our enemy approaches us and requests
it as they did nearly a month ago. We have always listened before.

"But as many of you already know, this Government"—he
gestured toward the platform—"has not listened this time.

"Instead of negotiating table with our enemies—in response
to an urgent request to achieve a new peace—we have arrogantly
ignored the request. Instead of being peacemakers, we have become war-bringers.

"The blame for this terrible warlike stance lies primarily with
this Government, under the administration of the current prime
minister and most especially her distinguished predecessor. I

cannot help but note, however, that there is plenty enough blame to go around. We here in the Assembly must share this blame as well, Mr. Speaker, for allowing this to occur. I am *ashamed* this day: I stand before you ashamed to be a servant of the Solar Emperor, as should we all. As should we all."

He stopped and took a sip of water, and looked around the chamber, as if gauging the impact he'd had so far.

"It would be a sad enough juncture for our beloved Empire if we merely had to acknowledge that our Government refused to talk peace but instead pursued this murderous campaign against the enemy. If that were all, we would have recourse." He focused his gaze on Julianne Tolliver, who sat in the prime minister's chair, her face scarcely hiding anger. They locked eyes for several moments.

"But that is by no means the worst that faces us today. For while the Government has stonewalled any attempt to dissuade it from this barbaric course—attacking civilian targets, taking no prisoners, rebuffing peace entreaties and the like—it has refused to confront the essential truth of this campaign so far: that it has *lost control of the fleet.*

"Somewhere beyond the edge of the New Territories, perhaps at A'anenu, perhaps even beyond the Antares Rift, the Imperial Fleet—despite explicit commands from His Imperial Majesty, Mr. Speaker!—is conducting *its own* version of this war. It will soon commit an act of xenocide that will solve the zor problem once and for all time, and leave our race's hands stained with blood that will never . . . *never!* . . . wash away. How did this happen? How did we become a party to this terrible, uncontrolled act of violence?"

He paused again, as if gathering his strength for one final effort.

"Today as we meet under the watchful eyes of our constituents across the Empire, we also work under the shadow of our first emperor, Willem the First." He paused, and gestured to the huge oil painting of the Empire's founder, resplendent in his admiral's uniform with the circlet and scepter. "The man who established the Solar Empire one and a half centuries ago was our original hero, our first great Imperial leader, our dispenser of justice and our lawgiver. In a time of conflict and turmoil, he united all of humanity in a common hegemony, he made the space lanes safe for commercial and private travels, and he encouraged investment in the expanding sphere of human influence.

"It has taken scarcely a hundred years for His Imperial Highness Willem, the founder of the Empire and of the Imperial House, to ascend from mortality into legend. I do not question his greatness," he added quickly, as murmurs began again. "Far from it. Who can say where we might be now but for Emperor Willem? But let us not forget," he continued, leaning forward at the lectern, pointing at the portrait, "that he established his just and fair and legal rule by military force. Agree or not, applaud or not, the throne that he established came from seizing sovereignty from the people.

"Before His Highness Willem the First founded the Empire, he was Admiral Willem McDowell of the European Space Agency. Though he was not viewed as subversive or traitorous when he was appointed to his flag, he was *empowered* by the very terms of that appointment. The European Space Agency placed under his command a squadron of starships, which were the means that allowed him to come to Sol System and hold the home world hostage while he dictated his terms.

"History is written by the victors, Mr. Speaker: this is a well-known precept that has stood throughout human history. With no way to stop him, our ancestors could not but accept his terms, and so the Empire was founded.

"Our emperors and the Admiralty have always been careful to prevent a recurrence of this event. By a system of checks and balances, no admiral has ever considered the possibility of seizing the throne that Emperor Willem established. No admiral—until now."

He paused once more (*for dramatic purposes, like some kind of damn showman,* the prime minister thought). The murmurs and undercurrent of side discussions in the chamber had quieted to a concrete, tomblike silence.

"Admiral Lord Marais, our heroic commander on the periphery, was appointed six months ago after Pergamum for the express purpose of defeating the zor enemy. He was empowered by the Admiralty document now entered in the official record." He waited a moment while the electronic representation of the emperor's warrant appeared on the personal screens of the Assembly Members. "I call your particular attention to the terms of the appointment: Lord Marais was empowered with complete discretionary power in the war zone under the terms of General Orders 6. For those unfamiliar with this particularly pernicious Admiralty directive, I should like to review it.

"This order dates back to the earliest years of our Empire. It was designed to allow commanders far from base to operate without constant referral to an absent superior officer. I will remind you, Mr. Speaker, that the technology of FTL communications was primitive in that era. As a matter of course, commanders were and are given their orders with General Orders 6 included, allowing them freedom of action.

"Because of General Orders 6, our admiral with our fleet is doing what he damn well wants in this war. Because of General Orders 6, he refuses to be countermanded. He refuses to be counseled. In short, because of General Orders 6 he refuses to be stopped." The increasing tumult in the chamber made Hsien raise his voice. "He may not stop until the zor are eradicated. *Until the zor are extinct.*

"This act of xenocide would be unparalleled in the long and violent history of our race, but it now appears to be a foregone conclusion. We will accept it as the price of having gone to the stars.

"What I fear—and what you should fear—is what he will do *next.* The answer to that question is written in our history. By combining absolute authority with a madman capable of destroying an entire sentient race, we may have sealed our own fates."

He was shouting now, against the pounding of the gavel and the shouts of "Mr. Speaker!" from those who wished to prevent him from uttering the final words. Somehow, he got them out.

"Prepare, my fellow Members, for the day when we tear down the distinguished portrait of our beloved founding emperor, and replace it with the portrait of our new emperor, Admiral Ivan Hector Charles Marais, Lord Marais."

The Lighting in the admiral's conference-room had been dimmed in deference to the zor prisoner, giving a sort of melodramatic overlay to the entire scene. Sergei had arranged for the marine escort to be led by Sergeant Boyd, newly transferred to the *Lancaster;* he and one other trooper remained in the room, weapons at the ready, as the admiral and Captain Stone took their seats. Sergei placed himself so that he could observe the zor and Sergeant Boyd, standing almost directly behind, near the door. If Stone was suspicious he did not show it.

"I welcome you aboard the fleet flagship," Marais began, once everyone had been seated. "I am Ivan Lord Marais, Admiral of the Fleet."

"Rrith of Nest Tl'l'u," the zor answered in passable Standard. "You have kept me alive, lord," he continued, without preamble. "What do you want of me?"

"Information only."

"And why do you think I will provide you this information?"

"Very simple." Marais gestured to the *chya*, which hung loosely from Rrith's waist. It had not been taken away from him, but had been secured in its sheath; during the trip across from the *Gagarin*, the zor had neither touched nor looked at it. "If you are willing to give me certain information, your life will be your own."

Rrith stared at Marais. "You will permit me to transcend the Outer Peace?"

"If that is what you wish, or what you must do, then yes."

"Pah." Rrith grunted. "I do not so easily cringe before a Servant of the Cast Out." His wings elevated in a faintly circular position; Sergei glanced carefully at Boyd, who shook his head.

"Yet you recognize the admiral as *esHu'ur*," Sergei said quietly.

Stone sat forward in his chair, frowning, his expression quizzical. Marais had neither moved nor changed his own expression, but his eyes betrayed a slight surprise.

"You will give me back my life if I choose to cooperate," Rrith repeated. "And if I do not agree?"

"If you do not, then when this campaign is over, I will bring you back to Sol System in confinement, under heavy sedation if necessary."

"The campaign is over, is it not, lord? You have A'anenu, you have all but the Home Stars. You have what any commander of the *naZora'i* has ever had, and far more. What more can you expect?"

"The campaign will be over when the zor have surrendered, *se* Rrith. Or when there are no more zor."

Rrith's hands clenched. He let his arms drop to his sides and folded his wings behind him.

"No mere *naZora'e* is capable of destroying the zor, the chosen of *esLi*." Boyd looked away; there was nothing in the zor's wing pattern that conveyed information. Rrith believed this statement.

"I am not a 'mere human,' *se* Rrith," Marais murmured. "I am the Dark Wing. I am your death."

The zor did not answer for many moments.

"*se* Admiral," the zor said carefully, "Do you understand of what you speak? You are a *naZora'i*. How can you claim to be *esHu'ur*?"

"I have chosen the flight of the Dark Wing; there is ample evidence that your people believe me to be such. They quote *aHu'sheMe'sen* in their dispatches, *se* Rrith. Neither it, nor the

*Legend of Qu'u,* nor any of the rest of traditional literature describes *esHu'ur* except in the broadest and most hyperbolic terms. I stand ready to do whatever must be done to bring about the end of this war.

"*Whatever* must be done, *se* Rrith *ehn* Tl'l'u. If that means that there shall be no more Nests, so be it. If that means that there shall be no more people, *so be it.* Very soon, we will be jumping for the Home Stars of the People." The zor made a sound, a sudden intake of breath like a gasp, but his face betrayed no expression that the humans could read. His wings rose in another distinct posture; Sergei looked at Boyd, who nodded. "If we are successful in defeating what defenses remain there, we will have the capability to destroy that world, and everyone on it. Do you not agree?"

Rrith said nothing, but Sergei could see his claws clench on his arms.

"Do you not agree, *se* Rrith?"

He grunted something and stared at the floor.

"The ability to destroy the zor makes me *esHu'ur, se* Rrith. There is no longer a question whether I can fulfill the role. I have already done so for thousands of the People and will do so again until I receive an absolute, total and unconditional surrender from *En'ZheL'Le,* the High Nest. If I receive no such surrender, the lives of all who oppose me will be forfeit."

"Do your home Nestlords know of this?"

"That, too, no longer matters. It is long past that stage."

Sergei hazarded another glance at Boyd. When he returned his attention to the table he noticed Stone staring directly at him. He felt a shiver in his stomach: whatever else was happening in the room, Stone had probably figured out where he was looking.

Rrith stood: not abruptly, but in a smooth, gliding motion that seemed to flow from one position to the other. He walked to one corner of the room, his back turned to the group. From where Sergei was sitting, he could tell that the zor had placed both clawed hands on his *chya.*

From somewhere, Sergei thought he could hear a faint humming, almost too high pitched for his ear to discern. It was enough to set his teeth on edge, and a chill down his back. Neither Stone nor Admiral Marais seemed to notice, and he did not wish to risk eye contact with Boyd.

Rrith turned, slowly, fluidly. The *chya* was in his hands; the bronze-colored blade caught the indirect light of the room and glinted crimson, as if a long trail of blood had run along its length. The blade hummed a moment and then began to glow, coruscating faintly crimson in the air around it.

The two Marines started forward, but Sergei, standing, held out a hand. Marais and Stone seemed frozen in position. The zor glanced quickly at Sergei, and then looked from side to side. The reddish light danced up and down his blade.

Rrith held the blade out, point up, holding it with the same hand-over-hand grip. Then, in one blindingly fast motion, he swung it over his head and down, embedding it in the deck with a crack and a flash. It hung there, humming, glowing with its own light.

"My life is yours, *esHu'ur,*" he said, bowing over the blade, his wings extended and spread about him like a cloak.

Two holographic images had already taken their places when Sergei entered the *Lancaster*'s ready-room. As if he really had stepped into a room aboard their own ships, the two captains' images stood on his arrival and waited for him to sit again before they took their places.

The two captains, Yuri Okome of the *Ikegai* and Sharon MacEwan of the *San Martín*, looked ill at ease and fatigued, though neither would admit it if asked. While the main body of the fleet had been sorting matters out at A'anenu, the two ships of the line with some small craft had been sent to nearby zor worlds left unprotected by the buildup at A'anenu. He'd already skimmed their report to know about their successes—and their discomfiture—but he felt the need for personal confirmation from them.

"I realize that you've just arrived insystem, so I appreciate you making yourselves available on short notice," Sergei began. "I received your reports, but perhaps you can review the high points for me."

MacEwan and Okome exchanged glances, as if neither wanted to speak first. At last Okome cleared his throat and placed his hands, palms down, on the table.

"Our command was directed to visit three solar systems within two days' jump of A'anenu. In each case, the system was expected to be lightly defended, most likely without jump-capable force. Our orders were to call upon the defenders to surrender and, if receiving none, to eliminate resistance.

"Defenders in each system did not exceed expected levels. Three to five defense boats, a handful of station-based fighters, some static emplacements. In each case, surrender was demanded, but none was given.

"The defenders' tactics, however, were not what we expected. For them to have fought us—tooth and claw"—Yuri Okome's scarred face almost betrayed a faint smile, but it didn't seem to convey much humor—"would have been reasonable, as would destruction of equipment or vessels, either to effect the destruction of our own ships, or to deny their own hardware to us. Neither tactic was employed."

"They let us kill them," Sharon MacEwan interrupted. Her face was lit with . . . what? Anger? Disappointment? Sergei wasn't sure how to read it, but he could see that MacEwan herself was confused how to respond.

"Please elaborate," Sergei said.

"They didn't fire their weapons. They didn't surrender, they didn't evade. They didn't even try to ram. They just—let us—kill them. As if they had planned to die, and our arrival provided a convenient excuse."

"Do you agree, Yuri?"

"Commodore." Okome leaned back in his chair and placed his hands on its arms. His left eyebrow raised itself slightly, as if of its own accord. "As you might be aware, I prepared a report on the battlefield response to defensive field 'cracking.'"

"Standard reading for officers of the line, Yuri. Go on."

"Aye, sir." Okome allowed a bit of relaxation in his grim expression. "With a limited amount of decision time available, a ship's captain whose vessel's defensive field is being successfully cracked has only one response likely to produce a positive result more than fifty percent of the time: a radical course change. Analysis has demonstrated that sudden maneuver often alters the field geometry sufficiently to dissipate the incoming fire.

"In at least two cases during our operations enemy vessels so targeted actually employed a maneuver for the exact opposite purpose. That is, instead of changing course to dissipate incoming attacks, these ships actually performed a course change to *intensify* them, leading to the . . . inevitable result. I have documented these incidents." Icons appeared above the table indicating log entries.

"During our return jump, I subjected our flight logs to close scrutiny, and I believe that I have identified three or four other instances of such suicidal maneuvers that were simply unsuccessful.

"Do I concur with Captain MacEwan? Yes, sir, I certainly do. I have fought and analyzed the zor enemy for most of my life and have no category into which I can readily put what I have seen during the past few days."

"My family has been in the soldier business for centuries," Sharon MacEwan said after a moment. "This is unlike anything in our experience. It's unlike anything we've seen in sixty years of fighting the zor."

"I am troubled by it because it serves no purpose." Okome steepled his fingers before him. "If you wish, consider this war as a large complex board game. If you achieve certain conditions or place your pieces in particular configurations, events occur that affect the course of the game. Sometimes it is necessary to sacrifice a piece to lure enemy pieces into a trap or away from an objective you desire."

Okome leaned forward, his eyes intense, his brows lowered, like some sort of grim portrait. "It is well within parameters to expect the zor to sacrifice pieces. Did they not do so elsewhere? Were they not ready to do so at A'anenu? It served some purpose to attempt to destroy the orbital base for it would have disabled us to be without troops for planetfall.

"And yet in three engagements since A'anenu was taken, we watched as zor vessels literally lined up for our guns, like a herd animal waiting to be gored by a carnivorous beast. I believe that my colleague"—he gestured toward MacEwan—"is troubled by these actions because they violate her image of war. I am troubled by them because they are simply impossible to understand."

MacEwan was clearly ready to launch some sort of ballistic rejoinder, but Sergei forestalled her. "Let me pose this question. If you believe that they went out of their way to be destroyed, why didn't they simply surrender?"

"I don't think it's the same thing." It was now MacEwan's turn to bore a glance into her commanding officer. "Surrendering and committing suicide aren't the same. If they surrendered—if they *could* surrender—they would expect us to grant them quarter. Which we would, of course."

"Meaning?"

"Meaning that they wouldn't die. It was like they wanted to die, that it was somehow better than surrendering. But why the hell didn't they *fight*?"

"Would it have made destroying them any easier? Would it have made neutralizing the Nests on the surface any easier?"

"Your point, Commodore?" MacEwan answered, her eyes full of anger. "Are you suggesting that I have not done my duty, sir?"

"No. You're drawing the wrong conclusion, Sharon." Sergei took a deep breath. "I'm suggesting . . . I'm tending toward agreement with our friend Yuri here. I know all about the Mac-Ewan tartan, and Bannockburn, and Bonnie Prince Charlie and all. I know about Anderson's Star, and Boren, and the rescue of the *Bolívar,* and how you won your White Cross. The wars with the zor haven't lacked for romantic grist for the legend mill, just the sort of thing that adds to your distinguished family tradition. I'll repeat what I said after L'alChan: I won't be giving you any medals for what you just went through—it wasn't about heroism, or drama or legend.

"It was just about destruction. Brutal, violent, but—at least in Admiral Marais' mind—necessary destruction. That's all that war is really about." Sergei looked away; he didn't want to see Sharon MacEwan's expression, as he expected to have had little impact with his remarks.

"Does the commodore have any further questions?" she asked quietly after a moment, though Sergei could hear a tightly leashed anger in her voice.

"No, I suppose not. Thank you for your time. Dismissed."

Sergei looked up in time to see the two images fade out. Okome's face, just before the holo ceased, had a curious expression: Sergei imagined that it was the sort of face that he put on when one of his Academy students worked his way through a difficult problem to reach a more difficult, unpalatable truth.

Even when the image had disappeared, the hint of a smile seemed to remain, a polite sort of mocking: *at last the truth is revealed,* it said. *Now you see.*

A s the departure from A'anenu drew closer, a sense of eager anticipation seemed to run through the ship. The magnitude of the act about to take place seemed not to have penetrated much past him, Sergei reflected to himself; in truth, the very nature of the destruction about to occur, and the intended object of that destruction, seemed to beckon them onward even faster. More and more crewmembers and officers seemed to be reading

Marais' book. One watch he came into the officers' wardroom during one midwatch to find a scrap of printout tacked to the bulletin board.

It was a quote from *The Absolute Victory:*

> One of the fundamental problems with humanity, all through its history, has been its inability—or unwillingness—to come to terms with the notion of personal violence.
>
> There is an unfortunate delusion that mankind is somehow above the emotion of hate and that individuals, and aggregates, should somehow repress that emotion rather than come to terms with it. Violence has been a part of human life since before the ability to record history even existed.
>
> We can no longer turn away from that fact; it is impossible to wall it away or to hide it in a closet. It is vitally important that we harness it instead and make use of it for the greatest possible good: to destroy the enemies of our race, and thus guarantee our own survival.

He felt the urge to tear it down, to summon his officers and dress them down until he discovered who had put it up there. It offended him and gave him a weak feeling in the pit of his stomach. But he did not, even though he reached his hand out to do so. He had spent fifteen years doing just what Marais had described: actively carrying out the hatred of the zor, reciprocating perhaps their own hatred for humanity. Now humanity stood on the threshold of ending that threat for good, and it represented the culmination of his career . . . whether he liked it or not.

Numbed, he left it up, and turned away, walking out of the wardroom, trying to fix his mind on something else.

## chapter 13

HISTORY TRULY IS WRITTEN BY THE VICTORS. SOME HISTORIANS HAVE EVEN SUGGESTED THAT THERE IS NO SUCH THING AS AN OBJECTIVE VIEWPOINT, OR EVEN AN OBJECTIVE OBSERVER. HUMAN NATURE, THEY WOULD SAY, PRECLUDES IT.

SIMILARLY, THE CONSIDERATION OF GOOD AND EVIL IS EXTREMELY SUBJECTIVE, AND THE CLOSER THE OBSERVER IS TO THE SITUATION, THE HARDER IT IS TO SEPARATE HIS PERCEPTIONS FROM THE ABSOLUTE TRUTHS. INDEED, IT IS NOT EVEN CLEAR THAT THERE ARE ANY.

—*By Fire and Sword: A History of the Man-Zor Conflict,*
by Ichiro Kanev (Gleason Publishing, Adrianople, 2310)

To humanity, realizing far too late what was happening hundreds of light-years away, Marais had become a villain, a madman with the capability to perform a monstrous act of destruction, the responsibility for which would not just lie with him but with them as well. Admiral Marais and his now outlaw fleet could not be stopped from completing that act, or taking whatever actions they desired afterward. The emperor and the Government had lost control.

He was a villain because he had been as good as his word. He was a villain because he had won. That it had been allowed was the most difficult thing to accept, and Marais, who had been been mentioned in the most glowing terms for weeks in the press in the Solar Empire, was now a name snarled in editorials and shouted out by demagogues.

When all of the preparations had been made, however, the fleet made ready to depart from A'anenu, having secured all of the remaining zor worlds on the near side of the Antares Rift. Their destination was not Zor'a but rather a location in deep space: somewhere within the empty quarter of the Rift itself, whence the attackers of Pergamum had come. While matters within the Empire rose toward boiling-point, the fleet moved on through the unreal night of jumpspace, preparing to meet with its destiny.

He heard the door-chime, and looked up from behind his work-desk. "Come."

Stone stalked into his office. There was obvious anger in his eyes, and it was scarcely withheld from his voice. "I just learned about Boyd, the Marine sergeant. Why was I not informed of this?"

Sergei did not answer for a moment, but looked the adjutant up and down. "You continually amaze me, Stone," he said quietly. "Staff flunkies like you are usually punctilious about matters like salutes and forms of address. I seem to recall that I am your superior officer, and worthy of some shred of respect."

"Very well, *sir*," Stone sneered, still angry. "If the commodore pleases, I should like to know why information concerning Sergeant Boyd has been intentionally withheld from me."

Sergei leaned back in his chair, still taking his time. "I didn't realize that you took such an interest in Marine troopers."

"This is no ordinary trooper, damn you," Stone replied. He was more angry than Sergei had ever seen him, and his spare frame bent over the desk, leaning on its front edge. "If you're holding out—"

Sergei stood up behind his desk so suddenly that Stone, straightening up as well, had to take a step back. Sergei was at least twenty centimeters taller and at least twenty kilos heavier; for his part, his anger put aside any threat he'd felt from Stone before.

"This is not the Imperial Court," he said at last. "This is His Majesty's ship *Lancaster.* I am the captain of this ship, and I hold the rank of commodore, responsible only to the orders of his lordship the admiral. During the past several months while you've been operating in the shadows I have had to tolerate your sneering, your condescension, your insults, and even your threats. I have had enough, *Captain.* Do you read me? Enough."

"Your duty—" Stone began, but it was clear that he had lost grasp of the momentum of the discussion. Sergei hurried on.

"You want to know about Boyd? All right. I have transferred him as well as the zor prisoner to this ship so that they are at the admiral's disposal, and so they may interact. It appears that Boyd has acquired some understanding of the zor language, and I deemed it appropriate that he make the acquaintance of the prisoner in order to help obtain the information that the admiral desires.

"I have made no secret of Sergeant Boyd's orders; neither have I restricted your access to the prisoner, even when Boyd has visited with him. Admiral Marais has been apprised of this in my official report. I assume that is how you learned of it. Now, what the hell else do you want from me?"

Stone did not answer that question, but his eyes were full of hatred. Sergei continued. "You've worked very hard at trying to question my credibility and my loyalty to the cause of defeating the zor, which seems to include pouring poison into the admiral's ear. But I've thrown my lot in with Admiral Marais, and expect to be court-martialed if I ever return to the Empire. That seems to be good enough for him. If it's not good enough for you, that's too damn bad.

"I've given the admiral my report on the subject, and the subordinate reports and records are on file for your scrutiny. If you have any questions, and can bring yourself to ask them civilly, then I'll be glad to answer them. Until then, get the hell out of my office."

Stone seemed to consider this for a fraction of a second too long for military politeness. Then he gave Sergei a salute, still radiating hatred, and stalked out of the room.

Sergei stood where he was for several seconds, almost euphoric at having vented his anger and frustration; then, somewhere back in his forebrain, he remembered the feeling he had had when Stone had suggested putting him out the airlock, and he realized that there was something further he needed to do.

I appreciate you taking the time, my lord."

"Not at all, Commodore." The admiral set aside his 'reader and gestured to a pair of comfortable chairs set up facing each other in a corner of his suite. Sergei followed Marais to the chairs, and took one of them. Marais took the other, then said to the air, "Computer, voice-lock this room on my orders. Marais, Admiral Ivan."

"Acknowledged."

"Now, Torrijos. What's on your mind?"

"I have a . . . delicate subject to discuss with you, sir. I just had a disagreement with . . . No, that's not really the way to begin.

"My lord, I would like for you to tell me about your adjutant, Captain Stone."

"Stone?" Marais looked at him quizzically, but not, Sergei noted, with any visible resentment or suspicion. "He's a curious little fellow, very efficient, with a phenomenal memory. He's very knowledgeable, and works hard at keeping me informed about what's going on in the fleet."

"Keeps you informed, sir? Is that his charter—to keep you informed?"

"Among other things, yes."

"Does that order extend to breaking into secure shipboard computer systems, monitoring private conversations, and issuing threats to superior officers?"

Marais sat forward. "Excuse me?"

"I have proof that he has done all of these things, sir. Computer systems aboard the *Biscayne,* the *Gagarin* and the *Lancaster*—and possibly other vessels as well—have been tampered with and there is strong evidence to suggest Captain Stone as the culprit. Private discussions between officers have been monitored, and the participants have received communications from Stone impugning their honor, insulting their performance and implying disloyalty. At least four officers have been threatened with fatal accidents."

Marais had no answer. Sergei was not a consummate judge of personality, but the admiral's body language suggested that he had not heard of any of this.

"I have been threatened as well, sir."

have been threatened as well, sir."
    Stone sat back in his chair. "That little bastard. Gone crying to the admiral. He won't get away with this."

He began to consider his options, looking around his quarters. Possibilities began to surface in his mind, one after another; slowly, his scowl began to soften into an unpleasant and disturbing smile.

issued no orders for this, Commodore, I assure you." Marais seemed genuinely ill at ease and concerned. Sergei hadn't known how this information would be received; he had considered the possibility that Marais was in fact directing Stone's actions, and to complain about them was a calculated risk.

In all of his time in service he had never been able to function in an environment where he could not trust his superior officer. Even aboard the *Ponchartrain,* an eternity ago, he had had some sense of where he stood. Now, isolated in jump, headed for a violent confrontation with mankind's enemy, and possibly without a legal leg to stand on in a court-martial, he realized that he had to trust Marais now.

"I am sure you would not, my lord. In fact, I am sure you are unaware of most of Stone's actions. It is clear that he has taken advantage of his position to act in your name."

"Why do you bring this to my attention now?"

"Sir, I'm not a social climber by nature. I'm interested in one thing: bringing this war to an acceptable conclusion, and I'm pleased and privileged to commit my knowledge and talents to doing just that. I was willing to tolerate Stone's disrespect, his insulting attitude, and even his threats. Up to a point."

U p to a point."

Stone stood and walked to a shelf, extruded from the wall of the room. He picked up a normal-looking 'reader, and placed his right hand in a particular configuration on the underside. There was a sharp *click* and the 'reader rotated in a strange, disturbing way, as if it were turning inside out. What emerged from this transformation was a sort of holographic display, showing a cross-sectional view of the *Lancaster.* Several areas were highlighted, with blinking red, blue or yellow dots.

He made an adjustment to the device, and it focused in on one of the dots, located in the quarters of Admiral Marais.

Stone smiled to himself broadly, an expression that might have brought a shudder to anyone watching—but there was no one there to watch.

•    •    •

My Lord. I have made no secret of the events that took place aboard the A'anenu orbital base. I have found Sergeant Boyd's account disturbing but compelling, and I have included his descriptions in my report. Both he and the prisoner are aboard the *Lancaster* for your convenience, and I have no additional agenda for either of them.

"Half an hour ago, Stone walked into my office and essentially accused me of 'holding out' on him. Not on you, sir: on *him*. I'm afraid I reached my limit. I threw him the hell out of my office, and decided that it was time that I presented you with an accounting of his activities. I knew that I would receive a fair hearing."

Marais rested his elbow on his knee, and his chin in his palm. "Do you wish to level charges against Captain Stone?"

"Very much so, sir. But I do not *need* to do so. In fact, if you wish it, I will refrain from doing so for the sake of harmony. What I wish to do is constrain Stone's activities. I will not tolerate any further insubordination, any more unscrupulous activity or any more threats. At the first infraction, I will put him in the brig, in irons if necessary, for the duration of the war."


. . . ꜰor ꜩhe duration of the war."

"Issuing threats, are you?" Stone said to no one in particular. He adjusted the device again; it focussed in even closer to the blinking dot. The screen showed two vague outlines, man-shaped, moving slightly back and forth. He reached for a control on the top of the device—

Suddenly, the chamber was filled with light. It was split into bright bands in each of several colors: red, orange, yellow, green, blue, violet. It was hard to tell where one band faded out and the next one began. Stone had to squeeze his eyes tightly to make out anything in the room: his hands, the furniture, the device.

"No, damn it," Stone said. "I've got to—"

"CEASE," a disembodied voice said into the room. The greenish band of color grew more luminous as this word echoed around the walls.

"But I've got to get rid of Torrijos," he said. "Marais needs me, and Torrijos will get in the way."

"NO." The red band brightened. "WE DO NOT DESIRE THIS ACT TO TAKE PLACE."

"WE WILL NOT CAUSE IT TO OCCUR," the blue band seemed to say.

"WE HAVE CHOSEN NOT TO PREVENT IT FROM BEING STOPPED," the violet band said.

"IT IS TIME FOR YOU TO DEPART," the green band said after a moment. The transformed 'reader became luminous and then vanished, leaving Stone empty-handed. "THERE WILL BE OTHER OPPORTUNITIES."

"But—" Stone began to protest.

"IT IS TIME FOR YOU TO DEPART," the green band repeated. The bands of color that had filled the room narrowed, until they became a path perhaps a meter wide, extending outward from where Stone stood. The features of the room had become dim and vague, and all around the path was cloying blackness. The rainbow path began under his feet and extended off into a distance he could hardly see.

Without looking back, Stone began to walk along the path. Soon the room and the ship had disappeared entirely.

In fairness to my adjutant, Torrijos, I would like to confront him with these charges. I know that you have evidence to support your claims, but I believe that Stone has the right to defend himself."

"I am willing to trust your fairness, sir. I—"

The bosun's whistle interrupted his comment. "Officer of the Watch calling the captain."

"By your leave, sir?"

Marais nodded.

"Torrijos here."

"Fordyce here, Cap'n. Sorry to disturb you, sir, but we've just detected an unusual high-energy reading from somewhere in officer country. I've already sent a detail to investigate."

"What kind of energy reading? An explosion of some kind?"

"No, sir. It doesn't match anything I've ever seen. Commander Wells and science section have been alerted, but they have no guess yet."

"Where exactly did it take place?"

"Stand by a moment, Cap'n—" Fordyce got some sort of confirmation from someone on the bridge. "Captain Stone's quarters, sir."

Sergei looked at Marais. Both stood at once. "I'm on my way, Pam. Ship's troops on standby. Captain out."

"Is that necessary?" Marais asked as they headed for the door of the admiral's suite.

"Just a feeling," Sergei replied.


Stone's quarters were no more than a minute away from the admiral's. There was already a marine squad waiting for him when Sergei got there. Chan Wells approached from the other direction, sensing-equipment in hand. No one had entered the room yet.

"Report," Sergei said.

Chan looked from Sergei to the admiral to the door. "I don't know what we've got, sir. Something just happened—like a surge in the space-fabric, similar to what happens when an FTL vessel enters jump."

"Huh." Sergei couldn't conceive of what that could mean in this context. The *Lancaster* was in jump, traveling faster than the speed of light in a dark and empty continuum, for all intents and purposes all alone.

The marines were standing about uncomfortably, waiting for something to happen. Sergei shrugged, and pushed the door-chime. There was no answer.

"Break it down," he said, and stood back. Marais and Chan Wells stood back as well. One of the marines opened the access panel and inserted a card-key, while the rest of the squad set up, ready to return fire if someone in the room came out shooting.

The door slid aside, revealing bright light within. The marines burst in, weapons ready.

"Captain?" a voice said from inside the room. Sergei walked forward, and stepped into Stone's quarters—

—Or rather, what had been Stone's quarters. Instead of furnishings, personal effects, or extruded furniture, the room was absolutely empty. The default lighting was on, but the walls were white and bare.

Marais stepped carefully into the room. Chan began to scan with his portable detector, but after a moment stopped and shook his head.

The admiral walked to the center of the empty chamber, and looked around, as if he was unsure what to do next.

"Bridge, this is the captain," Sergei said to the air. "Locate Captain Stone."

"Aye-aye, sir." Pam Fordyce's voice was strangely hollow in the empty compartment. After several moments, she spoke again. "Internal scan can't find him, sir. He might be somewhere in Engineering; equipment might shield his vital signs down there."

"Seal it off and search it. Captain out." He turned to Chan. "Why do I get the feeling we're not going to be able to find him?"

"That's impossible, sir. He has to be aboard the *Lancaster*. There is no other place."

"What do you mean, 'no other place,' Commander?" Marais asked.

"Precisely that, sir." Chan gestured around him. "The ship is in jump, Admiral. It is enclosed in a sort of bubble, we theorize, that travels from a specified location in realspace along a vector. We measure the vector's length by using ship-objective time, and determine its direction by precise measurement of the direction the ship was heading when we jumped.

"While we are here, we are totally out of contact with anything outside the bubble that encloses the *Lancaster*. Some schools of jump physics hold that the *Lancaster*, for the duration of its jump, is in fact the *entire* universe. There is nowhere for Stone to go, because there is *nowhere else.*

"If Captain Stone is not aboard the *Lancaster*, and our instrumentation is working, then obviously . . ."

"Obviously what?" Sergei asked, trying to follow his exec's train of thought, and unable to reach any useful conclusion.

"Obviously," Chan answered after a moment, "those schools of physics are incorrect."

Rrith opened his eyes, letting his meditative state pass away. Nearby Boyd was sitting on a cushion, studying his 'reader intently.

"*esGa'u*'s minion is gone," Rrith said, and closed his eyes again.

"What?"

But Rrith had allowed himself to return into trance, and would not respond to Chris Boyd's inquiries.

Without really noticing, Sse'e drifted into sleep, and felt the familiar dream-shapes gather around him. As it began to sort itself out, he extended his acute Sensitive's perceptions, and became an observer in the dream, unseen and unnoticed by the participants.

*esGa'u* was there, as often was the case in his dreams. The Lord of the Cast Out paced back and forth in his shrouded laboratory, as the sky broke open with storms. He could see past *esGa'u* to the windows, which showed the crouching clouds and the driving rain, sweeping across the plateau to the sorcerer's fastness.

He could read *esGa'u*'s thoughts, as always. *No surprise,* he thought to himself: *as all of this is a dream, acted out within your own skull.*

Or was it?

*Can you not hear me, Crawler? esGa'u* was thinking, stopping his pacing to look up through the high windows at the loosed storm, addressing *esLi. Can you not see what I have wrought for you? A pretty play, is it not?*

*The Faithful still follow you,* he continued. *They wait so desperately for your favor; they cease strife among themselves; and yet the Dark Wing still descends upon them. In your Name they are so bent upon their course of misbegotten truth and misplaced honor that their doom—which I have prepared for them—cannot be avoided.*

*It can only be embraced . . .*

*esGa'u* stretched his wings in the half-circle, the wing talons nearly meeting, the legs crossed and slightly bent in the posture of *esLi'u'eRa,* Loyalty to *esLi;* it was a gesture that could only be meant to mock . . .

*It is as I have planned, Lord Crawler, esGa'u* continued, his eternally handsome face twisted with glee. *For though it might destroy me, it cannot help but destroy you as well. Without worshipers to dutifully keep your name alive, you will perish, whether you think yourself a God or not. And the Dark Wing cannot fail while your narrow codes of honor will not let the People succeed.*

*Even now I hear the Awaited One's armies batter at my gates.*

The dreamer heard noises outside the sorcerer's laboratory, the sounds of battle on the steps.

*It is too late to teach your old wings new ways, esGa'u* thought, turning his proud head to the sky. *The Dark Wing comes to my door, esLi, my ancient enemy.*

*esGa'u,* sorcerer, Lord of the Cast Out, turned to face the door which was under attack even as he finished his last utterance toward the howling storm beyond the windows. But before he could open that door, it burst asunder, flying off its hinges and crashing to the floor, leaving a gaping dark hole.

Through that aperture stepped a human—the fleet admiral, the commander of the human force that was even now approaching the Home Stars. He wore none of the traditional accoutrements of the Dark Wing—no crimson sash, no medallion of the Unbroken Circle. His features did not even seem to be the same as they had been in other dreams.

*esGa'u* staggered back as the human stepped into the laboratory, flanked by other humans and . . . one of the People. In the human's hand was a plain white rod, the symbol of . . .

"The Bright Wing," the human said, clenching the rod in his long-taloned hand. He ignored *esGa'u* and turned to the dreamer's vantage.

"It is time, Lord," he said, "that I speak with you."

*Speak with you.*

*Speak with you . . .*

". . . speak with you. Eight thousand pardons, High Lord, for the disturbance of your repose. But your cousin *se* Hyos claimed it to be urgent."

The High Lord glanced down at his feet, which gripped the torus firmly, almost convulsively. He took a moment to clear the last dream-images from his sight, and sighed deeply. Then he launched himself into midair, and flew in long, casual sweeps, beating his wings in rhythmic eleven-counts, and reciting the Ritual of Waking to himself as he did so.

"Tell my honored cousin," Sse'e HeYen said at last to the audio pickup in his meditation chamber, "that I am pleased to grant his request. And," the High Lord added, coming to rest on a perch a dozen meters below *esLi's* torus, "and tell him that if his reasons for disturbing my meditation are insufficient, my *chya* shall taste his blood."

"... By your leave," came the reply, and then silence.

The High Lord stood on his perch and considered the dream he had just experienced. To some, dreaming was merely an act of mental exercise, performed during sleep; but it had long been held that the dreams of the High Lord represented the focusing of the collective unconscious, a talon extended to *esLi* Himself. Sse'e HeYen was disinterested in speculation about the truth of it all: *esLi,* or a manifestation, had appeared to him many times through those visions and he could not imagine that the Creator was somehow a figment of a Sensitive's fever-dream.

It was a paradigm, however, that the dreams of the High Lord had significance; in fact it had long been accepted that the dreams, which always seemed to be shrouded in metaphor, could be properly interpreted to yield the truth of what was to come ... It was as if the Sensitive who dreamed them was given a sudden vision of the future, and how the present flowed toward it.

Sse'e pondered what his vision could mean.

Some of it was clear enough: *esGa'u* was the eternal enemy of *esLi.* It was plain that beliefs regarding humanity had led them irrevocably to this juncture; yet to abdicate responsibility for destroying the human pestilence could only make the People *idju* in *esLi*'s eyes. But humanity had not been destroyed: it had risen again and again, and had now spawned the legendary *esHu'ur.*

It made the People *idju* to surrender, even to *esHu'ur.* But were the People not already *hi'idju* to have been defeated? Was it not better to end the matter now and perform the Ritual of Death for the entire race rather than to suffer dishonor any longer?

And yet a mystery remained. *esGa'u,* in the dream, spoke of the destruction of the People at the talons of the Dark Wing. But the human admiral had called himself the Bright Wing. Clearly, by his actions, he was the Dark Wing.

Could he be the Bright Wing instead?

Or—perhaps—as well?

The Dark Wing promised surcease, the eternal sleep of the honored dead. But the promise of the Bright Wing was life, continued devotion to *esLi*, a chance for redemption and renewal. Literature mentioned the theme of "condemnation to Life"; rather than permitting the Ritual of Death, *esLi* would condemn the hero to suffer existence further, that he might serve some greater Purpose at a later time. It was not difficult for a zor to consider himself *idju*, but it was truly a matter for *esLi* Himself to decide. Perhaps that was what *esLi* sought to tell him as he dreamed.

"The call from your honored cousin is complete," the audio pickup said.

The High Lord touched a depression on the wall, and watched a screen come to life, depicting his cousin's image.

## chapter 14

(From the records of the Investigative Subcommittee to Review the Battle of Pergamum, Naval Oversight Committee of the Imperial Assembly, 23 April 2311.)

MEMBER AVIDRA PRAMURJIAN *(Chairman, New Chicago)*: Please describe for the Committee how you reached this conclusion.

FIRST LORD OF THE ADMIRALTY: Certainly, Madam Chairman. If the Committee would refer to their displays . . . [*note vidrec attachment 2311-PCI4291-12*] an analysis of jump echoes for the original attacking force at Pergamum, as well as the reinforcing vessels, indicate a common point of origin.

By projecting these vectors, as you see, it is clear that they do not intersect with the location of any zor base on the Imperial side of the Antares Rift. Nor do they coincide with any location in the zor Core Stars. We have determined that they must have jumped from somewhere in the Rift itself.

MEMBER MIKHAIL SALEH (*Denneva*): Within the Rift?
Surely that's impossible.

FIRST LORD: Our calculations show it to be true. If you
would examine this display—

MEMBER SALEH: But the Rift is empty. Surely the Admiralty hasn't changed the laws of jump physics while the
Committee's back was turned. [*Laughter.*]

FIRST LORD: No, Assemblyman Saleh. We would require
the emperor's permission. [*Laughter.*] Let me clarify.
You are aware of the concept of the Muir limit and its
effect on the ability of a vessel to transition to jump—

MEMBER PRAMURJIAN (*interrupting*): First Lord, if I may,
perhaps you could provide the laymen on this committee with a brief explanation. I realize that you are not
prepared for a full lecture, but I am sure that any insights you can provide would be invaluable.

FIRST LORD: I will do my best, Madam Chairman. The
first diagram presented in an introductory jump-
physics course is the Muir-limit curve. It is an expression of mass plotted against range from that mass, and
represents how celestial bodies cause "dents" in space,
both in the real and FTL continua.

MEMBER SALEH: Don't jumping vessels create similar
dents?

FIRST LORD: Yes, that's right, but they are instantaneous,
and once the ship is gone, its "dent" is gone as well.

MEMBER SALEH: I see.

FIRST LORD: Mass concentrations represent a hazard for
interstellar travel; but if there were no mass concentrations, jump would be impossible. This is because jump
is basically probabilistic in nature: there is a probability
that the target destination will be reached, tending
toward one hundred percent—but only if the Muir limit
of the destination is within a narrowly defined range.

If the Muir limit is too high—deep in a gravity-well, within a solar system or too near a sun—or too low, in deep space or near a small, dim star—the probability of successful jump drops away. For this reason exploration of new solar systems is very risky—exact mass measurements are not known, thus increasing the chances of misjump.

Based on our calculations, our putative base must have a mass nearby. The absence of luminous stars, as well as the presence of dark matter, is what makes the Antares Rift a rift, after all; so our search was restricted to dark suns—collapsed suns and sun-sized planets that have spent their nuclear fuel.

MEMBER SIR EDOUARD KANEV (St. Catherine): You mean like a black hole or neutron star.

FIRST LORD: Not exactly, sir. Both black holes and neutron stars present problems. A black hole has relativity issues, and a neutron star would have excessively high gravity. What we're really looking for is a large planet or small, dying star with absolute magnitude above ten—at least a few thousand times dimmer than our own sun. We have identified seven likely candidates with sufficient mass to make jump possible . . .

MEMBER SALEH: Placing a base in the Rift would require considerable investment, isn't that true? If your estimates are correct . . . nearly a hundred zor vessels jumped from this supposed base to Pergamum.

A base capable of supporting that number of vessels even for a short time would have to be quite large.

FIRST LORD: We have prepared some estimates [*note vidrec attachment 2311-PCI4291-19*], which you will find on your displays.

MEMBER SUNG LIN (*Morgaine*): There would be little material on-site to build such a base, isn't that true?

MEMBER PRAMURJAN: In which case, the expense required to bring material to the desired location would be quite considerable.

FIRST LORD: And time, Assemblyman. Our conservative estimate suggests that it might have taken ten or eleven Standard years to complete.

MEMBER KANEV: That precedes the Treaty of Efal by several years.

FIRST LORD: Assemblyman, this construction effort must have preceded the Treaty of Las Duhr. That suggests that the attack on Pergamum or something similar was planned years ago—before the current war was even contemplated.

The lift hummed softly to itself as it rose, and Sergei went through the ritual he always used just before coming onto his own bridge.

It was important to be calm, and in control, but not relaxed. Years of command had taught him just how dangerous it could be to relax. People made mistakes that way. People died that way.

He breathed deeply a few times, and reviewed the section of the Naval Regulations he had memorized fifteen years ago for this very purpose. After his mind was clear, having been thus forced to concentrate, he straightened the cuffs on his uniform jacket and cleaned a speck of dirt from his right boot.

The lift opened, and he stepped onto the bridge of the *Lancaster.* Admiral Marais was wearing another variation of his full-dress uniform; he stood at the exec's station, examining a display. Chan Wells sat in the pilot's chair, but rose as soon as he saw Sergei.

"Captain on the bridge." The officers stopped their duties to turn and give him a salute, but remained sitting at their stations; Chan walked forward to meet him, extending the watch report for his consideration. "All systems at one hundred percent, sir."

"How long before end of jump?"

Chan looked at the large chronometer above the engineering station. "Two minutes, thirty seconds."

Sergei took the report and walked to the pilot's seat, offering Admiral Marais a salute, but nothing else; on the bridge of the *Lancaster,* at least, Sergei outranked him.

He examined the pilot's board distractedly, noting the current status reports by the watch officers in navigation, engineering, and life-support; he looked from station to station on the bridge and cast a quick glance at Marais, who was looking away. Finally he looked at the forward screen, which showed nothing but featureless darkness.

The lift-door slid aside. Sergei cast a quick glance over his shoulder and saw Boyd come onto the bridge. He was clearly unaccustomed to his surroundings. Sergei gestured him to a seat out of the way, and returned his attention to the pilot's board.

"Request captain's permission to leave jump," the helmsman said, without turning.

"Jump at your own command, Lieutenant," Sergai replied.

"One minute . . . mark," the helmsman said. An alert sounded through the ship. A tangible tension grew in the air, and with it a ponderous silence descended, only interrupted by the constant drone of the air circulators and the subaural tone of the engines from the aft part of the ship. Sergei could not help but glance at the chronometer as it ticked away the seconds.

"Ready defensive fields. Beat to Quarters," he said. It was impossible to arm the ship's defenses in jump; it had to be ready for the moment of transition. More than one warship had been surprised—and destroyed—by jumping unprepared into a hostile system.

The chronometer ticked down to zero. Slowly the forward screen faded from black to mercury-silver, streaming outward from some distant vanishing-point, until the streaks resolved themselves into stars.

Against the backdrop of a bright arm of the Milky Way, punctuated by patches of dark matter that lay closer, the *Lan-*

*caster*'s forward screen showed a huge metallic structure lit only by reflected light from stars and nebulae. Beyond, there was a huge, dark mass—the corpse of a long-dead star—hovering in the void.

"Report," Sergei said to Chan, as he watched lights wink into existence on the pilot's board in front of him. The chatter of ships reporting their arrival buzzed in the background.

"Nineteen ships have emerged from jump, sir. All units are reported operational. The base is four hundred million kilometers downrange."

"And the enemy?"

"We read something over forty vessels in the vicinity, sir."

"*Lancaster* to *Gagarin*. Get your wings in the air, Captain Bell."

"*Gagarin* acknowledging, sir," came Lew Cornejo's voice. "First squadrons will be launching in one minute."

"Excellent." Sergei quickly glanced at Marais, then at Boyd, then back at the pilot's board. The zor were deploying some of their ships from the base. "Open channel to all ships, this is the *Lancaster*. All vessels, ahead one-quarter."

There was chatter from the comm channels. Sergei watched as the ships that had launched from the base began to form a battle wedge, heading for his incoming vessels. "Open channel to the zor commander. This is His Imperial Majesty's ship *Lancaster*. I call upon all enemy vessels in this volume to surrender and be granted quarter."

It grew silent on the bridge. The majority of the Imperial ships had arrived; only a few stragglers were materializing near the jump point. The zor did not acknowledge, but were maneuvering into a peculiar formation as they closed in.

"*Sevastopol, Indomitable*, prepare to fire," Sergei said. They were the advance vessels and would be first to come in range.

The next moment, however, the comm officer turned from her station. "Captain, I am receiving a broad-beam transmission from the commander of the zor squadron. It doesn't seem to make any sense, sir."

Boyd said, "Sir, have you noted their pattern of deployment?" It was the first words he had spoken since coming onto the bridge.

Sergei looked at the forward screen. The ships, showing as half-illuminated globes, were arranged in a whorl like a seashell, with two vessels to port, one above the other. Then he looked at the pilot's board; the zor formation was fifteen, or perhaps thirty, seconds from coming in range of his own.

"Is there something about it I should know?" he asked, without looking away.

"It's a . . . *hRni'i*, sir. The glyph represents 'Fate,' but in a very deep sense."

"Explain."

"In this context, sir, I believe that they are seeking to surrender, but they are expecting us to recognize this pattern."

"Anne, what are the zor transmitting?"

"The translator is having problems with it, sir. It is some sort of poem, I think. Something about a captive, and a hero, and the . . . 'Mountains of Night.'"

Marais, who had been silent for the entire exchange, looked at the forward viewscreen, and said, "Mr. Boyd, what is the name of the glyph represented by the zor deployment?"

"*esHu'eyen*, sir. And if I may point out to the admiral, the zor have deployed eleven ships in the formation, no more and no less."

"Lieutenant," Marais said, "broadcast the following: *esHu'ur*'s wing has been touched by *esHu'eyen* and now demands the immediate surrender of this base and all vessels in this system. Those that resist will be cast to the Eight Winds."

Anne DaNapoli looked bewildered for a fraction of a second but quickly glanced at Sergei and, when he nodded slightly, proceeded to send the message.

Almost immediately, she turned back. "Captain, a zor commander requests permission to speak with . . . *esHu'ur.*"

Sergei looked at the pilot's board. "Nearly all of our own ships have arrived insystem, Admiral. We have the zor forward contingent outgunned. If this is a trap, we will certainly be able to retaliate."

"Very well." Marais concentrated his gaze on the forward viewscreen. "Lieutenant, please inform the zor commander that *esHu'ur* will speak with him."

"Advance units hold fire," Sergei said immediately. "Captain Bell, have your fighter wings stand off on my orders."

A 3-V of a zor appeared forward on the bridge of the *Lancaster*. His uniform was ornate, and a blue sash was belted around his waist. Some of his surroundings were represented as well, ghostly images arranged about him.

"My Lord *esHu'ur,* I am Hyos m'Har, of Nest HeYen," the zor said. Since the *Lancaster* was sending a visual image of its own bridge, his eyes darted around from figure to figure. Nonetheless he seemed to quickly settle on Marais. His words were translated by the ship's computer and reproduced in Standard in a close approximation of his own voice. "I command this base on behalf of the High Nest."

"I am Ivan Hector Charles Marais, Lord Marais," the admiral replied, not missing a beat. "This fleet is under my command."

"Mah-*rees.*" The zor tried the word for a moment, then retreated to the more formal title. "Lord *esHu'ur,* I am informed by the High Lord that you wish to speak with him."

Marais did not look away, but said, "Lieutenant, please check the translation on that last remark by the zor commander."

Anne's fingers across her console. "The translation was accurate, my lord."

"I have not contacted the High Nest, *se* Hyos." He paused for a moment, considering, and then continued. "In any case, I have demanded, and demand again, complete and unconditional surrender from this base. That is what I am here for. Discussion with the High Lord can come later." Sergei looked back at him, but only Marais' eyes betrayed confusion; his expression remained solid. "You will yield this station, or I will destroy it."

The zor commander said something offscreen. Marais looked at Boyd, who said, "They are discussing whether you are indeed the Dark Wing, my lord." The admiral nodded, watching the commander's wings ripple from one position to another.

"If that is the case, *esHu'ur*, then I am here to offer that surrender."

It was almost too sudden to believe, but after a moment, a cheer rang out across the bridge of the *Lancaster*. Marais cut off further celebration with a gesture. "If you are so empowered, *se* Hyos, we will take immediate possession of all facilities in the system, and your vessels should prepare to receive prize crews."

"Agreed."

"You will arrange the terms of surrender with my fleet commander, Commodore Torrijos." Marais appeared very ill at ease suddenly, and after adding a "You may proceed" to Sergei, walked off the bridge.


One of the paragon virtues of a good commander is his ability to adapt at once to new situations. While under the guns of the fleet's capital ships, prize crews and marine escorts from several ships of the line were ferried across to the eleven zor vessels that drifted in their seashell formation toward the Imperial position. Within an hour, all of them had reported directly from the bridges of those ships that they had them under control.

The combined fleet then began to move toward the inner reaches of the system, leaving a dozen ships at the jump point to secure against treachery. There was a three-hour journey ahead, traveling toward the great base, escorting the eleven captured vessels. The admiral left orders not to be disturbed, creating a confusing interlude on the bridge.

When the Imperial flotilla and its zor prize vessels closed in on the station, a small, unarmed system-boat launched itself outward, and came into range of the Imperial ships. It stood off and hailed the *Lancaster.*

"This is the *Lancaster,*" Sergei said, as the image of Captain Hyos began to materialize. "Go ahead."

The zor commander looked out from the screen, his alien visage unreadable. His wings were tucked behind him and Boyd, who had remained on the bridge, shrugged; there was no additional information.

"Captain," the zor began. "I am unsure how to proceed. There is no precedent for what we are about to do and the High Lord has given me to understand that *esHu'ur,* if he showed himself, should not be offended.

"I am aboard the barge you see approaching your vessels and I propose to receive you here and offer you the hospitality of the High Nest as we contemplate the details of the . . . *surrender.*" The translator had difficulty with the word; clearly there were overtones that it could not understand. "Would this be acceptable?"

"I will convey your request to the admiral, Commander. I cannot say for sure what he will or will not find acceptable. I do confess that we were not expecting this."

"The Eight Winds have blown us this way, Captain. The High Lord has dreamed, and we will do as *esLi* wills."


Marais seemed to accept the arrangement almost without question. He had been reticent and distant since Stone's disappearance, but this most recent turn of events had seemed to stun him almost to silence, as if it had removed his power of understanding.

At Sergei's suggestion a Marine honor guard and an escort of four senior officers, including Sergei himself, had been chosen to accompany the admiral aboard the barge. First, a Marine squad had been sent aboard to secure it and to guard against treachery. The zor commander had seemed to accept this affronting action with diffidence; by the time they reached the service airlock very little potential danger remained. Seabees had taken extreme care to secure the joint that had been quickly constructed to connect the two airlocks. They floated outside in the space between the vessels, ready to act if the integrity of the connection was compromised.

Silently the two officers reviewed the Marine honor guard, which had again been placed under the command of Sergeant Boyd; then Marais signalled to the bosun's mate to cycle the airlock.

A military march rolled through the intercom, and the slow pumping of the compressors began.

Though it was largely a ceremonial occasion, it was singular in the long history of war between man and zor: no zor vessel had ever struck its colors or allowed itself to be boarded. What was more, there was no precedent for courtesies and honors due a zor commander who surrendered.

But then there was very little precedent for anything that was happening during this campaign.

Sergei exchanged a glance with Chris Boyd; the younger man stood rigidly at attention, but he, too, looked nervous at the meeting that was about to happen.

The compressors sighed and finished their task. The airlock doors slid aside, and the group—Sergei, Marais, Marc Hudson, Alyne Bell, Bert Halvorsen, Tina Li, and the six-member marine contingent—advanced into the airlock. The doors shut with a hollow sound and the compressors started again, equalizing the pressure between the 'lock and the tunnel. This operation took only a few moments and presently they were walking along the fifty-meter section of tunnel, dimly lit by hastily strung lightcords. As they approached the zor end of the tunnel the other airlock cycled open to accommodate them.

There was a brief wait while the compressors equalized pressure on both sides of the bulkhead door. The hatchway, which was finely inscribed with *hRni'i,* slid up and out of the way and the group stepped onto the deck of the alien vessel.

A zor stepped forward to greet them in the reddish light. He was dressed similarly to the base commander, except that he wore a sash of crimson color, similar to the one worn by Rrith; it identified him as a Sensitive. A finely decorated *chya* hung at his waist.

"Greetings to you, *se esHu'ur,* and to those of your Nest," he said, in nearly flawless Standard. "I am Kasu'u m'Har, of Nest HeYen. Be at home on our humble vessel."

Marais made a polite greeting in return and introduced his officers.

"It is my honor," the zor continued, "to escort you to the presence of our base commander, *se* Hyos *ehn* m'Har of Nest HeYen, with whom you have already made acquaintance. *se* Hyos further begs the honor of your presence at his table along with your officers."

Marais again replied with a phrase. The zor turned, issued a command to the waiting group of uniformed zor, and led them away along a sloping corridor, the walls of which were engraved with *hRni'i,* forming an almost discernible pattern.

As they walked, Sergei's portable comm signaled. He was re-assured by the message from Chan that a "green condition" was in force—that there were no problems. Polite conversation and dress uniforms had done nothing to relieve his concerns about zor duplicity, Dark Wing or no.

The corridor turned, and ended in a wide ladder. The zor led the way, flying slowly up to the next level. The humans, agile in the low gravity, followed him up.

The upper level was even more dimly lit; clearly the zor had illuminated the lower area more brightly as a courtesy to their captors. Further, the atmosphere had a peculiar musty odor. Their guide led them through the gloom to a semicircular hatch and they entered between a pair of marine guards who looked singularly ill at ease in the alien surroundings. Without further comment Kasu'u withdrew, leaving the humans alone in the chamber.

If they had not already been aware of the alienness of the zor vessel, this chamber brought the point home. It was wide and high-ceilinged with a dispersed, multileveled structure, ranging from a high perch on the left three meters from floor level, to a depressed area in the center with cushions and a number of low tables. The rear wall of the room was partially occluded by a large torus suspended from the ceiling.

Sergei noticed Chris Boyd shuddering when he noticed the torus, and filed the observation for future consideration. Silently he beckoned the marines to take up positions around the room.

Their host entered through a narrow door on the right side of the room. He had a message-pad in one hand. Upon seeing the visitors he placed it on an ornate side table just inside the door.

"*esHu'ur*," he said. "I am . . . honored. May I offer you refreshment?" He spoke with care but it was clear that he was skilled in human speech, far more than Kasu'u who had escorted them there. His choice of using his enemy's tongue seemed to continue the overtone of conciliation that already had been suggested by the proceedings thus far.

He showed the officers to cushioned seats in the depression and assumed a position on a perch. With great care he decanted bluish liquid into exquisite goblets, and offered them around.

"To the success of our discussion," he offered. "This is *h'geRu,* a mild alcoholic drink extracted from a particular kind of nut found only on Zor'a. It is known to be safe for humans to consume."

Sergei looked at Marais and then beyond to where Chris Boyd stood near the door through which they had come. Boyd nodded and Sergei took a careful sip of the liquid. It had a pleasant almond flavor and only the slightest hint of alcohol. The de-

canter was equipped to keep it very cold, which seemed to enhance the taste.

Marais placed his goblet on a low table and folded his hands
in his lap. "*se* Hyos, there is much that we must discuss. In order
that decorum may be preserved in our negotiations, I must ask
about your level of responsibility within the hierarchy of your
people. That to say, sir, will it be necessary to renegotiate with
the High Lord as well?"

"Lord *esHu'ur*, I am of Nest HeYen, the High Nest. The
Lord Sse'e HeYen is the offspring of my Nest-father's elder
brother, making him cousin to me.

"To negotiate with me is to negotiate with the High Nest.
My authority extends over this base; but insofar as the High
Lord is concerned, I am given the right to straighten the flight for
him. Our agreements are binding"—he beckoned to the torus
behind him—"before *esLi.*"

Marais took a deep breath. There was a subtle yet perceptible
switch of psychological emphasis in the room; the zor Hyos had
been at the center of attention from the time he had entered.
Now, suddenly, the focus was on the admiral.

"*se* Hyos," he began, "I am prepared to accept the total surrender of all installations at this base. Though we both understand that I am under no obligation to guarantee the safety of any
persons or property, I will make that guarantee if I receive what
I ask.

"In like manner, I expect you to straighten the flight for me
to negotiate a similar surrender for the zor Core Stars. I do not
seek to touch your honor in this matter; I merely desire that you
assist me in concluding this war in a way similar to that in which
we reach agreement here.

"The alternative for your people will be annihilation. There
is no middle ground at this point."

The zor extended a taloned hand to the low table near him,
and took up the goblet. He carefully sipped at the blue liquid,

never letting his eyes leave Marais as he did so. After a few moments, he placed the glass carefully back on the table.

"*se esHu'ur,* it is hard for the People to deal with this situation, either individually or as a group. We are . . . Our entire culture is based on the notion that our Lord and Creator *esLi* constructed this universe for our own use, exclusively and without restriction. Our own religion asserts that other intelligences, if we were to find them, would be the servants of the Lord of the Cast Out—*esGa'uYal . . .*" He paused as Marais nodded, indicating that he recognized the word and what it meant. "It would be our duty and our right to eradicate them as unworthy of *esLi*'s Circle of Perfect Light. Indeed, we would be instruments of the Lord *esGa'u,* the Deceiver, if we failed to do so.

"We could not have envisioned that this evaluation could be wrong. We have, in a sense, been blinded by *esLi* Himself.

"The struggle between your race and the People has always been a holy war for us, Lord *esHu'ur.* We had believed that *esLi* intended us to eradicate you and to cleanse the universe—*our* universe—of the pestilence of humanity." There was a sharp intake of breath from the other officers; Marais remained as impassive as he could under the circumstances. "Yes, Admiral, Lord *esHu'ur:* we always assumed that we would defeat you ultimately. No matter how many times a warrior fell beneath the shadow of the Dark Wing, we took another step closer to your defeat.

"We never believed that there would come a time that one such as you would achieve victory over us." Hyos sighed, a suddenly human mannerism that seemed to belie his alienness and the alienness of the room in which they sat. "Defeat is a simple affair for the People. To live through a defeat is to be *idju:* so it has always been."

"There are somewhat different circumstances in force now, *se* Hyos."

"I agree, Lord *esHu'ur.* We cannot accept defeat without accepting dishonor as well. But another talon of this same argument is the undeniable truth that there is no sense in struggling against the inevitable. No matter what sense of personal honor one of the People possesses, he knows that he cannot in the end defeat *esHu'ur.* There is no escape from the Dark Wing, whether He comes sooner or late.

"We knew, long before you reached this base, that our options were two only. We could struggle against an inevitable defeat, or we could face the prospect of being *hi'idju: idju* as a race."

Marais was visibly shocked by this statement. Gathering himself together, he asked, "What would be the consequences of this dishonor?"

"That would not be for me to decide, Lord *esHu'ur.* The High Lord would have a clearer understanding of our obligations. But the possibility exists that there would be but one honorable solution to this situation.

"We would . . . give up our lives."

Marc Hudson sat forward. "I beg your pardon, sir," he said—and to Marais—"and yours also, Admiral Marais. But I must ask: Do you mean to say that you would commit suicide . . . as a race?"

"If we felt that was the only solution, we would."

"I cannot conceive of that, sir. It is impossible for me to believe that an intelligent race would destroy itself rather than change its beliefs. You could not accept our existence: now you can not accept that we have defeated you. Rather than live with the knowledge of that defeat, you choose to end it all. For good. Forever.

"*se* Hyos, that sort of stubbornness does not sound like an evolutionary advantage to me."

The zor tensed as Marc said these words. His talons clenched, and there was anger in his eyes that transcended the alien distance between them.

"There is no choice, if we determine that it is the only solution. If the High Lord commands . . . or if *esHu'ur* commands . . . the People will come to an end."

"I would never command such an action, *se* Hyos."

"Yet you *have* done so by your actions, *se* Admiral. You say so yourself: if we do not yield to the Dark Wing, we will be eradicated. What indeed is the distinction? With the one wing you order us eradicated by the talon of your servants, while with the other you would order us to transcend the Outer Peace by our own means. In the end we would all be gone."

Marais had no answer for this comment and simply waited for the zor commander to continue.

"For us to choose an alternative to our code of honor is to tear down the entire fabric of our society. It undermines our faith and the foundations of our social order: the sky is the ground, the ground is the sky. There are some of the People who might never accept the dishonor of defeat. They may fight on for generations, resisting until they are slain.

"When we began this war, we were told that *esLi* had turned His face from us and would not bestow His favor again until we eradicated our enemy. We believed that our will and *esLi*'s favor would bring us that victory.

"No one expected defeat. No one was ready to accept defeat. Now that defeat has occurred, no one is sure whether the prospect of total destruction is not preferable to the mercy of the Cast Out. If that were the case it would not matter if you destroyed us or we destroyed ourselves. The flight has been chosen: the thing would be done."

Marais seemed to size up Hyos HeYen for a long moment before he replied. "Commander, I have come a great distance, both physically and otherwise, to reach this place, this choosing of the flight. As Captain Hudson points out, it makes no sense for the People to choose to transcend the Outer Peace because they cannot accept dishonor. Some may find this unavoidable: perhaps those who bore the defeat most heavily.

"If you truly wish this outcome—and like my subordinate I can see no reason why your entire race might wish it—I am prepared to grant you the freedom to do what you will. If the High Nest will not agree to that surrender, I will make your moral quandary a moot question, except for those persons who have already accepted my offer and thus lie under my protection.

"What must be done before I receive a decision?"

The zor altered his wing position, bringing them around him like a cloak. He took up his glass of *h'geRu* and sipped delicately from it.

"There is a portion of the *Lament of the Peak, esHu'ur.* . . . In it, the Bright Wing has been imprisoned beyond the Mountains of Night by *esGa'u*, who hopes to use this fact to control it and thus dominate the World for all time."

Marais nodded as Hyos described the passage.

"But *esLi* is too clever for *esGa'u;* he knows that both Bright Wing and Dark Wing are part of the World That Is and that one cannot exist without the other. Thus though they are opposites, the Dark Wing delivers the Bright Wing from exile and the World is changed.

"When the great hero Qu'u was confronted with the imprisonment of the Bright Wing, he realized that he was powerless to aid it from escaping. He was even unable to save himself. It is no easy thing for a hero to admit that no expression of courage, fortitude or wisdom can have any effect. Qu'u had to concede his powerlessness. It is his lament that is named in the title of the story and it is his lament that we must now sing.

"The High Lord has dreamed, and in his vision you came to *him* and informed him that it was time that you spoke. I was given orders that if you came I should greet you by a sign that you would recognize if you were truly the Dark Wing. You recognized it and I have admitted that I am powerless to oppose you. I am powerless to prevent your devastation of the People. There is no sense in the People struggling, if the opponent they face is the Dark Wing Himself.

"But still the Lord *esLi* might deliver us. Though I can do nothing to sway you, I believe that it is incumbent upon you, *esHu'ur,* to go to Zor'a and meet with the High Lord Sse'e HeYen. It is he who will decide the path we must fly now and it is you who will guide him.

"Only in this way can honor be satisfied."

## chapter 15

"I believe that I first met Thomas Stone in 2307."

Marais took the decanter of fruit juice from the autokitchen dispenser and came back to sit in his usual armchair. Sergei leaned forward, elbows on knees, listening; the admiral's 'reader was recording it all. "It was after the *Bolívar* incident; I was a staff officer posted to the border area, part of Admiral DeSaia's strategic planning-team.

"There was a plan even then for an attack on the A'anenu Base, you know: of course, the Efal peace talks scuttled all that. It always disheartens me to think that this war could have been fought, and perhaps won, long before now."

"About Stone, sir . . ."

"Stone. Yes. He was a relatively new officer, with almost no service record. He had a letter from the station commodore at Mothallah, a nobleman named Willis: he also had a personal recommendation from my brother Stefan, who commands the facilities at Tuuen. He was—or seemed to be—a climber, a commoner with no Court connections and no patron."

"There are a lot of us out there, Admiral."

Marais looked into his cup, as if the next sentence might be swirling around in there. "I did not mean that pejoratively, Torrijos. I merely meant to describe Stone to you. Like many such officers, he had little in the way of leverage. He was self-effacing to a fault and had outstanding qualities that made him an ideal aide."

"An eidetic memory, for instance."

"That's right; he had certification from the New Chicago Institute. But it was more than that: while on staff with Admiral DeSaia, he proved himself invaluable to me. He seemed to know what I was thinking almost before I did. By the time the peace talks became serious I had already engaged him as my own attaché.

"When I was beached after Efal I obtained a captain's commission for him." The admiral smiled, as if distantly remembering something from the past, misplaced like an absent keepsake. "There we were on half-pay, a pair of military officers without postings. Money wasn't an issue. But rather than simply retire and enter my family's business, we began to take an interest in the conflict itself.

"I had spent rather a lot of my university time studying the zor, years before. A few months after the treaty was signed we were able to obtain diplomatic visas to travel to the zor worlds on the Imperial side of the Antares Rift, in order to look at manuscripts and examine zor culture firsthand. It wasn't hard to do; even though the war was just over, the aliens we met were remarkably accommodating. I suppose they tolerated our presence because they felt we were no more than *esHara'y,* barbarian servants of the Lord of the Cast Out, who could see nothing and learn nothing. Knowing the zor as I do now, though, I think that they might've viewed us as avatars of Shrnu'u HeGa'u."

"'Shrnu'u HeGa'u'?"

"A legendary general. He served the Deceiver, and sought so hard to insinuate himself into zor society that his own *e'chya* turned on him. They must have expected us to be consumed and crumble to dust at any moment."

Sergei took a few moments to absorb this information before he posed his next question. "When did you begin writing the book, sir?"

"It was about that time." Marais set his cup on the table. "We spent four months in zor-space and returned to Mothallah to consult their excellent library. From our investigations, it was clear that the zor took a completely . . . well, *alien* view of the war. Even characterizing it as a struggle between good and evil or a religious jihad had failed to do their point of view any justice. It was something totally different, so much so that we felt it necessary to articulate that view in order that a consistent and effective policy toward them could be formulated.

"It was like viewing a history from the other side of the 3-V. It all fell into place: why they had attacked Alya in the first place, what the motivations had been to break the various treaties, and what was likely to happen to the Treaty of Efal. Reviewing the six decades of conflict made us realize that we had listened to their words but never completely understood what they had said."

"We were never able to read their wings."

"Yes; of course, we can see that *now*—but there was never any reason to know it before. The zor must have assumed that we were ignoring them—as, indeed, we were.

"So, over the period of six months, we wrote *The Absolute Victory.* I received a stern reprimand from the First Lord of the Admiralty for it; if I'd been on active duty I would have been cashiered for calling Navy tactics into question—at least outside of a confidential briefing. No one in the Navy who had any sense believed that Efal would be any more successful than its predecessors. It was destined for the airlock, and everyone knew it.

"The book was picked up by a reputable publisher and made widely available. I don't mind admitting that I put some of my own funds into its distribution, but I hardly expected it to come into the emperor's hands. After all, I had accused His Majesty's Government of appeasement."

"But it *did* reach the emperor's hands," Sergei said. "But not by your means."

"No, Commodore. Stone had some contacts at Court at that time—"

"Though he had none when you met him."

Marais paused for a moment. "You're right, he didn't. But I clearly recall that he told me that he knew someone at Court who might be able to gain the ear of His Imperial Majesty. I was excited about the possibility, since an Imperial comment—especially a favorable one, but really, any publicity from the Court—would help the sale of the book. My family was—*is*—well known at Oahu, so it would have been natural for me to have a chance for an interview, maybe at some official function.

"The actual outcome was quite different."

"Quite so, my lord. It seems that you owe a great deal to Captain Stone, sir, if I may be so forward."

"What do you mean by that?"

"I mean no offense, my lord. You are here and your mettle has certainly been tested and proved. We are carrying out something very close to the campaign you described in the book—the same book that, whether His Imperial Highness likes it or not, was the catalyst for your appointment. Your present state isn't due to Captain Stone, but rather the way in which he acted to bring this state about."

"Stone did not write the book, Torrijos; I did."

"But he did help you formulate what you wrote. And he *did* arrange for the book to reach the hands of Emperor Alexander."

Marais' eyes had begun to fill with anger. "He was a tool, Commodore. Nothing more."

"He left my ship in jump, my lord. *In jump.* I have a mystery on my hands: an energy flux and a physical phenomenon that my science officer and his staff cannot explain. Just as I was calling his behavior and motivations into question he disappeared from the *Lancaster*, something that we consider to be impossible.

"Maybe twenty years in His Majesty's Navy has made me a skeptic, a paranoiac or worse. Maybe I'm seeing something where nothing exists. But I can't ignore an undeniable fact that whoever Stone was, or is, his agenda and motivations were not what they seemed. The cabin where he was quartered wasn't on the outside of the hull—he wasn't vented into nothingness. There was no sign of an explosion or an antimatter annihilation. There wasn't a molecule left behind. There isn't a joule of energy unaccounted for.

"Whatever Stone was doing, however he stepped into the picture and back out of it, it's clear he wasn't here on this ship or even on this campaign by accident.

"In short, Admiral—and I mean no disrespect, sir—I don't think that Stone was a tool as much as I believe that *you* were a tool. I'm not happy with that conclusion, sir. I have the greatest respect for you, and the strongest belief in what we are doing out here. I simply don't know what it is we're dealing with."

Marais' anger hadn't completely dissipated. "What does it mean, Torrijos, if you're right?"

Sergei had expected that question, but he still took a deep breath before answering. "I don't quite know, Admiral. I've been trying to think this through: Captain Stone has at least one power that we don't. Maybe someone directed Stone to get involved in this campaign, perhaps by finding you or someone like you. His actions helped make you admiral.

"Maybe he believed that with your talents and beliefs, and your—what should I call it? . . . your *will*—that you could bring the task to completion."

"Winning the war."

"At the very least, sir. I've been reviewing my interactions with Captain Stone over the past several months. I don't think that he ever took the enemy's religious overtones seriously, except in one respect: how they contributed to the fleet's ability to destroy the zor."

"He helped me write the book, didn't he? He read the same things I did."

"But I don't think he reached the same conclusions. Look at his actions: he sought to silence dissonant voices among the officer corps; he challenged the credibility of both the zor prisoner and Sergeant Boyd. I don't think he ever wanted any kind of understanding to take place.

"He wasn't pushing toward conquest, my lord. He was interested in seeing the zor exterminated."

"We always knew that would be a possibility."

"Yes, sir, we did. We always assumed that exterminating the zor was what we might have to do if we couldn't get them to come to terms with us. But the way I read it, Captain Stone wanted it to come out that way from the start. I'll bet that if Stone were sitting right here, though, he would counsel you against accepting such a surrender. He would say that it was a trap."

"Why would he want that?"

"I wish I knew, Admiral. Damn good question. But let me ask you this, Admiral: if someone out there wants us to destroy the zor, isn't that a good reason to think twice before doing it?"

He showed his badge to the guard at the desk while another submitted him to a retinal scan. Security was tight here at Langley: no surprise—this base, along with the rest of Callisto, was the exclusive preserve of Imperial Intelligence. Getting here was difficult enough, but entering this part of the sprawling complex was especially so—scarcely a dozen people in the Empire had clearances that got them through the door directly before him.

The knowledge that he was one of them and what made him

one of the privileged few—an eidetic memory, a superb analytical mind and (he always reminded himself, amused) an incredible humility—always reassured him that all was right with the universe. As he stood there and was identified, his mind was busy processing the information that chirped slowly and steadily from the star-shaped earring in his right ear. Keeping up was at least half the job; he always kept up.

"Everything seems to be in order, Captain Smith," the guard said at last and handed him back his badge. His current face looked back at him: self-assured, a half-smile creeping across it. The name SMITH, JOHN T., CAPTAIN, IIS appeared beneath.

Without comment he took the badge and placed it on his lapel, nodded to the two guards, and went through the door.

"Ah, there you are, Green."

The director and the five others in the room watched him carefully as he crossed the room. It was a large conference room, somewhat dimly lit, with a huge semicircular view of Jupiter in the background. Every time he saw that view it mesmerized him, if only for a few moments: he had long ago realized that 3-V could never do justice to the spectacle he witnessed outside—the storms that chased each other across the planet's gigantic surface, the mysterious Red Spot, the dances of the moons as they whirled around. You could forget yourself watching that.

But only for a moment.

He nodded and conveyed what might pass for a sincere smile to the director, an elderly woman of slight stature. He took the only vacant seat: a high-backed armchair with a green circular design worked into the table in front of it.

"Pleasant flight, I hope," the director added, as she slid a 'reader over to him. He smiled and nodded again and took a quick survey of the others: Red, a stern-looking dark-skinned man with a closely cropped beard; Yellow, a dapper Caucasian with a scar over his left eye that seemed to give him a perplexed look; Blue, an Oriental woman with liquid eyes and a posture that suggested a hunting-cat ready to strike; Orange, a thoughtful-looking woman with olive skin; and Violet, a huge, swarthy man whose very glance seemed menacing.

And the director, of course, and himself.

*Quite a group,* he thought to himself.

"I would like to thank you all for coming at such short notice," the director began, when he had taken his seat. "Normally a face-to-face meeting of this group would not even be practical or perhaps even possible. But given the present climate . . ." She let her voice trail off and made an offhand gesture. Smith noticed a swirl of storm seemed to be just forming on Jupiter's upper limb behind her; he wondered if it were some part of her presentation. "In any case, now that we're all here, I'd like to make sure we're all up-to-date on the current situation.

"Orange, perhaps you could summarize for us."

"My pleasure, Director," she answered, folding her hands in front of her on the table.

"As you all know," Orange began, "some weeks ago the zor placed a peace offer on the table in the way they have always done before: a tight-beam message was received at Mothallah on the frequency reserved for such communications, and relayed to our ambassador. A report of this offer was duly made to His Imperial Highness.

"The terms of the offer were simple: the zor agreed to voluntarily withdraw from their naval base at A'anenu if the Imperial Fleet would stand off that world. This would have made it impossible for them to maintain any effective military presence on this side of the Antares Rift, restricting them to their Core Stars and whatever areas of space they claimed outside of Imperial jurisdiction.

"The emperor was suspicious of treachery on the part of the aliens but agreed to order the fleet to cease and desist, pending the verification that the zor High Nest would be willing to take this step. He also sent a plenipotentiary ambassador"—she took a moment to pause and smile ever so slightly, as if to suggest that she knew something that the listeners did not—"to begin this verification. The Admiralty's latest information placed the fleet at the zor world S'rchne'e; the emissary was sent there. By the time he arrived, of course, the fleet had already departed and he was refused access to the necessary transponder codes and other information necessary to make his way into the war zone.

"There is evidence to suggest that the order to stand off was received by Admiral Marais' flagship; the fleet was at that time positioned *at* A'anenu. There is no logged acknowledgement.

"Lacking such confirmation, we cannot say with absolute certainty that Lord Marais acted in contravention of orders from the Admiralty or instructions from the emperor. All of the circumstantial evidence, however, suggests that he did—a fact that has caused no end of consternation in St. Louis, not to mention Oahu."

Orange looked from face to face. "The Tolliver Government worked to keep this fact away from the press and out of the hands of the Opposition, particularly Assemblyman Hsien." She smiled at Yellow, across from her. "Needless to say, we made certain that they could not keep this a secret. Our policy decision has caused a number of problems that I'm sure my colleagues will take up in due time.

"As far as the war zone is concerned, Marais' disregard of Admiralty orders allowed him to invest and take the A'anenu Starbase. The zor tried to destroy the base during this operation but were unsuccessful; A'anenu is therefore in Imperial hands more or less intact. As an additional bonus, it seems that one of the zor on the base was taken into custody alive, and is now aboard the *Lancaster.*"

This brought murmurs from a couple of those sitting at the table; Smith kept his face impassive, but the ramifications of this revelation were already running through his mind at high speed.

"Do we have a report on the prisoner?" the director asked. Blue leaned forward slightly, inclining her head. "Please continue, Orange."

"Another unforeseen consequence of this action is a perspec-

tive change on the part of Admiral Marais. It has already been reported that he has taken a peculiarly messianic view of his role
with respect to the war.

"In a staff meeting, on which subject we have a full account"—she keyed a reference number that appeared on the
'readers in front of the others—"he has proposed strategic and
policy decisions based on his interpretation of the zor perception
of his role; now he seems to have begun to believe himself to be
a sort of mythical agent of destruction.

"This remarkable mind-set is very much in keeping with the
admiral's personality. I believe that if he survives this campaign
he will undoubtedly seek the Imperial throne. The recent chain
of events only reinforce this position, which has been stated here
before."

"Where is the fleet now?" Red asked, absently stroking his
beard.

"Somewhere between A'anenu and E'rene'e," Orange answered. "There is no way to be sure. The majority of the fleet has
departed A'anenu, probably for the site of a zor naval base in the
Rift. After destroying this site, its next destination is E'rene'e in
the zor Core Stars. Based on the most recent experience on this
side of the Antares Rift, the aliens may not even be fighting back
at this time."

"Please clarify that last point," the director said, tapping her
stylus on the table.

"Several vidrecs are available to support the idea that since
the taking of A'anenu, the zor are not resisting their own destruction. A report presented by Captains Okome and MacEwan
is instructive." Text flowed to the 'readers.

She leaned back in her chair and folded her hands in her lap.
"Even with the mythological undertones, however, there is no
analytical basis to conjecture that the zor will do anything but
what they have already done. They will not surrender: Marais
will destroy them."

"What does our deep agent report?"

"Ah." Orange glanced at the director, who seemed to nod almost imperceptibly. "I'm afraid we were forced to pull our best agent out of the war zone. There was some evidence that his cover was about to be blown."

"Our eyes and ears—" Red began, a hint of anger in his voice.

"Gone," the director interrupted, holding her left hand up slightly. "We will have to rely on our noses. Does that conclude your report, Orange?"

"Yes, Director."

"Yellow, please review the situation in the Assembly."

"Certainly, Director." Yellow shifted himself in his chair. "We have been working closely with the Commonwealth Party's extensive information-gathering apparatus during the past several months. The opposition has certain advantages that the Government cannot possess, most prominently that it can associate with local organizations across the Empire; by comparison, no member of the Government would want to appear on a vidrec with them. In some respects this makes them much more vulnerable to our infiltration—especially in underrepresented areas of the Empire such as in the New Territories.

"In fact, the presence of Sir Stefan Ewing in the Imperial Assembly has provided the opposition with a rallying point. He has begun to say all of the right things about the actions of Marais' fleet—suggesting that the brunt of any zor counterattack would fall on the New Territories. Shortly after his election, he began to provide Assemblyman Hsien with information about activities in the war zone. We aided this effort as well," Yellow added, smiling, his scar making his left eye seem to droop sleepily.

"Hsien is writing his speeches," Violet growled.

"The voters do not seem to have any problem with his behavior at the Battle of Pergamum," the director said.

"His connections at Court saved him from anything worse than a graceful exit from active service," Violet added. "We should have been so lucky with Marais."

"We were," the director answered. "He was on the beach after Efal. If we hadn't lost DeSaia *and* Bryant and if McMasters hadn't been injured . . . If, if, if . . ."

"In any case," Yellow continued, "pacifists from all quarters have opposed the brutality of the war, from the first attack at L'alChan several months ago. Hsien for his part has played the part of populist outsider to the maximum: he has obtained the tacit or explicit support of pacifist groups as well as watchdog organizations such as Amnesty Interstellar and the Red Cross. With Green's help"— he exchanged a nod with Smith—"the emperor was made aware of Hsien's rising popularity and invited him to the Imperial Court near the end of the summer. The Government resigned shortly thereafter and a new prime minister was appointed.

"She, too, has borne the brunt of renewed attacks from Hsien and the other Commonwealth Party leaders, but has not yet lost a key division of the Assembly, and has refused the opposition's call for general elections."

"What evidence does Hsien have in his possession?" the director asked.

"Footage from L'alChan and S'rchne'e, as well as an official report on three systems neutralized by the *Ikegai* and the *San Martín*. This is the material that suggests that the zor have stopped fighting." Red was responsible for dissemination of intelligence; with the deep agent apparently gone from the fleet, he would have little to report.

"He's holding that back," the director said. "It didn't come out when he made that speech to the Assembly."

"No, you're quite right," Yellow continued. "Hsien's speech was so disruptive that the Speaker had to call a recess—but its thrust was considerably different than we had expected. Ewing, among others, had expected—and promised—a blast against brutality and xenocide in the war zone. Instead Hsien concentrated on what he perceived to be Marais' ultimate objective: seizure of the Imperial throne."

"He likened him to Admiral McDowell," Violet said, in a quiet voice that seemed to carry well. "He was very close to suggesting that the founding of the Empire was somehow . . . illegitimate."

*It was,* Green thought, but kept silent.

"Marais has been relieved of duty," Red interjected. "For what it's worth. It appears that all of the fleet in the battle zone and even some of the reserves are loyal to him."

"Does Hsien know this?"

"Whenever you want him to, Director," Yellow said, smiling again.

"That would be unwise," Violet interrupted. "Hsien assumes that Marais is acting alone or with a small coterie of officers. He also believes that certain 'sane' elements in the Navy will oppose him if he seeks to seize the Imperial throne. Let him continue to believe it." Violet pillared his fingers in front of him and leaned back deep into his chair. His voice had descended into a range that chilled even Smith. "If Marais tries and fails, Hsien may have an opportunity to become prime minister. Let him be beholden to the Agency."

"He already is," Yellow said.

"Your point is well taken," the director said. "Do you have anything further to report, Yellow?"

"No, Director. The situation in the Assembly is much as we had expected. Since Green reported on the meeting between the prime minister and Admiral McMasters, it was clear that the Government had no real power to control the situation but would do its best to keep that information from the opposition. The prime minister is considering asking the emperor to prorogue the Assembly, which I understand he is likely to grant. It's pretty much a deadlock right now."

"Very well. Blue, you have some information on the zor prisoner?"

"Yes, Director," Blue answered. She touched her 'reader and the screens on the other ones sprang to life, showing a short 3-V clip of a uniformed zor pacing about in a dimly lit chamber. "This is the zor Rrith, captured during the attack on A'anenu

Starbase. He is currently held aboard the flagship. He bears the crimson sash of a Sensitive though he obviously has not submitted to formal testing. He is aware of his current surroundings; you will notice a crude attempt by the Science Section of the *Gagarin* to simulate a zor Nest.

"Also—" She touched the 'reader again, and froze the clip. "Focus, 340 by 90, enlarge six times." The screen panned up and right and expanded the scene to show an object in the corner of the room: a sword in its scabbard, seemingly discarded on the floor. "Also, in this scene he seems to have tossed aside his ceremonial weapon, the *chya*—"

"That was left in the holding cell with him?" Red growled. "Fools . . . He could take his own life at any time!"

"What little we know of zor society suggests that the alien now considers himself to be *idju,* or dishonored," Blue replied, her voice conveying barely concealed patience. "By being captured rather than killed he has lost the right to take his own life. That is why the *chya* has been cast aside. However, Rrith was seen wearing the *chya* since this vid was taken.

"The decision to leave the sword with the prisoner was made by Admiral Marais himself; he evidently chose to accord some status to the zor."

"Absurd," Red said, but stopped short of further comment after a glance from the director.

"Despite this perception," Blue continued, "the zor was hostile and uncooperative. He was visited by a Marine from the *Biscayne* shortly after this video was obtained. While Rrith did not attack him, their exchange was unproductive."

"A Marine?" the director asked. "Why would a marine visit the zor prisoner?"

"I'm afraid I don't know, Director. Our agent was unaware of the visit until after it occurred and was unable to obtain a transcript or a vid of the conversation. Some technical problem aboard the *Gagarin,* I believe. But both the Marine and the prisoner have been transferred to the *Lancaster*. The zor has since been interviewed by the admiral."

"What was the outcome of that meeting?"

"Again, Director, I . . . We are short of hard data on this matter since our agent is no longer in place. We do know, however, that the prisoner left the interview still wearing his *chya*, so perhaps Marais *has* accorded him some additional status."

"We must have more information on this matter. Blue, see to it that we learn as much as we can about this prisoner, and about the Marine, if we can."

The director consulted her 'reader briefly. "Now, then— Green, please bring us up-to-date on events on Oahu."

"My pleasure, Director," Smith began. "As you are all aware, our emperor has rarely demonstrated a desire to control the affairs of his Government, even to the extent that his father did. He has more interest in horseback-riding and collecting three-hundred-year-old antiques than in following the conduct of the war."

"As is his privilege," Violet said levelly.

Smith looked at his colleague, then continued. "Still, he is not unaffected by the backlash. When the Imperial Court first learned of L'alChan, we decided on a course of action—to have the prime minister offer Admiral McMasters the opportunity to be appointed to command the fleet. There was good reason to believe the profile we had built: that McMasters, a career Navy man, would jump at the chance to supplant an upstart Imperial appointee of noble birth.

"The prime minister was unconvincing, as McMasters flatly refused the prime minister's offer. He predicted—correctly, I might add—that Marais intended to carry out the war exactly as predicted and exactly as described in his book."

"There was always some danger of that," Red remarked. "We knew that when the book was passed to His Imperial Highness in the first place."

"Yes," Smith replied, "of course. But it wasn't the most likely possibility, was it? When we conduct an operation we always deal in probabilities. There's a chance that someone won't react the way we predict; there's a chance that some unforeseen circumstance will arise, causing a mishap, and so forth.

"In any case, the emperor is more and more reclusive these days, as information about the conduct of the war reaches the public. Having to fire his longtime lapdog of a prime minister was a bit of a shock to him; his new prime minister is less accommodating but more able to withstand the shocks in the Assembly. He's leaving her to take a beating while he plays with his grandfather clocks and goes for rides on the beach."

"He *did* receive the opposition leader," Orange said quietly. She had remained silent and observant through the entire discussion after her initial presentation, but leaned forward now. "That meeting led directly to the resignation of the prime minister. Clearly that points to some interest on his part?"

"What happened at that meeting?" Yellow asked before Smith could respond.

Smith smiled. "Our great populist is quite different in the privacy of an Imperial audience than on the floor of the Assembly. Recall that this was long before he began preaching about Marais' grab for the throne; Hsien at that time was operating more on behalf of his party and in support of his own ambitions than anything else. He offered to serve as prime minister in a minority government and call elections at the emperor's command; he offered to support the war effort if Marais was instantly recalled and a peace offer made to the zor. Both offers were refused, as the good press from the victories outweighed the small amount of bad press from the atrocities.

"Hsien next suggested that the current prime minister could be made to take the blame for any misdeeds of the fleet and advised that Julianne Tolliver, a longtime political rival, be asked to form the next Government."

"Hsien asked—" Red sputtered, but the director held up her hand.

"Of *course* he did," she said. "However distasteful it might have been to him, it was certainly to his *political* advantage to do so. Tolliver is able to take the heat, while Hsien's reputation as an outsider remains intact."

"Unless word of this involvement reaches the public," Orange observed.

"Quite," the director said. "Please continue, Green."

"Thank you, Director. The emperor accepted Hsien's third suggestion, as you know. It is not clear that he understood Hsien's ulterior motive. When the assemblyman made his speech last month, accusing Marais of Imperial ambitions, the emperor was furious; afterward he commanded Hsien to come to Oahu to explain his actions, but Hsien had already gone outsystem. That left His Imperial Highness with a prime minister under attack, an admiral out of control, and an Assembly unable to take any action. It's no wonder he's spending so much time ignoring politics."

"We helped create this situation," Violet observed quietly.

"This isn't the situation we intended," Smith replied quickly. "We had expected something quite different—"

"Nonetheless," Violet answered, "we have dug a deep hole for His Imperial Highness. It seems only fair that we help get him out of it."

"If it suits the Agency's interests," Blue said coolly.

"This isn't some two-credit politician," he replied quickly. "This is the Solar Emperor, and I'll thank you to remember that. We have a loyalty—"

"—to the Empire."

"And to the emperor. Or had you forgotten your oath? I have *not*. We have created a compromising situation, because we helped to create Admiral Marais. I suggest that we solve His Imperial Majesty's problem in the most direct and forthright way possible."

"What would that be?" the director asked, though everyone at the table already knew, or suspected, the answer.

"Operation Tattoo," Violet said at once.

"As you know, Violet, sanctioning a figure as public as Admiral Marais requires the emperor's direct approval," the director answered carefully. "We would be fools to take that authority directly into our own hands. There is also the question of what impact that might have on the war effort."

"I hardly think it will undo the work he's already done," Violet sneered. "There isn't a zor naval base or even a zor settlement on this side of the Antares Rift. He's captured A'anenu; he's even captured a zor prisoner. The enemy has placed a peace offer on the table and I'm sure they would consider offering another."

"The aliens have given Marais mythic proportions—"

"Oh, come now, Director. You don't take that seriously, do you? Alien nonsense, mumbo jumbo, hand-waving—or should I say, claw-waving. Eliminating one man will make no difference in the grand scheme of things.

"On your other point, Director, I find it somewhat unpalatable that you are willing to balk at something so simple and tawdry as assassination, especially where protection of the emperor is concerned. You were willing and able to direct the Agency in an operation to place Admiral Marais in command of the fleet so that he could lay several zor worlds waste, kill millions of aliens and place tens of thousands of human lives in jeopardy—"

"It's hardly the same thing—"

"Oh no? Please spare me this peculiar bout of morality, Director. It is *exactly* the same thing. If we needed Marais to help set the Empire right after Pergamum, then we need have no qualms about having created him. If we need him to be gone at this point, then we dispose of him now. It is as simple as that."

The director looked visibly angry, but took a few moments to compose herself before speaking. "Your points bear a certain logic, Violet. I will take them into consideration. Is there any other input at this point?"

No one seemed willing to venture any comment.

"Very well, then. At the moment I believe that we have no basis for immediate action. If the emperor wishes to invoke Operation Tattoo, then we will carry it out. If Marais has the capability and the desire to be emperor then he will need an intelligence service at his disposal. As always, we will be capable of protecting and maintaining our own interests.

"In any case, we all have information to assimilate and duties to perform. This meeting is over."

The six agents stood, politely excusing themselves from the conference. Violet did not speak to his colleagues or to the director, but made directly for the exit.

"Red, Green, if you'll stay behind for a moment," the director said, as the group began to disperse. Smith exchanged a glance with his colleague but stood by his chair until the last of the other agents had left the room and the door had shut behind them.

"I half expected an outburst of the sort we just witnessed. I have concluded that Violet is not to be trusted since he may no longer be operating in the Agency's best interests. Red, you are to make sure that he has no access to Agency apparatus, commencing immediately.

"Green, you are to pay close attention to the personal welfare of the emperor and Prime Minister Tolliver. If necessary, you are to reveal your Agency connection and your status to those two people only. Are we clear?" She looked from face to face; both nodded. "Very well. Get back to work."

The two agents made their way out of the room. Neither said a word about their orders to the other. Behind, a storm began to swirl across Jupiter's mottled face.

chapter 16

ON THE PLAIN OF DESPITE,
THE LOST SOULS CANNOT RAISE THEIR FACES;
[*Sorrow of the Hssa*]
ONLY THE TRUE HERO            [*Honor to* esLi]
CAN TURN HIS GAZE TO THE SKY.

—*Lament of the Peak*

Ptal HeU'ur emerged from beneath the arbor just in time to prevent a scene, but he knew right away he was flying into trouble.

Makra'a, Nestlord of HeU'ur, stood near the entrance, declaiming angrily. His wings were held high in a posture of extreme affront, and he looked ready to draw his *chya* on S'tlin, the High Lord's *alHyu*. S'tlin, a middle-aged servant of small stature, stood respectfully and said nothing, but had placed himself so that Makra'a could not get past him without violence.

Ptal could already suspect why the Eight Winds had brought Makra'a here. Though he did not wish to confront his Nestlord now, he realized that he had little choice.

"*esLiHeYar,* my Lord," he said, quickly approaching. "Greetings to you, *ha* Makra'a, and welcome back to esYen." S'tlin stepped deftly out of the way and the High Chamberlain took his place before an obviously angry Makra'a HeU'ur.

The Nestlord lowered his wings to a more respectful level, and his voice came down with it. "*se* Ptal. You are looking well so far from the friendly sun of E'rene'e." It was an obvious jab at him for not having come home.

"Sometimes our duties pull us more strongly than our desires," Ptal answered. "*ha* Makra'a, is there some service I might do you?"

"I would speak with the High Lord."

"Eight thousand pardons, my Lord," Ptal replied. "I do not believe that *hi* Sse'e is receiving visitors this afternoon."

"He will receive *me.*"

"I do believe that your errand is urgent, my Lord, but when I was with him he asked that no one be admitted. Perhaps *se* S'tlin explained it to you already?"

"I am no offworld *L'le*-cousin who can be dismissed so easily, *se* Ptal. It is unpleasant enough to have to suffer the gibes of lesser Lords when they learn of the High Lord's plans and wishes even before I do, despite my many years of service. I do not suffer lightly the insult of being turned away by an *alHyu*, even the *alHyu* of the High Lord himself."

"I am sure that *se* S'tlin meant no insult."

"It is insulting to be merely *debating* with you out here, *se* Ptal," the Nestlord replied, his voice held level, his wings beginning to form the Stance of Impinged Honor. "You will disturb the High Lord on my behalf and I shall wait while you do so."

"*ha* Makra'a, I—"

"I will not debate this with you. I have abandoned my Nest in the face of *esHu'ur*'s shadow to wait upon the High Lord. Every sixty-fourth of a moon I spend here on Zor'a is too long to be away. You will tell him that I am here and would speak with him. If he will not meet with me I will take his answer back to E'rene'e. Go and do this."

Ptal HeU'ur considered Makra'a's statement for a moment and weighed whether he should refuse again.

"Very well," he said, after waiting another few moments. "Please come this way, *ha* Makra'a," he added, gesturing toward the entrance to the arbor.

Ptal expected to find the High Lord as he had left him just a few minutes earlier, perched in the center of the *esTle'e*, in meditation; instead, he was bent over, examining the progress of some of the colorful shrubs that circled the center of the garden. His *hi'chya* was sheathed at his side, and he looked up when Ptal and S'tlin approached.

"*hi* Sse'e," Ptal began, "I would not disturb you again except—"

"Except," the High Lord said, straightening up, his wings forming a posture of friendliness, "that someone of great importance demands my attention and seeks to disturb my rest and contemplations." Ptal moved to answer but the High Lord held up a hand. "A Lord of Nest, I would suppose . . . Makra'a, perhaps?"

"A dream, *hi* Sse'e?"

"*esLi* does not often send me dreams about Makra'a," the High Lord answered, his wings raised lightly in amusement. "No, I sensed the commotion outside and when you returned so quickly I realized that there were few who could demand service from you contrary to my own orders."

"Eight thousand pardons," Ptal answered, eyes lowered. His wings descended to a posture of apology. "If the High Lord feels that my responsibilities are compromised by my blood relationship with *ha* Makra'a, I will gladly withdraw from my post—"

"By *esLi*'s Circle of Light, no indeed!" Sse'e stepped forward and gripped Ptal's forearms with his claws. His wings settled into the Stance of Comradeship. "In these troubled skies, my good friend, I can think of no other who could fly with me so loyally and well."

He let go the grip and looked at S'tlin for a moment. "Have you had word of your son, *se* S'tlin?"

"My son, High Lord?" S'tlin seemed taken aback, almost embarrassed to be asked a question during the exchange. "Yes, I have, *hi* Sse'e. S'reth has performed the first Ordeal of Experience with great skill, and is now among the students at Sanctuary."

"Excellent, excellent. S'reth's Sensitive talent came on only recently," the High Lord explained to Ptal, who was also bewildered by the change in subject. "We have lost so many skilled in the Sensitive arts; it is good to see that *esLi* has granted us a few more.

"Now," he said, turning back to Ptal, his wings circling about him, "we should consider what *se* Makra'a wants." He gestured to S'tlin, who stepped away, formed a wing-position of homage, and took off into the air toward another part of the garden.

"I can conjecture, High Lord," Ptal said after a moment. "He wishes to know what is to become of his—of our—world, in view of *esHu'ur*'s imminent arrival."

"That seems likely. But that is directly linked to his expectations." The High Lord began to walk slowly through the garden; Ptal fell in step. "If *esHu'ur* intends to lay his world waste as he expects, then he is right to fear. In view of what Makra'a now knows, there is little else to expect given the course of the war.

"For all I can see, *se* Ptal, the Dark Wing may yet do so. I can only pray to *esLi* that his desire for blood has been sated."

"Do your dreams give you any indication?"

"Indeed they do, *se* Ptal, indeed they do. It is the reason that I can walk here in my garden, my mind at peace, while Lord Makra'a stands outside so upset. He does not know what has occurred at *Ka'ale'e* Hu'ueru, the Fortress of Dark—that signs have been given and recognized, and that the *HaSameru* has surrendered to *esHu'ur* there. And there are other things he does not know."

The High Lord stopped his progress and bent over to take

the stem of a bluish, many-petaled flower between two of his talons, turning it about gently as if admiring its delicate structure. "Though it is well concealed, the shadow of the Deceiver's wing is visible over this entire affair."

"The humans—"

"The humans are *children* in this game," the High Lord interrupted. "Children." He looked up at Ptal from his inclined pose. "They are *naZora'i*, of course, and no Nest-brothers of ours; but they are neither *esGa'uYal* nor *esHara'y*. They are not the enemy." He inclined his head even farther, taking in the flower's fragrance. "It remains to be seen if they ever were."

"High Lord—?" Ptal was unable to answer immediately. If this were anyone other than the High Lord, the statement would have been evidence of treason—or of insanity.

"Somewhere, a very long flight from the Golden Circle of *esLi*, is the real enemy of the People." He did not turn to face Ptal this time, but his wings elevated slightly in a pose of reverence.

The High Chamberlain could see Sse'e's talons tighten on the stem of the plant he was considering. "It is not the human *naZora'i* who we must defend against now, *se* Ptal. They have been maneuvered, just as we have been. *esLi* has made this clear by delivering us into *esHu'ur*'s talons. We might well have further to fear from the Lord *esHu'ur* but our real enemy is unknown. He serves the Lord of Despite. He is close, my old friend. He is close."

With a lightning motion almost too quick to follow, the talons of the High Lord sliced the stem neatly.

"And we *will* stop him," he added quietly, his wings arranged in the Stance of Reverence to *esLi*, his claws sliding back into their sheaths. For a moment the flower remained atop the stem, but then it toppled into the fine gravel below.

The garden was quiet but for the occasional waft of distant noise from the Hall of Homage beyond.

"Now," the High Lord said. "Let us hear what our kinsman Makra'a HeU'ur has to say."

•   •   •

The *Lancaster's* bridge was located at the top of the flat-tened sphere that composed the fore end of the vessel. At the bottom of the sphere was the shuttle bay, from which small craft could be launched; just above it, spanning the entire circumfer-ence of the ship, was an observation deck, giving a complete 360-degree view. During battles the deck was sealed for security and safety reasons, and it was closed to outside view while the ship was in jump. When it was actually available for use, the *Lan-caster's* crew visited during off-duty hours, a refuge from quar-ters or work posts. Line officers stayed away; they had their own wardroom.

Sergei also needed no such refuge. It was one of the privi-leges of rank that he had private quarters, a study and a ready room to call his own. Still, none of them had a 360-degree view, and he enjoyed the opportunity to mix with his crew.

Now, with the fleet still at anchor at the zor station in the Rift and the next move undecided, he took the time to visit to gauge the mood of his people.

He found the observation deck fairly crowded. As he came in, the crew nearest the door rose and saluted; in a few moments everyone on deck had followed suit. He acknowledged their salutes and waved them to sit, and then walked slowly along the elevated platform that surrounded it, looking out at the stars. Af-ter a moment things returned to normal in the wide, circular area; conversations that had been halted started up again, glasses clinked on tables, and the faint noises of games began to fill the background.

"What brings you down here, Bruce?" Sergei said to a famil-iar figure leaning against the outside railing.

Bruce Wei, Major of Marines, turned to face his commanding officer, saluted and smiled. "Just admiring the view, Skip." He gestured over his shoulder. "*Gagarin's* getting ready to change patrols."

"Let's have a look." Sergei walked to the railing and looked out where Wei pointed. The viewport had been set at a higher magnification directly in front of them, and the great fleet-carrier was lumbering into view. Sergei could see a wave of tiny specks emerge from its flight deck in a perfect pattern, bearing off to starboard and beginning a long lazy orbit around the *Gagarin*.

"You used to fly one of those, if I'm not mistaken, Skipper," Wei said, without looking away.

"When I was younger and had less sense." That drew a smile from his chief of security. "It was a long time ago, and I was damn lucky to live through it."

"I wouldn't take that job at ten times the pay."

"I'd agree with you *now*. But when I was nineteen . . . There's nothing like flying an aerospace fighter, Bruce. You can see the whole universe like it's in hand's reach. It's all under your control: speed, direction, distance; you're gripping the firing button."

"You get in range of Big Brother's guns, you're plasma."

"So you don't *do* that. You don't fly out of range of your wingmen, you don't try to pull any solo stunts. Combat's the worst, of course. But a lot of a fighter pilot's time is doing *that*." He pointed at one of the tiny fireflies. "Flying along in a pattern, watching the deep-radar, calling and acknowledging every fifteen minutes or half-hour. Gives you a lot of time to think." He leaned on the railing in front of him. "Wonder what that guy is thinking about right now."

"About the war, I'd expect, Skip."

"What about it?"

"Oh, nothing deep and philosophical, I'd expect. He's thinking what every soldier thinks every time the subject comes up: When am I going home?"

"Home." Sergei stood up, and a feeling of loneliness—*no,* he thought, *more like* alone*ness*—washed through him. "This is a long way from home, isn't it?"

"We're going to get farther away before we get closer, I'd

guess," Wei answered, crossing his arms in front of him. "Doesn't seem to be much choice."

"How do the crew feel about that?"

"I'm sure if you asked them they'd be foursquare behind you, Skip. And behind the admiral."

"That's what they're supposed to say. But what do they really *think*?"

"I'm not really privy to that," Bruce Wei replied, his expression not changing a millimeter. It was obvious that he knew damn well and wasn't going to tell Sergei a thing.

"You know," Sergei said, after a moment, "I think you're still the best damn poker-player in the fleet."

"Now, I hate to contradict my CO," Bruce said, smiling ever so slightly, "but I think I've got to yield that title at least for this cruise."

"Oh?"

"The admiral is the best damn poker-player in the fleet," Bruce continued. "I've always said that I could figure out whether someone was bluffing based on how often they blinked, but I haven't a damn clue which way this is going."

*Now I understand,* Sergei thought. "I don't really think I'm at liberty to discuss that with you, Bruce, and you know it."

"'Course I do, Skipper." He looked back at the window. "And you know that I wouldn't presume to ask . . . but you do hear things."

"'Things?'"

"Rumor going around," Bruce said, his voice reduced so as not to carry, "that the admiral isn't the admiral anymore, and isn't in any hurry to let anyone know. 'Course, there are ways for that situation to be turned around, too. Rumor going around that something really strange happened while we were in jump, and Chan's so unwilling to talk about it that it must be true.

"Rumor going around that the admiral's taken on a new title, maybe to replace the one he shouldn't be using anymore, and that the zor gave it to him."

"Rumors," Sergei replied, his mouth suddenly dry as he tried to remain impassive while his chief of security passed on these bits of information that he knew to be true.

"You know, Skip, it's hard to believe that in twenty years you've never really learned to play poker. If you'll excuse me," he said, saluting, "I've got duties to attend to." Sergei sketched a salute in response and turned to watch him go.

The fleet lay at anchor off the station that the zor called *Ka'ale'e* Hu'ueru, the Fortress of Dark. The human contingent was bigger now, enlarged by eighteen vessels that had joined it just after they had taken A'anenu. It had only been possible to keep rumors from the rest of the fleet for so long: eventually, what with communications as well as invitations and wardroom dinners, Marais' removal was common knowledge, though kept unofficially below the static level. There was still a comm silence in effect. Even if the Admiralty guessed where they were, there was no fleet that would try to track them here. They were alone.

Rrith, by the orders of Admiral Marais, had the run of the *Lancaster*, except the drive-rooms, the hangar deck and the bridge; he was unarmed except for his *chya* and was escorted everywhere, but was allowed to go where he pleased—though much of his time was spent on observation decks, gazing out at the stars, unapproached and unapproachable.

Three Standard days after Hu'ueru surrendered to the protection of the Dark Wing, Gyu'ur HeYen, commander of the *HaSameru,* and his officers were invited aboard the flagship. It was more of a courtesy between soldiers than a state visit, and the admiral politely excused himself from the gathering. In order to reduce the official nature of the meeting even further, Sergei delegated Chan to issue the invitation from the *Lancaster*'s wardroom.

"Look," he told Chan, "we've been operating in a vacuum since before A'anenu. This is a chance for us to really learn something about the zor."

"Having an enemy commander at the wardroom table is without precedent," Chan had replied. "That's not what the wardroom is for."

"It's a courtesy," Sergei had told him. "Having any zor aboard an Imperial vessel is unprecedented. But they're not necessarily the enemy anymore, and—" He had wanted to say, "—*and we're not an Imperial vessel anymore,*" but the words wouldn't come out. "I'm not ordering you to do this, Chan, I'm asking you. If the war is over, the officers of the *Lancaster* are going to have the first chance to try and understand our new friends."

Chan had sighed, as if trying to imagine the struggle to explain this to his fellow officers. "Very well, sir. Is there anyone else I should invite?"

"Sergeant Boyd," he said. "I realize this is unusual, too, but we'll need him."

"What about the prisoner?"

"Ask Boyd, but I suspect the answer is no. And unless I tell you otherwise, no mention is to be made of the prisoner during their visit."

His suspicion had proved correct. Boyd had circled around the subject with Rrith, but had determined that the zor's status was still *idju,* regardless of his personal commitment to Admiral Marais as the Dark Wing. He would not be able to sit at table with zor officers, no matter how much he might want to be with his own kind.

On schedule to the minute, a zor shuttle came onto the hangar deck of the *Lancaster.* The bright lighting had been toned down to the red part of the spectrum in deference to the guests, and the internal gravity had been set partway between their accustomed 0.6 g and the 1 g Standard aboard.

After their boat port opened, they glided slowly down to the deck, and landed in a triangular arrangement directly before Sergei, who stood alone to meet them. The ship's bell on the comm rang fifteen times.

"Captain," Sergei said to the frontmost zor, the commander of the *HaSameru*. "Welcome aboard the *Lancaster. esLiHeYar.*" *Please,* he thought to himself, *let me have pronounced it right.*

"*haKarai'i esHu'uSha'methesen,*" Gyu'ur HeYen replied. When Sergei inclined his head, wondering what the hell the zor had said, Gyu'ur added, "I am glad to feel welcome aboard the ship of a follower of *esHu'ur,* Commodore. You do me honor by addressing me in words from the Highspeech."

"You do us honor by your presence." Sergei gestured toward the exit. "My fellow officers await us in the wardroom."

"I understand," the zor said as they walked, his two companions, unintroduced, following behind, "that this invitation comes from them." His wings shifted slightly as he said this.

"A tradition in our Navy." They stepped through the hatchway into a red-lit corridor. It had been ordered clear; they walked along through the empty hall, following it as it curved gently to the left. "The executive officer—the second-in-command—presides at the officers' table, and can invite anyone he wants. It's . . . more informal than the captain's dining-room." He smiled, not sure as he did so whether the zor would recognize that visual cue. "They have even deigned to invite me."

*Chaos,* Gyu'ur thought to himself as he walked with the *naZora'i* commander. *An underling presides at table and can choose to exclude his commander?* "How singular," he said, spreading his wings in the Position of Polite Disdain. It was obvious the gesture was lost on the human.

"We were not sure how to begin dialogue between us, and thought an informal setting would be best."

"I understand. Who will be present for this . . . gathering?"

"Several of my officers, and a few invited guests."

"And . . . *esHu'ur?*" He stopped, his wings flowing naturally into the Cloak of Deference to *esHu'ur,* but the motion seemed so unexpected to the human that he almost stepped into Gyu'ur.

"Excuse me?" Sergei said, trying not to bump into the alien.

"Will *esHu'ur* be present?"

"The admiral is occupied," Sergei said, trying to determine whether Marais' absence was somehow insulting to the zor.

"Ah." The zor began to walk again and Sergei fell into stride, feeling as if he had lost control of the conversation. "Would you rather have spoken with him again?"

"You misunderstand me, Commodore. Speaking with the Lord *esHu'ur* is by no means a requirement for my officers and myself to attend your dinner. Had he been present, however, we would have had to . . ."

The zor seemed to be at a loss for words, so Sergei supplied some. ". . . hold your wings differently?" he ventured.

The zor stopped suddenly again, glancing back at his fellow officers. *He knows of this?* Gyu'ur thought quickly, holding his wings in the Stance of Elevated Understanding. It was a moment of revelation—a *sSurch'a,* a leap of comprehension.

For decades it had been clear that the humans had been like blind *artha* in negotiations, as if they had never seen the wing-component of the Highspeech, and had never been able to reply in kind. Their maddening array of facial expressions had been difficult to penetrate. Some scholars claimed to have studied them in depth, but it was impossible to see any consistency.

What was the human trying to say? That he could read the wing-part of the Highspeech? Or that humans had *always* understood them, and had chosen to ignore them?

It was a path he did not choose to fly at this time.

"Your choice of words is most apt, Commodore," he said at last, emphasizing his remark with the Posture of Annoyed Expectation.

• • •

Sergei suspected that the dryness in his mouth was the result of tasting his own bootsole. He led them to the lift and they ascended in silence to the middle decks of the ship and then through another cleared corridor to the door of the wardroom. He removed his uniform cap in conformance to wardroom tradition, and rang the door-chime; on the other side was a junior officer in dress blues, with whom he exchanged a perfunctory salute. Chairs moved back as the other officers came to attention.

Sergei walked into the room with the zor following close behind. He stopped at the seat to Chan Wells' right, at the head of the table. His exec stood, gavel in hand, waiting for all to arrive.

"Mr. President," he said to Chan, "it is my pleasure to present Gyu'ur m'Har *ehn* HeYen, the captain of the *HaSameru,* and his fellow officers. Captain," he said to Hyos, "the president of the wardroom, Commander Chan Wells."

Chan gestured with his gavel to empty seats near the head of the table and the zor took the places indicated.

Gyu'ur was initially bewildered by the tableau and found it somewhat disturbing that the humans had chosen to space the zor out among the others in the room. He found himself instinctively scanning for other exits. He could hear his *chya* muttering quietly to him.

All eyes seemed to be on him as they stood for a long embarrassing moment; then he realized that they must be waiting for him to speak.

"I . . . apologize in advance for any slight or dishonor my comrades and I might make during this visit, *se* President," he said to Chan. "Permit me to present my officers . . . my Chief Sensitive and honored cousin, Kasu'u m'Har *ehn* HeYen"—he indicated the crimson-sashed officer across and to his left—"and my First Navigator, Mres m'Chi'i *ehn* HeYen." He indicated the third zor farther down the table.

Chan looked down the table at the assembly. "My friends and comrades, it is customary at the beginning of a wardroom dinner to offer a toast to the Solar Emperor and Empire. In view of the rather unusual circumstances, I should like, if our guests would find it proper, to offer a toast both to the emperor and to the High Lord of the People. May they both prosper."

Hyos inclined his head.

"To the emperor and High Lord," all of the humans replied, lifting their glasses and drinking. After a moment, the three zor beginning with Gyu'ur raised their glasses as well, uttered the same phrase and drank.

Chan rapped the table with his gavel and the group sat. The zor took their seats carefully, The seats molded to fit their forms. Midshipmen began serving the first course.

"We have a small but lively group here to dine with you," Chan said to the zor captain. "You know our commander, of course. Each of the other officers is a representative of one of our ship's departments. Lieutenant Pam Fordyce is here from Gunnery; Ensign Pete Elway is an Engineering officer; Lieutenant Keith Danner represents comm; and Ensign Zhu Di is from Navigation. In addition to being executive officer, I am also chief science officer." He gestured toward the end of the table, between Elway and the zor engineer. "I am also pleased to introduce to you Marine Master Sergeant Christopher Boyd."

"*Karai'i esMeLie'e,*" Boyd said. *Be welcome, honored guest.*

The sudden fluency from the soldier caught Gyu'ur off guard. He altered his wings to a posture of surprise, just short of affront, though the chair seemed to restrain him somewhat.

"You speak as if you are worthy of the Highspeech, *naZora'i,*" he replied in the Highspeech. The human commander's face altered slightly, maddeningly unreadable.

"I am merely a Nestling with respect to speech, *ha* Captain," the marine answered, slowly, in the Highspeech. The others at the table seemed to be shifting in their seats as though uncomfortable. "I am much more able to hear—and see—the Highspeech than to actually speak it," he continued in Standard.

"Is this usual training for such as yourself?"

"No." The other's expression changed. Gyu'ur sensed— What was it? Embarrassment? A slight wing-signal from Kasu'u, looking up from the soup course, confirmed it. "I confess that I am changed."

"I do not understand."

The soldier opened his mouth to frame some sort of explanation but was interrupted.

Sergei felt the situation running out of control again, and silently cursed the marine sergeant. "Is there something wrong, Captain?" he asked, realizing as he said it how foolish it sounded.

"I am glad," the zor answered slowly, "that you are provided with an individual well versed in our speech. It will doubtless be useful as the evening progresses.

"Perhaps you, or your executive officer, can tell us a bit about the quaint custom of wardroom dinners."

Sergei smiled, trying to appear at ease, and cast a glance down the table and then at Chan.

"It's an old custom, at least as we measure it," Chan said. "More than six of our centuries ago, when our great voyages were on seafaring ships, quarters were so cramped aboard that only the captain had a private cabin. In fact, the captain usually had all the privacy he could ask for—quarters, areas of the deck for his own use, chart-room, pilot-house.

"Junior officers often had little to distinguish them from the crew. The problem was that officers needed a way to learn command skills, navigation, bookkeeping—everything that they'd need when they were captains on their own. Since there wasn't enough room for every officer to have his own cabin to study, a single one was set aside for all of them to share. Soon officers came to take their meals there and thus developed a certain camaraderie."

"I'm sorry?" Gyu'ur said.

"*e'djuye*," Boyd offered.

"Ah, yes, I see," Hyos answered. "Please continue."

"There is another purpose for the wardroom, of course." Chan took a spoonful of soup. "On a sailing-ship of old, the captain's word was law. Good or bad, right or wrong, he governed all of the activity aboard including decisions of life and death. Abovedecks none were allowed to dispute or disagree. But within the wardroom, officers could express their opinions freely, even when they disagreed with their captain. On a well-run ship they might even do so to their captain's face in the wardroom, if he granted them leave to do so. This is called 'wardroom privilege' and allows a captain to solicit opinions in private without breaching his own discipline."

"And this is . . . a well-run ship?"

Chan smiled and looked at Sergei. "Sir?"

"The best in the fleet."

The soup gave way to greens. Gyu'ur had resolved to try each course as a courtesy to his hosts; to his surprise, the salad was pleasing.

"Would it be forward to ask you about yourself and your ship?" one of the officers asked. It was Fordyce, the—comm officer? *No, gunnery,* he remembered.

"Not at all." Hyos glanced down the table at his First Navigator. "*se* Mres, would you care to comment on the *HaSameru* for our hosts?"

"As the captain wishes," Mres answered stiffly in the *naZora'i* tongue, his wings curling to indicate his distaste—a gesture seemingly not lost on the marine sitting opposite him. "Ours is the fourth vessel honored to bear that name, which means *'Warrior at Sunrise.'* It is four eights and five turns old— something less than thirty of your years."

"A rather old ship, then," Fordyce said.

"It is still relatively new by our standards," the Navigator said. "Though its design is from before the . . . from prior to the first contact of the People with your race."

"Our ship designs rarely stay in production for more than ten years," the human captain interjected. "Our newest ships were designed and built within the last five; the *Lancaster* is something of an anachronism, still in service after nearly twenty years."

"Rather like our captain," Chan Wells said, and the assembled officers made sounds of amusement—laughter, clearly at the expense of Commodore Torrijos.

Gyu'ur tensed, wondering what the reaction to this insulting behavior would be; but the captain did not seem to take notice of it, and directed his attention back to the astonished Gyu'ur.

"What about yourself, Captain?"

*Remarkable,* he thought to himself. "Since my status is not well defined at present I cannot find it dishonorable to speak of my lineage. I do not know what you might understand of us," he added, looking down at Sergeant Boyd. "We are of the High Nest, HeYen, of *L'le* m'Har on Ri'ier'e in the zor Core Stars."

"You're not from Zor'a, then?" Fordyce asked.

He began to arrange his wings in a posture that might have been sarcastic or even condescending, but mindful of the presence of the marine, thought better of it. "No, *se* Lieutenant. Less than one sixty-fourth of Nest HeYen actually resides on the home world. The same is true of the other ten Nests and is even more true of the Young Ones, Nest-brothers of the other Nests created after the Unification."

He paused to see if they understood his explanation so far. "I myself am honored to be a descendant of the m'Har lineage on Ri'ier'e, an honored clan founded several five-twelves of your years ago when our world was first settled. Almost three thousand," he said, after a moment of rapid calculation changing his own familiar radix-eight to the alien base-ten.

There were sharp intakes of breath around the table. The three People tensed; Mres' hand had strayed close to his *chya* but Gyu'ur gestured to him to relax.

"Eight thousand pardons," he said. "Did I say something improper?"

"Did you say . . . three thousand?" one of the officers—Danner, the comm officer—said.

Gyu'ur rechecked his calculations, unsure of the motive for the question. "Five five-twelves, seven sixty-fours, three eights and six turns since Gane'e HeYen built the Cliff Nest on m'Har plateau on Ri'ier'e. Three thousand and thirty-eight turns of the People or approximately two thousand, seven hundred and . . . ninety-five of your Standard years."

None of the humans spoke. "Have I offended?" the zor captain said at last.

"Twenty-eight hundred years ago," Danner offered slowly, "the most advanced civilization on our home world worshiped the sun and moon, believed that the Earth was flat, and was fighting with bronze weapons. At the same time your ancestor was building a settlement on another *planet.*"

"That is correct," the zor answered. "Our spacefaring capability is almost a thousand years older than that."

"Extraordinary," Danner said.

"I did not mean to offend."

"Did you mean to amaze?" Sergei asked, smiling. "I think you've succeeded."

"I meant only to state facts. Ri'ier'e, like the other ten systems in the Home Stars, was originally settled by slower-than-light vessels. It took almost two five-twelves of our turns before we developed jump capability."

"By that time," Danner said, "Alaric was sacking Rome." The other officers laughed.


Gqu'ur raised his wings in slight amusement, realizing the true astonishment of his dinner companions. Kasu'u indicated by gesture that the humans had relaxed somewhat; their laughter was almost self-deprecating, a truly alien notion.

"Our culture is older, and in some respects deeper, than yours," he said, as the salad was taken away and replaced by a main course featuring some sort of meat. "Yet your battle capabilities have always been the equal of, or greater than, our own. When our races first met . . . ah . . . we were roughly the same in strength, though we had been in space for ten times as long. We had reached the same level but at vastly different speeds.

"Two rivers," he said, placing his taloned hands on either side of his plate. "One flows rapidly from the mountains to the sea; a second wends its way, leisurely and patiently, until it reaches its final destination. Yet both are consumed by the all-encompassing ocean."

The naZora'i were paying rapt attention now, he noticed. "Our race is the patient river, my companions. We have turned when the High Lord's dreams direct; our course has rushed when esLi has demanded it but by and large we have pursued softer options.

"By comparison, you are the swiftly flowing stream. You drop heedlessly over precipices; you carve new channels. You traverse the land with scarcely a moment to take note of it. In the time it takes the patient river to go ten meters, the swift one has gone a hundred. Yet they both meet the same end.

"In short," he said, folding his arms in front of him, "your race began far behind the People; yet you have caught up with us and may have already passed us. Thus we are faced with the reckoning that esLi Himself has decreed."

"Adapt or be left behind?" the human commodore asked.

"No, *ha* Commodore, it is not that simple. For the patient stream it may be our destiny to have reached the ocean at last . . . and have nowhere else to go."

Sergei had heard the earlier comments of the base commander. *"If the High Lord commands . . . or if* esHu'ur *commands . . . the zor race will come to an end."* He also remembered Marc Hudson's comment that it didn't sound much like an evolutionary advantage.

*"esHu'ur*—the admiral—has far too much respect for your people to command such a thing," Sergei said. "I believe him to be capable of ordering the end of your race but not desirous of doing so."

"The High Lord will do—must do—as *esLi* commands," Gyu'ur said. "The High Lord has dreamed of the admiral, and is ready to accede to his request to speak with him."

"The admiral's request?"

"That is what I understand, *ha* Commodore. It was conveyed in the dreaming that your admiral has requested a meeting with *hi* Sse'e."

"And the purpose of this meeting?"

"It is not for me to know at this time."

"Captain." Sergei folded his hands in front of him and leaned forward; the zor leaned back very slightly as he did so. "You have fought my people all your life. I have spent my entire life as a military officer with the objective of destroying as many of your people as I could. We have clearly reached, and passed, a decision point from which there is no turning back."

"An *aLi'e'er'e,*" Hyos said. "Choosing the flight."

"We are on a different flight now, Captain," Sergei said. "The world has changed. After sixty years of enmity it may be possible for us to be friends. There is nothing stopping us—"

"Save *esLi,*" the zor captain said.

•     •     •

Three pairs of zor wings assumed the Stance of Reverence to *esLi* and the chairs strained to keep up.

"Will your Nestlords choose peace?" Gyu'ur added. "You and I, we are military persons. We can react to a changing situation. We can even accept a different direction. But we do not dispose; we merely carry out dispositions. What the High Lord or the human emperor—or the Lord *esHu'ur*, for that matter—commands is the path we must follow. To do otherwise, regardless of our own intentions or desires, is to betray our oaths to our respective lords.

"I find you engaging and gladly partake of the hospitality of your wardroom. Yet if the High Lord of the People, *hi* Sse'e HeYen, were to suddenly appear and command me to take your life, I would do so by whatever means—my pistol, my *chya*, or my bare claws if I had no other weapon. There is no other alternative. There is only duty.

"I am sure that you would do the same."

A profound quiet settled over the wardroom. The main course was cleared away, and dessert was served, along with coffee—Royal Kona, the same served at the emperor's own table—with conversation reduced to small talk and courtesies. The zor answered general questions and deflected specific ones; the humans listened, and wondered at what they heard.

At last, after a final toast, the three zor took their leave. The officers of the wardroom, and Sergeant Boyd, accompanied them to the hangar deck.

"We were most gratified for your company," Gyu'ur said as they stood at the foot of the zor craft. The hangar-deck gravity had been reduced to zor-normal 0.6 g, and the aliens' shoulders and wings seemed less hunched, more able to move fluidly and gracefully. "Among the People, we part by saying, 'May we meet again within *esLi*'s Golden Circle.'"

"I hope that it is much sooner, Captain Gyu'ur," Sergei answered.

"Life is fleeting, and its end is not for mortals to discern. Yet I, too, would hope that there is another flight, that the patient river has farther to flow."

"*esLiHeYar,*" Sergei said, and signaled to his officers, who came to attention and saluted.

The zor arranged their wings in a pattern, all three the same. "May you fly toward Light," Hyos responded, inclining his head. Then, all three stepped backward and launched themselves into the air, circling to the level of the shuttle's airlock, which opened to admit them.

## chapter 17

Well in advance of the *naZora'i* fleet a single, fast vessel jumped toward the Home Stars. During the battle at A'anenu, it had slipped away at the jump point with its precious cargo: the remains of a single elderly person traveling in state, an ancient, ornate sword lying on his chest. The ship was fired upon, but its defenses were adequate to protect it; in any case, the human commanders had much else to occupy them.

If they had known of its significance they might have tried to capture or destroy it; or perhaps, in some inscrutable human way, they might have done something even more unusual. It was a moot point: the vessel and its significant burden was able to escape into jump, as if *anGa'e'ren*, the Creeping Darkness, had reached out and enfolded them as it had done to Qu'u on the Plain of Despite.

It would be a fitting irony indeed if this single ship was one of the rare few that went translight and never emerged.

But six suns later, harmonizing with the exact *tick* of the navigator's chronometer, the ship emerged in normalspace at the Riftwardmost jump point of the home system. It was immediately escorted down into the gravity-well as it made its way home.

The ready-room door slid aside. Sergei looked up to see Chan Wells enter, a message-pad tucked under his arm.

"You're early," Sergei said, pushing his own 'pad aside and leaning back in his chair. "What's up?"

"I've been investigating that anomaly we experienced during the jump into the Rift," Chan answered, taking his own seat to Sergei's right. "As a matter of course I conducted a thorough review of the ship's logs all the way back to our initial jump from Sol System to try and see if there was any pattern or correlation."

"That's a mountain of data."

"You'll be happy to know that I employed the ship's computer to help analyze it," Chan said, letting a smile cross his lips. Sergei had to smile as well; that sort of remark was a rare example of his exec's sense of humor.

"I assume that you found something."

"Yes." He touched the controls of his 'pad, and a 3-V graph appeared, hovering above the ready-room table. "This is the energy pattern of the anomaly, both by Restucci and Muir distribution. It's not only of an unusual magnitude but also of a totally different structure than anything we've seen before. We were almost certain of this within a few minutes of the event, so this extended analysis really provides little additional information.

"Using this pattern as a guide, however, I scanned backward through the *Lancaster*'s log files and found at least a dozen similar surges. They were all of considerably lower magnitude, but were definitely measurable. I can provide you with chronometer readings for each surge, though I see no particular correlation between actual events and these energy bursts."

"Why didn't we pick up on them before?"

"Many of them were of such small magnitude that they would not attract undue attention, even from our meticulous Engineering staff. Three others were during equipment anomalies—power surges or minor failures of ship systems—and were probably ascribed to them. Two others occurred while the *Lancaster* was at General Quarters, and simply escaped our notice."

"Were there any events of this sort before Admiral Marais and Captain Stone boarded the *Lancaster*?"

"No, sir. The first recorded event corresponds almost exactly with the conclusion of Admiral Marais' address to the squadron at L'alChan."

"And have there been any events since Captain Stone's departure?"

"Only one, sir." At Chan's direction, the graph melted and re-formed with another, equally unusual energy pattern. "This anomaly was recorded shortly after the Rift space-station surrendered to Admiral Marais. It is markedly different from all of the others, however: if you will note, it is almost a mirror image of the one that first attracted our notice." He superimposed the previous graph over the current one, and they did seem to fit together. "I almost missed it," he added.

Sergei let it all sink in before replying. "Conclusions?"

"Difficult with so little data. Captain Stone's disappearance in a way that seems to be impossible, and the coincidence of all but one of the anomalies with his presence aboard the *Lancaster*, would suggest a correlation—but I don't know what it tells me, other than the likelihood that Captain Stone was not what he seemed to be. However, I cannot explain the last anomaly since it does not overlap Captain Stone's time with the fleet.

"I completed my investigation of these events more than two full days ago and spent off-duty time pondering the information. On a hunch, I extended my survey of the *Lancaster*'s ship's-log to include any energy transmissions to or from the ship, including weapons fire and communications, on the assumption that these anomalies either originated from, or were directed toward, some location outside the ship."

"Sounds like you found something."

Chan touched his 'pad, and the graphs disappeared. "Captain, I am not privy to the top security classifications for this mission, so it is possible what I have discovered is explicable either by the admiral's orders or your own. Therefore I am prepared to drop the inquiry and eliminate all record of it if—"

"Out with it. What did you find?" Sergei asked, cutting Chan off before he could protest further.

His exec's face showed a faint hint of relief. "I reasoned," Chan began, "that these energy surges might be some means of communication between Captain Stone and persons unknown using some unknown technology, since some of them occurred while the *Lancaster* was in jump. I thought that there might be a correlation between the energy transmission patterns and these anomalies that might provide us with direction and distance information."

"And was there a correlation?"

"Unfortunately, there was not. But I uncovered an entirely different set of transmissions, all occurring while the *Lancaster* was in normalspace, and all directed outsystem on an extremely high frequency band. I am fairly certain that these messages were intended to be concealed. Only someone searching exhaustively through ship's-logs would be able to find them and then only by accident as I did."

"You use the word 'messages.'"

"Yes, sir. They were encoded but I had little difficulty extracting their contents once I was able to identify them. They contain highly sensitive information: the fleet's destination, ship dispositions, copies of the admiral's battle orders, all addressed to someone—or somewhere—called 'Orange.'

"I considered the possibility that you were aware of these messages. I decided that if you were not, the importance of apprising you of them far outweighed the consequences of revealing that I was aware of them. The band used is usually reserved for communications of Imperial Intelligence."

Sergei didn't answer for a long moment as he considered

what his executive officer had told him. It was a shock to consider the possibility that someone, most likely an intel operative, had been aboard his ship sending back information from the war zone and had gone undetected until now.

"Are these messages still being sent?"

"The last message I found was sent just after A'anenu was captured. I looked at other channels, but found no others."

"Speculate for me. Do you suppose that our Captain Stone was the originator of these messages as well? After all, his disappearance was just after we jumped from A'anenu."

"That is possible, but we have no evidence on which to decide. It is even possible that the culprit is still aboard the *Lancaster* or perhaps aboard some other ship in the fleet, still sending messages to 'Orange.'"

"Damn." Sergei frowned, running a hand through his hair. "As if we don't have enough things to worry about, we have to consider the possibility that someone who might be in a position of authority is a goddamn spook." There was no love lost between active-duty soldiers and intel people; they'd stepped on each others' toes far too many times.

"All right, Chan. Recommendations?"

"I took the precaution of securing the ready-room from unwarranted prying before I reported here. It is thus likely but not absolutely certain that our spy, if still aboard, does not know that we are aware of this evidence. I would therefore advise no action at this time. We should keep our ears open, in case there are additional transmissions."

"Consider it an order. And not a word of this to anyone, do you read?"

"Loud and clear, Commodore."


The orange-red sun of E'rene'e beat down oppressively on the midmorning scene, but it did not seem to affect Makra'a HeU'ur. His steady eleven-count wing-cadences seemed to harmonize with the other sights and sounds of the vast jungle over which they flew. It was all Ptal could do to keep up with his elder cousin, but it was not like the High Chamberlain to admit defeat.

Ptal HeU'ur conceded that what he most wanted was a tall drink of *egeneh* and a comfortable perch with a soft breeze to draw away the sweat that seemed to leak from every pore. Every five-twelfth of a sun or so he admitted (with some asperity) that he really needed to get more exercise, war or no war. But he would not utter a word, or convey any sign with his wing-position, to let Makra'a know he was tired.

*If the old* artha *can do this, so can I,* he thought.

They had left *hiL'le* HeU'ur after a quick meal and a short-ened review of the day's Nest business. Makra'a had been pen-sive and moody since the word had come from esYen concerning *esHu'ur's* imminent arrival here at the edge of the zor Core Stars. At the Nest's Council of Eleven the night before, the Lord of Nest had been so angry that Ptal had wondered if the patriarch would oppose the High Lord's will in this matter. If he did so he would have made himself *idju*, along with whoever of Nest HeU'ur followed him. This madness had passed at last.

This morning, with the sun scarcely over the horizon, Makra'a had told Ptal that there was an excursion he intended to make. He had invited Ptal—*well, it was more an order than an invitation,* Ptal thought to himself—to make it with him. Makra'a's wing-position suggested that no amount of protesta-tion, official or personal, would gainsay the Nestlord's will. Thus they had set off from the cliffside *L'le,* flying across a multihued and verdant jungle, with the summer sun of E'rene'e rising be-fore them.

Ptal's patience, and his stamina, had almost reached its limit when Makra'a began to descend toward the jungle. There was a clearing directly ahead, perhaps sixty-four wings wide. The Nestlord was heading for it and Ptal gratefully followed.

Makra'a settled to a stop, the High Chamberlain only a few wingspans behind. The clearing was almost perfectly circular, as if the trees and undergrowth had voluntarily entered into a pact to keep their distance. In the center was a circular piece of gray stone, smooth from long exposure to weather, rising slightly to an octagonal platform in the center. It was unadorned, but Ptal's Sensitive talent detected the slightest impression from the stone. His *chya* hummed a discernible but unintelligible response.

The air was thick with humidity, so that the scene fairly shimmered; in esYen—indeed, in most of the cities on Zor'a—the climate was controlled artificially, so Ptal found it extremely uncomfortable. Makra'a gave no indication of discomfort; without a word he flew to the platform, his talons just above its surface, and landed. He placed his wings in the Stance of Reverence to Ancestors and stood still for several moments. Then at last he turned to Ptal and spoke for the first time since leaving the *L'le.*

"This place has been here for more than three thousand turns, *se* Ptal. Do you know what this is?"

"I would assume this is the Stone of Remembrance, *ha* Makra'a. If so, I am honored to be in its presence."

"Normally," Makra'a said, flying once again over the surface of the stone to land near Ptal, "this place"—he gestured to the clearing, as if taking it in with a single sweep of his wings—"is reserved for Nestlords and the High Lord. This is where the *le'chya* is conferred upon a new Lord of Nest."

He took a few steps away from Ptal, back turned to him. "More than three thousand turns ago Kanu'u HeU'ur landed on this very spot. Despite the hostility of the terrain and the climate, he pledged that his Nest would settle here and remain here: that adversity would be our strength and that we would not retreat once we chose a path to fly."

Makra'a turned around, holding something in his hand. "The history of Nest HeU'ur recounts that he brought a sample of soil with him from Zor'a." Makra'a's taloned hand opened to reveal a small plastic vial. "He broke it open over this spot, mixing it with the ground beneath his claws, and spoke the words that are the motto of our Nest: *se'e Mar de'sen.* 'Here I remain.'" He slit the vial open with one claw and let the soil drift out, pooling on the ground near his clawed feet.

Ptal was well versed in his Nest's history; but he knew the Nestlord wanted to make a point. He even suspected that he knew what it was. He did not answer, but instead placed his wings in the Posture of Polite Approach and waited.

"We have been here for three thousand turns, cousin. More than a hundred generations, from Kanu'u to myself. This world is in my blood. We have often said, we HeU'ur, that what our world lacks in hospitable climate it makes up for in difficult terrain. There is little to recommend the world of E'rene'e to our brother Nests: violent winds that will tear your wings from your shoulders, hostile mobile forests, heat and cold in extremes our weaker cousins find unpalatable. Yet some of the greatest warriors of legend learned their craft here, and our Nest is admired for its tenacity and its steadfastness. Our reputation is due in no small part to our world.

"And now . . ." Makra'a's wings seemed to droop from their proud configuration as if showing that they were the wings of an old patriarch after all. "And now you ask me to give it all up to a band of wingless *artha* because they have defeated us in battle and frightened our poor cowardly *hsth*-fly of a High Lord, whose prescient dreams would cause us to fly in circles until we collapsed." As he spoke, his wings rose to emphasize his anger.

Ptal's *chya* seemed to snarl as he listened. "I am still the High Lord's servant," he answered after a moment.

"And by the Eight Winds, you are still a member of Nest HeU'ur."

"Do not ask me to choose my loyalty, *ha* Makra'a."

"Pah. I do not ask any such thing, *se* Ptal. I am aware of where your loyalty lies and seek neither to force a confrontation nor to sway you. *esLi* Himself knows that would do no good; I spoke with the High Lord myself and could scarcely contain my anger."

"What in *esLi*'s name *do* you want of me, *ha* Makra'a? You say that you do not ask for my loyalty and yet you insult the High Lord. You fly me for an eighth of a sun to a historical landmark to praise the HeU'ur and challenge my loyalty to the High Nest. These are things I already understand: that you care for your land and your People, and you do not wish to follow the High Lord's wishes in receiving the *naZora'i*—"

"The *esGa'uYal*," Makra'a interrupted.

"The *naZora'i*," Ptal repeated. "What exactly do you want of me?"

"Truly," Makra'a said, his wings falling again, "truly, *se* Ptal, I do not quite know. This war with the aliens has been going on for my entire life. The present High Lord's father chose this flight because the Lord *esLi* directed him to do so. The Lord *esLi* told him that if the People were steadfast they could not lose. The People have truly been steadfast—not just the HeU'ur, but all of the People.

"How could we have lost? How can this be? Is this not just another trick of the Deceiver, a ruse to betray us? We have made peace with the humans before; let us do so again, so as to gather our strength."

"The enemy will not accept peace this time, *ha* Makra'a. You know this, and so does the Council of Eleven. Even the Speaker realizes that our last chance to turn the humans aside was at *Ka'ale'e* A'anenu. Somehow that effort was prevented. The humans were even able to capture a Sensitive—alive."

Makra'a tensed. "To what Nest did this *idju* creature belong?"

"To the High Nest, *ha* Makra'a. And the High Lord is unable—or unwilling—to judge the captive's status. The traitor has been invited along with a deputation to esYen, when the human fleet reaches it."

"Madness. If the creature sets foot upon my world I will tear his head from his neck with my bare hands if necessary."

"It is unlikely that the captive will come to E'rene'e, *ha* Makra'a. As he would be under the formal protection of *hi* Sse'e, to kill this person would render you *idju.*"

"More madness. A traitor is protected and a rightful act is prohibited. The Core Stars are delivered into the hands of the *esGa'u Yal*—eight thousand pardons, the *naZora'i*—and we allow a just war to be ended with an unjust peace. I might as well go to Sanctuary and cloister myself rather than continue as Lord of Nest."

"Is it truly so difficult to accept that we have met, and passed, an *aLi'e'er'e*?"

"I cannot read the signs and portents, *se* Ptal, so yes, it is. There are many of the People who will heed and accept the word of the High Lord in this matter. As a Lord of Nest I cannot accept his words without question—and yes, I have difficulty with what they portend. Guided by *esLi*'s mighty talons or not, *hi* Sse'e is mortal and therefore fallible. Perhaps *esGa'u* has already made him one of the *Hssa,* condemned to the Valley of Lost Souls forever, unable even to direct his gaze to the fortress of his tormentor.

"If there is any purpose in bringing you out here, my honored cousin, it is to tell you—in the presence of the Remembrance Stone, at the very heart of our beloved world—that I will not thwart the desires of my High Lord. I will not do it even if he is delivering us unto the very Plain of Despite.

"But it is difficult and perhaps impossible for me to accept this *aLi'e'er'e.* I may not be the only one of the People who has this difficulty. Before we are on a different flight it will be necessary for the High Lord to convince many others whom he might find considerably less tractable than the Nestlord of HeU'ur. I have told you; it will now be your duty to tell *hi* Sse'e."

Without another word and after the briefest obeisance to the stone, Makra'a launched himself into the air. A moment later Ptal followed, further burdened by the candor of HeU'ur's Nestlord.

• • •

Marc Hudson's image sat at the opposite end of Sergei's ready-room table. The other captain was relaxed, slumped back in his chair with his hands folded in his lap; a slowly turning 3-V image of a world hovered half a meter or so above the table.

"... Since I had so much free time on my hands, I had Science Section do a topographic survey of the solar system. What a hell of a place! For starters the sun is a K-type, but it doesn't behave like a Main Sequence K: it has a photospheric shell that seems to be fragmented, almost irregularly so, which leads to all kinds of solar flare activity. That in turn leads to electromagnetic irregularities in the planet's atmosphere, making comm broadcasts difficult and maybe even impossible at times.

"The world itself is no bargain, either. It's three-quarters Earth-size but lacks many heavy metals, leading to a gravity low enough for zor flight; it completes a rotation in just under sixteen hours. Overall, that's a bit faster than standard, which causes high winds and Coriolis effects, especially at high altitudes and near the equator. We counted nine active tropical storms and perhaps a dozen others capable of reaching tropical-storm status within the five Standard days or so. The mean temperature in the *temperate* zone is over thirty degrees C and it's almost unbearable at the equator.

"Our studies show that most of the lowland is extremely fertile, almost aggressively so—"

"'Aggressively' fertile?"

"Yeah. We scanned a large lowland area and found several locations with high concentrations of metal and plastics—clear markings of civilization—but the flyover showed nothing but forest and jungle. My exec concludes that there must have been settlements that were unable to prevent overgrowth. Considering that both communications and transport are at a disadvantage due to climactic conditions, it's no wonder that most of the settlements are in the foothills or the mountains."

"What about industry and agriculture?"

"I have some orbital-scan information, but I was politely but firmly denied access to the world's data banks until we go down there."

"Did you tell them—"

"Yes, I told them that the bogeyman sent me." Marc smiled crookedly. "I invoked the admiral's name and official zor-title but the Chamberlain of Nest HeU'ur, the highest-level bureaucrat who would talk to me, practically told me to stick it up my reaction mass."

Sergei couldn't help but smile in return. "Marc, you're going to set Standard back a hundred years. I'm not surprised at the natives' response; from what our guest has told Sergeant Boyd, this Nest is well known for being intransigent and stubborn—"

"Ornery."

"Rrith probably isn't familiar with that word, but I'd guess that's on the money. As long as they're not launching fighters or system-boats against you, we can wait for that data."

"Alyne Bell has two patrol wings in the air all the time, and they know it. There doesn't seem to be much danger that we'll be attacked. Still, you never know with these bastards, so I've maintained General Quarters and advised the *Inflexible* and the *Sevastopol* to do the same."

"Consider it an order," Sergei answered. "Now, as to—"

The ready-room door slid aside and Admiral Marais entered. Sergei stood and Marc's image rose as well; Marais gestured them to sit.

"As you were. Anything to report, Commodore?"

"Captain Hudson was just bringing me up-to-date, sir," Sergei said, sitting again; Marais took a seat alongside and looked at the slowly turning globe over the table. "Everything seems to be quiet, both in space and planetside, Admiral. Nothing has come insystem since we arrived."

"Excellent. If there is nothing further, Captain Hudson, you are dismissed."

"Sir," Hudson said, inclining his head and disappearing. The globe faded out as well, leaving the room curiously empty.

Marais did not speak for a long time. He sat with his hands folded and appeared to be lost in thought. At last he stood and walked around the table to stand before a large projection chart of the New Territories and the Rift.

"We have come a long way, have we not, Commodore?"

"Yes, sir."

"It is hard for me to imagine that this war is over. I imagine that it's nearly as hard for you. In some ways, it is probably more difficult for me since I had convinced myself—with help—that the war would only end one way and this wasn't it.

"In a few hours we will be negotiating the surrender of the High Nest fleet in the Core Stars and that will be that."

"I don't believe it is quite that simple, sir."

"No." Marais turned to face Sergei and stood, his arms crossed in front of him, his face serious, as if he were posing for his book's cover holo. "No, we've broken the restraints that the Admiralty and His Majesty's Government wished to put upon us. Even the zor are aware of that. After A'anenu, they didn't even bother to resume peace negotiations since they understood where the real power lay.

"It does place the Government in an uncomfortable position when we are done here."

"It places us in an uncomfortable position as well, sir." Sergei considered his words and then continued, "Thousands of sailors and soldiers stand accused of violating their oath to the Emperor and can only see one way to go home again."

"I do not seek the Imperial throne, Torrijos: not now, not ever."

"What *do* you expect to do, sir? Even if the Imperial Government were willing to let you retire to an agrocomplex on Tuuen, to spend the rest of your life dictating memos and sipping cool drinks, many, many people are left out in the cold if that is your decision. Society isn't kind to traitors, even if they have performed a noble service."

"I am not responsible for the Emperor's shortsightedness."

"No, sir." Sergei took a deep breath. "But you are responsible for the people under your command. They are unlikely to let you simply fade into the background like Cincinnatus."

Marais returned to his chair and sat down, then focused his gaze on Sergei. "It is all irrelevant for the moment. What we do in the next few days out here in the zor Home Stars, a universe away from Oahu, will have crucial impact on the future of the Empire. We must concentrate on the present before we address the future."

"With all due respect, sir, the men and women of this command need to know that you will not abandon them." He tried to return the admiral's stare with one of his own. "I think they need to know your plans before this matter concludes."

Marais thought about this for several moments, as if he were weighing the matter carefully. "Your recommendation?"

"I need to know what you intend to do. If the zor surrender to the fleet, will you conclude a treaty with them on your own authority as the Dark Wing?"

"Certainly. I have every reason to believe that they would hold to such a treaty."

"I believe they'd accept whatever terms you will offer them at this stage, so there's a good chance that the real fighting in this war is already over. If they decide to fight, we possess enough firepower to destroy them. In either case they no longer present a threat."

"But what if they decide to end their existence as a race, as Hyos HeYen suggested back in the Rift? What will we do then?"

"Do?" Marais slumped back in his chair once more. "What can we do?" He thought for a moment. Then he looked away, back at the wall-chart. "I imagine that we'll let them."

The thought of mass suicide chilled Sergei again, so he

pressed on. "No zor at all means no enemy for humanity. In any case, the Fleet's work would be done. What then? A return to the Empire?"

"I had always hoped to return. The end of the war might well be sufficient reason for the Admiralty and the emperor to set aside any minor disputes—"

"I beg to differ with the Admiral, but mutiny is hardly a *minor dispute.* What's more, even if the end of the war creates one hero, there will be no victory parade for lots of others. By agreeing to this mission and by understanding the importance of finishing this job, I have sacrificed the only career I have ever known. The emperor wouldn't give me command of an aircar after following you to the zor core worlds in defiance of his orders."

"Do you regret your decision?"

"Of course not, sir. But even if I did, it hardly matters now, does it? For officers like Alyne Bell, or Marc Hudson, or Yuri Okome, or me, following through on this was more important than their Navy careers. It was more important than letting the best chance to beat the zor slip away because people a few hundred light years away couldn't stand the sight of blood and couldn't let the job be done right.

"A century and a half ago a group of similar officers convinced another admiral that the governments back home were corrupt and unsuited to the task of directing human expansion to the stars. They made the critical decision to transfer their loyalty. No one has approached you with a crown resting on a velvet cushion, but you have already captured their loyalty. That means that they wish for you to lead: and wherever you lead they have already chosen to follow.

"That is why, sir, it is important that you explain your intentions. Not just to me so that I can advise you, but to the entire fleet. I believe they deserve such an explanation."

"Very well," the admiral said at last. "Inform all commanders that I will address them and their crews two watches from now.

It will take time for me to assemble my thoughts. They will have their explanation, Commodore." He folded his hands in front of him. "Then we will set about bringing this matter to a close."

Єyeh HeNa'a, the Speaker for the Young Ones, accepted the tiny cup of *egeneh* from the High Lord's extended hand, made the proper obeisance and sipped from it. Opposite him Sse'e HeYen perched calmly, his wings in a Position of Reverence to *esLi,* drinking from his own cup. The silence stretched out.

A private audience with the High Lord was unusual these days: Eyeh did not remember ever having spoken with *hi* Sse'e without at least *ha* Ptal present. For it to take place in the Chamber of Solitude, the High Lord's private place of contemplation, made it even more unusual.

The capital was in turmoil: every Nestlord had clamored for the High Lord's attention and he had denied every request. The Council of Eleven had even met without either High Lord or High Chamberlain present, but had been unable to reach any concensus about what to do or even how to do it without the advice and consent of the leader of the People. Then, abruptly, Eyeh had received an invitation from the High Lord himself.

It was difficult for Eyeh to keep apprehension or tension from his stance, but he noted neither of these attributes in the other's wings.

"I have had several dreams in the past few days, *se* Eyeh," the High Lord said at last. "I would like to share them with you."

"I am honored, High Lord."

"Perhaps you will find it less of an honor when I have done so," Sse'e answered, his wings slightly elevated in amusement. "Nonetheless, I value your opinions and courtesy.

"This is a most troubling time for the People. I certainly do not need to tell you that. Still, we are witnessing—and will witness shortly—the greatest transformation our People have ever experienced.

"While we perch here in the Chamber of Solitude, drinking our *egeneh, se* Ptal and *se* Makra'a negotiate with *esHu'ur* over the fate of E'rene'e. They will surrender it to him despite Makra'a's reluctance. There is no other path for them to fly. Then *esHu'ur* will go to Shanu'un and then Bas'a. Then he will come here to Zor'a."

"You have dreamed this, *hi* Sse'e?"

"In part, younger brother. In part I have deduced the logical next steps. *esHu'ur* will come here to esYen with his entourage and his prisoner—"

"The *idju* Sensitive captured at A'anenu? You would admit this creature to your presence?"

"My dreams tell me that I will do so and you should not trouble yourself about it, *se* Eyeh. You see, that term has very little meaning anymore."

Eyeh did not answer but his wings rose in confusion.

"I have come to the realization that we are *hi'idju,* younger brother."

Eyeh continued his silence as he began to comprehend what the High Lord had said. *idju* was personal dishonor: the violation of Inner or Outer Peace. *hi'idju* was a word that he had never heard spoken; it was accompanied by a wing-position he had never seen—though it was not the one he would have expected.

"*hi'idju,*" he repeated, as if trying the word to see how it sounded.

"It is the only way for the People to accept the outcome of the war, *se* Eyeh: to accept that we are *idju* as a race. It is also the only way for us to escape the *Ur'ta leHssa.*

"We must accept that the Lord *esLi* has sent us the Dark Wing in the guise of a *naZora'i* for a reason. Still, if He sought to have the People destroyed He would not permit an escape. Yet this admiral, this avatar of the Dark Wing, brings us not the death of our race but rather condemnation to life.

"Our destroyer will now become our redeemer. It is for this

reason that I did not create a new *Gyaryu'har* when *se* Kale'e transcended the Outer Peace at A'anenu half a moon ago; it is for this reason that I have directed *se* Ptal and *se* Makra'a to accommodate *esHu'ur* in his demands.

"It is for this reason that *esHu'ur* himself will come to es Yen. He shall receive the People, *hi'idju* as they are, in his hand. He shall receive what he wishes in tribute. He shall also receive the *gyaryu*, the sword of state, with which he shall lead us on a new flight."

"A *naZora'i* shall lead us?" Eyeh asked, incredulous.

"It is the only way, little brother. We chose this flight in my grandsire's time. We have created this outcome or helped to create it. *esLi* grant that this *naZora'i* admiral chooses wisely how it is completed."

After reassuring the Speaker and relating him further details of his perceptions and his dreams, Sse'e allowed his wings to droop and his voice to admit a touch of weariness. Without being directed, Eyeh withdrew, leaving the High Lord alone in the Chamber of Solitude.

The dreams of the High Lord were the guideposts by which the People's flight was chosen. It had always been so; years of training as a Sensitive, and study in the epics, legends and histories prepared a future High Lord for the sometimes baffling interpretation that followed prescient visions. *esLi* did not always direct the High Lord by words: sometimes His will was communicated in symbols. Sse'e felt that he had done his best in interpreting what he had received and communicating it to Eyeh and to others.

His last and most recent dream he had held back even from Eyeh. After scenes of great moment had played themselves out before his dreaming eyes, he had experienced one last vision. It took place in his Chamber of Solitude but he was only an observer. A vision of himself—or rather a younger version of himself, slightly different in appearance, like an older E'er or Dra'a, his two sons—stood perched at the very top of the Chamber as if in contemplation. Then, as he watched, the figure gave a deep obeisance to *esLi* and launched itself from the perch, performing lazy circles, slowly turning as it lost altitude.

But a dozen wingspans from the bottom Sse'e watched as the figure tensed its wings and leveled its path, so that instead of gently turning within the curve of the wall, it was aimed directly for it. As so often happened in dreams he could not summon his voice to cry out. He could only watch in horror as the figure crashed headfirst into the wall and then fell from its impact point to the floor below. Its lifeless face and crumpled wings communicated a sensation he had never experienced and which chilled him beyond words or stance to express.

In that lifeless image he saw *naGa'sse:* the Sensitive's blindness. Even in death a Sensitive's face is composed, for his *hsi* goes directly to *esLi's* Golden Circle. This terrible image, this transcending of the Outer Peace, bespoke a Sensitive's greatest fear— that the great gift of *esLi* would leave while the *hsi* is still in the body, leaving one mind-blind.

For it to happen to a Sensitive was painful; for it to happen to a High Lord would be devastating.

This dream had come to him twice already and each time the scene had been the same. There was a message he could not understand, unless it was a simple depiction of the future. It seemed ironic; the People were at their greatest despair and he could see a new path of hope and change that would lead them away from the *Ur'ta leHssa.* At the same time, his vision of a bright future was clouded by a portent of a High Lord's death, blinded and separated from the Inner Peace of the Lord *esLi.*

He counseled patience to himself. *esLi will give you understanding in time,* his inner voice said to him. *In the meanwhile, there is much to do.*

It seemed a trifling reassurance, but it was all he possessed.

## chapter 18

[Begin vidrec 210811-0143502.]

[Voiceover:] "Admiralty spokesman Commodore Sir Kenneth Tamori issued a statement at 1310 CT in response to published rumors regarding an enemy fleet.

"There is no truth to this rumor," Commodore Tamori announced. "Despite materials published on the net, we have accounted for all enemy ordnance and tonnage on this side of the Antares Rift. The fleet in the war zone has defeated the zor fleet and captured all enemy bases, including the primary base facility at A'anenu.

"The base that launched the attack on Pergamum six months ago has also been captured. The zor enemy no longer has the capability to launch any sort of attack within Imperial space."

Commodore Tamori's statement was accompanied by a number of vidrecs covering zor defeats, including A'anenu. The Admiralty refused comment on questions from net reporters.

[attached vidrecs:
210811-0143511, 210811-0143514,
210811-0143519, 210811-0143523]

[Begin vidrec 210811-0143503.]

A spokesman for the Commonwealth Party dismissed Commodore Tamori's statement as willful misdirection. "The Admiralty has no idea of the conduct of the campaign in the war zone, and has no idea of the present whereabouts of Admiral Marais' fleet. It could be in the Rift, in the zor home stars, or en route to Sol System to seize the throne."

There was no comment available from the Imperial Compound.

"Bogey near Number Three jump point, Skip."

Sharon MacEwan, captain of the *San Martín,* looked up from the Engineering report she was reviewing with her chief. "Do you have a confirmation?"

"*Ikegai* has it, Skip. She's closest." Mitch Sanders, the *San Martín*'s watch navigator, scanned the pilot's board. "*Sarasota* and *Piraeus* are next-closest, and they're already turning to intercept."

"Incoming call from *Ikegai,* Skip," said her comm officer.

"ID it, Mitch. Jack," she said to her comm man while crossing to the pilot's seat. "Get the two of them on the line, and Beat to Quarters." She sat down. "I'll take *Ikegai* now."

The General Quarters alarm rang out across the ship; the *San Martín* went over to battle stations. Yuri Okome's image appeared near the pilot's board.

"I have calculated a least-energy solution to intercept the intruder, Sharon."

"Do you have an ID on it?"

"*Cameron,*" Mitch Sanders said quietly.

"I have it as the IS *Cameron,*" Yuri said, giving a short, withering glance at the *San Martín*'s helmsman—his attention was suddenly focused on his station. Sharon could hardly keep from smiling as Okome went on. "It is a lightly armed patrol vessel. It does not seem to be a threat."

"Is it responding to comm?"

"Yes, to inform me that they wished to speak to the ranking officer here at A'anenu." Okome's voice betrayed no emotion, but he allowed his scarred face to take on a slight hint of annoyance. "I informed them that I would pass this on and await orders."

"What's the *Cameron*'s course and speed?"

Okome named a course, which would take the ship into the gravity-well. "She's traveling at a high rate of speed, but dumping velocity quickly."

"Good. Order her to heave to. Fire across the bow if you have to—" Sharon saw the hint of a smile cross Yuri Okome's face; he'd find a way to "heave to" one way or another. "And let them stew out there. I'll issue similar orders to the other two ships nearby. Everyone else is ordered to keep clear.

"They want to speak to the CO; let them send a boat to the orbital base. I'll meet them aboard the *San Martín* in"—she looked at Mitch Sanders, who held up two fingers—"about two hours. Oh, and Yuri, if they try to bug out you bring them down. If they're just out here to have a look, they'll be staying longer than they intended."

"I read you loud and clear. Okome out."

"Nice work on the ID, Mitch," she said to her navigator as Okome's image disappeared. "Give us a course to the orbital base in the asteroid belt. Nice and easy; we're in no hurry."

"Ready," he said after a moment.

"All ahead one-third," Sharon said, leaning back in the pilot's chair.

She called up what the *San Martín*'s computer had available on the *Cameron*. As Yuri had said, it was a lightly armed patrol vessel; it was usually assigned as a courier in the New Territories, but never ventured out into the front lines. It was commanded by a Captain Carlos Hsien.

*Who the hell is this Carlos Hsien?* she asked herself. *That name sounds familiar . . . This is a gutsy move, especially right now. The Empire is in an uproar, because the admiral isn't following orders from home anymore. Everyone from the fleet who's coming aboard with him is probably already aboard; those that didn't want to follow him to the zor Core Stars or return to protect A'anenu have jumped for home; the* Cameron *isn't likely to be a late defection.*

*What does he want?*

They'd arrived here a week ago, jumping from the zor base in the Rift. The admiral had taken a pared-down squadron led by the *Lancaster* into the zor core while a contingent remained behind at the Rift Base. Another group with the *San Martín* as flagship had returned to A'anenu to protect the fleet's way home. About a quarter of the ships that had participated in the attack on the Rift Base had been unwilling to continue under Marais' command and had been allowed to depart for Imperial space . . . an unusually risky decision on Marais' part, but it was necessary to make sure that everyone who remained was committed to the admiral's cause: completion of the war on his terms.

The comm traffic out here at A'anenu made it clear that no one truly knew what was going on: there was even a rumor that a zor fleet had evaded Marais and was on its way into Imperial space, with Mothallah or New Chicago or some other heavily populated world as its target.

Even if they'd known what was really going on, it would have been difficult for them to believe. While diplomats and politicians back in the Empire fretted about what was to happen next, Admiral Marais was going to Zor'a to supervise the surrender (or perhaps the mass suicide) of the greatest enemy in the history of mankind. It was practically impossible to believe it.

The *San Martín* arrived at the abandoned base in the asteroid

belt in just under two hours, and was already waiting when the
shuttle boat from the *Cameron* came into range. The *San Martín*
took nav control and maneuvered the boat into its shuttle bay.
Sharon gave orders to direct the passengers to a conference-room
on the Engineering deck. Whoever they were, and whatever their
agenda, she wanted them as far away from the bridge as possible.

As soon as the boat was aboard she went to the conference-
room. Her exec and first cousin Sean MacEwan was waiting
there along with the *San Martín*'s Major of Marines, an old veteran named Claude Symmes. He had spent most of his career
aboard ship. Yuri Okome's holo image was also present, sitting at
the far end of the conference-table.

"Report," she said, taking her seat at the head.

"The *Cameron* hasn't moved since we ordered her to heave
to," Yuri said. "They followed orders to the letter; your shuttle-
deck chief told me that you have three guests—two officers and
a civilian."

"A civilian? Who is it?"

"I believe there's a still vid, taken while they disembarked."
Yuri gestured toward Sharon's message-pad. She touched a control and a 3-V image swirled into view on the adjacent wall.

"Hsien," she said quietly. "No wonder that name sounded
familiar. That's Tomás Hsien, the leader of the Commonwealth
Party. What's he doing out here?"

"We will know soon enough."

Sharon dismissed the image of Hsien just as the door chimed.
"Come," she said, and the door slid aside. Two naval officers entered, offered smart salutes, and stepped aside. A distinguished,
well-dressed third person came past them into the conference-
room.

He had an air of authority about him, as if he were sizing up
the room and the people in it with a single glance. He was clearly
unaccustomed to the somewhat cramped accommodations of a
ship of the line, but he was by no means uncomfortable; he

sketched a bow to Sharon and nodded to the others present. The two officers that accompanied him seemed all but forgotten in this brief moment of introduction.

"You would be Captain MacEwan," Hsien said. "Allow me to introduce myself. I am—"

"I know who you are," Sharon answered. "Please be seated, Assemblyman."

"Thank you." Without losing a beat, Hsien took a seat near the head of the table. "May I present Captain Carlos Hsien and Lieutenant Jillian Kwamee of the *Cameron.*"

Sharon gave them the briefest of glances. They took seats at the far end. It was clear to her that they were here for show and nothing else.

"You have taken a risk coming here, Assemblyman," she said, turning her attention back to Hsien. "This is a war zone. You could have been blasted out of the sky, coming out of jump like that."

"I was willing to take that risk."

"You must want something."

"Information only. I come empty-handed, Captain: no treaty, no official representation from the Government, no orders for the admiral . . . not that any of those things have any meaning, I suppose. Where is the admiral, by the way? I had hoped to speak with him."

*And not with some flunky,* his words seemed to say to her. "The admiral is not here."

"While a true statement, that does not answer the question."

Sharon quickly glanced at Yuri and then back at the assemblyman. A number of ships would have reached Imperial space by now; the outcome of A'anenu would at least be common knowledge.

"The admiral is in the zor Core Stars. The zor have surrendered, sir. The war is effectively over and Admiral Marais has won it."

"That's a very broad statement, Captain. Surely it is not up to the admiral to decide whether the war is over or indeed won."

"Who is it up to, then?"

"I should think that the Imperial Assembly"—Hsien placed one hand over his chest like an orator—"would be the proper arbiter of those decisions."

"The Imperial Assembly was willing to accept a peace offer that was a damn sight short of winning the war, sir. I would think that the Assembly has no understanding of the situation, and is in no way qualified to deal with it.

"But we digress: if you're not here in some official capacity then why *are* you here?"

"I represent only myself, and the people of—"

"Spare us your well-known populism, Assemblyman," Yuri Okome said quietly, cutting across Hsien's sentence. "This is not the Imperial Assembly, sir. I suspect that the only value your political position carries is that we are listening to you."

"All right." Hsien's half-smile seemed to fade away, revealing a sterner, more serious expression. "Let me lay it out for you, then.

"The emperor has dissolved the Imperial Assembly. There are rumors of every description running through the Empire. There's damn little information to confirm or deny them. I want to know what's going on."

"What happened to your spy?" Okome asked. Hsien looked up sharply, as if surprised by the question. After the shortest moment the façade dropped back into place.

"My sources of information are no better than anyone else's. I will not waste words on you, Captain; I am no more brave than anyone else—I am simply more determined. Regardless of the outcome of this war there will still be a Solar Empire.

"It only remains to see who will be its emperor."

"Sir, I—"

"Now *you* try to dissemble, Captain." He folded his hands before him on the table. They were well manicured and smooth—

the hands of a politician, that had never felt worse than a paper cut. "Let us set aside the matter of whether the war is over or not. Six months ago no one expected or anticipated that Admiral Marais would do what has been done. It is clear to me that the consequences of these acts are far greater than the simple military solution.

"The entire balance of power in the Empire will radically shift according to the admiral's next move. I wish to know what that next move is. *That* is why I am here: to confirm my suspicions that, in view of the circumstances, there is no other course for Admiral Marais other than to claim the throne."

"I don't know one way or the other, Assemblyman. I'm not convinced."

"Then you're a damn fool. You are the scion of a family with a long tradition of military service, unsullied by words like 'mutiny' . . . or 'treason' . . . yet in the view of nine-tenths of the people of the Solar Empire, *you* are a mutineer and a traitor. You have willfully and deliberately disobeyed the direct commands of His Imperial Majesty, instead following the orders of a mutinous admiral. Neither purpose nor motivation nor even outcome matters. The emperor has already passed sentence.

"There is only one way for you to return to the Solar Empire as anything other than a criminal," Hsien said, fixing her with an intense glare. "You must return in the service of a new emperor. You and Captain Okome here and every other officer and crewmember in this whole damn mutinous fleet has a stake in following this through to the end, and that means delivering Admiral Marais to Oahu as the Solar Emperor."

Sharon MacEwan was aware of Marais' reluctance to seize the throne; yet she understood Hsien's point. It was impossible for the emperor—the current one—to set aside the charges against Marais or anyone who had chosen to follow him; Marais had done just as Hsien said, and there were consequences to following it through.

"What do *you* get out of all of this?"

"Even if there is a war fought over the throne, there will come a time when the Imperial Assembly will return. I expect to be a Member of that Assembly."

"By throwing your lot in with Admiral Marais now."

"By making sure," Hsien replied carefully, "that the admiral is aware of his options should he choose to pursue the throne and by offering crucial assistance at a critical time—for a price."

"What makes you think he'll accept?"

"Nothing. I haven't asked him yet; I'm not sure what his answer will be. However, Admiral Marais has his supporters in the Empire. If he has done what you say he has done then the threat of two generations is gone. I don't think very many people will shed tears over the end of the war."

"What happens if the admiral declines your, shall we say, 'generous' offer?"

The careful smile returned to Hsien's handsome face. "Then I denounce him for the traitor he is and rally support for the emperor against a xenocidal usurper."

"I see. And if I simply put you in the *San Martín*'s brig and throw away the key? Or if I push you out the airlock without a pressure suit?"

Hsien allowed the tiniest bit of fear to appear on his face when she mentioned the last alternative. Then he quickly answered, "In seven days, if I have not communicated instructions otherwise, a vid of a speech will be released informing the people of the Solar Empire of my heroic effort to appeal to Marais out here at A'anenu, to ask him to give himself up and to bring this terrible war to an end . . . as well as my apparent demise in the attempt, of course. I'm sure that will help Admiral Marais win over the hearts and minds of his future subjects."

"I see."

"I would far prefer to survive this experience. When I decided on this course of action, however, I had no illusions that a fleet capable of carrying out attacks on helpless worlds like L'alChan would not hesitate with a few human lives.

"I think," he said at last, "we have said all we can say to each other. I would like to meet the admiral."

"As I told you, he isn't here."

"I suspect that you can contact him. What is more, I am sure you will not take it upon yourself to make this decision. I will wait, either aboard the *Cameron* or in your brig, as you wish."

She turned to Major Symmes, who had sat silent through the whole exchange. "Get him off my ship."

Symmes stood and bowed very slightly to Hsien. "If you please, Assemblyman." Hsien needed no further urging; he and the two officers rose and accompanied the major out of the conference-room.

"Well?" she asked her exec when the door had closed.

"He's a slimy bastard, all right," Sean said, rubbing his carefully trimmed beard. "We can't say yes or no and the admiral doesn't have any guarantees even if he listens to Hsien."

"The assemblyman is correct," Okome said. "We cannot make this decision ourselves."

"He knew that when he came here. He probably also knew that Marais wasn't here."

"Then what was the point of this charade?" Sean asked. "Why did he bother coming aboard the *San Martín* to explain his position? He should've saved his breath for Admiral Marais."

"He knew that we would need convincing to carry this message to the admiral," Sharon answered. "He must have believed that it was important to coerce us, rather than going direct to the source. I was a damn fool to tell him where Marais is; he probably didn't know."

"The information does him little good," Yuri answered.

"True. All right, gentlemen. Suggestions. What do we do?"

"We'll have to contact Admiral Marais," Sean said. "No choice, given the time limit."

"Sean is correct," Yuri added. "It will be too easy for the *Cameron* to intercept any comm message, however. We will have to send a vessel."

"You have one in mind."

"Subtracting the *Ikegai* from the defenses of A'anenu is of little consequence. I am already aware of the content of this meeting; like you, I am one of the officers selected for the admiral's original squadron. Presumably I am trusted. A close escort can cover the required distance in a relatively short time."

"Besides, you'd rather be there than here."

"I am offering logical arguments for the choice of the *Ikegai*, Sharon. Personal preference does not enter into the decision. Which is yours to make, I might add." He smiled slightly, as if completing a lecture at the Academy.

She looked at him for several moments. He was right on all counts.

"Very well. I'll cut some orders and prepare a dispatch for you. Get ready to get under way in eight hours—no, make it four. We should give the admiral as much time as possible for this decision."

"Aye-aye," Okome said, and his image disappeared.

"You know," Sharon told her cousin, "I think that's why the MacEwans always stuck to soldiering instead of politicking. There's always the danger that one of us might take the nearest club and crush somebody's skull; it's always better when there's a legitimate enemy in reach."

The trip down to the surface of Zor'a had been uneventful, but once down the admiral and his entourage began to realize how alien a world it was.

The vermillion sun of Antares beat down, making the day stiflingly hot. This was compounded by the heavy, humid air. In addition, the lower gravity made the humans feel light-headed.

A group of zor awaited them at the bottom of the shuttle's gangway, and others maneuvered through the air nearby, cradling weapons idly. Marais descended first, his gaze straight ahead, followed by Sergei, Alyne Bell, Marc Hudson, Tina Li,

Yuri Okome, the zor Rrith, and a squad of marines in dress uniform led by Chris Boyd.

The officers did their best to concentrate on the descent to the tarmac, while Rrith moved like someone in a dream. Boyd had all he could do not to be overwhelmed by impressions and sensations that were familiar and new all at the same time.

At the end of the descent, one of the zor reception committee stepped forward to meet them.

"I am Dres HeShri, Master of Sanctuary. I am the chief teacher of young Sensitives when their talents emerge. I was the teacher of your . . . guest."

"*se* Rrith has spoken well of you, *se* Dres," Marais replied. "I hope to have an opportunity to visit your domain."

"*esLi* guide you," Dres answered, a bit cryptically.

Marais introduced the rest of his officers and then the group climbed, somewhat relieved, into a pair of aircars that had been provided for the humans and their escort. As the cars rose and then flew along, Marais and his entourage had an opportunity to see the huge metropolis of esYen up close.

As they left the sprawling spaceport behind, they began to approach the complex inner city, which consisted of tall, thin skyscrapers with perches projecting at all levels along the walls with narrow flying-bridges connecting them at dizzying heights above the ground. They were interspersed with wide stone arches and curiously shaped megaliths. All were adorned with *hRni'i.*

In fact the ground level seemed to have little meaning, as the city of esYen—the capital of the zor hegemony—was accessible at almost any height . . . at least for someone capable of flight. As they moved along, they could see many zor, but none approached the aircars too closely.

At last they settled to a landing several stories above ground level. The humans disembarked a bit shakily, since there was no railing on the edge of the platform and it looked to be a thirty-meter drop. They made their way under a high octagonal arch into the upper level of a huge entrance-hall. A narrow staircase—really a series of perches a meter apart and half a meter or so below each other—gave access to the hall below.

"Jesus," Marc Hudson whispered under his breath, as the group walked slowly down to the polished marble of the ground floor.

The entrance hall was nearly a hundred meters wide and perhaps sixty meters tall. They had entered just over halfway up. Zor, some armed with slug-throwers or beam weapons, but all wearing the ceremonial *chya*, watched silently.

Sergei felt a thousand pairs of eyes watching him from mezzanines and balconies, and from perches scattered around the walls. Far off, like a whisper on the wind, they could hear a chiming sound.

It was alien and it was frightening because of it. Three hundred years of interstellar travel had opened Man's horizons, but an alien environment like esYen was an assault on the strongest bastions of the psyche, slamming shut all of the open doors of the mind. More than sixty years of war to the knife accentuated this emotion and Sergei had to restrain the feeling to draw a weapon, if only to reassure himself.

He wondered to himself what the average zor watching him was thinking, gazing into the faces of the race's conquerors. Some of the zor that watched silently were confronting, for the first time, the personification of what might be the death of their race. Only a few had met with the humans at the Rift Base or on E'rene'e. Most were as unfamiliar with their enemy as humanity was unfamiliar with them.

Still, as Sergei looked carefully about, he didn't sense suppressed anger as the crowd watched the humans and their escort descend to the polished floor. But the subtle clues of anger and hatred might not translate neatly from zor to human.

As they reached the floor level, the Chamberlain, Ptal HeU'ur, turned to face Marais. His expression, like the pattern of his wings, was unreadable to most of the humans present, but it was clear that he was speaking to the quiet crowd of zor as well. He spread his wings wide and performed an elegant bow before the admiral, and his entourage did the same.

Dres HeShri said quietly to Marais, "The High Chamberlain of the High Nest," indicating the zor waiting for them.

"*esHu'ur,*" the Chamberlain said. "I am Ptal HeU'ur, Chamberlain to the High Lord. I welcome your return to the High Nest."

"I am honored," Marais replied.

"Lord Marais, if you will follow, I shall escort you into the garden, where the High Lord will receive you." He turned and, never looking back to see if the humans followed, passed under an archway and down a long sunlit arbor. The embassy, led by the admiral, strode after him.

The corridor opened out to a wide arch. Ptal HeU'ur beckoned, indicating they should enter; without hesitation, Marais walked forward.

Sergei's first impression of the garden was of a giant aviary or greenhouse. The ceiling, if there was one, was invisible; instead, the familiar cobalt-blue sky hung over a huge well-ordered tropical forest. No zor escorts followed them into the garden, so they stood in a small clearing, waiting for something to happen.

Something did. While Sergei stood uncomfortably in his dress blues, a plant which reminded him of a sunflower rose on its stalk and stretched itself out toward him, *sniffing* at the arm of his uniform jacket. Sergei knew, as an experienced commander, that there were many forms of life in the universe and most of them could be harmful to humans under the proper circumstances.

He tried to edge out from under the plant, which had now developed an affection for the cap tucked under his arm. A row of sharp-looking teeth had emerged from the stamen of the flower and began to tug at the brim, trying to pull it away from Sergei's grasp.

His right hand reached for a weapon, but before he could make a move a zor voice called out, "Sr'can'u!" and the flower gave up its struggle for the cap, retreating meekly and wavering on its stem at the edge of the undergrowth.

A moment later a tall, thin zor emerged from around a bend in the path and walked to the plant. He gently stroked its stem and reached into a pocket in his cream-colored robe, drawing out a small cluster of reddish berries. He fed the creature one berry at a time and then held the stem. All the while, the zor spoke to the plant softly in the Highspeech.

At last he turned to the startled group of humans and offered them a slight bow.

"Good day," he said. "You are Admiral Marais."

The admiral nodded. "Yes, sir."

"It is my pleasure to welcome you at last to Zor'a, Admiral. I am Sse'e HeYen, High Lord."

The High Lord ran a taloned claw along the length of the plant. "My apologies for your cap," he said to Sergei. "Sr'can'u is very curious and *very* impolite to strangers."

"Quite all right, sir," Sergei replied, examining the rips the teeth-marks of the plant had left in what had once been his best cap. "I beg your pardon. Is Sr'can'u some sort of pet?"

"I am afraid I do not quite understand what you mean. He is an intelligent being, a symbiote . . . a guardian of this garden. He is quite friendly if you make sure he knows his place." His wings changed position slightly. He spoke two more words to the plant and then let go of the stem.

"Let me offer you refreshment," he said, and escorted the group through the garden to a wider clearing, where low backless chairs and perches were set. A small table held metal goblets and a dispenser.

The humans arranged themselves on chairs. Rrith remained standing to the side. The High Lord dispensed *h'geRu*, the same liquor that had been offered to them before.

"Please, cousin." The High Lord gestured to an empty perch and elevated his wings slightly as he spoke to Rrith. "Join our companions in a toast to . . . What shall it be, lord?"

"It is your choice, *hi* Sse'e," Marais replied. "But it should at least include an offering to the Lord *esLi.*"

"To *esLi,* then," Sse'e said, extending a goblet to Rrith who arranged himself carefully on a perch. *"esLiHeYar."*

They drank the liquor slowly. "I prefer *egeneh,* myself," Sse'e said at last. "It is something of a . . . learned taste?

"You have come a long way, Admiral. I hope it is not inconvenient for you to have come here, to the High Nest."

"It is a privilege and an honor, lord."

"The privilege and honor are mine, Admiral. In the short time you have waged war upon the People you have brought us from enmity to admiration, until at last we stand on a precipice with bound wings, waiting for the Eight Winds to blow us into the abyss.

"As I am sure you are aware, the People began to travel in space long before you did, though we began to explore the stars beyond our area much more recently. Like everything we have done, our explorations had reinforced our convictions and our beliefs about our place in the universe and about our relationship with the Lord *esLi.*

"Sixty of your years ago all of that was suddenly altered. The presence of humanity, indeed its very existence, threatened the People—not just our way of life, but the very beliefs that held us together. After this discovery my honored father, who is now one with *esLi,* had a dream. *esLi* appeared to him with His face turned away. The Lord of Lords told our High Lord that the scourge of humanity must be wiped away or we would be forever *idju.*

"Ask our cousin here what it means to be *idju. se* Rrith, I am sure you are uncomfortable to be here in my garden with your status thus in doubt."

Rrith did not answer at first, but the High Lord seemed to be waiting patiently. At last he said quietly, "I do not consider my status to be in any doubt, High Lord. When I failed to activate the *saHu'ue,* my status became all too clear."

"There we differ," the High Lord answered. "Your status is really no different than mine or than most any of the People's at this time."

"*hi* Sse'e—?" Rrith's wings assumed an unusual position.

"'A single tear is lost in the ocean,'" the High Lord quoted. "The People have had a terrible confrontation, one brought about by the intervention of the admiral. We are *hi'idju,* my young cousin. We are dishonored as a people.

"As you stand here in the High Nest you, as well as the rest of the People, face the certainty that everything you fought for, every goal we as a people sought in our war with the *naZora'i,* has been ground into dust.

"To one of the People," the High Lord continued, addressing Marais, "*idju* is worse than death: it is condemnation to a most unbearable sort of life. We believed then and we have always believed that to win back the favor of *esLi,* we must fight you and destroy you. Regaining the favor of *esLi* was the most important thing. After all, had not *esLi* Himself told us so?

"Yet we failed somehow. Now we are *hi'idju*—by our own self-judgement. As all know"—and the High Lord cast a telling glance at Rrith—"there is usually only one alternative available to regain the sight of *esLi*: self-destruction."

"I would not ask for that outcome," Marais said quietly.

"It is not for you to ask, nor for us to look to you, Admiral." He seemed to choose that title deliberately, rather than *esHu'ur.* The High Lord extended his talons briefly, as if suppressing anger, or perhaps frustration. "When you took up the mantle of leadership of your fleet, this was an *aLi'e'er'e:* Choosing the Flight. If you were one of the People, we would say—in retrospect, of course—that the Lord of the Bright Circle guided you to that position.

"When you chose your methods and means and did not stay

your hand from doing what we had always believed to be too distasteful, too unpleasant for humans, this, too, was an *aLi'e'er'e.* Whatever the reason, *esLi* in His wisdom allowed that event to be carried into fruition.

"When your young soldier"—he gestured to Chris Boyd, who looked back in surprise from where he stood at parade rest—"used the *esLiHeShuSa'a* and joined minds with me for a moment, this, too, was an *aLi'e'er'e,* one which was not of your design, but which gave us quite by accident a critical means of understanding.

"And at the time you stood on the bridge of your flagship before *Ka'ale'e* Hu'ueru in the empty talon of space you call the Rift, you could have destroyed those who acknowledged you as the Dark Wing, as *esHu'ur.*

"Yet you did not. This was the most important *aLi'e'er'e* of all.

"Did not my cousin Hyos say to you that the People would destroy themselves if *esLi* willed it, or if *esHu'ur* commanded it?"

"Yes, *hi* Sse'e. I replied that I would never command such a thing."

"You were as good as your word. Your actions showed compassion and mercy. But these are not traits of *esHu'ur* the Destroyer. Did you not worry that your claim to be the Dark Wing might have been overturned in that moment?"

Marais paused for a moment as if he needed to choose his words very carefully. "I spoke the truth then, High Lord, as I hope to be doing now. If I am who I claim to be, must I carry this forth to its logical and terrible conclusion? Is that the choice you offer me? Will you only recognize me as the Dark Wing with your dying breaths?

"I did not come to Zor'a to be the second to an execution or assistant to a mass suicide. Surely there is another course."

Somewhere far off in the garden a bird whistled, a sharp trill of joy. The High Lord stopped and cocked his head slightly, listening for a moment, and then turned his attention again to the humans.

"There is a strong tradition in our own literature and culture, called 'condemnation to Life.' As a scholar in our traditions, I am sure that you are aware of it. Even for those who are *idju* there is the possibility of redemption if the Lord *esLi* wills it. Since *esLi* is far more wise than we and since His reasons are not always known to mere mortals, He will sometimes command one of the People not to destroy himself so that he can live for some greater purpose.

"Admiral, I believe that all of the People have been called in just this way for some reason I do not yet know."

"How do you know this?"

"Some fraction of a moon ago I had a dream, in which you and your companions were prominent. Even my cousin *se* Rrith was present."

He turned to Rrith, began to say something, and then continued. "Admiral, your dream-image spoke to me, telling me that we had to meet and discuss matters. *esLi* spoke through you to me, I believe, for He garbed you as a traditional figure in our beliefs."

"The Dark Wing," Marais said.

"No, Admiral. This interview would have been much different if that were the case. You were not the Dark Wing in my dream. You were the Bright Wing, the giver of life, the opener of minds. And so I believe: that you and your fleet have ultimately come not as destroyers, but as the *givers* of life. *esLi* has chosen to condemn the zor to life, and now they stand ready to follow you, the Bright Wing, who will open their minds and change their lives."

Marais was stunned, almost physically taken aback. He stood abruptly looking from face to face: at his officers, at Chris Boyd, at Rrith and the High Lord in turn.

"Lord Sse'e, I . . ." He ran a hand through his silvery hair. "I do not know . . ."

"Consider this, Admiral." The High Lord resettled himself on his perch, spreading his wings slightly for balance. He laid his taloned claws in his lap. "We are at a crucial crossing-point, a place where the lines of history for our two races cross: this, like each of the other situations I have described, is *aLi'e'er'e,* Choosing the Flight.

"When we first encountered your race we were guided by a belief that you had to be eradicated . . . for the Lord *esLi* told us so. It was not disharmonious with what we had always believed and what our culture had always told us. It was in keeping with the violence of our culture and with the way in which we had always reconciled our Outer and Inner Peace.

"I have come to believe, however, that by having the capability to destroy us—and then *not doing so*—that you, too, are working the will of *esLi,* who intended that we be defeated by you and be placed at your mercy. It is now time that we widen our perceptions of the universe: clearly you as the Bright Wing will bring us to do that, and help us survive to serve *esLi* in whatever manner He has planned for us."

"And what does this really mean, *hi* Sse'e?" Marais fixed the High Lord with a glance. "What if a High Lord decides in fifty years that it is time to make war upon humanity once again?"

"Why would we try again, Admiral? The point is moot. Surely the humans of that time would not spare us. We always believed that humanity would not be capable of doing what you have done. That mistake is one we will *never* make again. To secure this, I have decided to present you with something which will make your position clear to all of the People."

The High Lord stood and walked between where Sergei and Marc Hudson were quietly standing. Behind them on an elevated stone platform was a narrow metal box intricately worked with *hRni'i.* Sse'e took the box up and carried it gingerly back to where Marais stood. Neither Rrith nor Chris Boyd could avoid an audible intake of breath: clearly they knew what was coming.

Marais opened it along its long edge by working an elaborate

catch. It held an ornately scabbarded sword, clearly of a significance greater than even the High Lord's *chya*. The humans in the
room could sense its power, as if that area of the High Lord's garden had suddenly become highly charged.

For his part, Rrith stood transfixed, unable to tear his gaze
from the sword.

"This is the *gyaryu*, the sword of state," the High Lord said,
gesturing for Marais to take it from its box. "A tradition of the
People says that in the Time of the Warring Nests, the Lord *esLi*
sent the great hero Qu'u to the Plain of Despite to recover it
from the fortress of *esGa'u* the Deceiver. At Qu'u's death, the
sword was given into the hands of the warrior whom *esLi* chose
to bear it: not the greatest, nor the most powerful, nor anyone
who would wield it wrongly.

"The warrior who wields it is called *Gyaryu'har*, and is the
one who personifies the promise of the Bright Wing, the redeemer of the People. You shall be the *Gyaryu'har*, Admiral, for
*esLi* has chosen you."

"I must . . . consider this . . ."

"That is as it should be," Sse'e answered. "But if you accept
this role, this bright burden, the war between your race and mine
will be over, for all time." The High Lord stood, and extended a
claw toward Marais.

Marais reached out his hand, and grasped that of the High
Lord.

"Come, Admiral," Sse'e HeYen said. "Your People await."

In response to the door-chime Sergei heard the admiral's
voice say, "Come."

The door parted and he entered. Admiral Marais was sitting
on a makeshift chair that was trying to accommodate him; beside
him on an elaborate stand lay the *gyaryu*, the zor sword of state.
Chair and stand were set on the highest step of a wide staircase
going nowhere, which somehow fit the rest of the layout of the

room provided by their zor hosts. It was composed of a checker-board array of platforms, arranged so that they ascended and descended to various parts of the room. Some areas had furniture, mostly wide perches and backless chairs, while others were simply empty.

On one wall of the room a stone disk hung in midair, with space within for a good-sized zor to stand upright. Behind it the wall was tinged faintly orange, perhaps to suggest the dawn of Antares.

"You asked to see me, sir."

"Yes." Marais gestured to another chair opposite and Sergei navigated the room to reach the admiral. He set his uniform cap beside him on a table and sat where indicated.

"A drink?"

"No, thank you, sir."

"Commodore," he began, "I am in sore need of advice."

"I'd be happy to help, sir."

"The High Lord has presented me with a dilemma." Marais looked at Sergei, his expression somewhere between concern and surprise. "I believed that when we came here to Zor'a, the end of the war was a foregone conclusion. The zor faced overwhelming force and had enlarged their perception of the fleet, and me in particular, to mythical proportions. We were on the verge of either destroying the zor or causing them to destroy themselves.

"And yet from this remarkable turn of events something entirely unexpected has evolved. Instead of having to take the step of destroying the zor utterly or having them destroy themselves, the High Lord has given me this." He pointed to the *gyaryu* carefully. "It is a token of their belief in a new direction for their People, a new understanding between themselves and our species. Yet it is more than that. Much more."

A strange expression seemed to come over Marais' face as he said these words.

"I'm not sure I understand, sir."

"It's not at all clear that any of us, any human, truly can understand. I must try, however. I must try.

"The zor have presented me with an artifact of great symbolic significance, but it is more than that. They have given me a token which legitimizes me before all of the People, providing them with an escape from the prison of dishonor that they and I have built for them. If I accept the *gyaryu,* the zor will accept the end of the war, for now and for all time.

"If I do not accept, the zor will again be faced with dishonor as a race—*hi'idju.* There might be only one way out of that dilemma. If I choose to decline the *gyaryu,* the zor will likely die as a race, either by their own hand or by continuation of the war."

"If that were the only consequence, my lord," Sergei said, "I am sure that you would simply accept the sword."

"Quite right. There is more to it than that. You heard what the High Lord said about the *Gyaryu'har*—what he does, what he is: I would be representing the Bright Wing, the Illuminator of the Path of *esLi.*"

"I'm not sure I understand the significance of the Bright Wing, sir. If *esLi* is the principle of Good, and *esGa'u* a representation of Evil, how do the Bright Wing and Dark Wing fit into the scheme?"

"Like everything else in the zor cosmology, it is hard to explain. The zor have not two, but *four,* significant powers—I do not know if you could term them all deities—that participate in the *enLi'hiRe,* the Flight of the People. Chiefest among these is *esLi,* the bringer of life, the Lord of the Golden Circle.

"*esLi* represents perfection, the harmony of Inner and Outer Peace. He is the being with whom zor hope at last to unite. Zor Sensitives theorize that the major part of a zor's *hsi,* or life-force, does become part of *esLi* at death."

"An overmind of some sort."

"Yes, that's right. *esLi* is an amalgamation of the life-force of all of the People who have gone before and thus is the source of power, of inspiration and of precognition. The High Lord is supposed to be guided by *esLi* through prescient dreams.

"At the other end of the spectrum is *esGa'u,* the Deceiver. He is represented as a brilliant sorcerer, one of those who refused to accept the loss of being that unison with *esLi* entailed."

"Satan."

"That's a bit of an anthropomorphism, but it's a reasonable parallel. In any case, by their own volition, he and a number of his followers—the *esGa'u Yal,* a term often applied to our race—chose to become Cast Out from *esLi's* perfection. The Deceiver's role is to oppose *esLi,* and in general to steal *hsi* that might make *esLi* stronger."

"You said that there are four powers."

"That's right. On either side of this axis are two beings, *esTli'ir* and *esHu'ur,* the Bright and the Dark Wings. While *esLi* and *esGa'u* seem to be personifications of active forces of good and evil, the Bright Wing and Dark Wing are agents of nonpersonified force, like a storm or a harvest. They are neither good nor evil, and they are intertwined in ways so fundamental that neither *esLi* nor *esGa'u* can permanently affect them."

"Is this why they believe you could destroy them even though—I assume—*esLi* is omnipotent?"

"From what I understand, that's true. *esLi* cannot prevent a powerful hurricane; nor can he prevent the eventuality of the destruction *esHu'ur* brings. But *esGa'u* cannot cause an immensely powerful plague; nor can he cause any illumination of the correct path that *esTli'ir* provides.

"In zor legend, *esGa'u* even captures the Bright Wing for a time, only to find that the Dark Wing has become the Bright Wing and the Bright the Dark, so his Plain of Despite suffers accordingly while the world above is saved.

"In one of the old texts the four powers are placed over the silhouette of a zor. *esLi* appears at the head, *esGa'u* at the foot, and *esHu'ur* and *esTli'ir* form the two wings. At the center is the self, the *hsi*. *esLi* and *esGa'u* pull in two different directions, while the two wings push. A well-disciplined zor holds the *hsi* in the center."

Sergei thought about Marais' explanation for a moment, and then said, "What does it mean for you to be both the Bright and Dark Wings? What are they implying?"

"I suppose it makes sense." Marais leaned forward, elbows on knees, in a most unadmiral-like pose, a sort of anti-*zazen*. "If the Bright and Dark Wings are intimately connected, it might be logical to represent them with the same individual. It certainly puts an entirely different light on the zor view of humanity, and of me.

"It also puts a different cast on our present relationship with the Solar Empire."

"Forgive me, Admiral, but I don't see how. We both heard the report of Assemblyman Hsien's interview with Captain MacEwan. Based on what Hsien said about opinion back home, our standing with respect to the zor hardly enters into the discussion. If anything, the public consensus is that we have made the zor into even more implacable enemies."

"Okome also said that Hsien expected me to try for the throne and that he would aid that effort in exchange for certain concessions. But if I were to do that, I would legitimize our war but never justify it. *Here* is an opportunity for a breakthrough." He sat back in his chair again and looked directly at Sergei. "We have a chance to understand each other, something that has been impossible for more than sixty years. We have come close to the abyss and stepped away from it.

"A coup against the Solar Emperor would be seen in the long term as nothing more than an attempt to escape the consequences of mutiny and treason. It would be clear to the zor, at least, that we were not acting on behalf of humanity as a race. It would be possible for a future emperor to rekindle the conflict, perhaps even on the same scale as this one. If *hi* Sse'e's belief is correct, human and zor must grow closer together to thwart some common enemy. My own experiences support this belief."

"My lord, I must point out to you that there are still grave consequences awaiting the men and women in this fleet if you simply retire into the background."

"I am aware of that, Commodore." He stood up and walked away from Sergei, toward a high balcony that overlooked the main entrance-hall of the High Nest. Halfway there he turned, as if practicing some dramatic stage gesture. "I do not intend to simply retire. I believe there is a way out of this cul-de-sac that preserves what we have done, that opens the way for friendship between the two races, and that also preserves honor on all sides—even that of our newfound friend, Assemblyman Hsien."

"I am anxious to hear it, sir."

More than thirty parsecs away, in a small stateroom aboard the IS *Cameron,* Tomás Hsien leaned back in his armchair and considered the situation. It was obvious to him, as well as the Assembly Members who had sent him out here to A'anenu, that there was only one course of action left for the Imperial fleet: to return and seize the throne, much as Willem McDowell had done almost two centuries earlier. But even with the military might he possessed he had needed help in the UN General Assembly to bring enough of humanity to his side to avoid an even more hideous bloodbath and become emperor.

*This* future emperor would need help as well; Hsien was sure of it. When he finally had his patrician ass planted on the throne in Oahu, he would need guidance as well—of the sort Hsien was more than willing to provide.

Hsien smiled to himself, Buddha-like, and closed his eyes, imagining the changed face of the Solar Empire.

chapter 19

Jump scan record, 10/01/2311, 1927 Standard: Forty-three vessels recorded arriving at Kensington Starbase. Thirty-four Imperial IDs [ID beacon sigs attached].

Jump scan record, 10/02/2311, 1134 Standard: Forty-three vessels recorded departing from Kensington Starbase.

Jump scan record, 10/04/2311, 1103 Standard: Forty-three vessels recorded arriving at Cor Caroli Starbase. Thirty-four Imperial IDs [ID beacon sigs attached].

Jump scan record, 10/04/2311, 2256 Standard: Forty-three vessels recorded departing from Cor Caroli Starbase.

The scramble siren rang loudly through the ships, down the corridors, in the holds and hangars, and across the intercoms. Pilots dived for their suits and then ran for their cockpits; starships went to red alert, flung themselves into long predetermined standard orbits; crews of shuttles and boats ran for their vehicles, preparing to take off at a word from the portmaster. Traffic control was swamped in an instant, but the flawless precision drilled into the crews by months of training made its job almost superfluous.

Michael Mbele was aboard the starship *Charlemagne* when the siren rang. The *"Charlie,"* as its officers and crew called her, had been on a routine patrol between Pluto Base and Sol's Number Six jump point, the closest to the icy outermost planet's current orbital position. Mbele had made a habit of visiting or flying with all of the elements of his command here at the outskirts of the Sol System.

He told himself that he'd expected to be sitting at his desk writing some damn memo when they finally turned up. He stood on the bridge watching activity erupt at all stations. As yet there was no visual contact with the intruders, but Mbele could see two dozen blips on the pilot's board at a half-million kilometers' range. The transponder codes indicated that they were traveling at a high rate of speed: at least half-C, aimed directly at the Sol System gravity-well. As he watched, several others appeared.

Half–light-speed meant they had jumped a significant distance. Based on the distance jumped and the number of ships, it had to be Marais' fleet. Records of jumping vessels between the New Territories and the inner Empire had made their arrival a dead certainty.

McMasters had been dead right, the old bastard: Marais *would* come to Sol System, probably to claim the Imperial throne. It was impeccable timing—Imperial Guards had already withstood a half-dozen terrorist assaults on Imperial facilities on Oahu and elsewhere; the Assembly had long since been prorogued and sent home to steam; civil traffic had been slowed almost to a standstill while anti-Government protesters roamed major cities in mobs calling for Marais' head, or the emperor's, or something else.

Madness, and all because of one man . . . who did what he

had promised. And now he was here: the destroyer of a sentient race, with a fleet behind him.

And he was here to seize power.

Mbele reached inside his uniform jacket and pulled out a packet. He touched his right thumb to the seal to open it, and drew out a single sheet of real Admiralty stationery: his orders, in case the inevitable occurred. It had never been farther than five meters from his body since McMasters had handed it to him a month ago.

It was brief but went directly to the point.

Chan, report."

"Short-range scan indicates thirty-six arrivals so far, Commodore, including all nine zor vessels. The defensive fleet has scrambled and is on an intercept course with us."

"Who's in command there?"

Chand touched a keypad beside him at the exec's station. "A Captain Mbele commands Pluto Base, sir."

"Michael Mbele?"

"That's correct, Commodore."

Admiral Marais had stood silently at the rear of the bridge through the entire exchange. Now he leaned forward and said, "Do you know him?"

"His midshipman's-cruise was on the *Gustav Adolf*, Admiral." Sergei swiveled the pilot's chair to face Marais. "He's a good officer."

"Gun-happy?"

"No, sir, quite the opposite. Very levelheaded. I know Admiral McMasters always spoke quite favorably of him . . . a post in Sol System speaks for itself."

"Indeed so." Marais squinted at the pilot's board, which showed the intercepting vessels closing on their position.

"Your orders, Admiral?"

"Open a comm channel with this Captain Mbele. All ahead one-quarter."

"Aye-aye, sir."

The communications officer on the *Charlie* turned suddenly. "Hailing signal from the starship *Lancaster,* Captain," he said. The *Charlie*'s captain looked at Mbele for orders.

"Acknowledge, Ensign."

"Visual coming up, sir." Near the *Charlie*'s pilot's board, a 3-V image appeared, showing part of another bridge.

"This is Captain Michael Mbele, commanding Sol System—" He stopped suddenly. "Commodore Torrijos."

"Hello, Michael."

"Commodore Torrijos, your fleet is outlaw. It is my duty to inform you that, under Imperial military law, you are under arrest. Prepare to heave to and be boarded."

Mbele did not seriously expect this request to be heeded, since the fleet had been outlaw for three months now and had crossed hundreds of light-years to seize the Imperial throne. However, it was his official duty to say it.

"We make no dispute about our status or your legal right to make those demands. However, we will not at this time allow your command to board."

"Then I regret that I must—"

"Hold it a damn minute," Sergei continued, interrupting Mbele's next formal statement. "My command will agree to maintain a near orbit to the closest jump point and not enter the gravity-well if you in turn keep a reasonable distance."

"You are in no legal position to make demands."

"For what that statement is worth, Michael, you're right. But there's a lot of firepower out here that says we can and will do what is necessary to keep you from forcibly boarding vessels in our fleet. Now we have a request of you."

"A request."

"Admiral Marais wishes to speak with Admiral McMasters regarding the disposition of our fleet and our allies'."

"'Allies'?" Mbele glanced at the pilot's board. There were several dozen ships in close formation now, and at least fifteen of them registered as enemy—not Imperial—vessels. "Who—?"

"There are a number of zor ships with us."

"Zor *allies*?"

"Yes, that's right. The war is over, Michael. Now get McMasters."

The observatory in orbit around Pluto had been hastily evacuated. The two dozen resident astronomers had been removed by military transport two hours after the sudden arrival of the outlaw fleet from jump. Now it was empty but for a half-dozen marines Ted McMasters personally trusted. That was no small matter; his loyalty to the emperor demanded that he not place his own person at the mercy of an avowed enemy of the state.

What was more, his survival instinct was very strong. Someone who had eradicated a sentient race would probably not think twice about venting him into space.

From the bridge of the station, McMasters could see the admiral's barge preparing to dock. It was unarmed, as Marais and Mbele had agreed; the fleet had kept its distance as well.

What game could Marais possibly be playing? He had the force at his disposal; half of Sol System was under martial law or rioting against the emperor.

McMasters gripped a railing in front of the viewport and looked down at his hands. The calluses and burn-scars had faded somewhat, retreating as paperwork replaced engineering; but the veins still stood out, and the muscles under the skin were bunched and knotted.

He had worked his way to flag rank step by step over thirty years. He was a lifer, and proud of it: he had the scars and the record to prove his devotion to the Empire. He had fought the enemy without flinching or wavering.

Yet it still seemed impossible to grasp that Marais had defeated the zor. What he also could not grasp—and he imagined that it eluded most of his fellow citizens as well—was the manner in which the fleet had gone about it. The visual evidence from the zor border worlds had affected him. It was not so much the cold efficiency of the acts as it was the gross destruction, perceived with horror by less-trained eyes. The execution of the campaign had been flawless: no military leader could have asked for more.

McMasters felt a slight thrum through the deck as the barge's airlock connected with the station.

But what sort of a man would have asked for such a campaign in the first place?

And the answer came into his mind almost immediately.

*Only a madman,* he thought to himself. *Only someone whose reason had been consumed by hatred, whose resolve had been driven to insanity through the singular pursuit of one driving ambition, and whose goals had as yet only been partially achieved.*

Angered by the thought, but frightened as well, Ted McMasters turned from the railing to face the admiral of the outlaw fleet.

The hatchway sighed open. Two shipboard marines took up stations on either side of the door and exchanged long glances with McMasters' own marines on the station bridge. Following in their wake came Admiral Marais, dressed in an everyday uniform set off by an ornate scabbard hung at his belt. Something not completely perceptible drew McMasters' attention to the sword contained within it.

Marais walked forward to McMasters and gave him a brisk salute.

"All right," McMasters began. "I'm here. Just what is it you want?"

"I thought it best that we talk to you directly," Marais began. He walked to the railing and looked out at the stars. It looked for a moment as if he'd never seen them before.

"There isn't anything you could say to me that you couldn't have said to Mbele."

"Is that so," Marais replied, without turning.

"Yes, damn it, that's so. Just what do you have in mind, *Admiral*?" McMasters' voice was tinged with anger, almost sarcasm, when he said the word. "Or let me say it more directly. Why have you come here?"

"The answer might surprise you."

"Nothing would surprise me anymore, Marais. Including armed treason against the body of the emperor."

"Oh, but it's not that at all." Marais turned to face McMasters again. In his mind, Ted McMasters had pictured an expression of hatred or even of frenzy on Marais' face: instead there was a paternal, almost gentle expression. "You see, McMasters, I've come back for the best of reasons: to vindicate myself."

"How?"

"In the traditional way. By a full court-martial, which I believe will acquit me and all of my officers and crew of any misconduct or wrongdoing in the pursuit of lawfully given orders to defeat the zor race and render it unable to trouble the Empire. I have accomplished my task, McMasters. The war is over and my commission has expired."

McMasters looked from Marais' face to those of the two marines at the door and then back to Marais again.

"Are you out of your mind?" McMasters finally said quietly, almost as an aside to Marais. "Do you have any idea of the charges? You should already be *dead*. Insubordination isn't the half of it. Treason isn't even the worst of it. Xenocide—" He ran out of words to express himself.

"It isn't about that. It's about the orders given me by the emperor himself." Marais reached inside his uniform jacket and slowly drew out a packet bearing the royal-blue insignia of the sword-and-sun. "They state quite clearly that my mission gave me absolute authority in the war zone for the duration of the emergency and empowered me to take whatever steps I felt necessary to carry out my task.

"I contend that I have in no way compromised the trust placed in me. No word or deed has contravened the absolute letter of these orders. On that basis I intend that the Imperial Navy shall acquit me of all charges."

"And how do I fit into this insanity?"

"Very simple, McMasters. You, as senior ranking officer in the Imperial Navy, are going to take any and all steps necessary to assure that I am judged fairly and according to the Universal Code."

"And if I refuse?"

"That seems unlikely. You are well respected and fair-minded, and you would not condemn a fellow officer without giving him the opportunity of a fair trial."

"Fair—" McMasters walked to the railing where Marais stood. "You have no idea what you're proposing or what's been going on while you were incommunicado, destroying the zor beyond the edge of the Empire. It almost would have been better if you had never come home."

Marais locked glances with McMasters. The moment seemed to stretch out into infinity, until it was interrupted by Marais' voice.

"I had a task to accomplish, given me by the emperor himself. I carried that task out and finished it while the politicians and the weaklings here and elsewhere in the Empire tried to stop me. The zor haven't been exterminated and at last we have peace with them.

"I should know: for I am now a part of their High Nest."

"*What?*"

Marais turned to one of the marines that had accompanied him. "If you would ask *se* Rrith to come up here?"

The marine nodded, saluted and turned and left the bridge.

"The zor are a proud race, McMasters. It was almost impossible for them to accept defeat at the hands of humanity. It was possible that the race might have committed *mass suicide* as a result of our victory; but the High Lord has told me himself that he perceives a greater purpose for the zor, decades or even centuries in the future.

"The High Lord is a powerful Sensitive with enormous precognitive ability. I believe that he is correct: that the talents and character the zor possess will be of use in the future, and it is much better for us to have them as friends than enemies.

"We have done something that has never been done before.

"We have befriended the zor."

Marais gripped the rail and stared out into the dark night of space. There was a long pause, as if he was weighing where he might take the conversation next.

"In our own way we have perceived this struggle as narrowly as the zor have. To them, this was a war based entirely on xenophobia. Previous commanders had used halfway measures and unwarranted trust to bridge the yawning gulf that such a fear generated between us. My tactics, though repugnant to some, accomplished the desired objective: an end to the wars between zor and human—for all time.

"But it is possible that there are even greater consequences. The universe is not an empty place. We might find other races, perhaps more powerful and less amenable to either my tactics or the pastoral political techniques used in the past. Perhaps then the capabilities of our two races combined would better serve."

"Wait a minute," McMasters said. "Are you telling me that you believe that there's some sort of cosmic bogeyman"—he pointed toward Pluto and the arm of the galaxy beyond—"floating around out there somewhere, waiting to eat our lunch, and that we're going to ask the help of a race we've bitterly fought for sixty years, to protect us against them—just because a precognitive member of that race says so?

"If you intend to base your entire court-martial defense on that idea, you'll be in an asylum so fast your head will spin. And I'll sign the damn papers myself."

"It sounds foolish in that light, I agree. But I believe I already have more concrete evidence that there are potential enemies out there we haven't discovered yet."

"Oh?"

"You remember my aide, Captain Stone?"

"Yes. What about him?"

"He—"

"Excuse me, Admiral," said the marine, approaching the two flag officers. He was accompanied by a zor wearing a white sash and a ceremonial robe. McMasters turned suddenly.

"Admiral McMasters," Sergei said, "may I present the High Lord's envoy, *se* Rrith ehn Tl'l'u."

Emperor Alexander Philip Juliano punched his ring finger angrily down on the access-tablet and the huge viewscreen faded once again to opacity. Alexander was really more frustrated than angry; his rule had not been an easy one. It was hardly what he had expected when the mantle of government had suddenly dropped on his shoulders eight years before.

It had seemed easy then, when his father, the emperor John of blessed memory, died suddenly of a massive heart attack while engaged in heated argument with one of his ministers.

There had been much made of the incident. Sometime during all of the pomp and ceremony that had transferred the Imperial dignity from his dead father's shoulders to his own, Alexander had arranged for the unfortunate fool to be given a posting as permanent Imperial emissary to Tolman's World, a cold and desolate place about as far from the Imperial Court as mankind had yet journeyed.

As in that incident, use of the tools of power had fallen easily into young Alexander's hands. His father had taught him well; manipulation of the Imperial Assembly, the major corporations, and the many propaganda instruments at his disposal had made him appear kind and just, while firmly entrenching him in power. It was not an easy task considering the size of the Empire.

He had made all of the right moves, it seemed, except one. But that one . . .

He stood up, looking back at the velvet-upholstered throne on its little platform. The audience chamber was empty and half in darkness; he had sent the ministers and the courtiers away, dismissing them with no less rudeness than he felt they deserved.

A faint breeze played at the curtain and he walked to the window to look out at the moonlit night. He could hear the waves crashing to the shore down below the cliffs of Diamond Head, while the steady tramping of boots on the lower plaza reminded him of the guardsmen that protected him from his own people here in the isolated Imperial Palace.

*Think clearly,* he told himself. A madman had been given control of a fleet and likely destroyed an alien race. Forget for a moment that this particular race had been attempting to do just that to humanity for two generations. Forget for a moment that at least some councillors and ministers thought it was a great triumph.

To most people, it was an act of incalculable brutality. That Marais was able to do it could only imply that the emperor condoned the act, and indeed had ordered it in the first place. Marais the Butcher became Alexander the Butcher.

*God.*

Alexander conjured up in his mind a history class sometime in the future . . . *"Today we will discuss the great murderers of human history—Jenghiz Khan, Ivan the Terrible, Adolf Hitler, Joseph Stalin, Hwa Chiang, Alexander the Butcher . . ."*

It hadn't been that way at all, though: Marais had gone off on his own and couldn't be stopped, not from Sol System. He hadn't been following the will of the emperor at all. He was a traitor, nothing less.

But to admit *that* would be to tell Alexander's subjects that an appointed military commander with the full confidence of the Imperial throne behind him had done exactly what he damn pleased and gotten away with it. It was absolutely unthinkable. This flouting of Imperial authority could bring about total chaos and the end of the Empire. Not to mention its emperor.

"Sire?"

Alexander whirled to face the intruder in his empty audience-hall and saw his new prime minister step out of the shadows into the moonlight.

"It is very disconcerting when you sneak up on me like that, Julianne," he said at last. "Besides, I want to be alone now."

Julianne Tolliver, the Imperial prime minister, scowled at the emperor. "There is hardly time for that now, Your Majesty. Less than thirty-six hours from now Marais will arrive at the Admiralty in St. Louis. Less than twenty-four hours later the court-martial will begin."

"I don't give a damn."

"Your Majesty has a hell of a bad attitude."

Alexander narrowed his eyes at the prime minister. "And just who do you think you are, and who do you think you're talking to?"

"At the moment I am your prime minister, Sire. I know that I am addressing the Solar Emperor. However, if Your Majesty is unwilling to carry out responsibilities associated with his exalted position, I can assure Your Majesty that he will soon require another prime minister. You told me yourself that I would be permitted the freedom to speak—"

"Very well, Madam Prime Minister." Alexander sighed deeply. "What must I sign?"

"Nothing yet." The prime minister walked to the window and looked across the courtyard, as if surveying the landscape. "Marais has requested the court-martial, Sire. I mistrust the man's intentions. He must believe that he is likely to be vindicated on the charges. He will, after all, be tried by his peers in the military."

"Meaning?"

"Moral issues will hold little sway over them, Sire."

"The man disobeyed *orders,* Julianne. He deliberately ignored a direct command to cease and desist; he avoided an Imperial envoy sent for the same purpose; he made his own treaty with an alien race—"

"He returned to Sol System with a military force," she said, interrupting him. "Who knows whether he will use it if the court-martial finds him guilty?"

"What do you think we should do?" He turned away from the window and crossed his arms in front of his chest. "Your emperor awaits. Advise."

"Operation Tattoo still remains a possibility, Sire."

"A barbaric alternative."

"In the face of all that has happened? After all of the blood shed in this war, what would be the significance of the death of one man?"

"He is a leader of the zor."

"I don't believe that, Sire, any more than you do. We have the zor home worlds hostage; *that* is the power we need over them, not some mystical nonsense. It wouldn't wash at the court-martial in any case."

Alexander thought to himself and sighed deeply. "Very well, Julianne. Give the order. Operation Tattoo has my permission to proceed."

She smiled, the moonlight catching her face half in light, half in shadow.

"By your leave, Sire."

## chapter 20

"Violet is missing."

The Director of Imperial Intelligence looked up from her 'reader. The mottled face of Jupiter behind was covered with swirling storms; by comparison, the director's face was calm and settled. She gestured Smith to the chair with the green emblem in front of it.

"Yes, I know. Please have a seat, Green." She returned her attention to the 'pad. Smith sat down and cultivated patience, watching the planet's atmosphere slowly drift. At last the director looked up at him.

"Why don't you tell me what you know, and I'll fill you in on the details."

"Violet had taken his 'retirement' well, as you know, taking up residence in the Winnipeg arcology, pursuing studies in ancient history, I believe. He has spent much of the intervening time doing research, and generally keeping to himself.

"Two and a half Standard days ago, he attended a lecture at Winnipeg University, dealing with the campaign of Xerxes against the Greeks. As usual, one of my department monitored him during his journey—she was even in the lecture hall as well—but when the presentation ended, Violet had disappeared.

"He did not return to his apartment that day or since. A check of transit systems leaving Winnipeg revealed nothing. He does not own a private vehicle and there is no record of rental or purchase of a vehicle by someone answering his description."

"A family member, perhaps?"

"Violet has no family on-planet, Director. We have been monitoring his off-planet communications—"

"If he had any ulterior motives he would know that you would do that. Go on."

"We have been monitoring him very closely, Director, as you ordered," Smith continued, trying to contain his annoyance. "He was treated as a Class One suspect, a potential enemy of the state."

The director folded her hands in front of her and fixed Smith with a grim visage. "If you monitored him as closely as you say, then how did you lose him?"

"I . . . cannot say for sure." Smith thought a moment, then added, "Violet was a member of the inner security circle for many years, Director, longer than most of us, including me. I can only assume that some member of the detail assigned to him has been turned and aided his escape."

"Had you not guarded against that contingency?"

"Director, I assure you that everything possible was done to assure the integrity of the agents assigned to this case. No member of the team had ever previously worked directly with Violet; the psych profiles for them showed no inclination toward Violet's rather extreme political views. But until he was removed from inner security Violet had access to all of the records, documents and technology we now possess. He must have anticipated your decision. There are a hundred things he could have done to turn the situation his way.

"We could only have anticipated a few of them even if the Agency had decided simply to assassinate him. Many, many contingencies could have been prepared. I suspect that one of them is being carried out at this moment."

The director didn't seem to like this conclusion, though it must have been one she had reached several minutes ago. Violet was an experienced member of the inner security circle, a fox among the foxes—and now he was somewhere out of sight, a fox among the sheep.

"What do you believe he will do next?"

"I can only conjecture, Director, but I believe that he will attempt to kill Admiral Marais."

It was predawn, the darkness above and below grudgingly giving ground before the coming morning as it always did; the earth and the sky readying for the metamorphosis that day always brought. From the window Sergei could see all of the great naval spaceport, a hive of activity as always, as the shuttles launched into the sky every few minutes as he watched. The huge metropolis of St. Louis lay beyond, a diadem of light and dark.

He had hardly slept, had not expected to sleep. Now he had given up on the idea entirely as he watched the megalopolis a hundred meters below his vantage slowly come to life.

Like a passenger in a 'copter who has been en route for several hours and arrives only to still feel the illusion of motion, Sergei found it difficult to fix his attention on the seemingly frozen instant of time that was the present. Events had tumbled one after the other in rapid succession, and his training as a line officer had permitted him to accommodate it all and respond to it.

Scarcely seventy-two hours had passed since the fleet had come out of jump; there had been an extended negotiation with Ted McMasters, and then with the First Lord of the Admiralty and the new prime minister, and finally with the military governor of the St. Louis district. Finally, under the escort of eight system-boats, six representative vessels of Marais' fleet had come into the gravity-well, their weapons-ports closed, their defensive fields lowered. Led by the *Lancaster,* they had cruised through the asteroid belt, crossed Mars orbit and anchored at last part-way between Earth and Mars. It had been a strange few hours, stranger and more frightening in its way than any experience of the campaign.

There had been comm silence: absolute quiet except for the automatic beacons directing navigation. It might have been merely for psychological effect, but it worked. Even Marais, whose coolness and poise had returned during the exchange with Ted McMasters out at Pluto Base, seemed worn and on edge as a result.

*Very curious,* Sergei reflected to himself as the last echoes of the bell slowly faded in the distance. The zor, whose race had been on the brink of destruction, had welcomed Marais and his fleet as heroes and as worthy conquerors. It had been a difficult decision on Marais' part: accepting the *gyaryu* and all that it en-tailed had caused him to completely change perspective on the fi-nal outcome of this war. Choosing a court-martial proceeding rather than simply returning to seize the Imperial throne seemed to suit Marais' sense of honor far better.

They were heroes to the zor, despite the destruction and death and the bitterness of the war. But to humanity, for whom this blood had been shed, they were outcasts and pariahs of the lowest order—villains, monsters, barbarians. At the spaceport the crowd had been a kilometer and a half away from where their shuttle had landed, but they had been able to see the cordon of police holding the crowd away from the gates of the shuttlepad. The epithets that rang out and the ugly mood of that crowd had made the public opinion of Marais quite clear. The 3-V had con-firmed and redoubled it for Sergei as he sat in his room on the floor that had been hastily cleared for Marais and his contingent. Marines under McMasters' personal command, with strict orders not to speak to their charges, "protected" them from the wrath of the public that teemed, even now, in sight of the spaceport gates.

The door-chime interrupted his reverie and Sergei stood and walked to the door, wondering who the hell would ring it at 0500. He opened it and found Rrith standing there wrapped clumsily in a robe.

"*se* Commodore," he said, and inclined his head respectfully. "I hope I am not disturbing you but I heard you stir and wondered if you desired company."

"Sure, come in." The marine posted outside Sergei's door was standing well back, his rifle ready but lowered. Sergei ignored the trooper and stood aside to let Rrith enter and then shut it without looking. "I was just sitting and thinking."

"Unable to sleep?"

"That's about right," Sergei replied, and dropped into the plush armchair near the open window. Rrith perched on a low chair by the bed. "Is something troubling you, *se* Rrith?"

"I am aware that there is a delicate situation, *se* Commodore."

"Sergei."

"*se* Sergei." Rrith inclined his wings a trifle under the robe, as if seeking to communicate some feeling that Sergei could not understand. "There is some difficulty between *esHu'ur* and his superior, the human High Lord. I confess I do not completely understand—it clearly touches on the zor, but I am not sure. Does the human High Lord wish to pursue the war?"

"It is hardly that simple. The emperor wishes . . ." Sergei thought for a moment wondering how to phrase it. "The emperor did not wish that the outcome be the way it was."

"I fail to see why, *se* Sergei," Rrith replied, a hint of confusion creeping into his voice. "You won the war. Did the emperor wish you to lose?"

"He did not order the invasion of the zor Home Stars and was willing to sign a peace with you after A'anenu."

"That would have accomplished nothing. We would not have accepted the admiral as *esHu'ur* and we would have been compelled by *esLi* to attack once again."

Rrith settled himself in his seat, his face half lit by the brightening sky and half in the shadow of the darkened room. "I have read through the admiral's book, and he was quite clear about the necessity to take the war to Zor'a. Did you not tell me that the emperor also read the book, before he empowered *ha* Marais to fight us?"

"Yes, he did. It is what convinced him to give Admiral Marais his commission. But he never expected the task to be carried out, at least not as Marais said he would. He thought of it as rhetoric and so did I." Sergei leaned his head on his hands and sighed deeply.

"Rhetoric? I am not sure I see. Did the emperor believe that the admiral had lied about his intent?"

"No, he simply considered it exaggeration. Our military is influenced by the political intrigues of the Imperial Court and Lord Marais' friends there had convinced the emperor that such a choice would be politically expedient."

"'Politically expedient'?"

"If Lord Marais was defeated, the emperor would have someone to blame close at hand; if he won, then His Highness could take credit for having found a victorious admiral. Then Marais could retire and become prime minister and reap the benefits of his victory."

"It seems very duplicitous to me, if I may say it, *se* Sergei."

"Politics is a duplicitous art, *se* Rrith," Sergei replied, looking up at the sky slowly paling in the east. "It's fitting to consider that our admiral goes to trial today not as a loser but rather as a winner, and that those whom he fought to defend are his enemies, while those he fought against are his friends."

"And how will this . . . trial . . . end?"

Sergei stood and walked to the window, through which the first echoes of the morning were passing.

"Lord Marais is a man with very high standards, especially those he sets for himself. He truly believes they will acquit him of the charges." He turned to face the zor. "He believes that justice will prevail, and recognize that what we did needed to be done."

"Do you believe that the outcome will be so favorable?"

The disk of the sun was verging on the horizon now, preparing to rise like an angel of the day to greet the slowly waking city.

Sergei took a long time to answer. "No," he said at last. "Right or wrong isn't the issue. To soothe the public conscience, to disassociate the Service from what we did—and had to do—they will destroy him.

"In a way they really have no choice."

Behind him the sun rose, casting a long shadow from his toes outward.


Three hollow raps of a gavel brought the courtroom to silence. Admiral Theodore McMasters, flanked to either side by two flag commodores, sat down carefully in his chair, followed by the rest of the assembly.

"The court will come to order. We are convened by the authority of the Solar Emperor, Alexander Philip Juliano, long may he reign, in his capacity as Commander-in-Chief of all Imperial Armed Forces. This is in accordance with Article 5 of the Uniform Code.

"Commander Sir Joseph Aronoff has been named by the Admiralty to act as trial counsel on behalf of the Solar Empire in this court. Does the defense have any objection to Commander Aronoff?"

Captain Lynne Russ, Marais' counsel, stood and inclined her head toward McMasters. "No objection, sir."

"Commander," McMasters said to the trial counsel.

Aronoff, an angular, gaunt man of middle years, stood and walked to the pedestal placed near the wide table of the tribunal.

"The prosecution is prepared to proceed with this trial in the case of the Imperial Navy against Ivan Hector Charles Marais, Lord Marais, Admiral, who is present in court," he began. "In a pretrial meeting with Captain Russ, the composition of the court, counsel, and recorders have been established to the satisfaction of both the Empire and defense counsel."

"The court is assembled," McMasters announced. "All members of the court will now be sworn."

The counselors, Marais, and the reporter and the tribunal rose.

McMasters raised his right hand, and Aronoff followed. "Commander Sir Joseph Aronoff, do you swear that you will faithfully perform all the duties incumbent upon you as a member of this court, and that you will pursue the truth and just cause of all matters relating to the case currently before this court?"

"I do, sir," Aronoff replied gravely.

McMasters administered a similar oath to Captain Russ and then to each of the two other members of the tribunal. At last Aronoff came before the tribunal and raised his hand, McMasters following.

"Admiral McMasters," he said, "do you swear that you will faithfully perform the duties incumbent upon you as a member of this court, that you will faithfully and impartially try, according to the evidence, your conscience and the laws applicable to trials by courts-martial and the laws of war, and that you will not disclose or discover the vote or opinion of any particular member of the court, upon a challenge, or upon the findings of a sentence, unless required to do so in due course of law, so help you God?"

"So help me God," McMasters replied. He took a deep breath as Aronoff returned to his seat.

"This court is now assembled. Unless required to be present for other reasons, all persons expecting to be called as witnesses in the case of the *Imperial Navy versus Ivan Hector Charles*

*Marais, Admiral Lord Marais,* will withdraw from the courtroom."

Marc and Sergei stood and quietly made their way out of the courtroom, along with a few other officers who had been sitting in the rows behind Aronoff.

"Commander," McMasters said, "you may read the charges."

Aronoff rose once more. He stood straight and only occasionally glancing downward at the tablet on the desk before him. In between, his hawklike eyes precisely swept the nearly empty courtroom, resting on one or another of the principals briefly before moving on as he spoke.

"The accused is charged with violations of the Uniform Code of Military Justice. These most serious charges are preferred by the First Lord of the Admiralty on behalf of his Imperial Highness, acting in the capacity of Commander-in-Chief of Imperial Armed Forces. For the record, it shall be noted that the accused has initiated the request for this court-martial as a means to obtain official exoneration for his acts and conduct while serving as the Admiral of the Fleet during the current conflict with the zor.

"By your leave, sir," he said, his cold eyes briefly resting on Ted McMasters, "as trial counsel, I beg to express the Judge Advocate-General's admonition that the tribunal be strictly enjoined from allowing this fact to enter into the judgement of this tribunal one way . . . or the other."

After a suitable pause, Aronoff continued to speak.

"Charge One, Violation of the Uniform Code, Article 92, 'Failure to Obey Order or Regulation,' and Article 90, 'Disobeying Superior Commissioned Officer.'

"In that Admiral Lord Marais, having received a lawful order dispatched on 8 August 2311 from the First Lord of the Admiralty on behalf of his Imperial Majesty's Government to cease and desist from continuing operations against the enemy and return to Pergamum Starbase, did willfully ignore that order and treat it with contempt as well as all orders subsequent to that date.

"Charge Two, Violation of the Uniform Code, Article 104, Section D, 'Aiding the Enemy: Communicating, Corresponding or Holding Intercourse with the Enemy.'

"In that Admiral Lord Marais on 23 September 2311 or thereabouts did conduct private and irregular negotiations with a hostile power, as represented by the alien Sse'e HeYen, titled High Lord of the zor; and that the accused did enter into a treaty with said hostile belligerent thus usurping the rightful province of His Majesty's Government."

Aronoff's eyes fell on Marais. Under the harsh phosphors in the courtroom Marais seemed pale and wan; but the defendant's gaze was turned downward at a 'reader on which he was making notes.

"Charge Three," Aronoff continued, "Violation of the Uniform Code, Article 99, Section C, 'Misbehavior Before the Enemy: Endangering the Safety of a Command through Disobedience, Neglect or Intentional Misconduct.'

"In that Admiral Lord Marais, through continued prosecution of the war against the zor after the issuance of the aforementioned order of 8 August, did jeopardize the safety of his own command and the Solar Empire in the face of an enemy of unknown size, power and capabilities.

"Charge Four, Violation of the Uniform Code, Article 93, 'Cruelty and Maltreatment of Persons Under Command.'

"In that Admiral Lord Marais during the prosecution of the campaign against the zor, did plan and order the execution of xenocidal acts. These acts were extremely cruel and brutal, and are contrary to the standards established by humanity and tradition and contrary to the law of war as it touched upon the rights of civilians and noncombatants as well as in opposition to the deportment of a war-zone commander toward same.

"Charge Five, Violation of the Uniform Code, Article 133, 'Conduct Unbecoming an Officer and a Gentleman.'"

Marais' head snapped up to face Aronoff at the reading of this charge, with an expression of surprise on his face. The charges had been presented in written form to the defense in advance, but the trial counsel retained the right to append any charges at this time. Of course, the charges thus added were subject to challenge.

But there was no way to challenge Article 133.

Misconduct was subjective in the minds of the members of the court. It was no secret that since 133 was vague, it could be used when a trial counsel believed that he had the court on his side but might not have enough evidence to convict on other charges.

"In that, in his methods, words and acts, Admiral Lord Marais did act in a manner which compromised his standing as an officer and that his conduct has made him unfit to serve as an officer in His Majesty's Armed Forces."

Marais and Aronoff held each other's eyes tensely as the trial counsel paused for a breath.

"Furthermore," Aronoff added, looking away at last, "that the accused did falsely represent the tenor and the moral turpitude of the entire human race and that his conduct and brutal prosecution of this war against an alien race will have justifiably made them our implacable enemy. This is a situation that no one except perhaps the accused himself would have desired, and which is now and forever irreversible."

"Captain Russ," McMasters said into the ponderous silence, "how does your client plead?"

Russ and Marais rose together. "Sir, the accused, Admiral Lord Marais, pleads guilty to all specifications of Charges One through Four. He maintains, however, that the specifications as the trial counsel presents them are *insufficient* to convict him of the asserted charges.

"The accused also affirms, sir, that Charge Five, which was not originally part of the charges presented to the accused in the pretrial hearing, is a baseless accusation for which no proof exists. He therefore affirms his innocence of both the charge and any specifications the trial counsel may care to present."

McMasters turned to Aronoff as Marais and his counsel sat down once more. "Commander, you may proceed."

"Thank you, sir." Aronoff touched the 'reader in front of him. He rose and crossed the room as the lights dimmed. A wallscreen lit up to show a copy of an Admiralty order. "With the permission of the defense counsel," he said, turning and inclining his head to Russ, "I enter the following dispatch into the official record as Exhibit One."

Russ nodded.

"The order shown," Aronoff said, "was dispatched from Admiralty Headquarters on 8 August 2311. It was addressed to the accused. It bears the signature and sigil of the First Lord of the Admiralty, and it states in part that upon the orders of the First Lord the fleet should cease and desist from further activity against the zor and return to Pergamum Starbase to await the arrival of an officially empowered negotiator. The comcode bears the automatic recognition signal of the IS *Lancaster,* the flagship of the fleet on station.

"The prosecution calls as a witness Lieutenant Jan DeClerc, communications officer of the *Lancaster.*"

The bailiff opened the courtroom door and spoke Lieutenant DeClerc's name. A young man in dress uniform entered after a moment, advanced to the court table, and offered a salute. As Aronoff administered the oath to him, he glanced at Admiral Marais who returned a tight-lipped smile.

"State your full name, grade, organization and station."

"Lieutenant senior-grade Jan Michel DeClerc, middle-watch communications officer aboard IS *Lancaster,* sir."

"Did you serve under the accused?"

"I had that honor, sir."

"Were you on duty on 8 August 2311, Lieutenant?"

"Yes, sir."

"Please describe for the court what took place."

"The fleet was investing the zor naval base at A'anenu, sir. Captain Hudson's squadron was in the gravity-well; other forces were engaging the enemy fleet. We received a tight-beam message bearing the high-priority code of the Admiralty—"

"Excuse me, Lieutenant. Please examine the communiqué entered as evidence. Is this the message you received?"

"Yes, sir. I did not examine its contents when it was received, but I did note them after the battle."

"Did you deliver this message to Admiral Marais?"

"I informed him that we had received it, sir."

"What was his response?"

"He ordered me to file the message."

"Did you inform him of its origin and priority?"

"Yes, sir."

"What was his reply? In your own words."

"He . . . ordered me to file it, sir. He told me he didn't give a damn if . . . it had the personal code of God Almighty, sir."

"Did he give you any further orders on this subject?"

"He ordered me to maintain comm silence, sir."

"Thank you, Lieutenant," Aronoff said, turning and walking to his seat.

Captain Russ stood. "Sir, I wish to introduce a piece of evidence, and then I have a question for Lieutenant DeClerc."

"Proceed."

Russ touched a spot on the 'reader before her. The screen changed to show another document bearing the Imperial seal.

"If it please the court, the following document is offered as Exhibit 2 by the defense: Special Orders 17 for the year 2311 entitled 'Admiral of the Fleet, Empowering of.' It is dated 1 March 2311 and is addressed to the accused, and reads as follows:

"'By the power vested in us as Commander-in-Chief of Imperial Armed Forces, you are hereby empowered by this order and by the provisions of General Orders 6 to take overall command of the Imperial Fleet and to engage the enemy. You are authorized to take whatever measures are necessary to secure the safety of your command and the safety of the Empire for the duration of the current emergency.'"

She glanced at Aronoff, who shrugged. She approached the witness stand. "Lieutenant, you have stated that you were ordered to ignore a communication from outside the A'anenu system and that you were ordered to maintain comm silence. Would you state the regulation regarding comm silence as you understand it?"

"The commanding officer may order comm silence at any time, Captain, if he or she believes that breaking it might endanger the mission. General Orders 33 addresses it."

"Thank you for your expert testimony, Lieutenant."

"The witness may stand down," McMasters said, and DeClerc stood, saluted again and left the courtroom.

"Sir," Russ said to the court, "the accused contends that this alleged violation is in fact a misrepresentation of his responsibilities as governed by Special Orders 17, General Orders 6 regarding the absolute authority of a commanding officer in a war zone, and General Orders 33. Admiral Lord Marais was correct in refusing communication at that time, and in fact was under no responsibility to either acknowledge or obey the orders thus given—not at that time nor later. By the time the content of the message could be examined, the A'anenu Base had been taken; any plenipotentiary would be operating with critically outdated information."

Aronoff looked up sharply and stood. "Objection, sir. The defense is contending a point of military law which directly contradicts the Uniform Code. The accused was ignoring a lawful order by his direct superior, the First Lord of the Admiralty."

"Captain Russ?" McMasters asked.

"By the provisions of General Orders 6, the accused had no direct superiors in the war zone. As I have stated, by the time the order from the Admiralty could be considered, the accused had good reason to believe that the order might no longer be relevant. His original orders in any case overrode any instruction to the contrary. Special Orders 17 specifically provided him with the widest possible authority for the duration of the emergency.

"If counsel—or the court—desires a definition of what constitutes military emergency, I will be happy to quote the appropriate section of the Uniform Code."

"Sir," Aronoff replied, "the intent of the orders is clear. The precedent governing right of recall is well established—"

"The intent is not at issue here," Russ interrupted. "What is more, counsel does not seem to recognize that the nature of Special Orders 17 is entirely different from previously documented orders to supreme commanders. The accused was fully empowered by those orders to do *whatever* was necessary. The extraordinary success with which he performed his task amply demonstrates the emperor's wisdom in having chosen him for it."

McMasters looked from Russ to Aronoff, and then briefly at Marais.

"Objection overruled, Commander," he said at last. "Captain Russ is upheld in her contention."

Admiral Marais emerged from the building with a grim expression. It had been a long and tense day, during which neither Sergei nor Marc had been summoned to testify against or in defense of their commander; they had spent most of it away in an uncomfortable lounge, which seemed to be designed to maintain a high level of anxiety.

Though he realized later that the next events only took seconds, Sergei later remembered it as if it had happened in slow motion. Marais was coming down the steps of the building with Captain Russ at his side.

Suddenly, the universe exploded into a flurry of light and sound. A 'copter, swooping low over the building, fired its weapons, laying a staccato pattern of fire along the lane to the building. Sergei leaped instinctively, knocking Marais to the ground: somehow the shooting from above missed him as he sprawled over the admiral. As the 'copter sped into the sky, he noticed Lynne Russ down on the pavement holding her arm. Sirens were ringing out across the complex, and Sergei could see MPs running toward them with their rifles ready.

Marc Hudson was sprawled on the neatly manicured lawn, bent double, clutching a gradually darkening chest wound. His eyes were jammed shut.

The 'copter was vanishing in the distance, with scrambling VTOLs in pursuit even as he watched.

Sergei stood quickly. "Corporal," he shouted at the ranking MP, "cordon off this area immediately. No one is to come within a hundred meters of this building." He helped Captain Russ and then Marais to their feet, and moved to Hudson's side.

Hudson opened his eyes a crack and squinted at Sergei, a pained expression on his face.

"I think . . . I got hit, Sergei." Then he smiled. "Boy, that sounded . . . pretty stupid . . . huh?"

"Don't try to talk." Sergei looked up at the sky, wondering if any other 'copters were on their way. "Can you walk?"

"That's . . . what I got legs for . . . isn't it?" He slowly tried to pull himself to his feet, but collapsed to a sitting position on the grass. Almost curiously, he removed his hand from his chest and looked at the blood that had leaked through his uniform.

Then he collapsed onto the ground unconscious, just as the members of the court-martial tribunal were coming out of the building. Ted McMasters dropped his briefcase and ran down the lane to where Sergei squatted.

"Help me move him inside, Admiral," Sergei said to McMasters. The two men lifted Hudson's inert form and carried him quickly up the lane and up the steps.

Through the window in the empty Judge-Advocate's office, Sergei looked out at the lawn. MPs and base security personnel were swarming outside and a 'copter had landed close to the building.

Hudson, still unconscious, was laid out on a large wood table; a young lieutenant from the base staff was administering first aid, but it was clear that Hudson would quickly need more serious medical attention.

Sergei turned away to face McMasters, who had just finished a call.

"Any word on the 'copter?"

McMasters sighed. "It got out of the base's airspace. How in God's name a 'copter could strafe this building in broad daylight without having been intercepted—"

"It seems fairly clear," Marais interrupted. He sat in a leather armchair, his features half in shadow. "It was allowed to do so."

"Are you implying—" McMasters began, but Marais cut him off.

"I imply nothing. In fact, Admiral McMasters, I need imply nothing. This trial is being conducted with the utmost level of secrecy at Westmoreland Air Force Base in the middle of Iowa, a few hundred kilometers from our quarters. It is being protected by the finest security the Admiralty can muster from His Imperial Majesty's Armed Forces.

"But a single 'copter just strafed us and was somehow able to evade a scramble of aircraft pursuing it.

"If I am not mistaken, you cannot say just where this 'copter is currently located.

"Is this a *satisfactory* representation of the facts, Admiral?" Marais said, his voice scarcely concealing a sneer.

"Admiral, you suggest—"

Marais stood and walked from the corner. "Is this a satisfactory representation of the facts?"

McMasters clenched his fists. "Yes, it is."

"Then I deduce, Admiral," he continued, walking up to McMasters and facing him from a few feet away, "that the attempt just made on my life—and the lives of my officers—involved the collusion of someone with the hierarchy of the Admiralty or His Majesty's Government.

"Since I know you to be a man of honor, I rather suspect the latter."

"You're talking about the Imperial Government, Admiral. You are impugning the name of the emperor himself."

"If I am correct," Marais replied quietly, "then the Government—and the emperor himself—just tried to kill me out on that front lawn.

"I am well aware of the state of public opinion about my fleet and this trial. I am still willing to defend myself and my actions through legal channels. But I *will* take whatever steps are necessary to protect my person"— he gestured toward Hudson's body on the table—"and my officers."

"Meaning?"

"Meaning, Admiral, that this trial will move to the starship *Lancaster*."

"I cannot sanction—"

"It will move to the *Lancaster,* or it will end now." Marais turned to Sergei. "Commodore, please signal your vessel for a shuttle."

Sergei looked at Marais and then at McMasters: it was a tableau backlit by the bright gray light filtering in the window.

McMasters looked away at last. "The emperor will have to be informed."

"Inform him, then."

Sergei took a comm from his uniform jacket and depressed a button.

"Wells here."

"Chan, this is the captain," Sergei said. "Send a shuttle with a full complement of marines. And send Dr. Clarke—we have a casualty."

"Aye-aye, Commodore."

"This issue is now joined, Admiral," Marais said. "When that shuttle arrives, my officers and I will board it. If you wish to continue these proceedings, your court may come there."

• • •

The agent was waiting in the nightclub in the alcove beneath the archaic twentieth-century clock. The music and the feverish activity that accompanied him were actually quite easy to shut out. He suspected that it might be a much more difficult task for the person who was to meet him tonight. The thought of the other's discomfiture, however, made him feel more at ease in the raucous atmosphere of the nightclub; it would make the evening's discussion even more enjoyable.

Absently he ran a finger along the scar over his left eye. It was an unconscious habit, but whenever his conscious mind caught himself doing it—as it just did at that moment—he remembered how that scar had come: from the end of a lightning-fast blade, held by an alien intent on slicing him to bits. It was an alien he had enjoyed killing, even though he could hardly see it by the time the opportunity arose. The wide-angle spray of an automatic weapon had killed the zor all the same.

His hatred of the zor had stemmed from that defining moment. Given the serious nature of his interaction with the aliens, such a mind-set was hardly surprising. Given the history of conflict between the two races it didn't even require an apology.

Though they protested from one end of the Empire to the other about the terrible atrocities of Admiral Marais and his renegade fleet, it would not surprise him if they changed their tune completely if the admiral chose to overthrow this emperor and replace him.

*After all, nothing is so highly praised as victory,* he thought to himself.

His reverie was interrupted by a familiar figure attempting to cross the dance floor. A moment later an observer positioned at a strategic vantage gave him a signal. *I'll deal with that dereliction of duty later,* he told himself, and composed himself to meet the visitor.

The person made his way to the alcove and approached the agent slowly, as if hesitant at the last moment to complete the tryst. The agent gestured to a seat opposite.

"Please make yourself comfortable, sir," he said. "Can I fetch you something to drink?"

"I don't think so." Tomás Hsien, Member of the Imperial Assembly, looked around as he sat down like a hunting cat searching for rival predators. As the agent expected, he appeared uncomfortable in this public venue. To his credit he was doing a good job of concealing it from all but the most studied observers. The agent complimented himself that he fell into the latter category.

"There must have been somewhere slightly less public we could have met," Hsien said after a moment, rearranging himself in the chair as it conformed to fit his shape.

"Of course there was, Assemblyman," the agent answered, running a finger again along his scar. Hsien seemed to follow the gesture, ever so slightly perplexed by it. "That would have aroused suspicion. This way, this meeting will be simply dismissed as a discussion between a Member of the Imperial Assembly and a potential patron." The agent raised his glass by the stem and touched something underneath; the raucous sound became muddled and distant, and even the bright lights of the dance floor seemed to mute. "Ah. That's better."

"I don't know as there's anything I could tell you that you haven't already learned. I found no trace of your eyes and ears, though I understand that the fleet command was aware of an agent."

"I'm sure that they disposed of him efficiently. That doesn't concern me right now; I want to know more about your meeting with the admiral."

"I can't tell you any more than I've already reported."

"Indulge me."

Hsien's eyes narrowed. "Why are you so interested? He seemed to have no interest in my power or connections and told me directly of his intentions. From all I've seen, he's carrying those intentions out to the letter."

"Someone tried to kill him today," the agent said.

"*What?*"

"A 'copter launched an attack on the admiral and members of the military court. There were casualties but Marais was unhurt. He assumes that the Agency was behind it, with or without orders from the emperor."

"And were you?" Hsien asked levelly.

The agent began to reply angrily and then stopped, realizing it would do no good. "Of course not. If we wanted Marais dead, he would be dead. We had nothing to do with this attack."

"But you want to know who did . . . wait a minute. You don't think that I—"

"No, I don't think that you had anything to do with it. There are several people in your camp who would be willing, and even a few who might be capable. But you really have nothing to gain by making Marais a martyr for the militarist wing of the Government: it would get them too nicely off the hook for losing control of him in the first place.

"Similarly, we have no desire to see him killed at this time in that fashion. But someone, or some group, clearly did.

"So tell me, Assemblyman. What happened out there? What did Marais say to you?"

"I've already told—"

"Tell me again."

"Very well . . ."

The doors slid aside to show the *Gagarin*'s observation deck, a huge room with a 360-degree view of the vicinity of the huge carrier. A careful observer could pick out the sickly pinkish-red globe of the nearer gas giant, and the orange-yellow sun of A'anenu in the same region of space. But the most dominating impression was of thousands and thousands of stars. In all

directions the dome of dark sky was filled with the light of distant suns, except for a wide swath that cut through the star field
like an angry black welt: the Rift, the boundary across which lay
the zor Core Stars.

The deck was empty but for a pair of marines at the lift and a
single figure sitting with its back to him in one of the chairs on
the far side, facing the Rift. Hsien made his way across to it, feeling small compared to the awesome night of stars that hung overhead.

"Assemblyman," Marais said, turning his chair and gesturing
to a seat. He was wearing an ornately scabbarded sword.

"Admiral," Hsien replied, sitting.

"*anGa'e'ren,*" the admiral said, gesturing toward the Rift
that dominated the view on this side of the observation deck.
"The Creeping Darkness. The zor believe that the Rift is the
habitation of servants of the Deceiver. They believe that it is
slowly growing, seeking to swallow all light."

"How quaint."

"You are a most interesting person, Mr. Hsien," Marais said,
leaning one arm on the side of his chair and interlacing his fingers. "I wouldn't have thought that any Member of the Imperial
Assembly would risk his life so readily for a mere political maneuver."

"I hope there's more to it than that, my lord."

"I rather think you'll be disappointed." Marais turned away
again, to look out at the Rift. "You don't know much about the
zor, do you, Mr. Hsien? You've spent your political life talking
about them in the Hall in Genève and you don't really understand the first thing about them."

"I understand they mean to exterminate us. That seems to be
a fairly important point."

"But you don't really know why, do you." It was a statement
rather than a question, intended—or so it seemed to Hsien—to
make him rise to the bait to defend himself somehow against the

rhetorical reply that was sure to come. He passed on the opportunity, and waited for the admiral to continue.

At last he did so. "They meant to exterminate us because our very existence was an affront to them. We offended them by simply *being.*"

"I note that you have reverted to the past tense."

"The situation has changed." Marais stood and walked away, one hand resting on the hilt of the sword. "Everything has changed and we must change with it."

"I find it hard to believe that the zor have dispensed with their xenophobia. Based on what I have read of your book, their only alternative must be to fight to the bitter end. It is *we* who have changed—at least those who have carried out this campaign—by sinking to the level of the zor."

"You find that distasteful."

"Of course I do. I have no great love for the zor, but I find xenocide more than a bit unpalatable. Don't you?"

"If I told you that I did, would you believe me? Think of it, Assemblyman. I am the person you have railed against in the Assembly Hall. You have accused me of atrocities, of mutiny, of treason and most recently of seeking to seize the throne in Oahu. Yet here you are more than a hundred parsecs from the home world, seeking . . . what? What is it you want?—accomodation with this monster you seek to destroy? Most duplicitous, Assemblyman. Most opportunistic, Assemblyman. *I* find *that* distasteful."

"I am impressed with your rhetoric, my lord. You would have made a fine politician."

"I should vent you into vacuum for saying so," he replied, his face softening slightly from the angry expression that had seized control of it. "But tell me, Assemblyman. What would you say if I told you that the war is over?"

Hsien felt a chill for a moment, as if a cold breeze suddenly blew across the observation deck. The starry dome above seemed

more distant, the Rift loomed larger and more menacing. Marais'
expression never wavered.

"You've done it, then." He looked at the sword again, but
Marais didn't comment.

"I've been to Zor'a. But we haven't destroyed the zor. Instead, something extraordinary has happened. The zor have fundamentally changed their worldview: so much so that there is no
longer any need to continue the campaign. The war is over and
we have won it, but we have done so without having to eradicate
them. Better yet, they have not found it necessary to eradicate
themselves. We have transformed enemies into allies."

"Allies? Are you *mad*?"

"We can go to the flight bridge and look at the pilot's board
if you like: there are twenty-one zor naval vessels present in this
system at this moment. Several of them will be accompanying me
back to Sol System."

A hundred possibilities and a hundred consequences ran
through Hsien's mind as he considered the implications. He had
no doubt Marais was telling the truth: there were zor ships in the
system—the *Cameron* had ascertained that much before he came
over here to the fleet-carrier. But to consider them allies was an
entirely different sort of mental leap. And allowing them into Sol
System, where a single, suicidal vessel could seek a glorious death
crashing into Buenos Aires, or London, or Genève . . . .

. . . or Oahu . . .


. . . then he told me that he had no intention of becoming emperor," Hsien said at last, looking away from the agent at the
throng in the club. "He said he was coming back here to be vindicated by due process.

"He said that the zor had given him some kind of position in
their government, a sort of King's Champion. I assume that's
what the sword was about. I imagine that a military court
wouldn't think much of that."

"What do you believe?"

Hsien did not answer for a moment. Then he sighed and leaned back, rubbing his forehead with the thumb and forefinger of his right hand. "I believe that our Admiral Marais is more cunning and more ruthless than Admiral Willem McDowell. There is a strong possibility that this trial is just window-dressing: the real action will come afterward. Either he will be exonerated and will be free to do as he pleases, or he will be convicted and will disregard the result. He's no fool," Hsien added.

The agent's expression never changed.

"Do you expect him to be the next Solar Emperor?"

"Well." Hsien stood up and gave the agent an ironic little bow. "That's really up to you, isn't it?"

"Assemblyman—"

"If you will excuse me," Hsien said, appearing quite interested in putting distance between himself and the agent. He strode away purposefully, under the watchful but concealed gaze of the agent's observers.

The emperor took pleasure in his little anachronisms. It was one of the privileges of rank, the ability—and the leisure—to engage in pursuits that were no longer in vogue, or in general use. He collected old 2-V equipment and recordings—*films,* actual photographic media, rather than vids; he sailed in the calm waters off Waikiki without benefit of motor; and he rode horses along the beaches and through the rolling meadows of the Imperial estate. It calmed him when stresses closed in on every side; it gave him a spiritual link with emperors of the past as he rode along with his cloak billowing behind him.

This afternoon as he rode along the golden beach he was extremely ill at ease. He reined in his horse at the top of a bluff and waited as a personal skimmer made its way slowly across the shallow water. Its occupant was a nondescript man in casual clothes, no different than a thousand other pleasure-boat pilots plying the coasts of Hawaii; the only suspicious aspect was that he was allowed to approach so close to the Imperial presence.

Alexander waited as the skimmer approached. Behind him on the cliffs two sharpshooters stood ready to act on a motion of his hand.

The civilian drove the skimmer up onto the beach and killed its grav field. It settled slowly to the ground, and the driver stepped out of it to stand before the emperor. He bowed with what seemed to be the minimum required deference.

"Your Majesty summoned me," he said.

"You're damned right," Alexander began, his voice rising slightly. "What the hell—" He stopped, realizing his voice was echoing across the empty beach. He lowered his voice somewhat and glared at the other man. "What the hell sort of incompetence prompted you to try and kill him that way?"

"Your Majesty seems to have a low opinion of Imperial Intelligence, if I may say so, Sire."

"You give me no reason to hold any other opinion. Because of your bungling, Marais and his cohorts have removed to orbit and the court-martial tribunal will be virtually his prisoners. What—"

The other man raised his hand. "A moment of Your Majesty's time. We did not attempt to kill him. In point of fact, we do not know whose work it was. We—"

"The prime minister informed me that the 'copter was brought down. Did you—"

"We examined the 'copter thoroughly, Your Highness. It is true that it was requisitioned from Offutt Base under the authority of the Agency but nothing was found in or near the craft after the interceptors forced it to ground in northern Missouri. In fact, there was evidence that it had not flown a single kilometer since it left Offutt."

"That's impossible," the emperor said. "The black box should show that it was used." He looked past the Intelligence officer out over the ocean, distracted for a moment by something.

"The evidence . . . or lack of it . . . is clear, Sire. Someone tried to murder Marais and has covered his tracks so well that the Agency has not yet been able to track him down."

"And the identity of the person responsible for the 'copter?"

The Intelligence officer smiled curiously. "The most mysterious fact of all, Sire. The officer who requisitioned the 'copter is a naval officer listed as missing-in-action during the most recent campaign.

"His name," the officer said, "is Captain Thomas Stone."

THE ACCUSED [AT A GENERAL COURT-MARTIAL] SHALL
BE PERMITTED TO REQUEST A CHANGE OF VENUE FOR
THE FOLLOWING PURPOSES:

- TO EMPANEL A FAIR AND IMPARTIAL COURT;
- TO RELOCATE A COURT TO A LOCATION CLOSER TO
  THAT OF CONSEQUENTIAL EVIDENCE; OR
- UNDER UNUSUAL CIRCUMSTANCES, TO GUARANTEE
  THE SAFETY OF ONE OR MORE MEMBERS OF THE
  COURT, OFFICERS OF THE COURT, OR THE DEFENDANT.

—Uniform Code of Military Justice, Article 28 (d) (2).

The barge settled to the hangar deck. The internal systems
switched over to the *Lancaster*'s power supply with a scarcely
perceptible drop in power. Ted McMasters stood and reached for
his briefcase and caught a glimpse of James Aronoff doing the
same.

"I don't like it at all, sir." Aronoff placed his case on his vacated seat and meticulously straightened his uniform jacket. "This
is most irregular."

"We're not dealing with a very normal situation, Commander."

"I don't see it that way, Admiral. My superior feels the same way. A court-martial is a court-martial and—"

"The court has certain responsibilities toward the accused. We have been negligent."

Aronoff picked up his own case. "Something happened. It was beyond the court's control."

"Someone tried to *kill* him. And us. And you, for that matter. The same stray fire that caught Counselor Russ could have caught you as well. Be realistic, Aronoff. How would you expect Marais to react? He evidently trusts the crew of the *Lancaster*—"

"His fellow traitors," Aronoff snorted. "Unless the defense can demonstrate otherwise. I must remind you, Admiral, that these people did not hesitate to carry out murder on a massive scale. We are not safe aboard this ship."

McMasters took a deep breath before replying. "Admiral Marais gave his word—"

"It has no value."

"His *word,* damn it," McMasters continued, his voice bordering on anger. "It is worth quite a bit, Commander, unless *you* prove otherwise to *me.* The admiral is a peer and a gentleman. You will bear in mind that at the moment he is *still* an admiral in His Imperial Majesty's Navy.

"He gave his word that we would be received appropriately and be allowed to depart when this discussion was ended. I accept his word and respect it."

"Without a second thought?" Aronoff stepped closer, and tried to read McMasters' intentions in his expression. "Without fear for your life if Admiral Marais suddenly changes his mind and decides that he's on the side of the zor or that he wants to be emperor after all? And here we are aboard the *Lancaster* surrounded by would-be traitors. We'd be inconvenient baggage, wouldn't we? Don't you worry about *that,* Admiral?"

McMasters waited a moment before answering. "Yes. Of course I do. But the continuation of these proceedings are in my hands. There are probably millions of people who simply want to have his head: but no lynch mob gets even close on my watch. I'm going to do my duty and make sure he receives as thorough and as fair a trial as I can manage.

"I've got a job to do and I'm here to do it, Commander. I expect you to do yours as well." He turned on his heel and walked toward the barge's airlock. Aronoff could do nothing but follow.

'ʟʟ be in the ready-room if you need me, Captain Smith," the young captain said at last. He saluted smartly and walked across the landing-field toward the group of buildings at the edge.

Smith sat in the pilot's seat of the 'copter and watched him go. At last he assured himself that the officious young man had turned his attention to other matters.

It had been an effort to get him to leave. As he considered the matter he realized that it had been an effort to get even this far: the Admiralty didn't seem to keen to let anyone—even Imperial Intelligence—get close to the 'copter that had attacked Marais' court-martial. But they were no match for a warrant bearing the emperor's official seal.

They had let him on base and let him have access to the craft, protesting all the way that they'd gone over it a millimeter at a time and had found nothing. He had smiled and ignored them; finally the last of them had gone away, letting him begin his examinations. No doubt someone had a spycam on the interior of the craft.

*Let 'em spy,* he thought.

He opened a small traveling-valise and took out a device very similar to a handheld sensing device. It had been altered in an intel research lab to pick up things that might normally go undetected.

Setting the device on the floor of the cockpit, he set about removing the faceplate of the dashboard.

This 'copter, like most other aircraft, carried a "black box" that measured the direction, distance and speed the craft had traveled. Every time there was a change in flight pattern, a packet of information was transmitted to the black box. It was normally impossible to alter without leaving a trail. A team had already been over every square centimeter of this 'copter including its black box, and had found nothing; but there was every indication that not a single kilometer had been flown since before Marais was attacked.

There were certainly ways to alter a black box. Some of them would be extremely difficult to find. The Agency knew half a dozen of them.

Smith unlatched the faceplate and pulled the formed plastic away to reveal the avionics control pad. The sealed trip-recorder was bolted securely into a frame directly beneath the steering column. He carefully detached it and set it out on the deck.

Close examination of the black box showed no obvious tampering; the seals were still unbroken and there were no apparent scratches or dents. He wasn't surprised: even though it was well shielded, the easiest way to modify a black box was to do it electronically. This left the box itself untouched. But even doing it electronically left behind evidence his equipment would readily detect.

*At least I hope so,* he thought to himself. The people who had been over this bird would have already done some of this. But they could have missed something . . . or they could have been ordered to miss something.

He began to move the sensing-wand slowly over the exterior of the box. Unbidden, an image of Violet came into his mind's eye: a large, swarthy man with chiseled features and dark hooded eyes. Violet had been a member of the Agency's inner circle, and presumably had arranged for this Captain Stone to attack Marais. All of this smacked of his style: devious in planning and in covering the tracks, but blatant in the act, almost sloppy; *no,* he told himself, *actually sloppy.* There were too many things that could go wrong; because of him, it would be even more difficult if the emperor ordered Operation Tattoo.

He dismissed the thought. Lack of Agency loyalty from a member of the inner circle was disturbing enough; a poorly executed operation made it even worse. He concentrated on the matter at hand, carefully tracing the edges and surfaces of the black box.

"Now isn't that interesting," he said when he was done. A 3-V graph hovered in the air before him. It showed an energy pattern; it was of a type he'd never seen. With a few keystrokes he changed the structure of the graph, using different displays to try and make sense of it. It didn't seem to match any recorded energy pattern—it seemed to change from moment to moment as if responding to some harmonic he couldn't detect.

*Like a starship's defensive field,* he thought. On a whim he displayed it using Restucci distribution, a mathematical representation used to track the seemingly random alterations in starship fields. At once it resolved itself into a sort of cone with a single focus on the top of the black box and emanating outward. The focus was just above where the trip-recording electronics would be.

Smith sat back and put down the wand. The earlier team could have missed this pattern or dismissed it as equipment malfunction. Of course, they could have known to expect it and simply ignored it. If Violet had turned them . . .

More and more his thoughts turned to Violet. He must have known he would be isolated; he must have made arrangements far in advance so that he would continue to have access to Agency resources.

Having Stone as his operative certainly would have helped. Stone was the admiral's adjutant, or had been until his disappearance . . .

Smith touched the control pad and brought up Stone's personnel record. As soon as it appeared, displacing the coruscating energy pattern, he sat forward so quickly that he bumped his forehead on the exposed avionics pod.

"February 2307," he said to no one in particular. Violet had become a member of the inner circle in . . . September? October? of 2306.

It fit almost too perfectly. Violet becomes a member of the inner circle of the Imperial Intelligence Service. He brings Stone into existence. Stone has all of the right credentials. He's introduced to Marais at Mothallah . . .

*What happened then?* he asked himself, rubbing his forehead. Did Violet let things get out of hand? Did Stone mess up and have to disappear—only to turn up here to finish the job? Or was it Violet's intention all along for Marais to be built up to become a serious threat to the throne? Was the attack intended to fail and simply interrupt the court-martial?

His eyes drifted back to the energy pattern. He still didn't know what to make of it, so he let his thoughts continue to wander.

*What about Stone?* he thought to himself. *Think, damn it. This has to make sense somehow.*

A naval officer—a fairly highly placed one, aide to the admiral—disappears on campaign. There's no death report, no missing-in-action . . . no evidence that the *Lancaster* was even *hit* while he was aboard. He was present when A'anenu Base was taken; and he was absent when Rift Base surrendered. He couldn't very well disappear from jump so he clearly jumped ship at A'anenu. He'd somehow made his way home to carry out Violet's direction to kill Admiral Marais. Or not.

If he was Marais' aide, why the hell didn't he kill the admiral while he had the chance? Did Violet want Marais to finish the job with the zor first? —But he didn't finish it, did he?

Surely Violet hadn't intended for things to go this way.

And how did Stone get home from A'anenu? An accomplice. He needed an accomplice.

*Hsien!*

He'd read the report on Hsien's little excursion to A'anenu before Marais came back from the zor Core Stars. He'd been over the assemblyman's description of his meeting with the admiral aboard the *Gagarin.* On the surface it all fit together the way Hsien had described it, but Smith hadn't been able to swallow it. Something didn't ring true.

If Hsien were working with (or more likely working *for*) Violet, he had the best reason in the world to get out to A'anenu— to fetch Stone. Something must have happened, something that had made it too hot for Stone to stay aboard the *Lancaster.* If Hsien had been able to return with someone with as high a clearance as Stone, there were certain avenues still open to Violet even without Agency inner-circle access.

He called up the *Lancaster'*s ship's-log provided by Orange's deep agent before they'd had to pull him out. There had to be something there, something that indicated why Stone had left the flagship.

Twenty minutes later he was wondering to himself whether he had built the entire chain of deductions on sand. From all of the evidence at his disposal, Stone had been aboard the *Lancaster* until well *after* A'anenu was taken. Without access to the rest of the ship's-log, there was no way to tell what had happened. Indeed, there was no way to establish any sort of connection.

There was still the energy field. Something had been done to the flight recorder, something he could isolate but not identify. It appeared to be his only clue to Stone, and perhaps through him to Violet. If Smith's suppositions were correct, Violet had had access to some sort of equipment capable of producing this sort of field and—

*Wait a minute,* Smith thought to himself. *If he's got something that produces this field, what are the odds that he's used it more than once? And what are the odds that the world datanet might be able to find another emanation? He may not even be making any attempt to shield it.*

A few minutes later, Smith had his answer.

•    •    •

The front viewscreen showed the Earth half bathed in shadow. Sergei sat in the pilot's seat, ostensibly reviewing the weekly performance report that was displayed on the viewing-tablet in his lap. The matter was scarcely able to hold his interest in view of what was going on several decks below. McMasters and the trial counsel had come aboard despite a carefully worded protest from the First Lord of the Admiralty; Marais in turn had ordered the *Lancaster* and the other five ships to the Earth-Moon L-5 point. The Sol System defense fleet was badly out-numbered and outgunned; but it would only take one properly placed missile striking the fuselage of the *Lancaster* to spill Marais and the rest into vacuum.

Part of Sergei's attention was diverted by Marc Hudson. He was currently in the *Lancaster*'s sick bay recovering from multiple wounds. Though still too badly injured to be moved, Hudson had been extremely animated when Sergei visited him an hour earlier.

Hudson had looked annoyed and uncomfortable half propped-up in the hospital bed. "Doctor's orders, Commodore, but he won't let me stand up when you come in the room. He won't even let me stand up to . . ."

"No need." Sergei had pulled a seat up by the side of the bed. "How are you feeling, old soldier?"

"Mostly intact. Nothing I haven't done to myself tinkering in a workshop—" He laughed, but the laugh had transformed into a cough partway through. When it subsided he had looked at Sergei and added, "Seriously, I'm very glad to be alive. Damn. We go off and fight the zor and practically kill them off, we run the risk of getting dumped into hard vacuum, and then we come back and get shot at by our own people."

"Not our own, I don't think."

Marc's face darkened. "What do you mean?"

"Interceptors from the base forced the 'copter to ground and found that there had been no pilot—in fact, there wasn't even any evidence of a 'copter penetrating Westmoreland's airspace."

"So where'd it come from?"

"Offutt. The quartermaster at Offutt registered a requisition for the craft by a Captain Thomas Stone."

Sergei saw a look of surprise appear on Hudson's face. Sergei had apprised him of what he'd learned about Stone's disappearance between A'anenu and the base in the Rift. "Is this some kind of joke?"

"If so, I don't know who would be playing it. But remember that very few people know that Stone is missing, much less how. And given his position, there would still be fairly high-level clearances in his name. Given that we're not exchanging data with the Admiralty, they might not know that Stone is gone. Sound like an intel job to you?"

"Yeah." Hudson tried and failed and then tried again to adjust his position on the bed. Sergei braced his arm, and the injured captain seemed to relax a bit into his new position. "Yeah, sure does. It's an easier explanation than the alternative."

"Which is . . ."

"That it's really Stone. That the guy who *walked* off the *Lancaster* in the middle of a jump is out there somewhere, waiting for another chance to bump off our Admiral—" he made a gesture toward his bandaged chest—"and anyone else who happens to get in the way."

So he sat in the pilot's seat on his bridge, feeling small and powerless, wondering how the interview was proceeding, and wondering to himself whether anything out there was watching as well.


McMasters sipped carefully at the hot mug of coffee and then set it down in front of him and folded his hands.

"Admiral Marais," he said, with a side glance at Aronoff who sat frowning. "I realize the position that we're in. But I simply cannot convene the court here aboard your flagship."

"I trust Commodore Torrijos' security," Marais answered. "I don't trust yours."

"I understand your position, my Lord." McMasters picked up his mug again, then set it down. "I ask you to understand mine. You have chosen to move this—dispute—to a court of military justice. In so doing you have angered a number of people who simply want you dead. It seems that someone does not want this process to reach its logical conclusion.

"I will not let anyone, lone assassin or conspirator, civilian or military, prevent this court from completing its duties. Your security is my concern, but you must understand that I must *not* give any hint of partiality. Even if I had your word on the terms, moving the proceedings to the *Lancaster* would give the appearance of coercion. This would completely destroy their purpose."

"What do you suggest?"

"A change of venue. A mutually acceptable site where your personal safety can be guaranteed."

"It was guaranteed before," Marais snapped back.

McMasters was about to reply when Aronoff quietly interjected, "The Code does not require this or any other concession to be made to the accused, Sir. Admiral Marais has two choices: to accept the proceedings of the court including venue, or to reject them and give up his desire for vindication. I'm sure that the Judge Advocate-General would not look kindly at this attempt at . . . *accommodation.*" He said it as if it were a dirty word. His feeling toward Marais was scarcely concealed.

"I don't give a damn about the opinion of the Judge Advocate-General," Marais answered. "It's not up to him."

"I don't think there is any need for ultimatums, Commander," McMasters said and sipped his coffee. "And I don't think we can easily ignore the forms, Admiral. If you were the captain of a system defense boat accused of cutting into shipping lanes, this trial could proceed quickly and easily. There'd be no one trying to kill you and there'd be no need to discuss a secure venue.

"There are only a few alternatives. The court-martial cannot take place on any ship under your Lordship's command. Any low-security base on Earth would be just as susceptible to the type of attack we just saw and a potential assassin might not miss next time.

"My preference is for a location that is reasonably secure but with fairly limited access. I suggest that it be moved to Moonbase Grimaldi."

"As opposed to Mare Imbrium," Marais said. Mare Imbrium was the site of the original Moonbase, built by the UN in the early twenty-first century. Over time it had grown to a population in the millions, boring deep into the lunar soil. It had spread wide enough that it could be seen from Earth with the naked eye.

"Grimaldi has limited access. It's located near the edge of Nearside and is off the main freight and passenger approaches. It would be fairly obvious if someone came close enough either overland or from space."

"What about the *Lancaster*? Will you allow it into Lunar orbit?"

"No," Aronoff said. "The JAG's office will not operate in a threatening situation like that. We object."

McMasters looked from Marais to Aronoff and then into his coffee cup, as if contemplating the proper words. "The Commander is right. I will not let the *Lancaster*, or any of your vessels, closer than the Earth-Moon L-5 point. However, if you wish to temporarily assign a small contingent of your own Marines under the base commander's authority, I can see allowing it."

"That's pretty damn irregular—" Aronoff began, but McMasters waved him off.

"I'll authorize it. I assume that they are for personal safety only," McMasters added, and Marais nodded. "If you'll accept Grimaldi, I'll inform the court. We can reconvene in twenty-four hours."

"I agree," Marais said at once.

"I will have to consult with the Judge-Advocate General," Aronoff answered. "I cannot imagine what his reaction will be."

*Tell him he doesn't have a choice,* McMasters thought to himself. *No choice at all.*

With the resources of the Agency at his disposal it was not difficult for Smith to pin down the recorded emission of the unusual energy field. It had appeared in the Hilton Head arcology off the east North American coast, less than twenty-four hours after the attack on Admiral Marais.

It was too coincidental for a suspicious man like Smith. It pointed directly at Violet, as surely as if a warning beacon had been lit from the top of one of the two-hundred-story buildings. Smith was fairly sure that even though it was tenuous, it was significant, especially if—as he assumed—Violet did not think that the Agency had made the connection.

Smith was unwilling to tip off the former inner-circle agent. He had finally concluded that he would have to go to Hilton Head himself, rather than send an Agency team or call in local or military authorities. He had considered and rejected a dozen plans of action before making that decision; in each case, doubt crept in as he considered how in Violet's place *he* might catch wind of the tail and move on, submerging into the anonymity of Earth's high-tech highly mobile society.

It was all he had to go on. *He* was the only person he trusted. Other than a single message to the director on Callisto, giving only the specific location and time at which the signal had occurred, he was acting completely on his own.

With a different ID and slightly altered features, a civilian Smith boarded a commercial craft bound for the Raleigh-Durham megalopolis. He lost himself in the latest 3-V for two hours; the flight seemed much longer than that. The news was full of the trial, and of the war: bright pastel maps showing the conquests of Marais' fleet, some video squirts of the interior of the zor High

Nest that had reached the public somehow—*I know damn well how*, he thought to himself—and interviews with leading members of the Assembly, mixing disgust for Admiral Marais with scarcely disguised glee at the successes of the recent war.

*So it begins*, he told himself. *Backing and filling. We'll be off the hook in no time. Demonize the admiral, and take advantage of his successes.*

*You slimy bastards*, he said silently to the 3-V screen, where an analyst was carefully outlining the possible alternatives for the Government if the war was truly over.

If the war was over . . .

If, of course, Operation Tattoo had the desired effect . . .

And if both of those were true and some ship's-captain didn't get it into his ramrod-straight head to hold St. Louis or Genève or Buenos Aires hostage to try and make someone else emperor.

It was a positive relief for Smith when the flight to R-D was finally over. He traveled light, with only a small carry-on for his equipment; he was able to make his way quickly from the aircraft to a rented vehicle. Within minutes he was flying toward the coast where the six huge buildings that composed the huge off-shore arcology loomed against the eastern horizon.

When Hilton Head Arcology had first been built in the mid-twenty-first century it had been part of the Carolina coast, overlaying a barren tidal waste that environmental damage had rendered useless. The land had long since eroded away; the huge interconnected skyscrapers that were home to several million now seemed to float upright in the bright blue waters of the Atlantic Ocean. The arcology had grown to accommodate this condition, and even turned it to its advantage: it lent a certain isolation—there was only one ground-level road to the place, stretching out across the water for more than a kilometer to where the buildings stood.

With a brilliant sunset approaching behind him, Smith's first close-up view of the arcology showed it bathed in sunlight. Its tens of thousands of solar reflectors dazzled his sight and made the polarizer on the rental's windscreen work hard to keep up.

Hardly expecting to see anything useful, he reconnoitered the address from which the signal had emanated: an outside apartment more than a hundred stories up on the west side of the southernmost building. The windows on the building provided ample reflected light . . .

Except for one.

Curious, he adjusted the controls on the forward windscreen to magnify that area. A quick calculation from his portable comp told him that it was on the same floor as the apartment he sought. The bright light interfered with the view, but after a moment he began to make sense of it. Each apartment had a floor-to-ceiling window that could be polarized in sections. Whether it was transparent or opaque, the outside coating was designed to be a solar collector; this added to the dazzling brightness of the westward-facing facade. An absence of any reflection from one particular apartment likely meant a failure of the polarizing window . . . or perhaps worse.

He mentally calculated the distance the window in question stood above the surface of the water that gently lapped around the massive pylons holding up the building. Filing away that bit of information, he headed the craft for a landing-space in a low-level garage.

Trying to remain nonchalant and innocuous, Smith rode up the elevator with his valise in his hand to the 115th floor. Scenarios played themselves out in his head as he considered the possibilities of what he might find. No one else was getting off at 115; he stepped off alone. He waited for the doors to close and the lift to disappear and then turned left and followed a corridor toward the apartment in which the signal had apparently been generated.

It took him several minutes to locate the correct door. The arcology was a rabbit-warren of connecting passageways and corridors; at last he stood before it with a small pistol concealed in one sleeve and his valise in his off hand. He rang the door-signal but heard nothing within, not even a chime.

He hesitated for a moment, carefully thinking through whatever traps might be left in the door. He ran his fingers lightly across the door's surface and along the crack between the door and the frame, knowing it was unlikely that something so casual would set off a trap.

Finally he reached into his valise and withdrew a small disk and placed it over the electronic lock. It took only the smallest adjustments before it showed a steady green light; depressing a stud he stepped back, letting the pistol slide into his hand as the door retreated into the wall—

"Holy shit," Smith said to himself, looking across the blank floor of the apartment's outer room and into the rays of the setting sun flooding into the room through the open wall opposite, 115 stories above the Atlantic Ocean.

Agents are trained to handle a wide variety of situations and rarely get very far if they have inhibiting phobias. Fear of heights or flying or the dark are the ones that wash out promising agents most often; Smith had never had a problem in any of these areas. His personality traits and psych scores had always been exemplary. In the service of the Agency he had gone to plenty of places under all kinds of conditions and had never had much of a problem with the environment.

Still, it took extra reserves of courage to step through the door into the empty apartment with the open-air wall and to slide the corridor door shut behind him. The breeze was bitterly cold and it whistled around the wall with the sound of a moaning chorus, making the scene before him even more bizarre.

The apartment was *empty*. Not in the sense of a vacated room, where extrusion points or power outlets dot the floor or walls ready to do the next inhabitant's bidding—but completely absent of features of any kind. Floor to ceiling, wall to wall, there was nothing at all there. It was as if someone had come along and erased the room, leaving a blank slate like a completely blank computer screen.

Smith reached out and touched the nearest wall and found it smooth, offering almost no friction.

He bent down and removed the sensor device from his valise. He moved the wand slowly out in front of him, taking a step at a time, feeling as if the great orange-yellow orb of the sun were staring at him through the wide-open wall opposite. He found himself in the center of the room after several steps but he did not venture closer to the opening.

The wand found the energy emanation almost at once. Slinging the detector over his shoulder, he advanced, wand in one hand and pistol in the other, through the doorway into what once might have been a bedroom.

It was there he found the body.

His first reaction was purely reflexive. He dropped the wand and dropped into a crouch, his pistol coming up to a firing position aimed at the human-sized and -shaped figure that lay diagonally on the empty floor, bathed in the orange rays of the sun streaming through the missing wall. It took several seconds before the unchanging scene convinced him the shape wasn't going to move.

In fact, it wasn't clear that it ever had been able to. It wasn't even clear what it was. It had a human shape: torso, legs, arms, head—but no apparent clothing or facial features. The legs and arms seemed to be made of bone with some kind of thin reddish-gray goo streaked across them. The chest had a bone structure like a rib cage but it was half buried by the internals, exposed so graphically that Smith had to look away as he fought down his gorge. As for the head . . . it had all the appearance of brain matter, as if someone had removed the skull and split the contents open to reveal what lay beneath.

If it had been human, it was clearly dead by now. After he re-covered with a few deep breaths, Smith was able to pick up the wand and run a quick analysis. It confirmed that what he was looking at was organic and human.

As he crouched in the empty room, perversely fascinated by the horror that lay a meter or two away, he suddenly realized what it was he was looking at.

Bone. The reddish-gray ooze on the outside was probably bone-marrow. Like the brain, it was on the outside. The contents of the body including the brain were outermost. It was only a guess but he knew it somehow to be true: this *was* a human body that had been . . . turned inside out. What had been the contents were now the outer shell. Hidden within the mass of body parts, arranged on the exterior of the horribly altered corpse, were the features of the victim.

Nothing Smith knew—and he was aware of more technolog-ical developments than most members of the Agency, let alone the population at large—was capable of doing this. It had some-thing to do with this strange energy fluctuation—which meant it had something to do with Violet.

As Smith recalled, Violet would be just the sort of person to leave this sort of grisly calling-card if he was done with someone.

Which meant . . .

. . . that this was likely the mysterious Captain Stone who had been used to try and kill Marais. There wouldn't be any way for the Agency—or anyone else—to interrogate him and thus track Violet to ground.

Except there was the matter of means. How had this been done? And who would do it?

*What kind of person?* he thought.

Moments later, a powerful signal on a carefully monitored band was crossing open space, aimed for the Agency headquar-ters at Callisto.

## chapter 22

The long shadows of perpetual sunset dominated the landscape of Grimaldi Crater near the rim of Luna's Nearside. While Earth above went through phases, the position of the sun never changed, providing a frozen landscape and a source of constant energy to power the military base there.

Grimaldi Base had been built in the 2120s, half a century before the huge, mostly civilian installation at Mare Imbrium. It was one of a half-dozen military facilities used for low-g training, EVA exercises, and research. All of the others had gradually been abandoned as their equipment became outdated or their purpose became redundant or their budget was cut. Grimaldi had hung on tenaciously.

Its layout had originally been star-shaped with a large central hall and wide spokes leading off in several directions. Over time the areas between the spokes had been sealed and opened up, obscuring the orderly design and leading to a fairly disorderly sprawl. The circular hall with its high transparent walls showing the lunar landscape and sky beyond was still the center of the complex. All paths seemed to lead there and the regular inhabitants of Grimaldi, as well as its distinguished—or notorious—guests, seemed to pass through it regularly.

Sergei and the other participants in the trial had been quartered in the southeast wing of the complex in guest billets that hadn't seen use in a long time. Grimaldi's quartermaster had gruffly apologized for the lack of amenities, and had put his service staff through its paces getting the rooms ready by installing 3-V and replacing burnt-out lights and clogged air-circulation filters.

It felt rather like a low-security prison, and Sergei supposed it had been intended that way when McMasters chose it as a compromise alternative to the *Lancaster.* In order to disabuse himself of that feeling, he made a point of taking a long walk as soon as they were settled. His route took him to the circular hall, which he found empty.

It had clearly been designed for style as well as function. The floor, rather than being metal or plain tile or rubber, had been inset with what appeared to be marble flagstones—*lunar rock,* he supposed to himself—laid out in a large mosaic pattern showing a stylized representation of Earth's globe in blue and white embordered by two olive-branches whose stems touched at the bottom. The pattern, like the rest of the uncolored flagstones, showed considerable wear—the result of countless footsteps across them.

"United Nations," a voice said as he stood there contemplating it. He turned to see Alyne Bell approaching him.

"Excuse me?"

"The emblem." She came up to stand beside him. "In the floor. It's the old emblem of the UN." She pointed to it with the toe of one boot. "Disbanded by—"

"Willem McDowell. I know." Sergei looked from the emblem to the *Gagarin*'s captain. "Our first emperor, who didn't trust in the honor of politicians and bureaucrats."

"You think Admiral Marais does?"

Sergei smiled. "I remember once asking you a similar leading question about the admiral. What kind of answer are you looking for, Alyne?"

"I'll skip the most obvious one—what you think is going to happen in this trial. What do you expect to be doing when the trial's over?"

"I don't expect to be commanding the *Lancaster.*"

"Nor I the *Gagarin.* Or anything else, for that matter. My career is probably over."

"At least insofar as the Imperial Navy is concerned. I imagine that whatever happens, the admiral will leave the Solar Empire and probably return to Zor'a."

"If he isn't assassinated."

Sergei looked up through the transparent ceiling of the circular hall at the star-strewn sky above. "Yeah. If he isn't assassinated. I expect I'll go with him, if he'll have me."

"You'll go to *Zor'a*?"

Sergei smiled again, halfheartedly. "I don't think I'd be very welcome in Sol System. Yes, I'd go to Zor'a. Maybe when this is all history I'll come back again as a visitor."

"You spend your entire life concentrating on destroying the zor, and now you're going to move in with them."

"Admiral Marais gives the human race the greatest victory it's ever known—without exterminating the zor, no less—and his reward is to be villainized and to be shot at. They're going to get all the credit, you know, Alyne. These hypocrites in the Imperial Assembly and the emperor in Oahu. A hundred years from now this'll be mankind's greatest victory, not Admiral Marais'.

"And all because he *won't* commit treason, he *won't* try to become Solar Emperor. As for the rest of us, because we knew what he was doing was right, we're going to become exiles or worse. We were too brave to be cowardly or something."

"You paint a pretty cynical picture, sir."

"Can you blame me?"

"No," she admitted. "No, I suppose I can't." She looked away again, up at the unchanging stars, picking out constellations that seemed somehow alien and unfamiliar.

Under tight security at the Imperial medical facility in Dakar, a weary forensic surgeon emerged from the operating theater. Captain Smith stood as she approached, trying to read something in her expression.

"I've never seen anything like this. Every part of that body was turned inside out. Every organ, every bone, the position of each nerve and muscle and vein. Death was most likely instantaneous, but I couldn't guarantee that. If it wasn't . . ." She looked down at her hands, still covered by thin surgical gloves, that had been handling parts of the body.

"Did you determine the identity of the corpse?"

"We've compared dental records," the doctor began. "It wasn't easy with the jaw—inverted like that. Once we determined the radius of curvature, though, we were able to figure out who it was." She pulled a portable 'reader from her belt and handed it to him.

Smith took the 'reader and looked at the forensic data and then at the corresponding ID: an Imperial Intelligence service record.

Violet.

It came as such a shock to him that he almost dropped the 'reader. For it to be the man he'd believed was behind all of this was a stunning revelation. Smith envisioned the horribly transformed corpse in his mind, remembering it as he'd first found it in the open room high above the Carolina coast, and made a guess at the approximate dimensions of the man it had been. It was big and broad enough to match Violet's burly frame.

"It's not really my place to say this," the doctor said as Smith handed the 'reader back to her. "But I'd like to get my hands around the neck of whichever bastard in Special Ops came up with whatever did this."

"It wasn't one of ours."

"But—"

"You were right, Doctor. It's not your place to mention it." Unwilling or unable to carry the conversation further, Smith turned on his heel and walked away.

Iwill ask the defense counsel, the trial counsel and the other members of this court to take into account the rather unusual circumstances of this court-martial before we proceed. Let us have no illusions about the importance of this trial, or the absolute necessity that the truth be revealed and that justice be done."

McMasters settled several sheets of printout on the table before him, and folded his hands on top of them.

"Commander Aronoff, you may proceed with the presentation of the final charges against the accused."

Aronoff stood. He seemed a bit less unruffled than he had in the Earthside courtroom; the assassination attempt and the subsequent events had apparently disturbed him, as had the Judge-Advocate General's ready acquiescence to the choice of Grimaldi as the new venue. But it did not seem to have quenched the fire that had burned in his eyes from the beginning of the trial.

It was representative of the counselor's tireless quest for truth. To him, the case could be decoupled from its context; it could be judged strictly according to the bible—the Uniform Code of Military Justice.

It made him the perfect trial counsel for this case, both from the perspective of the defense and that of the Admiralty.

"Charge Four against the accused," he began, "addresses an alleged violation of Article 93 of the Uniform Code, which deals with maltreatment of prisoners or other persons held in custody. This article is wide in scope but stipulates a specific mode of conduct toward subordinates as well as toward noncombatants and civilians. It is this latter case that concerns us.

"It is the contention of the Navy that the actions of the accused with regard to civilians and noncombatants is in flagrant violation of this Article of the Code and demonstrates an attitude that is not only in callous disregard of regulations, but also of the tradition of humanity which upholds the sanctity of human life.

"The prosecution will now enter as Exhibit 4 a vidrec from the fleet-carrier *Gagarin* following the destruction of the zor base and outpost at S'rchne'e. By your leave, sirs," Aronoff said, inclining his head toward the tribunal.

"Captain Russ?"

"No objection, sir."

Aronoff signaled to an aide. The lights lowered and the viewscreen lit, showing the flyby log compiled by the fleet-carrier as part of the official record of the fleet. Aronoff and the members of the tribunal watched stonily as the vid played; Marais looked away, seemingly concentrating on a hairline crack in the surface of the table.

The log had as great an impact as when the deed was newly done. The scenes of destruction were revealed. The wars with the zor had been bloody and violent, but had been fought largely in the lonely and sterile reaches of interplanetary space—never against the civilian population of the zor.

The images from within the Nests depicted the birthing- and rearing-chambers of the most dangerous enemy in human history; they left their mark on the members of the court.

Some parts of this vid had already made it to the civilian press, but the impact of the entire flyby log was far more significant. When the lights came up again, even the members of the tribunal looked wan and pale.

"The accused," Aronoff began while the last striking footage was vanishing from the screen, "has stated that these actions will assure us a lasting peace with the zor. Indeed, he has claimed that the zor now hail him as one of their leaders.

"It is the contention of the Navy, however, that these acts of brutality will make those zor who have not surrendered more implacable enemies. By the act of xenocide, he has lowered himself and *the entire human race* to the same level of brutality which we find so reprehensible in the zor. This atrocity"— Aronoff gestured at the now empty screen—"and others of its sort are as evil as the attacks on Alya, Chandler or Pergamum. We can only look upon such acts with shame, to think that a human being committed them against *defenseless* civilians.

"A review of standing, general and special orders concerning the relationship between the Navy and noncombatant nationals of foreign powers shows no modification to Article 93. As a result, the offenses stand as evidence for unwarranted violation of the Article."

McMasters turned to Captain Russ. "The defense may now speak to the charge."

Lynne Russ stood carefully, her bandaged arm hanging slightly crooked at her side. "The defense," she began, "wishes to separate the two component parts of the trial counsel's argument—first, that the accused had no authority to commit such acts, thus placing them within the scope of Article 93; and second, that such acts would alienate the zor so as to make them our implacable enemies—a charge for which there is no corresponding violation in the Uniform Code. In any case, the defense rejects this idea out of hand as blatantly false.

"The position of the zor on S'rchne'e and elsewhere is patently clear. This is a war zone; the zor made no attempt to withdraw any personnel but instead left them in the line of fire. These zor were *not* innocent bystanders: they were nationals of a foreign—alien—power, whose very existence threatened humanity. It is utterly foolish to claim a special status for the civilians on the zor worlds captured during the recent campaign. Trial counsel himself recognizes the zor granted our civilian personnel no such status when they attacked Alya sixty years ago.

"What is more, the obligations of the accused under Article

93 concerning the safety of his command, and General Orders 6, which granted him absolute authority in the war zone, mandate that he had every right to carry out those acts the trial counsel feels are so reprehensible and so contrary to the long, ostensibly pastoral history of mankind.

"In short, the defense asserts that the charge of mistreatment is inapplicable, and can in no wise be applied to the accused, as he acted with all authority in a war zone to protect his command from potential hostilities."

She leaned forward on the table, her eyes narrowing at the tribunal. "The trial counsel also proposes to rest his argument on the issues of barbarity and inhumanity. The defense responds to counsel's argument by pointing out that as a race we lack any real pacific tradition. Even by comparison to the zor we are an exceptionally violent species.

"The prosecution's argument seems not to be that acts committed by the accused are violent; clearly that is a part of warfare, our stock-in-trade. It is rather that he finds it unacceptable that the violence did not take place within some easily palatable context—one that counsel and our tribunal and indeed the rest of the human race might be able to swallow.

"That sort of judgement belies the truth of this exceptionally bitter conflict: that the tactics designated as 'brutal' and 'barbaric' are in fact the ones that *succeeded.* Commander after commander was unwilling to take the final step to fight against the zor using their own tactics; diplomat after diplomat granted concessions—"

"This is not a forum for criticism of foreign policy," Aronoff interrupted, rising to his feet. "If Captain Russ wishes to make this into a debate over the policies of the government, she should go on the 3-V and stay out of a court of military law."

"I see," Russ answered. "It's within your compass to lecture the court on morality and propriety but when the foundations of these arguments are challenged, their relevance is questioned?"

"This isn't about propriety, it's about—"

"Order!" shouted McMasters, slamming the gavel into sudden, heavy silence. "Trial counsel and defense counsel are admonished to direct their remarks to the President of the Court. Commander Aronoff, do you have an objection to lodge?"

"I do, sir." Aronoff seemed to gather himself, exchanging angry glances with Russ. "This line of peroration pursued by defense counsel strays far afield of the legal issues under consideration by this court."

"If the court pleases," Russ replied, "trial counsel was more than happy to issue moralistic judgements as a part of *his* arguments."

"Both parties will restrict themselves to examination of the relevant facts of the case." McMasters turned to Aronoff. "Take your seat, Commander. Captain Russ, proceed with your remarks but restrict yourself to the issues."

"Yes, sir." She stood upright once more. "The accused contends that moral judgement of the actions taken under the Imperial sanction is absolutely inappropriate. Article 110, which addresses the responsibility of an officer toward vessels under his command, is thus adhered to with no chance that there will be any threat from a hostile party. In combination with the authority vested in the accused as Admiral of the Fleet, the charge against him is completely unsupportable." With one last angry glare at Aronoff, she sat down.

A private message-signal appeared on Prime Minister Toliver's console as she was discussing agro-subsidies with an obsequious Member of the Assembly in preparation for next week's convening of the parliamentary body. Based on the priority of the message, and the sender—the Director of Imperial Intelligence, on Callisto—she concluded that it was orders of a more important magnitude. She dismissed the assemblyman, pleading an important interruption.

After securing the comm channel she began to play back the message. It was a short text burst: *"Tattoo postponed. Unknown intervention prevents completion of task. Vidrec attached. Message ends."*

Tolliver was furious, but resisted the impulse to immediately call the director and dismiss her from her post. With her left hand clenched into a fist, she punched a button and began to display the vidrec: a forensic report showing the result of an autopsy performed at the high-security medical facility in Dakar . . .

Smith had left Dakar on the first available airbus and had swapped it for a lunar shuttle at Orly in Paris. He might have cut a few hours off his trip by commandeering a private vessel to take him directly to Grimaldi, but he still didn't want to give any advance warning.

The events of the last twelve hours, from his discovery at Offutt to the revelation at Dakar, had left him unsure how to proceed. Violet was unquestionably dead, by some means he could not even imagine; Hsien was at his home in Bavaria, and the Agency datanet indicated that he'd been there since the meeting with an inner-circle agent days ago. Whatever his part in this, it didn't directly include Violet's death.

That only left one suspect, the only lead he had: the mysterious Captain Stone, who had seemingly sprung into existence four and a half years ago just after Violet was appointed to the inner circle. Smith had run out of clues on Earth, but there might be information that could be had up on Luna from Admiral Marais himself.

*Will he even talk?* Smith asked himself during the short shuttle flight. He admitted to himself that he didn't know; he didn't even know, if he were in Marais' position, whether he'd have anything to say.

There were just no other directions he could go.

•   •   •

At Mare Imbrium, Smith used his clearance to obtain a GEV and a driver to make the two-hour trip to Grimaldi. A space-to-ground shuttle might have been faster, but far more obvious: if he hadn't tipped anyone off yet, he might still retain the element of surprise.

Less than a kilometer from the Grimaldi installation the vehicle was halted, boarded and thoroughly checked by a squad of Marines, including two bearing the insignia of the *Lancaster*, an item that was not lost on Smith (though it surprised the hell out of the driver). With a marine at the helm the GEV was driven under escort into the compound, and Smith was allowed to disembark.

Bogey, fifteen degrees to starboard," the *Charlemagne*'s helm officer said. The captain of the *Charlie* settled into the pilot's chair.

"ID it," he said. "And get a visual."

"It doesn't have an ident-beacon," the helm officer replied. "And it doesn't have a profile that matches anything in our database." He made some adjustment on the helm board. "Should be coming up in visual range now."

Its appearance was that of a hazy, multicolored strip, not much bigger than the smallest spaceship. Its composition was indistinct but it was clearly an energy phenomenon rather than a comet.

Whatever it was, it was moving at almost three-quarters the speed of light, an impossibility for either a comet or a space vessel.

"What the hell . . . ?" the *Charlemagne*'s captain asked no one in particular. "All right, damn it. Lieutenant, plot a nearest-intercept course and execute. Let's see what we've got."

"Aye-aye—" the lieutenant began to say; but suddenly, with no warning and no explanation, the energy field changed direction—a maneuver that required huge amounts of energy to perform.

In seconds the field was receding from range, at a speed that was impossible for the *Charlie*—or any other ship—to follow.

As Marais and Lynne Russ entered the circular central hall, Smith approached quickly to cross their path.

"Admiral, may I have a word with you?"

Marais eyed him suspiciously, examining Smith's uniform. "Do I know you, Captain . . ."

"Smith, sir. No, I do not believe we've met." He withdrew his ID from a jacket pocket and showed it to Marais. "I have some questions for you."

"Captain Smith, I am very tired and have preparations to make before the court-martial is concluded. Can't it wait?" He began to turn away.

"I don't think so, sir. It's about Captain Stone."

That got Marais' attention; his head snapped to focus on Smith, and the agent felt the admiral's gaze bore into him. Marais took a moment to size up Smith and then said, "What about him?"

"Perhaps we could take this up in private . . ." He glanced from Marais to Russ, who appeared annoyed at the interruption.

"Very well. My quarters are in the southeast wing." He gave a room number. "Meet me there at"—he glanced at a chronometer—"1830 hours. Half an hour from now. Is that soon enough for you, Captain?"

Without waiting for an answer, Marais threw a salute his way and walked across the hall and into another corridor. Smith returned the salute to his retreating form, and then just stood there and watched him go.

•      •      •

When he rang the door-chime to Marais' quarters, the door slid aside at once. Marais was not alone; Lynne Russ, his defense counsel, sat at a desk in the corner. Commodore Torrijos and the admiral occupied armchairs near a low table. He stepped into the suite, saluted again, and crossed to the unoccupied chair to which Marais gestured.

"My counsel is present, Captain Smith," Marais said, gesturing toward Captain Russ. "I won't answer any questions she might consider improper in view of my legal status. I've also asked Commodore Torrijos to join us; you may find his insights valuable.

"Now: Why are you here?" This last sentence crossed the boundary from cordiality to stiff formality. It had the undertone of: *Why are you wasting my time?*

"I understand that Captain Stone was your adjutant for quite some time, sir, including a substantial portion of the recent campaign against the zor."

"That's right."

"I also understand that he was aboard the *Lancaster* for that period but left it at some point prior to the fleet's arrival at Zor'a . . . at A'anenu, perhaps?"

Marais and Torrijos looked at each other, but Smith was unable to determine what message might have passed between them.

"He left the *Lancaster,* Captain."

"Did you dispatch him, or did he leave on his own?"

"He . . . left on his own," Marais replied, appearing somewhat uncomfortable.

"When did he leave?"

Marais didn't answer for a moment. He looked at Torrijos, who shifted slightly in his chair. "He departed en route to the zor base in the Rift," Torrijos said at last.

"I'm not sure I understand—"

"I'm damn sure *I* don't understand," Torrijos said, cutting him off. "He left the *Lancaster* somehow, while the ship was *between* A'anenu and the Rift Base."

"He left a ship in jump?"

"I realize that it's hard to believe, Captain. Yes, he did."

"You'd be surprised what I'm prepared to believe, sir. You say he left the ship. Can you tell me anything about it?"

Torrijos looked briefly at Marais, as if for permission. The admiral returned the tiniest of shrugs. "I was in conference with the admiral when it happened. The bridge reported an unusual energy fluctuation." Smith felt his stomach jump suddenly but he tried to show no sign of it, and Torrijos didn't notice. "We went to his quarters—where the spike had occurred—and we found it empty."

"Empty?"

"Everything was gone. Stone, his effects, every bit of equipment, every piece of furniture. The cabin was empty down to the walls. Chan—my exec—reported that at least a millimeter of wall-surface was gone as well."

Smith's mind was racing, trying to put this new information into play. Torrijos' description matched the room he'd found at Hilton Head . . . except there was no body. He must have conveyed some sign, because he felt Marais' gaze bore into him again.

"What is it, Captain?"

"Commodore Torrijos," Smith said, "do you have a log record of the energy fluctuation?"

"The *Lancaster* will have it. I can obtain it for you."

Smith unclipped his 'reader from his belt and set it on the low table. He called up his own record of the pattern he had found in the 'copter and the similar pattern he'd detected at Hilton Head. They appeared in the air above the device, swirling and changing slowly.

"Looks like you're already ahead of me," Torrijos said.

"No, Commodore Torrijos." Smith adjusted the device, freezing the pattern at a single moment in its cycle. "These patterns were recorded less than twenty-four hours apart, a long way from the *Lancaster*'s jump from A'anenu. The first comes from the vehicle that attacked the court-martial a few days ago. The second comes from a high-rise apartment building on the Atlantic coast."

He laid out almost all of the evidence he'd acquired from both locations, including the body he'd found in Carolina. He carefully excluded the identity of Violet and his suspicions about the plot that involved him.

"So," Marais said at last when Smith had finished, "Stone is still at large somewhere, with the capability to . . ." His sentence seemed to fail for lack of inertia.

". . . turn people inside out. And walk out of a starship in jump. And he seemingly wants to see someone in the court-martial dead. I assume that would be you, sir."

Marais thought about this for several moments, then looked up at Smith. "If we assume that your evidence is conclusive and your reasoning is correct, Captain, what do you expect to happen next? And what do you intend to do about it?"

"I assume that Stone will seek to attack the court-martial again," Smith answered. "I intend to stop him."

"Really." Marais stood up and took a step away from the table, then turned suddenly. "You intend to make us bait for this attack."

"I wouldn't quite phrase it that way, sir—"

"No, but I would. Let me see, Captain Smith. Your *Agency*"— he said the word with venom, as if he resented letting it pass his lips—"wants to catch this Stone, find out who he's working for, maybe get hold of his technology. And if I get turned inside out accidentally, that's too damn bad. Isn't that it, Smith? Isn't that what your precious Agency has in mind?"

"I think you ascribe more malice to us than we deserve, sir." Smith folded his hands in his lap and took a deep breath. "If you please, Admiral, consider this: there is an enemy out there, some-one who can do things we thought impossible and who *clearly* has an agenda. We can't predict when or where he'll strike, but we can *guess* and we can try to be prepared.

"Of course you're at risk, sir. So am I. So is this entire facil-ity. But that's true whether the Agency has sent me here or not—he isn't coming here to attack the Agency; he's coming to attack *you* and we have to assume that he'll keep trying until he suc-ceeds.

"I don't know how and I sure as hell don't know why, sir. But this may be our only chance to find out."

Marais leaned on the back of his chair, looking abruptly tired. He looked from Torrijos to Smith and back again.

"All right, Smith. What do you want me to do?"

## chapter 23

IT IS ONLY ONE WHO IS THOROUGHLY ACQUAINTED
WITH THE EVILS OF WAR THAT CAN THOROUGHLY
UNDERSTAND THE PROFITABLE WAY OF CARRYING IT ON.

—Sun Tzu, *The Art of War*, II:7

Lieutenant Pam Fordyce was at the *Lancaster*'s conn when astrographics reported an object moving at high velocity toward the inner system.

"Di, what the hell is that thing?"

"Unknown, Lieutenant." Ensign Zhu Di's hands flew over the controls at the helm station. "It's a matrix of some sort of energy . . ." He named a figure somewhat larger than the annual energy output of the sun. "It's moving at nearly three-quarters light-speed. It will cross our path in approximately . . . three minutes."

"Is it a vessel of some sort?"

"Unknown."

"Comm, summon Commander Wells to the bridge and get Mare Imbrium for me."

"We're out of the Sol System comm link, Pam," Keith Danner answered from the comm station. "They won't answer our hails unless ordered otherwise."

"Anything on system comm?"

"They're under orders to maintain comm silence, but . . ." Keith made several adjustments on the board in front of him, then tapped a subordinate to relieve him, and walked to the pilot's chair. "From the look of things"—he gestured to the 3-D pilot's board—"some folks are already scrambling toward it."

"Two minutes thirty," Di Zhu said, as Chan Wells came on the bridge and received a preliminary report.

"Where did it come from?" he asked. Pam yielded the conn and took up a position on the other side of it from where Keith stood.

"From what little info we've been able to receive on comm, neither Ganymede Observatory nor Titan Base observed the object coming insystem. Jodrell Bank picked it up a few seconds after we did. It's as if it just . . . appeared."

"That's impossible," Pam said. "Ships don't just appear."

"Then I must conclude, Lieutenant," Chan said, turning slightly aside to look at the gunnery officer, "that the object in question is therefore not a ship.

"So. What happens if that field of energy strikes our defensive fields?"

"I couldn't be sure, Commander," Pam answered. "We would absorb some of it, I would assume. If it was sufficiently dispersed, it would simply radiate; if on the other hand it was concentrated enough to overload our fields—"

"It could destroy the *Lancaster*," Keith finished. "And everyone on it. With relative ease, I'd think."

"We have three alternatives." Chan settled himself better in the pilot's seat. "We may attempt to destroy the unknown object, thus risking the consequences; we can wait and see what it does; or we can get out of its way."

Chan looked at the screen, which now was mostly filled with the coruscating energy-field. "Do you have a trajectory for that thing, Lieutenant?"

"It will strike Luna in just under two minutes, Commander. Near the dayside rim."

"Grimaldi."

"Almost dead-on, Commander."

"We'll have to warn them. Keith, raise Grimaldi. Interrupt the proceedings if they'll let you, but tell them what's coming if they don't already know."

The object streaked past, a blurry multicolored strip, dumping velocity as it descended toward the lunar surface.

Smith stood in the back of the hearing-room observing the prosecutor as he stood and arranged his notes in front of him. Other than Marais, Torrijos, Captain Russ, Aronoff and Admiral McMasters, no one was aware of his identity. No one seemed to take much notice that a bailiff had been replaced.

He didn't really know what to expect this morning. Marais had agreed after some protest to assist him, effectively playing the role of lure for whoever might make another attempt on his life. Smith, for his part, was present to make sure that the admiral's life was protected. The usually unflappable admiral seemed distracted and pensive; the others simply looked nervous.

At last McMasters gaveled the proceedings to order and nodded to Aronoff.

"The Fifth and final Charge brought against the accused in this court-martial is that of conduct unbecoming an officer and a gentleman." Aronoff leaned forward, his tall angular frame drooping over the table, his hands splayed to support him. "This is the most difficult charge of all, members of the tribunal: it is a matter which requires great subjectivity and great insight into the ideals established by the Service both in the letter of the regulations and the spirit thereof. It is not so much whether actions are legal or not within the Uniform Code, but whether the Imperial Navy wishes to take upon itself the onerous burden of sanctioning such actions.

"The Navy has elected to prefer such a charge in this case because of an almost overwhelming revulsion of the means used during the recent campaign to defeat the zor. A stain upon its honor would inevitably result from the sanctioning of those means. It is the Navy's contention, therefore, that it can not condone the use of *any* tactic or strategy to carry out its appointed tasks—that a war fought with dishonor and won, is worse than a war honorably lost. It is the burden of the defense to disprove that contention if it can."

"I am willing to take up that challenge," Lynne Russ replied. "Or perhaps I should say that the accused is willing to take it up. The defense calls Captain Marc Hudson."

Smith stepped out of the hearing-room and shortly thereafter returned, helping Marc Hudson walk to the witness stand. Hudson looked pale and drawn, but affected a wry grin as he passed the bench where Marais sat. After the oath was administered, McMasters indicated that he could sit while giving testimony.

"Please state your exact name and rank," Russ began.

"Captain Marcus Abrams Hudson," Hudson replied.

"What is your relationship with the accused?"

"I had the pleasure of serving under him from April as captain of the starship *Biscayne.* I participated in fleet combat actions and also directed the assaults on R'h'chna'a and A'anenu."

"Did you speak with the accused frequently?"

"Yes, Captain."

"Describe for the court your impression of the demeanor of the accused. How did he behave toward his fellow officers? Toward those under his command?"

"He always treated me with the respect due my rank. I observed the same behavior toward other officers."

"Did he burst into anger frequently? Was he prone to rages? Did he foam at the mouth or writhe on the deck—"

"Objection, sir," Aronoff said, his voice betraying annoyance. "Defense counsel is making a travesty of this testimony."

"Sustained. Captain, you will observe the proper earnest in your questioning."

"Sir, *I* must now object. The learned trial counsel has spent this entire trial trying to depict the accused not only as a violator of regulations but also as some sort of madman, insane with killing-lust. I wish to ascertain, for the record, whether the accused ever exhibited overt signs of madness."

"Objection," Aronoff said again. "The witness is not expert in these matters."

"Sustained."

"I withdraw the question." Russ said. She looked around the court at Aronoff, who seemed to be fuming, and at the members of the tribunal.

"Captain Hudson," she continued after a moment, "you participated in a campaign against the zor that was extremely destructive, costly in civilian lives, and—according to certain evidence produced by trial counsel—not sanctioned by the Admiralty.

"What is your time in service?"

"Twenty-six Standard years this January."

"Would you consider yourself something of an expert in matters of military strategy and tactics, given your extensive service to the Crown?" She gave an annoyed glance at Aronoff, who frowned back at her.

"I would say so, yes."

"What is your evaluation of the conduct of Admiral Lord Marais as a fleet commander during the recent campaign? Did he acquit himself properly of his duties?"

"He won the war, Captain."

"Objection," said Aronoff. "The witness cannot speak ex officio: that is a matter for the Crown to decide."

"Admiral," Russ replied hotly, "the witness is answering the question. The perception that the accused won the war is an evaluation of the military accomplishment of the accused. It is therefore valid."

"Objection overruled. Defense may proceed."

"I beg to remind the court," Aronoff interrupted, standing, "that this decision will permit the witness to engage in rhetoric which might influence the cause of the accused but which is in no way evidence."

"Does the trial counsel wish to lodge a formal protest?" McMasters said, turning to face Aronoff.

Aronoff did not answer right away, as he seemed to gather himself for a response.

Suddenly the lights in the conference-room went out. The steady whirr of life-support, a sound to which they were all so accustomed they could hardly hear it, was abruptly silent.

After a moment the emergency lighting came on, dim and yellow. It bathed most of the tribunal in shadow but left the defense table and part of the far wall well-lit. Marais stood, one hand going to his belt for a weapon that wasn't there.

Smith was completely in shadow. He drew his pistol.

"What the hell is happening?" McMasters said from the dark, as a bright, multicolored light began to form in the lit area of the room.

"Perhaps I can answer that, Admiral."

Marais slowly raised his eyes and looked across the room at the man who had suddenly appeared there.

He did not look much different than the last time they had seen him: pale and almost skeletal, his face caught in that expression partway between a scowl and a sneer. He held something in his hand which generally resembled a pistol, though it was clearly of an unknown design.

It was pointed directly at Admiral Marais' chest.

"All right, Stone," Marais said at last. "Answer."

Stone said nothing for a moment as he looked from face to face, surveying the room. Two marines, Sergei, Marc Hudson, the three members of the tribunal, Marais, Captain Russ and Aronoff stood or sat as if a part of some tableau.

"I am here, my dear Admiral," Stone said at last, "to kill you."

"Now wait just a damn minute—" McMasters replied, standing. Stone turned the alien pistol toward him and McMasters froze.

"This weapon has a most unusual effect," Stone said. "I will be happy to demonstrate its effects if you'd like."

"That won't be necessary." Marais let his hands drop to his sides, and McMasters did so as well. "I assume you intend to explain yourself at last."

"Of course." Stone smiled slightly, and Marais looked suddenly diminished.

"The problem, Admiral Marais," Stone began, "is that you have failed to play your part as originally intended. You had the greatest opportunity ever afforded a human: the opportunity to utterly and completely destroy a rival species and demonstrate the superiority of your own. Yet at the last moment you refused to deliver the coup de grace.

"That is a fatal weakness, Admiral. It is one that has plagued humanity throughout its history. Humanity is too violent to be civilized and too civilized to be ruthless. It will be your downfall in the end.

"But since you failed to do what was necessary, it is obvious that you cannot be allowed to live. If humanity will not destroy the zor, then surely the zor will have to destroy humanity. The destruction of their precious 'Dark Wing,'" he sneered, "should assure that."

"But there was no need—" Marais began.

"*Of course* there was need, you fool," Stone interrupted. "What do you think this was all about?"

"Tell me," McMasters said. "What is this all about?"

"This is a conflict between races. My employers determined that it was best that humanity defeat the zor, whose fanatic predilections made their evolutionary chances significantly less than their more adaptable human opponents. With my help, Admiral Marais wrote a book that described the single available solution to the quandary into which humanity had placed itself: the destruction of the zor by fighting them on the same terms as they fought humanity. The rest you know: Marais carried the plan forward up to the critical stage, at which point he allowed the mystical nonsense that passes for zor religion get in the way of carrying out his historical mission—to eradicate the zor."

"Mystical—" Marais interrupted, but Stone cut across his words.

"Your precious Admiral," Stone said to McMasters, "had even begun to believe that he was 'the Destroyer' their myths had foretold. This ridiculous messianic complex stayed his hand when he should have slain. Humanity has proven itself incapable of dominance."

"By showing mercy?" Marais asked.

"When did you show mercy *before*? At S'rchne'e? At A'anenu? Even the pathetic creature that you saved on A'anenu Naval Base, the zor Rrith, did not want your precious mercy."

"There is a chance to reconcile our diff—"

"Even the reconciliation that might exist while you live will be broken, Marais. Humanity and zor cannot live side by side. It has been foreseen."

"What else has been foreseen?" Marais asked. "How else have humans and zor been used as pawns in your game?"

"Regrettably," Stone said, a smile curling around his lips, "you will never know." His finger tightened around the trigger of the weapon. "Good-bye, Admiral Marais."

At the last moment, his head turned toward the figure moving quickly out of the shadows. Marais dove for the floor while

Stone altered the aiming-point of his weapon toward the oncoming Intelligence agent. Both weapons fired at once—

A beam of multicolored light lanced out and engulfed Smith as Stone fell to the deck, his right arm and a good part of his right side vaporized by the heat of Smith's pistol.

Smith writhed and twisted as if in the grip of the horrible energies that danced around his frame as he fell to the floor, a gurgling scream escaping his lips before it was suddenly, violently, cut off.

There was a single crash, and a burst of bright light as the alien weapon shattered into a thousand pieces on the metal deck.

The smell of blood and charred flesh filled the air.


In the High Lord's *esTle'e* Sse'e HeYen perched in contemplation, his wings arranged in a posture of submission to *esLi*. In his mind he stood on the parapets of Sanctuary, two days' flight from esYen. Dres HeShri, Master of Sanctuary, perched nearby.

"The servant of *esGa'u* has been destroyed," the High Lord said suddenly.

"*hi* Sse'e?" the Master asked, his wings in the Posture of Deference to the High Lord.

"Yes, my old friend?"

"Why did the *esGa'uYe* not destroy the *Gyaryu'har*? Surely the *e'chya*—"

"Pride," the High Lord answered. "The Deceiver's servant was so sure that he could thwart the Lord *esLi*'s desires that he did not do the deed at once. He was stopped just as in the past.

"Though I am sure that he will try again."

"We must be ready," Dres HeShri said, his wings descending to the Stance of Approaching Danger.

"Indeed we must," the High Lord agreed.

A chill wind, unbidden, blew across the high towers of Sanctuary in the High Lord's mind's eye, and both zor settled their wings about them like cloaks to defend against it.

•    •    •

The court did not reconvene for twelve hours. The intel agent was dead, and more than dead—his body was horribly transformed: it looked as though it had been turned inside out. Stone's corpse seemed human enough.

The courtroom was moved to another, more heavily guarded area of the complex, just in case it wasn't over yet.

"If it please the court, I should like to address it," Marais said after the court-martial was again in session. "I will then be ready to submit to the court's judgement."

"If any member of the court would wish a postponement . . ." McMasters began, looking from Russ to Aronoff to Marais and then at his fellow judges. "Very well." He looked at Aronoff. "Does the trial counsel—"

"If the accused will agree to be sworn as a witness on his own behalf, the Navy has no objection to a statement."

"Admiral, do you swear that any statements you may make will be the truth, so help you God?"

"I do, sir."

"Very well," McMasters replied, folding his hands before him. "Please proceed."

Marais stood and walked slowly to the center of the courtroom, his hands held behind him.

"We have just witnessed the revelation of a bizarre plot. I believe that this plot had as its primary objective the destruction of the zor race. I was to be the agent of that destruction.

"It is well within the capability of the human race to accomplish this feat. While some may argue that our essential humanity might be lost thereby, it is incumbent upon us especially as military men to realize that if our survival as a race depended on doing this thing, we could and would do it. Without the restraints imposed by 'standard procedure' and the shackles of 'traditional morality,' I took it upon myself to carry out a policy that could have led to that eventuality.

"I did this for one reason only: because I felt that it was the *only way* to free humanity from the scourge of perpetual war with the zor. I assert that I had the right and the mandate to do this.

"My learned counsel has asserted this right and this mandate throughout this court-martial. Whether this would make me a villain or hero was never of any importance to me. I expected that once I began, there would be those who would attempt to stop me. By choosing to carry out my orders in the way I did and by having the support of devoted fellow officers, I made that impossible. I expected that the zor would resist with their entire being. I knew that this might bring about their total annihilation.

"But something happened out there. Instead of opposing me to the bitter end, the zor began to perceive this conflict in a larger context. I was identified as a mythological figure: the Dark Wing, the bringer of destruction. My adjutant, Captain Stone, had helped bring us to the edge of the abyss: a few hours ago he dismissed this aspect of our conflict as 'mystical nonsense.' To him it was merely an attempt by the zor to rationalize defeat, something they had never before truly experienced at our hands.

"Yet this 'mystical nonsense' is the very essence of our position, my position, relative to the zor. As the one capable of destroying the zor as a race and as the one *willing* to do so, I truly was the Dark Wing: in the most tangible and factual way. I was and am capable of doing that very thing. By human *morality*"— he almost spat out the word—"I am some sort of monster.

"And by zor morality I am some sort of hero."

He looked down at his feet for a few moments.

"Yet after all is said and done, the most significant aspect of this war is not what we did to the zor but what we *could* do to them. By shattering their worldview I brought them around to a completely different conclusion: that in the debris of their society I have given them a new direction. In the zor vernacular, it is an *a'Li'er'e:* a choosing of the flight.

"This is because I am not just the Dark Wing to them: I am the Bright Wing as well." He touched the hilt of the ornate sword that lay on the table where Captain Russ sat and for a moment seemed to look off into the distance.

"I admit to the destruction of their Nests. I admit to the killing of their warriors. I admit to the razing of their planets. But when they chose *this* flight it was no longer necessary to do any of these things. They have acknowledged this by giving me this sword and naming me *Gyaryu'har.*

"The plotting of Captain Stone and his mysterious employers, changes nothing except to warn us of other, potentially more powerful participants in this conflict. In this context a reconciliation between zor and humanity is even more significant. Who knows what else is lurking out in the unknown darkness of space, beyond the reach of our widest-ranging ships?"


Sergei found Admiral Marais in the observation lounge that stretched along the north side of Grimaldi Base. It overlooked a flat desolate plain studded with boulders that cast huge shadows in the bright sunset; a half-full Earth hovered partway up in the sky, showing the African continent through partially obscuring clouds.

Two Marines stood at a respectful distance. The admiral had not been alone since Stone's attack a dozen hours ago and even in quiet meditation he carried two shadows with him.

Sergei was almost unwilling to disturb Marais, but knew there would not be another chance with the court-martial reconvening in an hour or so. He cleared his throat and Marais turned to face him. His weary expression relaxed into something close to a smile.

Sergei saluted but Marais extended his hand and Sergei took it. "Quite a sight," Marais said, gesturing toward the lunar landscape beyond the observation windows.

"Yes, sir." Sergei leaned on the railing, trying to collect his thoughts. "Sir, I feel there is something you should know."

"There is?"

"Yes, Admiral. We—I mean to say, a number of the officers who served under you—wanted to make clear that they are still behind you, sir. Most all of us, myself included, find the prospect of returning either to naval service or to civilian life somewhat unappealing and we were curious about your future intentions."

"Intentions?" Marais crossed his arms in front of himself and shrugged. "That's still up to the court to decide, don't you think? They might well decide to take me out and shoot me."

"Even if they did, sir, I don't assume you'd let that happen."

"I don't believe that either the High Nest or my loyal officers would allow it. But there is also the possibility that I will be exonerated."

"And all hell will break loose if that happens."

"Admittedly so." Marais leaned on the rail himself, his face illuminated in the light and shadows of the outside landscape. "More likely it'll be somewhere in between. I would think that exile, voluntary or involuntary, would be the outcome.

"In which case I'd go back to the High Nest and serve it in the capacity to which *hi* Sse'e appointed me."

"Admiral . . ." Sergei turned again to face Marais. "My lord, I believe that a number of us would be willing to accompany you. If you'll have us."

Marais seemed a bit surprised by this admission. "I would welcome it, but I expect that this exile would be for life. Are you all willing to accept that? It would mean severing your ties with everything—"

"We're aware of the consequences, my lord. For some of us our careers are already over. For others, the jackals in the Navy would dead-end them. We knew what we were getting into before and we know now."

"I see." Marais' expression became sad but it was tinged with anger. "You know," he said at last, "when I chose this course, I had a fair idea of the basis on which this court-martial would be decided.

"I expected the accusations of disloyalty and disobedience. I flouted the authority of the emperor and certainly disobeyed the spirit of my orders in order to win this war. But when they accused me of violating Article 133, I realized that the outcome of the trial was almost irrelevant.

"Both the military establishment and the civilian government will take the fruits of this victory while washing their hands of the responsibility. It was an unpleasant task even for me. I am not as heartless as some of my fellow officers might have thought." As Sergei began to frame an objection, Marais held up his hand. His proud face looked suddenly tired and old.

"Somehow I should have known that it would end this way, that humanity would make me a villain though I have won them the greatest victory humanity has ever had. It is weakness of character, nothing less.

"The zor suffer from no such weakness. And they acclaim me their *Gyaryu'har.*"

"Admiral, I—"

"Torrijos. Sergei. You have served the Empire well; you have served me well. I wish that the Solar Emperor would give you the rewards that you have earned. But if you are to be denied as well, then I'd be happy to have you along."

Sergei looked away from the admiral and his eye caught the Imperial crest, the sword-and-sun, emblazoned on the door of the accessway. Respect for that emblem and what it represented was deeply ingrained in him; a lump still came to his throat when the Imperial anthem was played.

Somehow it all seemed irrelevant now. The Empire—his Empire—had betrayed Marais for permitting this to happen.

"I'm with you, sir," he said at last, extending his hand to the admiral. After a moment Marais took the hand and shook it in a firm grip.

•        •        •

The court-martial was reconvened at five hours low watch, as the Hawaiian Islands were drifting from shadow into light: dawn Central Pacific Time. The members of the tribunal were in full dress standing behind the table, upon which lay a bound copy of the Bible and the white wand of office indicating McMasters' Imperial authority to pass sentence on the charges. Aronoff, entering at the same time as Marais and his entourage, walked to a podium opposite.

Marais stood at attention in the middle of the courtroom, flanked by his defense counsel. Sergei and Marc Hudson stood behind them.

"Admiral Ivan Hector Charles Marais, Lord Marais, the court has heard evidence given by your counsel and the trial counsel, Commander Aronoff. Is there any additional evidence or information that should be imparted to this court before sentence is given?"

"No, sir," Marais replied.

"Commander Aronoff, is there any additional evidence to offer before the court passes sentence?"

"No, sir."

"Very well. Commander, you will repeat the charges brought against the accused."

Aronoff examined a tablet before him.

"Item, Violation of Article 92, 'Failure to Obey Order or Regulation,' and Article 90, 'Disobeying Superior Commissioned Officer.'

"Item, Violation of Article 104, Section D, 'Aiding the Enemy: Communicating, Corresponding or Holding Intercourse with the Enemy.'

"Item, Violation of Article 99, Section C, 'Misbehavior Before the Enemy: Endangering the Safety of a Command through Disobedience, Neglect or Intentional Misconduct.'

"Item, Violation of Article 93, 'Cruelty and Maltreatment of Persons under Command.'

"Item, Violation of Article 133, 'Conduct Unbecoming an Officer and a Gentleman.'"

"The accused has entered a plea of 'not guilty' to all charges. Does the accused wish to alter his plea before the court offers sentence?"

"No, sir," Marais replied.

"The court will now pronounce sentence.

"Inasmuch as the accused was empowered by General Orders 6 and Special Orders 17 to carry out a campaign against the zor using whatever resources were put at his disposal, and inasmuch as these orders empowered the accused with absolute and unquestioned authority in the war zone, the court is obliged to dismiss Charges One through Four against the accused.

"The very nature of this trial, however, and the circumstances which have surrounded it and which originally brought it about, have made the necessity of a judgement in the case of the fifth charge a more difficult one." McMasters looked at Marais squarely and then down at the table before him. "The court must not consider simply the legal issues here but also the consequences of condemning or condoning the means by which the military achieves the ends which the civil government seeks.

"Perhaps the methods employed were necessary, Admiral. In desperation, there can be no sacred cows: if humanity had no choice but to carry out the brutal acts to which you have admitted, then you were well within your legal right and authority. But that does not make these acts any more excusable. We are a violent race; we are involved in a deadly war. But the ethics of our profession are not disposable at whim. You have taken this course; as you say, you have chosen this flight. You must accept the consequences.

"The court finds you guilty of the fifth charge, and sentences you to exile from the Empire effective at once, subject to pardon from His Imperial Majesty."

McMasters reached for the gavel.

"Excuse me, sir," Sergei said, stepping forward and withdrawing a data crystal from his pocket. "I wish to enter these documents as a part of the official record of this trial."

He walked to the table and placed the crystal before McMasters, who looked at him curiously.

"Would the commodore be so kind as to explain what is on this record?"

"Certainly, sir." He pulled a sheet of printout from his pocket and dropped it on the table. "It contains my resignation from the Imperial Navy along with the resignations of sixty-three officers under my command who served under the Lord Admiral Marais during the recent campaign.

"Under the circumstances, sir, we cannot in all good conscience continue to serve His Imperial Majesty."

"Sergei—"

"Our decision is made, sir. What is more, I ask that it be made a part of the record of this trial."

McMasters looked at his old comrade for several seconds. Part of him wanted to object, to delay the matter before it was irreversible—but another part of him realized that it had already gone too far.

He reached for the gavel and brought it down on the table. "This trial," he said levelly, "is concluded."

The ꜰʟᴇᴇᴛ of nine zor vessels approached the jump-point marker. The escort fleet was already beginning to draw away, making the alien ships harder and harder to discern through the viewport at Pluto Base.

Ted McMasters stood before the port unmoving, alone; there were others on the deck, but no one chose to jeopardize his or her career by approaching the admiral.

He wondered if it could have been different and then discarded the thought as soon as it crossed his mind. It was possible the conflict that had raged through all of his natural life was over, as a result of the efforts of one man.

But he doubted it. The military had made Ted McMasters pragmatic and pessimistic and solutions like that didn't happen that easily.

Even if the zor could be reconciled, there was still the unknown threat presented by Stone and his mysterious employers. Somewhere out there—he let his glance drift out at the star field, into which the zor ships were rapidly disappearing—was a threat much greater than the zor themselves. Against that threat, mankind would always have to be vigilant. Stone had failed: Man is not an easily predictable creature. He was probably not the only such agent.

The distant blur of the zor vessels lengthened into streaks. The nine ships, the first of their kind ever to visit the Sol System, were fading into the other-darkness of jumpspace. Though he did not know it as he watched them disappear, none of the humans would ever return to the Empire.

Some would hail that as justice done.

It took less than six months for the Imperial Government to conclude a treaty with the zor High Nest, despite protestations on all sides. Julianne Tolliver's majority in the Assembly vanished before the leaves were all gone from the trees in Genève. The Commonwealth Party, led by Assemblyman Tomás Hsien, forced a vote of no confidence long before the final peace accord was presented to the Assembly for its consideration. In the elections that followed, the Dominion Party was reduced to minority status for the first time in almost a century and Emperor Alexander was forced to appoint Hsien as his new prime minister.

The remains of Captain Stone, along with the transformed corpse of Captain Smith, were turned over to the Imperial Intelligence Service for examination. Neither they, nor the few bits and pieces of the bizarre alien weapon that could be recovered, gave any clue to the nature of Stone's employers, their true motives, or their origin. Other than the two bodies there was no evidence that anything had occurred at all. To no one's surprise, the Agency deleted references to the incident from the official logs.

Despite vilification of the previous war and dire warnings

about a return to hostilities and the continued threat of a still-living Admiral Marais, Prime Minister Hsien signed the Treaty of E'rene'e on February 12, 2312, a year after the attack on Pergamum, closing the book on the final conflict between man and zor.

Later that day, while reviewing upcoming legislation in the Assembly, Prime Minister Hsien was interrupted by a door-chime.

"I left orders not to be disturbed," he said looking up, as a visitor stepped into his newly redecorated office and closed the door behind him. The man was a Caucasian; he wore no uniform or other insignia, and seemed little different from any other well-dressed businessman he might meet at Grand Passage except for the scar over his left eye that seemed to give him a perplexed look. Hsien thought he'd met him somewhere before but couldn't put a finger on when or where.

"Who the hell are you?"

"My dear Prime Minister," the man said. "My name is Smith." He showed Hsien an ID badge indicating him to be an Imperial Intelligence agent. "I was sent to discuss certain matters with you."

"I don't have time right now."

The agent made a noise suspiciously similar to a *"tsk, tsk"* and pulled an armchair up on the opposite side of Hsien's desk and sat down. The new prime minister was obviously angry, and his hand moved toward his 'reader console.

"Mr. Hsien. I believe you should consider rearranging your schedule."

"Why should I even bother with you? If I need your Agency's help, I'll call the director. You've meddled too damn much in the affairs of Government and I'll have no more of it."

"Mr. Hsien," the Agency man repeated, as if he were lecturing a schoolboy, "after the long and fruitful relationship between our organization and yourself, you're trying to take the ethical high ground?" He chuckled, stopping short of full laughter.

"You have a problem with that. All of you"—he clearly meant the Agency—"seem to have an ardent desire to manipulate events and people any way you wish. Well, it's a new day now and I won't be manipulated."

"Oh?" The agent's smile disappeared. "You seem to have conveniently forgotten, Prime Minister, that six months ago you took a charter flight to A'anenu to offer your services to Admiral Marais, whom you demonize every day in the Assembly. You wouldn't want that to get out, would you?"

Hsien colored. "That's blackmail, you bastard," he said quietly.

"The Agency views it as an insurance policy, Prime Minister," the agent replied quietly. "Now, are you ready to discuss matters or not?"

Hsien didn't answer, but by his lack of response the agent could see his acquiescence. "Good. I'd say," he added, the crooked smile returning, "that you and I will be getting to know each other quite well."

The dream state came on slowly as he meditated, Inner and Outer Peace in harmony. He cleared his mind, knowing that something was to come, but he was unsure what it could be.

The storm raged beyond the high windows of *esGa'u's* fortress on the Plain of Despite. The Lord of the Cast Out would not turn to face Sse'e HeYen, but spoke to him addressing the walls of his fastness, gazing perhaps at that eternal storm.

"You have thwarted me," *esGa'u* said. "The Dark Wing has not taken you; the Bright Wing succors you. The pride of your fathers"—*esGa'u* lifted one wing in a disparaging gesture—"trampled and strewn to the Eight Winds, High Lord, for you have let an alien conquer you.

"Do not believe that you can learn each other's ways before the darkness comes. Do not believe that there is a bridge across that alienness.

"It will make you weak to make peace with these *humans.*" *esGa'u*'s voice spat out the word as if it pained him to say it. "There is greater power than either of you can ever overcome.

"While you live, I will not warn you again, Sse'e HeYen. It is done."

The dream state melted then as Sse'e HeYen felt himself settle into his body, the last glance of *esGa'u* he received troubling him severely as the Lord of the Cast Out turned to face him.

Chris Boyd woke with a start several floors below, bathed in a cold sweat. It was happening less and less frequently, as the Master of Sanctuary taught him to bring his talents under control; still, he knew that sometimes when he slept his mind sought out other, alien minds, and shared their dreams.

He swung his legs to the floor and stood shakily, making out only the outlines of his ornate bedchamber in the near-darkness. He walked slowly into the 'fresher and turned on the light. He began to dry his face and hands with a towel.

The dream-images haunted him still as he looked in the mirror and saw his own bleary-eyed face staring back at him. He knew that he had shared a dream, a prescient one, with the High Lord; the precision with which he knew this frightened him. He would discuss it with Lord Sse'e in the morning, but he would probably not sleep anymore tonight.

As he walked into his sitting-room to look for a book to keep him occupied, he found himself casting his mind back again and again to the last of the images: the figure of *esGa'u*, the legendary Satanlike Lord of the Cast Out, looking over its shoulder toward him, its face frozen in the image of Captain Thomas Stone.

The Solar Empire has its peace. The price of ending two generations of conflict is more than simply the exile of the commander, regardless of politicians' honeyed speeches or civilians' uninformed analysis. Humankind must come to terms with this victory if it is ever to lie comfortably with the zor and accept that there is no cause for future conflict.

In a way, nothing has changed. Sun Tzu wrote that only those who were acquainted with the evils of war could succeed in carrying it out.

For sixty years generals, diplomats and politicians let an artificial and totally superfluous code of conduct interfere with their education. We abandoned this code at the outset.

They never placed the conflict in the same framework that the enemy did. We chose another course.

They never fought to win because they could not bear to do what needed to be done. We did what needed to be done, and we would have won even if the zor had not brought the war to an end.

The exile of commanders from the recent conflict does not absolve the human race from responsibility for enemy deaths. Regardless of the hand that holds the sword, the blood is on everyone's hands. Turning away from this truth does not change it. Sending away the instruments of the deed does not change it, either.

The bridge from conflict to peace has long since been crossed in the eyes of the zor. *There is nothing more to fight about . . .*

. . . My sitting-room overlooks the city of esYen, the capital city of a world that sent its natives into space thousands of years ago. It is the home of the High Nest and the High Lord; in the three years since the Treaty of E'rene'e it has become home to two races. Humans here are a tiny minority, but they are accepted: not as intruders, not as strangers, and certainly not as conquerors. Humans are accepted as people; this is a major change of perception for the zor. We are learning to understand each other. This is essential: not only for our own welfare and comfort, but as a foundation for the future, when other challenges emerge from the unknown.

Our strength is that we have two perspectives instead of one: what the zor see and understand, and what we see and understand. Our weakness is that we took so long to reach this stage, at the cost of so many lives. The recent war did not cause irrevocable differences between our two races; curiously, the war reconciled such differences.

I do not rejoice in the need to commit the acts that brought us from war to peace. I do not glorify in the destruction, the violence, the death. Would I choose to return to the Empire instead of to remain in exile, with my fellow soldiers who accepted the means to achieve this end? Of course I would. However, I do not regret the means, because the end is so important: a lasting peace between zor and human, permitting us to use our resources for more important causes than to continue to destroy each other. That is the lesson that this awful war must teach us.

I believe that history will show that there was no other choice.

—*A Letter from Exile,* Ivan Hector Charles Marais
(saLi' a' a Press, esYen, 2315)